When Hell Freezes Over

WHEN HELL FREEZES OVER

For Sarah, with
my very best wishes
to a fellow musician.
Enjoy!

Rick Blechta

Rick Blechta

RendezVous
Crime

Text © 2006 by Rick Blechta

LE CONSEIL DES ARTS
DU CANADA
DEPUIS 1957

THE CANADA COUNCIL
FOR THE ARTS
SINCE 1957

We gratefully acknowledge the support of the Canada Council for the Arts for our publishing program.

RENDEZVOUS PRESS
an imprint of Napoleon Publishing

Printed in Canada

11 09 08 07 06   5 4 3 2 1

Library and Archives Canada Cataloguing in Publication

Blechta, Rick
        When hell freezes over / Rick Blechta.

(RendezVous crime)
ISBN 1-894917-41-3 (pbk.)

        I. Title. II. Series.
PS8553.L3969W44 2006   C813'.54   C2006-903893-7

Also by Rick Blechta

Knock on Wood
The Lark Ascending
Shooting Straight in the Dark
Cemetery of the Nameless

As editor:
Dishes to Die For...Again

Fondly dedicated to my son Jan
who helped greatly in this book's design
and is someone of whom I'm ordinately proud.

CHAPTER 1

I must make it clear from the start that ultimately I did have a choice—but that's always easy to say in hindsight. Right?

You hear about this sort of thing all the time: the "I don't want to get involved" syndrome. To myself, I'd rationalized my behaviour over the years as "minding my own business", something I'd honed to a razor's edge. How many times had I thought to myself or even said out loud while watching the telly that *I* wouldn't have been fool enough to jump into such-and-such a situation? I'd shake my head at the apparent stupidity of whichever person had come to the aid of someone they quite often didn't even know.

But as it turned out, when a life or death situation actually thrust itself into the safe little cocoon I'd wrapped around myself, I discovered one really doesn't have any time for choice-making. It turned out to be more a matter of reaction, cause and *immediate* effect.

When a person you've never seen comes running up to your vehicle, screaming for help, you could respond with a gut-reaction stomp on the accelerator and lie to yourself later that you'd been startled, which was why you'd taken off. I've thought about that a lot. Perhaps I would have been happy with the course my life took afterwards if I'd done that. Perhaps not.

Having spent a rather long day visiting my mum, (who steadfastly refuses to move from our old terrace house in Bacchus Road, Winson Green, Birmingham), I'd gone to bed early on in my old room, but had woken in the wee hours. Finding myself unable to sleep, I'd made the decision to start my trip north rather than wait until morning. A quick note to mum, (who was used to this sort of thing), and I was on my way.

As I drove along the deserted streets, my mind was wandering around in the foggy memories of my early years. I slowed for a traffic light next to Dudley Road Hospital, where I'd been born forty-nine years earlier. Before the car had completely come to a stop, a young woman yanked the passenger door open and fairly leaped headfirst into the seat.

Stunned, I turned to say something marvellously intelligent like, "What seems to be the problem?" when she froze me with a panic-stricken wail.

"Goddammit! Get me the hell out of here!" When I still didn't throw the Jaguar into gear, she grabbed my arm and yelled right into my face, "Don't you understand? If they catch us, they'll kill us both!"

What finally got my blood and the car's petrol pumping was the sight in my rear view mirror of two human mountains sprinting out of the darkness a hundred feet behind. They paused only momentarily before pointing in our direction. Almost immediately, a car hove into view back in Aberdeen Street, accelerating towards the two men.

Only then did I decide I would run first and ask the questions later.

Birmingham, England, has the reputation of being a tough city, even though the city fathers have spent a great deal of money in recent times trying to dispel its blue collar proclivities. However, there's no denying that there are areas no sane person would venture into after dark without a large group of mean-looking friends.

I knew that, because I'd grown up hard against one of Her Majesty's toughest prisons in a tough part of a tough city the locals call Brum. The only way I'd kept my face pretty and possession of all my teeth was by being exceptionally fleet of foot and adept at keeping a weather eye out for potential trouble. Even though my family had lived in the city for three generations, the plain fact was that a lot of people in my neighbourhood took exception to us being of Irish descent. My brother, Bobby, had always been too proud to run from a fight, resulting in his face (and head and ribs and kidneys) being rearranged violently on several occasions. Entertaining no illusions on that score, I'd scarpered whenever trouble had beckoned. Bobby I'd always considered a bit of a fool for standing his ground.

The car behind us accelerated past the two running men, and it wasn't hard to figure out that the driver's plan was to cut me off to give his friends the few moments they needed to catch up. Fortunately, their saloon car would be no match for my classic Jaguar E-type with its 265 horsepower engine.

Throwing the gear shift forward, I left thirty feet of rubber as I sped off. At the next roundabout, I wrenched the car around onto Ladywood Middleway, my goal being the city centre, hopefully busy with nightlife, even at this late hour. If someone wanted this woman badly enough to chase her down a public thoroughfare, I wanted to have the greatest number of people and definitely a few constables around in the event they caught up with us.

The years away from my native city betrayed me, though, as I turned into Broad Street. Nothing looked familiar, and the streets were steadfastly unpopulated. A cold rain began falling, perhaps explaining the lack of late-night clubbers. Keeping one eye to the rear, one to the front and a third I didn't know I possessed looking for the law, I made my way as fast as I could. Normally, traffic would have been at a crawl.

As we approached the roundabout at the bottom of Broad Street, I flicked a quick glance to my left. My passenger had her head down between the seats and all her attention out the rear windscreen. I took a hard, tires-squealing right in hopes of losing any pursuit in the side streets near the Gas Street Basin, which I knew well. Instead, I found a street narrowed by construction hoarding, fences and torn up paving. The place had the look of absolute desolation, not a soul in sight.

I downshifted, unsure of my bearings. Where was this? Had things changed so much?

"Why are you slowing down?" she asked. Unmistakably American: New York, or that general area, although when she'd first jumped in the car, I could have sworn she sounded British. "You don't know where we are, do you?"

I checked my mirrors before answering. No sign of the car. Perhaps the driver, stopping to pick up the two runners, had lost track of me.

Perhaps.

"Something like that," I admitted, slowing to a stop.

"You don't *live* in this city?"

"I was born here, but I haven't lived here for twenty-five years."

Whatever she was about to say in answer came out instead as a sharp intake of breath as a car appeared around the corner ahead of us. We both gasped until a passing street light revealed that it had a white bonnet. Maybe they could tell me where the hell I was. I started forward again, cutting the distance between us.

Flashing my lights at the other car, I was in the act of rolling down my window when it swerved right in front of me, forcing me to hit the brakes as hard as I had the accelerator earlier. Three large men leaped out, two from the front seat and one from the back—a different three men, and they too, looked as if they meant business.

Striding forward, the one from the back seat brought a two-foot length of pipe down very hard on the Jaguar's bonnet. The metal crumpled like aluminum foil.

"Out...now!" was all he said, his accent revealing him as a local.

A thousand things went through my head, and for the first time I thought of opening my door and bolting the way I had so many times in the past. But that had been when it was only *my* skin, *my* danger. This time I had someone with me who was squeezing herself back into the seat as if she wanted to disappear into the leather upholstery.

The man with the pipe came up on her side of the car as his companions were approaching mine. He tapped on her window almost gently with the piece of metal. "Out. I'm not kidding."

The girl—she looked to be younger than I'd at first thought—had the knuckles of her right hand pressed against her mouth and merely shook her head, her eyes wide with fear.

Crash! With a lightning flick of his arm, the window exploded all over the inside of the car. What would have happened next, I dare not think, but right at that moment, a car screeching around a corner behind us seized the attention of the three villains. Glancing in the mirror, I confirmed it was the black car and groaned inwardly. I probably couldn't handle even one of these brutes, and now there would be six.

The black car stopped quickly about five yards behind me. Its occupants got out slowly, and stepping in front of their car's headlights, became three huge silhouettes as I looked at them through my rear view mirror.

Our attackers had stepped away from the Jag and stood tensely, the man with the pipe tapping it gently into his open palm. "Get out of it," he hissed at the newcomers.

His two companions on my side of the Jag stiffened, and a quick glance in the mirror confirmed that behind us the middle man had pulled a gun.

I saw my only opening before bullets started flying and whispered, "Grab hold of something," out of the corner of my mouth, then slammed the car into gear.

Driving solely on instinct, I lurched forward, yanking the wheel as hard and fast as I could to the right. As the rear end swung wildly around, the three in front ducked for cover while the three behind must have been taken by surprise, because no shots were fired.

I almost made it by the car in front, but in yanking the wheel to get around it, the back of the Jag swung wildly and caught the nearside rear wing solidly before bouncing off. Straightening the wheel, we took off, making a hard left over a canal bridge as if the very hounds of hell were after us. I suppose they were.

I have no idea whether the two groups of thugs decided to have it out on the street right there, or jumped into their respective vehicles to give chase. I drove as if traffic laws didn't exist, going through lights and screeching around corners like some crazed Hollywood stunt man as my passenger braced herself as best she could.

I *finally* began recognizing landmarks, but even then I only slowed down marginally. Very few cars were about, and no police that I could see. Every block or so I checked behind us but saw no sign of pursuit. At last, up ahead I glimpsed the familiar silhouette of an official vehicle.

When I began to slow, my passenger gripped my arm for the second time. "Don't stop, please!"

"Why not? Those bastards nearly trashed this car and were trying to kidnap you and God knows what else!"

"I know, but we mustn't stop for the police. You have to get me away from here!"

Okay. I had time to think *this* one out. It wasn't a matter of reaction only. I could have stopped. I *should* have stopped. A lot of things would have turned out differently if I had.

But in my mind's eye, I can still clearly see us driving sedately past that police car as if nothing were out of the ordinary.

Even though I'd surprisingly decided that we weren't going to seek official help, there was still the matter of the smashed window to be dealt with. I didn't know of an all-night breakdown service, and I wasn't about to head back the way we'd come to roust me old mum out of her bed to ask her. There was no one around any more who I knew well enough to call on for help at 4:38 in the morning. The over-riding factor, though, to every alternative passing through my mind, was putting as much distance as possible between myself and those two carloads of thugs. Perhaps my "flight from fight" tendency had finally asserted itself, but in a more grown-up form: I now had a car in which to run away.

So I did the only sensible thing possible: got on the Ring Road with the goal of getting to the M6 and driving north—the way I'd originally meant to travel.

At speed on the highway, the wind howled through the jagged remains of the passenger window with a vengeance only winter and seventy-miles-per-hour can produce, making it even more imperative to get the thing covered over. Miraculously, neither of us had been cut on the glass littering the interior of the car.

By the time I'd begun considering the situation, Stafford appeared to be the logical choice for what I needed: not too close to the city and of sufficient size to have a twenty-four hour service station. It also had a railway station where I could dump the girl, one with connections to other lines. As chance would have it, I'd been in the area the day before to arrange transport back to Canada for a musical instrument I'd purchased.

"Why are we getting off?" my companion asked as we exited the motorway.

"We need petrol," I told her, "and we have to do something about that window."

She looked over and smiled feebly. "I want to thank you for what you did...stopping for me. I'm very sorry about your nice car."

"That's just the problem. This isn't my automobile. It's borrowed."

"Oh..."

"Oh, indeed. This Jaguar is the apple of its owner's eye, and he is *not* going to be pleased with what's happened."

Ahead, all I could see was darkened buildings and very few cars. Finally, we rounded a curve and ahead on the right saw a brightly lit Esso station with an attached Tesco Express and cash point, just what we needed.

I pulled up to a pump and got out gingerly, carefully shaking off the numerous little chunks of glass littering my clothes. My passenger also got out, looked around for a bit and decided the paper towelling the station provided would have to do for sweeping out the glass she'd been sitting in.

After filling the car, I checked out the damage to the body. It was as bad as I'd feared. Not something that couldn't be put right, but it was "going to cost a mint to put this to rights!"—as I could hear Angus bellowing when he saw it. I asked the night attendant, an elderly Sikh, if he could help out with something to cover the window. I fed him a story about yabbos and a fight outside a pub. The old man sympathized and came up with a translucent plastic garbage bag which I stuck on with a roll of gaffer's tape I found in the car's boot. He also loaned me a dust pan and brush to help with the glass removal, but made me swear to pick up any chunks that fell on the ground.

Using the cash point, I got some extra notes to pay for the petrol, bags of crisps and peanuts along with two cans of Coke. The old gent also got a five-pound note for his trouble.

Returning to the car, the girl was already sitting inside. Not wanting to talk to her through the sheet of plastic, I went around to the driver's side and got in. "Can I drop you at the railway station?"

She looked startled. "Drop me? Where are *you* going?"

I started the engine. "I'm afraid I'm off to Argyll to return this rather sad-looking automobile to its rightful owner—although I'm afraid it's going to be a memorable homecoming." I smiled at her. "He has a temper as red as his beard."

"Where is Argyll?"

"Scotland. Northwest of Glasgow. You *do* know where Glasgow is?"

"Of course I do," she answered sourly. "Can't I go with you?"

Now I was startled. "Look, this whole situation is surreal enough without prolonging it. I don't know you. I don't *want* to know you. I'll drop you at the railway station, and you can go wherever you want to go. The sooner you're out of my life, the sooner I can start to work thinking up an explanation for poor Angus as to why his car looks the way it does. I only have a eight-hour drive in which to accomplish *that* feat. I wasn't kidding about his temper. Now, where can I drop you?"

At my words, she looked even younger. It said something about her that she didn't fall back on that age-old ploy of women: rivers of tears. I would have booted her arse out of the car for that. Oh, I could see that she considered it for a moment, but I wasn't her daddy, and perhaps she saw from my expression that it wouldn't work.

The girl was not what I would call drop-dead gorgeous, but there was definitely *something* about her that made you want to look twice or maybe three times. She had huge hazel eyes in an oval face. Her mouth seemed a bit too large, but that could have been due to her choice of bright red lipstick. Her very fair complexion and thick, dark brown hair (pulled back at the moment) made her look rather like one of those women in Old Masters paintings. As for the rest of her, she had on a long, heavy coat, so I couldn't tell much. Physically, she seemed much like any young woman in her twenties: everything had pretty well assumed its final form, but life hadn't yet imprinted much in the way of character. Only her gaze, steady, patient and intelligent, belied the fact that she was simply just another cute specimen of the human female. One could get lost in those eyes...

She sighed deeply. "Okay. My name is Regina Mastrocolle. I'm from the States."

"I'd noticed that," I responded dryly.

Ms Mastrocolle made a face. "You can't drop me at a station or a bus stop, because I have no idea where to go, where I'd be safe. Those men found me once. I have to assume they can do it again."

I nodded. "That seems logical."

"I also have a pretty good idea who they are."

"Explain."

"The first group of men work for my father."

"*Your father?*"

"He hired them to bring me home."

"You've run away?" When she nodded, I had a sinking feeling in the pit of my stomach. "How old *are* you?"

She drew herself up a bit at that. "I'm going to be twenty-five in a month."

"Then why 'run away', as you put it? A woman your age should be able to just leave, if she chooses."

"You obviously don't know much about Italian families—and you've never met my father. He is *il Padrone*. The boss." And from the way she looked at me, I could see that she had a bit of *la padrona* herself. "Look, obviously I'm in trouble. I'd like to put as much distance as possible between myself and those people you met earlier. You said something about Glasgow. Would it be possible to drop me there? I'll pay for the gas." She smiled engagingly. "Whaddayasay?"

Now *that* last sentence had sounded like a New Yorker. Only they run words together like that. It had the calculated effect on me, and I put the car into gear.

"Okay. I'll take you as far as Glasgow. Just one question. You said that one group of men worked for your father. Who was the other group, then?"

She turned those big eyes in my direction, and they looked troubled. "I don't know."

CHAPTER 2

Surprisingly, the weather held for us on the long run to the Scottish border—a real blessing. My hurried patch job on the smashed window wouldn't have lasted long against heavy rain.

When you're travelling any distance in the British Isles during winter, the one thing you can be sure of is that the weather will change several times during the course of your trip—unless you're exceptionally lucky. Thankfully, we had been so far that day.

Just passing the junction for Liverpool, into that long, boring stretch where the M6 passes through Lancashire, the fact that I could barely feel my toes finally penetrated my sluggish brain. The heater in the car just couldn't keep up with the cold air flowing in around my trash bag patch job. I pulled into the next rest area to get something warm to drink and maybe a bit to munch on. Neither of us had felt like crisps or Coke, although we'd polished off one of the bags of nuts I'd bought.

Regina disappeared into the Ladies, and I am ashamed to admit to the momentary inclination to jump in the car and roar off. I settled for buying coffee for her and tea for me. The scones appeared stale, so I grabbed two muffins instead. I sometimes think that rest area food is supplied by grocery stores that want to get rid of their out-of-date products. Judging by the expression on the woman at the check-out, the stores might be shipping off their out-of-date employees, too.

As I pulled back into the line of early morning traffic, Regina took a sip of her coffee and frowned. "God, this is bad!" She must have thought better of her outburst, considering that I'd bought her the coffee unbidden, because she quickly added, "At least it's hot."

"You may have hit upon the reason so many Brits drink tea. Assuming the tea packet isn't horribly stale, it's usually your own fault if the muck doesn't taste good."

Regina took a few more sips, then staring straight out the windscreen and not at me, said, "Considering all you've done, I guess I owe you some sort of explanation."

"Perhaps it would be better not to tell me. I helped you out of a tight place, and that's it. I really don't need to know any more."

"But I don't have anyone I can talk to about it."

"Don't you have any friends who can help you?"

"No. And I certainly can't go to any of my relatives."

"A priest?"

"I don't know *who* I can trust," she answered in a low voice. "You seem kind, and you're old. I mean you're older than I am. Maybe you can help me help me figure out how to deal with this."

"Look, this is silly. You don't even know my name. You know *nothing* about me."

"I know you're kind and generous. I know that you can be trusted in a crisis." Regina flashed a quick smile. "So what's your name?"

"Michael Quinn. As I told you, I'm originally from Birmingham, but I live in Canada."

"Where?"

"Toronto. I run a backline instrument rental company."

"A what?"

"It's part of the music business. Say you have a band that doesn't want to tour with their own equipment; you need amplifiers, a drum kit, keyboards and the like. I supply them. Backline refers to things that form the back line on the stage."

"Sounds, um, interesting. Do you rent to famous people?"

"Sometimes. Mostly it's trade shows, showcases, smaller tours from the States or Europe, things like that."

"How long have you been doing this?"

"Since I arrived in Canada fourteen years ago."

"What did you do before that?"

"I was a musician."

Regina smiled again. "Okay, now I know all about you. So can I talk?"

I didn't see any way out of this unless I simply told her to shut up. "All right. What's the problem between you and your father?"

Judging by the way she'd been speaking, I figured Regina would just lay out the whole problem, and we'd discuss it or something. In reality, it seemed her words had been more bravado than anything else. She turned her head away, staring down at the space between her seat and the door, and I could distinctly hear sniffling.

After a few minutes, she straightened up, wiped her nose on a tissue she took out of a coat pocket, sniffed once or twice more and looked at me. "I'm sorry. I promised myself I wouldn't cry about this, that I was old enough not to start bawling."

I shrugged. "It's okay."

"No, it's not. I'm going to have to be strong if I'm going to get out of this."

"It might be easier if you started at the beginning and told it like a story. You know, give yourself a bit more distance."

So Regina began speaking and continued almost non-stop as we drove past Lancaster and up through the rolling hills of Cumbria, one of my favourite stretches of road in the world. *This* is what England looks like in my mind when I think of it back in Canada: grass-covered, treeless hills rolling away into the distance, long valleys filled with orderly fields, sheep everywhere you look. The M6 flows through this countryside like a tarmac snake, not conquering the landscape as many modern roads do. It's a pleasure to drive.

I hardly noticed it that day.

Without her saying as much, it quickly became clear that Regina's family had money—*a lot* of money. They lived in Greenwich, Connecticut, an area known for its posh homes. She'd grown up in a privileged household: servants, a swimming pool, tennis courts, a country club membership, all the trappings of wealth. Being an only child and her mother having died when she was eleven years old, her father had spoiled her rotten.

"Papa decided that I should go to school in Europe, that he couldn't properly care for a young lady. His business took a lot of his time. Our family originally comes from Abruzzo, but I was sent to a boarding school in Switzerland. The school was good, but it was a very lonely time for me. In the summer, I would go to Italy to visit family, and Papa would join me for a few weeks."

"So you haven't really lived in the States all that much."

"Not since my mom died. A few weeks at Christmas, between semesters sometimes, but never for very long. We'd vacation in

Europe, skiing or something. At home, there wasn't much to do. It wasn't easy to make friends, you see."

"Why not?" I asked, smiling. "You seem talkative enough."

Regina looked at me. "Are you teasing me?"

"No. What I meant is that you don't seem to have trouble striking up a conversation."

She nodded at that. "I was never let out on my own. Papa had bodyguards, and I couldn't go anywhere without one and sometimes two. You can imagine what *that* was like."

"Not really," I said, even though I did have *some* inkling. "Why would you need a bodyguard? Is your father a diplomat or something like that?"

"No. He told me he was a businessman. He owned a lot of real estate and some businesses, and he had enemies. Besides, there *are* people around who would like nothing more than to kidnap the child of a wealthy man and hold her for ransom."

"So it wasn't very nice being at home."

"In some ways, it was *very* nice. I'd have my papa all to myself. We'd play tennis together, swim. This past summer, he began teaching me to play golf. I had a few cousins in the area, too, but they're a lot older than me and also boys, so they kept their distance—except for Angelo. He was my favourite, because he teased me and called me his little sister. But they all seemed to be afraid of Papa. He can be very scary when he's angry.

"You're right, though. More and more it felt as if I was in prison, kept apart from people, even after I finished boarding school. I attended the Sorbonne in Paris and had no friends. I didn't tell you, but my mother was French—that's a bit odd in traditional Italian families."

"Did you visit your mother's relatives?"

"I've never met them. There was a falling out over the marriage, and Papa won't have anything to do with them."

"Sounds pretty grim. He obviously loosened the reins when you went to university, though, didn't he?"

"I thought so—at first. He arranged for me to have rooms in a private house. An older couple with one or two other student lodgers. I was majoring in Art History, and studying took up a lot of time. Sure, there were boys who asked me out, but it never developed into anything. They'd just drift off. I couldn't understand why, until one of them told me that he'd been approached by someone who asked him a lot of questions and made it clear that we were being watched."

"What did you do then?"

"I called my father and told him how angry I was. He flew right over and sat me down. 'You still need protecting,' he said. 'I'm doing what any father would do to protect his daughter.'

"I told him he was being ridiculous, that I was old enough to take care of myself. We had a big fight about it, but in the end, I got Papa to promise that he wouldn't interfere in my life."

"But he continued to, didn't he?"

"Was I really being that naïve? Is it so obvious to everyone else?"

"No, it's just that in my experience, when someone as seemingly strong-willed as your father capitulates so completely, then they're up to something."

"Exactly. Anyway, for the next three years, I went out on a few dates, but no one came along that really stirred my blood, and besides, I was engrossed in my studies. I'd decided to become a specialist in the restoration of damaged paintings. Papa spoke to some people he knew and got me a job with Galerie Longchamps in Paris. Research took up most of my spare time, too.

"Last fall, a man turned up out of the blue. I met him while I was eating lunch in a café—and he didn't give me the cold shoulder after a while like the others. He was great fun to be with. He teased me like Angelo had. What was wonderful was that I knew Papa would approve of him. Jean-Marc came from a proper family. I think I may have even been falling in love with him.

"Then one night I came down from my rooms and was waiting for Jean-Marc on the street when I saw him getting out of a car about two blocks away. He leaned back down and was talking to someone through the window. I wondered about that and drew back into the darkness of the doorway as the car drove past. I recognized the man as someone I'd once seen with my father.

"Jean-Marc walked up shortly after and pretended that he'd come on foot all the way from his parents' apartment. You should have heard the load of garbage he tried to feed me about his walk over! I told him he was despicable and that I never wanted to see him again. Without another word, he just turned on his heel and left. That was last week."

Regina looked silently out at the rolling countryside for several minutes, trying to regain her composure. I spent the time accelerating past a long line of cars.

"Better slow down or you'll get pinched," she said. "Next morning, I got on the first plane to New York. This was it! I was through having my life stage-managed!

"No one had any idea I'd left Paris. You should have seen the expression on the maid's face when she answered the door!"

"'Where is my father, Consuela?' I demanded.

"'Your father is in a meeting. You must not disturb him.'

"'The hell with that!' I said, pushing her out of the way.

"I stormed down the hall to his study, where he holds all his business meetings, and burst through the doors. There were a lot of people in the room. Some of my cousins and an uncle. Angelo was there. They looked totally stunned to see me.

"In the middle of the room was a man tied to a chair on a big sheet of plastic. He'd been badly beaten up. His face was covered in blood. Papa...my father was standing next to him, holding a gun against the man's head."

I almost lost control of the car. *"What?"*

"I have no doubt they were going to kill him, and only my walking in had prevented it. My father handed the gun to Angelo, grabbed my arm, and dragged me up to my room, where he practically threw me in and locked the door. The very strange thing was that Papa didn't look angry. If anything, he looked, I don't know, scared.

"Papa returned about an hour later with a dazed expression on his face and sat down heavily on my bed. 'The day that I have dreaded has arrived.'

"I'd had enough time to figure out a few things for myself. All those years of lies! Pretending he was simply a businessman. It was easy to see what had been going on now that the blinders were off. So many strange things suddenly made sense.

"He broke down! The only other time I'd seen him cry was when Mamma died. He begged for my forgiveness. He had sworn on the grave of my mother that I would never know, never be a part of his real life. I saw how easy it had been to fool stupid, naïve Regina! Ship me off to school. Keep me away from the house. Never for an instant let on where the money was *really* coming from. No wonder my cousins have always seemed so tentative around me. *They* knew! They were obviously part of it.

"I told him I wanted to be left alone. He went out like a whipped dog. It was a very strange thing. Angelo came in soon after and talked to me for a long time, telling me that Papa had only deceived me to protect me and to honour the dying wish of his wife. 'Your father is what he is, and your mother knew that when she married him. She thought she could change him, at least that's what your father says,' Angelo told me. 'We all told him you would find out someday anyway. Now it's happened, and your father is afraid you hate him, Gina.'

"Angelo tried to turn on that old charm, but I knew his hands were as bloody as my father's. 'What happened to that poor man downstairs?' I demanded.

"Angelo said, 'We were only asking him some questions. We needed to frighten him. I know it looks bad, but I swear he answered our questions, and we cleaned him up and sent him home.'

"'Liar!' I screamed, completely losing control. 'I can see it in your eyes, Angelo! This is nothing but a house of lies! I am such a fool! How could I have been so incredibly blind all these years?'

"I stayed in my room for three days. I wouldn't see anyone. Consuela left my meals on a chair in the hall. In the night I could hear Papa pacing the hallway outside my door. Finally, I decided what I would do.

"Next morning, I went down to the sun room where Papa always has breakfast, acting as if nothing was wrong. Papa's expression when I walked in was a mixture of fear and hope. It broke my heart to see it. In many ways, he *had* tried to be a good father. It didn't change anything, though.

"Sitting down at the table, I looked out at the grounds, pretty with some freshly fallen snow, and asked Papa how he was feeling. Consuela hurried in with orange juice and coffee for me. I ordered a big breakfast with all my favourite things. Everyone seemed very relieved.

"We made small talk, never referring to what had happened. I spoke of returning to my job in Paris and told him I wanted to pick out some new clothes to take back with me. He asked where I wanted to shop, and I told him Bloomingdales in New York City. Angelo could take me. Papa agreed right away.

"It was easy to convince him that I didn't have my credit cards with me, because I'd left Paris in such a hurry. Papa reached into his pocket and peeled off five one-thousand-dollar bills. I pouted and said I wanted to buy some special things. He gave me ten thousand in all."

I whistled. "Ten grand out of his pocket?"

Regina nodded. "He is always doing things like that. He once gave a thousand-dollar bill to a parking lot attendant just because he bowed when Papa got out of his car. You'll laugh to hear it, but I thought that was the way everyone behaved. He can be so, I don't know, courtly is the best way to describe it.

"Angelo arrived about an hour later, and we drove down to New York. He asked me what made me change my mind about things, and I told him that I couldn't change the way my family was, but they *were* my family, and that was that. He seemed really relieved.

"It wasn't hard to lose Angelo. He's a sucker for a pretty face, and I found the cutest salesgirl in that store to help me pick out dresses. Angelo was so busy chatting her up, he didn't notice me slip out of the dressing room. I'll bet he got hell from Papa!

"I took a cab to the airport and boarded a plane for London with only the few things I'd bought at Bloomies. When we landed, I hopped the first train for Birmingham—don't ask me why—and there you have it. I'd booked the B&B online and thought I'd just stay there until I figured out what to do. You know what happened next, although I don't know how they found me."

"The computer. If you looked up anything on the internet, you left a trail."

"But Papa hardly knows how to turn one on!"

"You *are* naïve," I said, and she bristled a little. "Your father may not know how to use a computer, but he doesn't need to. I'm certain his organization has men who know how to use them very well indeed. Nobody can survive in business these days without major computer skills—even the kind of business your father is involved in."

"I suppose you're right," she said.

"Bet on it. I wouldn't use a cash point or credit card for the same reason if I were you."

"Surely he doesn't have access to that kind of information!"

"Would you care to put a wager on it? He could."

Eventually, as we approached Scotland, and the rain which had been threatening during the entire drive finally started falling. In a short time, it had turned to sleet.

"What shitty weather!" Regina observed as I slowed down against the driving onslaught.

"This is Scotland. My friend Angus describes life in Scotland like this: 'You're born wet and cold and eventually you die.'"

He's only exaggerating slightly.

We had to pull into the next service area to patch up the repair job on the window. I toyed with the idea of stopping in Glasgow at least to get the window repaired before returning the car to its owner, but the weather report changed my mind. The temperature would continue falling during the afternoon, and more snow or freezing rain could be expected, especially in the Highlands. Argyll starts on the northern edge of Glasgow more or less, but is actually part of the Highlands, and I did not want to be out in wretched weather on some of the roads we had to travel.

Shortly before noon, about fifty miles south of Glasgow, we hit a long line of traffic: a breakdown or accident, no doubt. As we crept forward, sleet, helped along by a stiff north wind, came almost vertically at us and soon covered the road in a slick coating. Driving became treacherous, even at slow speeds. Making a decision, I asked Regina if she wanted to spend the night at Angus's, since I didn't want to take the time to drop her in Glasgow. Night came very early at this time of year.

"He has a ramshackle old place north of a town called Dunoon, just over the Firth of Clyde."

"Does he really have a savage temper?" she asked timidly.

"His bark is worse than his bite. Angus is big and loud, very Scottish, but all bluster. I'd trust him with my life. You'll like him."

She nodded. "All right. I wasn't looking forward to being by myself another night."

So we skirted around the southern end of Glasgow and turned west to Gourock and the ferry to Dunoon. The traffic eased a bit as we made our way along the River Clyde on the A8 through Port Glasgow and the seemingly endless town of Greenock.

I toyed with the idea of stopping for the night and trying to complete the trip in the morning when the weather forecast was better. That way I might also get rid of the girl. I did *not* wish to become any more embroiled in her mess than I already was.

Then the sleet let up, turning to rain. The ferry was in its slip and boarding at Gourock, and it looked like we'd be able to make it to Angus's before nightfall.

Only once before had I made a worse decision.

CHAPTER 3

Crossing the Firth of Clyde from Gourock to Dunoon was something I hated to contemplate, much less experience—even on a calm day. The Quinns will never be sailors, if I'm any indication. Look up seasickness in any dictionary, and my photo will be front and centre.

Alternatively, we could have got to Angus's by driving through Glasgow, up the western shore of Loch Lomond, crossing inland through the pass at Rest and Be Thankful then down the Cowel Peninsula. That was a hell of a long detour, especially in bad weather—compared to a twenty-three minute ferry crossing.

The water, kicked to life by a wind straight from the Arctic via the Hebrides, had a lot of the passengers on the ferry looking decidedly queasy. I spent the entire trip with my head hanging over the side, retching like a dog. Regina, after seeing she could do nothing to help me, went inside the boat to keep warm.

After many months at sea, our voyage came to a merciful halt. My mouth felt like the bottom of an ashtray as I got back into the car.

Angus's place was located on a mostly single-lane B road, running over the hills from just north of Dunoon towards the Isle of Bute, a beautiful and enjoyable drive in good weather. That afternoon, with sleet again beginning to fall, the trip was automobile hell, consisting solely of trying to prevent two lives from coming to a premature end by sliding across the ice into a tree, another vehicle, a rock face or falling off a cliff. The laybys are decidedly narrow, and full-length transports zip over the road without a care. Even the thought of meeting a Mini Cooper had me breaking out in a sweat.

That Regina proved to be a nervous passenger didn't help matters. "Jesus! You didn't tell me your friend lived in the back of beyond," she said after a particularly nasty slide that ended far too close to a rocky outcrop. "Why would anyone live in this desolation?"

"There's a good reason," I said, pulling hard on the wheel in an effort to straighten out.

After another hair-raising quarter of an hour, we'd slid our way down off the hills to the end of Loch Striven, passing the small hydroelectric power station there, then started up the steep road on the other side. If it hadn't been recently sanded, we'd never have made it. About halfway up the hill, I turned left off the road and down the icy drive, gingerly pulling to a stop next to a beat-up green Land Rover Angus had purchased from a local sheep farmer.

The drive ended in a few boulders, all that kept the unwary from tumbling down a steep slope and into Loch Striven below. In summer, the grass-covered hillside would be dotted with contentedly munching sheep while gulls, calling raucously, wheeled in the air above. The ever-present wind blowing up the loch would carry the wanderlust-inspiring tang of seaweed and salt water on its wings.

"*This* is why my friend chooses to live in the back of beyond," I said, indicating the breathtaking vista with a sweep of my hand.

Even with the heavy, leaden sky, driving sleet, and the teeth of a frigid wind bearing down at the bad end of a January day, the view was still worth taking in.

In clear weather, you could see far down the loch towards Bute. Angus's stone farmhouse, clinging to the side of its hill like some sort of mad architect's nightmare, had, in the owner's words, "as fine a view as many a laird would pay good money to possess." There was no place in the world Angus would rather live than in *this* place in his beloved Argyll. No matter where he might be, organizing the loading of mountains of gear on the never-ending tour of some band on the other side of the planet, or getting on yet another tour bus, his heart and soul were always firmly here.

I'd barely had time to switch off the engine when the "Laird o' the Manor" bounded out the side door, no shoes, no coat, red beard and long red hair blowing in the gale. "Michael! I've been keeping my eye out for you since noon, what with this weather and...*bloody hell!*" Poor Angus braked to a halt and gawped, shock covering his face. "What have you *done* to her, you bloody great bastard!"

I got out. "I'll pay for the damage in full, Angus. It was beyond my control."

"But *what happened?*"

"Well...it's like this," I began, but got no further.

Regina was out of the car, hugging her coat around her to keep out the wind. "It's my fault."

"Who the hell are *you*?" Angus demanded.

"Michael stopped to help me and...this happened." She faltered, looking rather intimidated by Angus's bristling beard, not to mention his bristling tone.

"All right," I said to both, "can we at least go inside to talk about this? It's brutal out here."

"Oh, yeah, right," Angus responded. "In we go, then."

Life at Chez Angus revolved around his sitting room and kitchen, which shared the front wall of the house, both of which had enormous picture windows framing the vista down to the loch. We'd spent many an evening sitting in front of one or the other, drinking single malt and talking quietly while daylight drifted away to darkness. There were three other rooms on the ground floor, and I don't think I'd ever done more than stick my nose in them.

Stomping our feet in the hallway, I noticed that the sitting room beyond looked as if an avalanche of loose paper had recently passed through, leaving the floor, tables, furniture, every horizontal surface buried.

"Please excuse the mess. I'm in the middle of doing my taxes. I didn't know that Michael would be bringing a guest, or I'd have straightened up a bit."

I let the little dig (and major lie) slide. Regina stood in the doorway, and it finally twigged with Angus that she expected someone to help her off with her coat. Behind her back, he raised an eyebrow, but kept his thoughts to himself as he took Regina's coat, hanging it next to mine on the pegs beside the door.

We picked our way through the sitting room and into the kitchen, where it was warm and steamy and smelled as if Angus had been doing his laundry in the new little washer/dryer set he'd recently purchased—a big step up from the old laundry tub and drying room.

"Can I get you something to warm you? Coffee? Tea? A wee dram?"

"A dram for me," I said. "I need it after that drive."

Regina seemed hesitant, then shrugged. "I'll have some, too."

Angus went over to a cupboard. "Then I'll just have to join you."

Sitting down at the table, he lined up three smallish tumblers and poured an amber measure into each. From a pitcher of water, he then doled out the merest splash into each glass. As we each took one, Angus intoned, "*Slainte mhath*!" and swallowed his scotch in a gulp. Slamming down his glass, he fixed each of us with a hard stare. "Now tell me just what the bloody hell happened to my beautiful automobile!"

III

"I still think you're a great fool to get yourself boxed in like that. *I* wouldn't have slowed down until I'd put a hundred miles or more between myself and those bastards," Angus said from over by the stove, where he was cooking. "I'm lucky there's anything left of my car!"

Regina and I had given Angus an edited version of what had taken place the previous night. Even though we hadn't discussed what to say beforehand, working in tandem, we supplied enough information to satisfy him, the interesting thing being what we'd left out. I felt it was up to Regina if she wanted to be as frank with him as she'd been with me. She said nothing. I also left out the part about the handguns. They aren't seen that much in the UK—being highly illegal. Knives and pieces of pipe Angus could understand. Guns were a different matter. He would have questioned those. So as far as he knew, two carloads of thugs had been after Regina, and she didn't know why. I'd happened along, tried to help, and the bashed-in Jaguar was the result.

"It just shows you can't go anywhere these days," Angus told us unnecessarily.

By that time, we were all growlingly hungry, and Angus offered to make some neeps and tatties and sausage—about the only thing he eats or can cook, for that matter. Regina had to have it all explained to her and looked as if she'd rather be served something else, but in the end gamely decided to take a chance, the alternative being a bowl of porridge.

"It'll be good. You'll see," Angus said as he came over and poured another 'wee dram' in each of our glasses. "I have some rather splendid venison and oatmeal sausages."

Regina looked rather appalled. "Venison and oatmeal?"

"Aye, lassie. Tuck into a couple of those, and you'll soon be farting like a hero!"

The poor girl coloured deeply and hastily took a gulp of her whisky—too big or too quickly because she began coughing, to the point where Angus had to pound on her back.

In the end, it turned out to be an excellent, warming meal. We sat in candlelight and watched the weather outside deteriorate. When we finally pushed our plates away, Angus poured more whisky. I was definitely beginning to feel tight.

"So, did you buy the instrument, Michael?" he asked.

I nodded. "The lads at Rugeley did a fine job restoring it. It's a good investment."

"But a mellotron? Those buggers are more trouble than they're worth!"

I shrugged. "They're hot right now. Studios will pay a good buck to rent them, and besides, the things have always fascinated me."

"What are you talking about?" Regina asked.

"Some silly instrument Quicksilver here came over to the UK to purchase."

"That's the second time you've called Michael 'Quicksilver.'"

Angus raised an eyebrow at me. "Didn't you tell her?"

"Tell me what?"

"Our Michael used to be a bloody great rock star. Called himself Michael Quicksilver."

"That was a long time ago," I protested.

"Why does that name ring a bell?" Regina said, half to herself.

"Ever hear of a band called Neurotica?" Angus eyed me mischievously, knowing full well how uncomfortable I was becoming.

"Yes!" Regina said. "I remember my older cousins playing their CDs all the time when I was about ten." She turned to me excitedly. "You were in that band?"

"Ah, yes, I was," I answered neutrally.

"He *was* the bloody band!" Angus roared. "Wrote all of their early hits!"

"Angus, that's not really true," I protested. "Rolly co-wrote them with me."

"Bollocks! Those were *your* songs, and no one knows that better than me. I was there! You know 'Don't Push Me'? Our Michael wrote that. Neurotica's biggest hit, too. Keeps him in mell-o-trons, it does!"

"That is so cool!" Regina said excitedly, humming a few bars of the song. "I remember seeing a clip of your band playing 'Don't Push Me' on *Saturday Night Live.*" She peered closely at me. "Yeah, you're him. How come you didn't say anything, Michael?"

"He doesn't like to talk about it," Angus answered for me.

"I left the band pretty early on," I clarified.

Regina seemed surprised. "But why?"

Angus poured himself a larger drink than his previous ones. It was going to be one of those nights. "He doesn't like talking about *that,* either."

"Can't we just drop it?" I asked.

"I don't want to talk about it if it makes Michael uncomfortable," Regina added.

Angus eyed me. "Speaking of which, Rolly called yesterday."

My stomach tightened. "What did he want?"

"To know if you'd changed your mind. Somehow he got wind you were in the UK."

"And I suppose he wanted you to talk me into it."

I could tell from Angus's expression that was *exactly* what the lead singer and "guiding light" of my former band had asked him to do, same as always. Idiot! Just because I'd remained friends with our old road manager didn't mean I harboured *any* good feelings for Rolly or wanted a thing to do with him.

"There would be very good money in a reunion of Neurotica," Angus stated.

He'd reminded me of that before, too. Two days earlier, as a matter of fact, when I'd been through to see him—and to borrow his car for the trip down to Birmingham. It was supposed to have been an enjoyable little ride down and back. A chance to spend some time with me mum. Decompress a bit...

"You can tell Rolly the answer is still, and will always be: when hell freezes over. *That's* when it will bloody well happen! I've moved on."

Angus looked at me from under his bushy eyebrows for a long moment before asking softly, "Have you then, lad? You could at least talk to him."

"No. If he's so hot to re-form the band, he can use what's-his-name to play keyboards."

"Rolly and the others want you and *only* you. None of the replacements could ever hold a candle to what you brought to the band, and even *they* acknowledge that. Come on, don't have such a stiff neck!"

"No."

Regina, silently watching the rising heat between Angus and me, decided a change of subject was in order. "Tell me about your house, Angus," she slid in effortlessly. "It looks as if it's very old."

He took the bait (and another drink). "Nay, lass. It's barely four hundred."

My old friend soon was off with his standard exposition on the history of the house, its outbuildings, the property, the immediate area, Argyll ("Don't ever trust a Campbell, lassie!") and would eventually get to an overview of all Scotland from the beginning of time if she showed the slightest enthusiasm.

I stared out at the snow blowing onto the hillside below and a distant gleam of light from another lonely house on the opposite shore of Loch Striven.

When would Rolly ever get the message?

Some time after eight, Angus showed us to our rooms, since we were completely knackered. With amusement, I noticed he gave Regina (whom he'd taken to calling The Princess) the room *I* usually got—it being closest to the loo, a very cold excursion on a winter night in the unheated upstairs.

Angus surprised me by producing a flannel nightgown for The Princess, probably a leftover from one of his failed attempts to form more than a passing acquaintance with a member of the fair sex.

He seemed quite taken with her in his own way. Seen without a bulky coat buttoned up to her chin, Regina certainly merited a second glance. She seemed taller, probably because of her slenderness and long neck. And even though she had on the regulation clothing of the young set these days, designer jeans and sweatshirt, Regina *did* exude a certain, I don't know, *regalness*, something which probably owed its origin to the way she was brought up. So, The Princess it was.

She again thanked both of us for our kindness, and as Angus stomped off to his room, she told me in a low voice how fortunate it was that I'd happened along. "You're kind of a knight in shining armour, you know, although reading between the lines from what was said tonight, you'll probably find that embarrassing." Leaning forward, she kissed my cheek. "Thank you, Michael."

Even though I'd missed a night, as usual sleep remained far away, and a half hour later, I was trying to decide if I wanted to read a bit, when someone knocked softly on my door.

"Are you awake?" Regina whispered.

"Yes," I called out, clicking on the bedside light. "Come in." When she'd slid in the door, I added, "You'll excuse me for not getting out of bed but I'm, ah, not dressed at the moment."

An indefinable expression flitted across her face. "Sorry to have bothered you. After all you've done for me, it's not fair to keep you awake, but..."

"What is it?"

She sat down on the chair by the door. "I guess it's a delayed reaction to what happened. I mean, you can imagine what a rollercoaster this past week has been. Back in my bedroom, alone with my thoughts, it finally hit me what kind of danger I was in—*am* in. I know my father truly loves me. There's no doubt of that. It's just...it's just..."

I sat up a bit straighter. "It's just that you haven't yet accepted what you've found out about him."

She nodded her head, her big eyes staring at me. "That's *exactly* what it is. You see everything so clearly, Michael."

"I wish that were true."

"It is! You've known *exactly* what needed to be done right from the beginning. You've let me talk when I needed to talk and were quiet when I needed peace to think. And you brought me here. I don't know how I would have been able to bear being all alone tonight. I'm so frightened!"

I nodded. "I wouldn't want to be in your position. Finding out that your father's, um..."

"He's a criminal, Michael. You can say that. I've had the past week to think of *nothing* else. My father has almost certainly killed people. I'm the daughter of someone in the mob."

"I'm so sorry for you," I said lamely.

"I knew you'd say something like that." Regina stopped and sighed heavily. "I feel as if I've been forced to grow up because of all this. Oh sure, I was out of school. I had a good job in an exciting city, but it's as if I've never been out from behind my father's shadow. He's always had someone watching over my shoulder, protecting me, shielding me from life. I'm wondering now what would have happened if I'd tried to do something he wouldn't have approved of."

"Like what?"

Regina looked straight at me. "Like taking a man into my bed."

I was astounded. "But you told me you'd had boyfriends. Didn't you ever...I mean..."

She laughed ruefully. "I felt that was something I couldn't do until I was married. Papa had forced that into my head from an early age. 'Men are not to be trusted, little Gina. They only want one thing from pretty girls like you!' A few times over the years, someone *has* come on to me, but I always put them off. I don't think I want that any more."

Regina stood up and undid the two buttons at the top of her nightgown. Being made for someone larger, it slipped easily over her shoulders and dropped to the floor.

She stood there for a long moment, lit only by the meagre light of a forty-watt bedside lamp. I was once again strongly reminded of an old painting, this one by someone with a more lusty view of his subject matter. Regina's body was quite beautiful.

What she was offering stunned me into speechlessness. She saw my confusion and padded over to the bed. "Slide over," she said matter-of-factly. "It's colder out here than I thought it would be." She felt deliciously cool and soft as I meekly let her join me.

I finally found my tongue. "Regina, this is crazy! Have you really thought about what you're doing? I mean—"

She put her hand over my mouth. "Hush! Yes, I *have* thought about it, about doing something crazy and out-of-control. I want to be my own person, dammit! Not some china doll that's locked in a glass case for people to stare at. I want to live! I want to know what it feels like to be with a man." She giggled, instantly sounding much younger. "You just happened to come along first." She opened her hand. "See? I even have condoms."

"I don't think this is a good idea, I mean, well, I'm old enough to be your father."

"Then you should know how to do this properly! The only way you're going to get me out of this bed is to throw me out." She quickly flipped herself on top of me, and looking down, asked, "Do you think you can do it?"

"What if *I* don't want to do this?"

Regina giggled again. "It certainly feels as if you do!"

"You're not fighting fair," I groaned.

"Angus told me that you're forty-nine, Michael. Do you mean to tell me that you haven't figured out yet that this sort of thing is *never* fair?" She leaned down and kissed me, wiggling around deliciously and making it even harder to think clearly. "At least I already know how to kiss."

"Yes, you do," I answered. "Regina..."

"No, Michael. No more talking. My mind is made up!"

I must have done a good job because, lying back a half-hour later, she was sweaty, flushed and slightly out of breath when she laughed delightedly, "Good God, Michael! Is it always like that?"

I was definitely out of breath. "Not always—in my experience."

"No wonder Papa never wanted me to know about it! I could easily become addicted."

"I'm glad you liked it. You were quite wonderful." I reached out and stroked her cheek. "Now, it's time we got some sleep."

She propped herself up on one elbow and used a finger to play with my chest hair. "No! I want to do it again."

"Have a heart! Neither of us got any sleep last night."

Her expression turned delightfully petulant. "No. Now!"

After the second time, I was ready to pass out from exhaustion and was asleep almost the moment my head hit the pillow.

Caught in the Act

Neurotica impresses in Manchester debut

If you haven't heard about Neurotica, the latest hot thing out of the Midlands, well get your head out of the sand! We caught them last night as opening act for The Clash in Manchester. Trust us when we say Neurotica won't be opening for anyone for very long after their debut album is released next week.

We'd like to be able to tell you who they remind us of but we really can't. They certainly aren't like the current crop of punk guitar thrashers, and I definitely wouldn't call them a pop act, but there are elements of both in their material. Neurotica can blast and strut with the best of them for sure, but their music certainly contains more than a nod in the direction of Peter Gabriel via XTC.

As is usual for the warm-up group, they got about half the wattage from the sound system and lighting, and initially about half the interest from the audience – other than a few hundred of their fans scattered throughout the stadium. That didn't last long. This band commands your attention from their very first note.

Unlike the usual guitar-laden bands so popular these days, Neurotica sports a full-blown keyboard virtuoso going by the name of Michael Quicksilver. This is certainly a musician to keep your eye on. Not one to go in for arse-wiggling antics, he just stands there and gets on with it. With a full keyboard rig, Quicksilver comes equipped with all the sounds, but unlike so many others, he actually knows how to use them. Some of the changes of texture he achieved were simply breathtaking. His match in virtuosity is guitarist Johnny Bowen, some of whose solos absolutely pinned the crowd to their seats, but who also knows when to back off. Quite refreshing approach, really, one we wish more guitarists used now and then.

The rest of Neurotica are workmanlike blokes, the standout here being frontman Rolly Simpson. Blessed with a clear voice and swaggering stage manner, he's sure to warm up the young ladies in the audience, being somewhat reminiscent in looks to Robert Plant.

Neurotica was midway through "Don't Push Me", their debut single release (already previewing on the Beeb) when the sound system "failed". Could it be The Clash was getting nervous?

You heard it here first: "Don't Push Me": monster worldwide hit. There's also a tour in the States for this summer. – SIMON STONE

Disappointment felt at start

CHAPTER 4

The change in the weather as we landed in Toronto came as quite a shock. While Scotland had been snowy, damp and miserable, the temperature hadn't come close to the effect of the glacial air mass that held southern Ontario in its grip. To top it off, when I'd left town, the weather had been more like March than January.

I left the plane, feeling gritty and hung over, the result of almost no sleep over the past two days. The cold bit right to the bone, going some way towards jolting me out of my stupor.

Boarding a plane in Glasgow twelve hours earlier, I'd asked for an extra pillow and given the flight attendant strict instructions not to wake me for any reason, then spent the trip in that peculiar twilight world where you're not sure whether you're awake or asleep. I'd done the same thing on the connecting flight from Heathrow. Consequently, when I eventually opened my eyes, it felt as if I hadn't really slept at all.

I should have stayed another day at Angus's, gotten the sleep I needed and taken the flight back to Toronto on which I had actually booked a seat, but...I couldn't.

Face facts, Quinn, I said to myself, *Angus was right. You turned tail and ran.*

While it had still been pitch black out, I'd carefully pulled away from Regina's warm body, and making certain I didn't wake her, I'd grabbed my clothes and suitcase and beat it.

As expected, I'd found Angus already up and sitting in the dull glow of a floor lamp in the middle of his sitting room, attempting to wrestle his tax receipt avalanche into submission. "Good God, Michael, it's only half five! I thought you'd be asleep for hours yet."

"I have to get back to Toronto. Will you drive me to the airport?"

"But your bloody plane isn't until tomorrow! You're going to pay through the nose to change your ticket if you leave now. Why the haste?"

"Something's come up."

"And what about the lassie?"

I tried to keep my face suitably blank. "I assume she's still asleep."

Angus fixed me with a curious expression. "I noticed on my way downstairs that she didn't sleep in her own bed last night."

"I *am* aware of that," I answered phlegmatically. "Are you going to take me to the airport?"

"Does she know you're leaving?"

"What difference does that make?"

"I think it might make *a lot* of difference to *her*," my friend answered as he got to his feet.

"Look, you're not my bloody nanny. I know what I'm doing."

"Do you? You weren't always like this."

"And you know *why* I am like this now," I said, taking my overcoat from the peg by the door.

Angus put his beefy hand on my shoulder, turning me to face him. "Michael, that was long ago. I'm not saying that what we did was right or wrong, but we did it, and it's over. Time to put the past to rest."

"Who's to say I haven't?" I shook off his hand and picked up my suitcase. "Maybe I just don't want the bother of having someone mixed up in my life right now."

"You did last night."

"Yes, and I'm regretting it already."

"What about all the other things? You know this exile you've put yourself in? This life you're living isn't the one you were destined to follow. Why deny it?"

"Look Angus, old friend, we've been down this road before, dozens of times. Nothing has changed. I'm through making music. It doesn't interest me any more."

"Bollocks! Then why the hell are you still hanging around on the fringes of the music business? You *do* want in again, and you're too stubborn or too *stupid* to see it!"

"Take me to the airport, or don't, but I'm leaving," I replied tensely.

"All right, all right, but I'll take you only as far as Dunoon. After that, you're on your own. I am *not* crossing the Clyde," he answered, as he grabbed his coat.

The roads were in better shape, but the ride was hardly less hair-raising, since daylight was still a few hours away. At least Angus knew the road well, and the Rover had better traction.

As we descended from the hills to sea level, I came to a decision. "We weren't strictly on the level with you last night about the Jaguar."

My friend continued staring straight ahead. "I'm aware of that."

I was startled. "How?"

"Because whoever smashed my automobile had to have been very angry. You're not the type to cause people to behave that way, and from what I've seen, neither is your lassie."

"She's *not* my lassie!"

Angus shrugged. "So what did happen?"

I gave him a more accurate version, still leaving out the part about Regina's father. It was up to her to tell him about that.

"So six great lumping bastards were chasing one wee lassie? There's more to this story than you're telling me."

"Be that as it may, I'm telling you this so you'll know."

"Know what?"

"Look, they might show up at your door. These are people you don't want to mess with."

"You did."

"Only because I didn't have a choice. Just take this as a warning. If I were you I'd go on holiday to the south of France or head to the Caribbean."

"No one chases me from my place!"

I slumped in my seat, having known before the conversation had started that it would end like this. Well, at least I'd tried to warn him. I just hoped he didn't get punched in the nose or knocked around if they showed up. Angus always was as stubborn as a mule.

He put his hand on my arm as we pulled up at the ferry dock. "What am I supposed to tell The Princess when she wakes up?"

"Here, I'll write a note," I said, taking a scrap of paper and a pen from my coat pocket. I scribbled a few lines and handed the result to Angus.

"*I've had to go back home suddenly. Glad to have been able to help you—and get to know you. Best of luck in the future. You're a really great person.*" Angus shook his head. "That's cold, Michael, very cold. And what am I supposed to do with her after she's read this? After all, *you* brought her here."

I opened the door, letting in a blast of cold air. "She's a big girl. Let her decide."

III

While waiting for my bag to come down the chute in the baggage claim area, I got on the phone to my business, knowing full well that I should have called them the day before.

A crisp voice answered, "Quinn Musical Equipment, Canada's backline specialists. How may I direct your call?"

"Let's see, Kevin, how about connecting me with the Department of Phone Answering Bullshit?"

"Oh, it's you boss! Where you calling from?"

"The airport. I came back early. Anything up that I should know about?"

"That huge order for the DataSwitch tour went out right on time, no hitches. We got a call about quoting for the Downtown Jazz Festival, and a little walk-in business. Not much else since the last time we talked."

"You *did* get a certified cheque and have DataSwitch's road manager sign the damage waiver, didn't you? Remember what happened the last time those idiots used our equipment."

Kevin didn't try hiding his bored tone. "Yes, I remember: most of it had to be thrown on the scrap heap, because they'd decided to pull a Who the last night of their tour and trashed everything. You remind us about that at least once a week."

Even though it mightn't sound like it, I had a good crew, and I cut them a lot of slack in how they spoke to me. But when it mattered, they knew who the boss was, even though I seldom had to exercise that particular power.

"Well, if there's nothing requiring my urgent attention, I'm off home, and I will see you first thing in the morning. I'm knackered."

"Oh, yeah, I forgot one thing," Kevin said. "Betty the Customs Bitch just called to say they had a large flight case that came in. They'll have it cleared by morning. She wants to know if we'll pick it up, or should they deliver it. Is it what I think it is?"

Kevin had called Betty the "Customs Bitch" ever since he'd put the make on her and she'd laughed him off, but she was good at her job and gave me great service.

"Must be," I answered. "We weren't expecting anything else. That was bloody fast! I only bought the mellotron three days ago!" The lads at Rugely Electronics had the reputation of always being prompt with everything. "I'll phone Betty and take care of it."

I made that call, saying we'd pick up the mellotron the next morning, grabbed my bag, retrieved my car from the long-term car park and headed downtown.

During the forty-minute drive, Angus lectured me about my disappointing life. He didn't have to be in the car to do that, because I could hear his voice perfectly well in my head. "You can't keep running away from life, Michael, because when you finally decide you want to take part in it again, you may find it's too late."

III

Much as I generally prefer being alone, I could never feel comfortable in a place as remote as the one Angus had chosen. It was rather odd that gregarious Angus lived in the middle of nowhere, while withdrawn Michael always went to ground in the middle of a city.

My present digs suited me quite well: a loft renovation just west of Toronto's downtown core. I'd bought the place when it wasn't yet trendy to live in a renovated factory. Now they're all turning into yuppie enclaves, and the prices have gone right out of sight. Since I didn't want people (primarily the lead singer from my former band) to know where I live, I'd taken great pains to preserve my anonymity. The phone number was unpublished, the ownership of the loft was through a numbered company, and even my staff only knew how to reach me via cell phone.

Angus had commented on all that, too, the first time he'd visited. Regardless of whether his observations about me bore any credence, from an early age I'd always preferred my own company much of the time and didn't find it strange nor wearing.

My place was in a four-storey, rather imposing brick structure almost a century old. They'd made typewriters and other office machines there, before the firm finally went belly up in the sixties. I'd paid a very good price for my loft because the developer had run short of cash before completing the renovation of the building. I'd got wind of that and offered to pay for mine up front at a reduced price.

I occupied the southeast corner of the top floor, the best spot because of the fantastic view of the Toronto Islands and the downtown core. The floors were the original wood, sanded and polished. It had twelve-foot ceilings, and not a lot of furniture: comfortable stuff, mostly old pieces I'd picked up at yard sales, and a few upmarket pieces that had caught my eye. The walls, painted in cream and brown, also had some art of the abstract kind. Early on, I'd succumbed to buying a big stereo but generally listened to recordings through headphones. My two extravagances were books I'd bought over the years which took up eighteen feet of wall, and a nine-foot Blüthner grand piano which sat in the outside corner of the sitting room, where I could look out the window as I played. Since my downstairs neighbour was seldom in the country, I could generally bang away whenever it suited me.

Putting my suitcase down in the entryway, I went over to the thermostat and cranked up the heat several notches. Outside, the wind was raging to the howling point, and I could tell from the way it drove tendrils of cold in around the windows that the night would see the temperature plummeting to the bottom reaches of the thermometer. After closing the curtains in order to keep as much of the frigid air at bay as possible, I headed down the hall to the kitchen with the idea of brewing a pot of tea.

Even though they'd been there so long I hardly noticed them any more, something caused me to stop and examine the gold and platinum recording awards that hung the length of the hall.

Several were for *Don't Push Me*, Neurotica's debut album, named after the song Regina, twenty-four years my junior, could sing. It had been a hit before she was born, for Christ's sake! I didn't know which made me more depressed: the fact that I'd slept with someone so young or the fact that her knowing my tune drove home so solidly that the best point in my life had taken place over a generation earlier.

I hadn't aged badly, the reward for a careful life, I guess. The passing years had done good things for my face, seemingly bringing out the strong points and hiding the weak. I'd kept most of my hair, and there was little sign of grey among the brown. Years of slugging equipment in and out of trucks had kept me trim, that and the fact that I skipped meals too often. Turning away from the present, I looked into the past, a promo photo taken in my twenty-second year at the end of the hall, showing a six-foot lad with long brown hair and a rather ascetic, sharp-featured face. What I couldn't deny, though, was the untroubled expression of a person who had the world by the tail and his whole life ahead of him. *That* certainly was no longer in my eyes, but life has a way of obliterating those sorts of things.

Those had indeed been heady days, everything happening so fast. One month we were just another struggling Brummy bar band with a solid local following, and the next, we had management and a major record label paying for us to record at a posh London studio. In short, we were being groomed as Rock Stars. *Don't Push Me* turned out to be the success everyone had predicted. The album quickly went gold, then platinum, and eventually double platinum, meaning that we sold a boatload of recordings. The single did equally as well.

The tours had always been the best part of it for the rest of the band. The excessive lifestyle had suited them all—especially Rolly, who embraced it with Bacchanalian gusto. I lived for being in the studio. I enjoyed most the time after everyone had left for the day with the hangers-on, spending hours experimenting, re-arranging, tweaking, looking for that something special that would take every song to the next level.

I made two albums with Neurotica and left them with enough material for a third. Although I didn't have anything to do with recording it, to my sad satisfaction, it showed in its mediocre sales. Rolly and I always took writing credit for the songs, me for the music and Rolly for the lyrics—even though towards the end he was too busy becoming a legend to do more than a cursory job. ("Yeah, yeah, Michael. Sounds fine to me. You might want to fix up the chorus a bit. The lyric's bloody depressing.") The material on the second album was consequently almost completely mine. It was during the tour in support of its release that the whole thing had imploded for me.

The kettle sang its steamy note, jerking me back to the present, and I sat brooding for almost an hour over two cups. It hadn't been a good idea to visit Angus. I didn't like it when the old trouble got stirred up.

Regardless of what I'd said, I also felt guilty about leaving Angus with a twenty-four-year-old problem named Regina. Heaven only knew how she had taken it when she'd woken up to find me long gone. But her problems were not something I could or would get involved in. When it counted, I'd done my bit and helped out a fellow human being. What had happened between us afterwards had all been her idea. If she now felt any remorse or anger about it, then it was her problem. Right?

So how come I didn't really believe that?

III

Next morning, I pried myself out of a pleasantly warm bed and looked out at a snow-covered city. The wind had died down during the night, and white stuff was falling in big lazy flakes.

Dressing, I couldn't help feeling silly about the night before, allowing myself to wallow in self-pity over how life had changed the cards I'd been dealt. A lot worse could have befallen me.

I'd built a successful business, and I still had a generous income from the royalties of my youthful musical endeavors. I could indulge myself when I wanted, buying silly unneccesaries such as the BMW M3 which sat in the parking garage in the basement of the building, the Blüthner in my sitting room, and now the ultimate silly musical toy waiting in a shipper's warehouse at the airport.

A quick glance at the clock showed me I'd better get my arse in gear if I wanted to pick up my latest vintage keyboard before noon. Toronto traffic could be horrible with even a small amount of snow. It's an odd thing that in a wintry country like Canada, few drivers in its largest city seem capable of driving in even moderately bad weather.

On my way to the customs broker, I phoned up the shop, getting Johnny, my newest recruit and a total keener for the job. Sensing that about him right from the beginning, I'd given him his own key earlier than I normally would have with a new employee. My intuition had so far proven correct. He was always first to arrive and last to leave.

"Welcome back, boss!" he said when he heard my voice. "Kevin told me that you'd scored on your big game hunt 'over 'ome'. Are we picking it up today?"

"Yes. I'm on my way to the shipper's warehouse to sign the papers and pay the charges. Bring the small van and meet me in an hour."

"You bet! This is going to be so cool. I've never seen one of the big mellotrons up close."

"You're probably going to be pretty sick of it before long, Johnny-my-lad, since it's to be *your* responsibility to maintain it."

III

As usual with these things, it took two times longer to bail out the mellotron than I'd planned, with the result that it was past twelve when I rolled into the industrial mall in the northern Toronto suburb of Unionville, where I had my business. Kevin and my other employee, Hamed, were busy loading our fourteen-foot box van with a small mountain of equipment rented for a movie shoot at a downtown location. Seems someone had taken it into their head to make a film about the trials and tribulations of a rock band on the road in the late sixties. Spare me!

"Where's the 'tron?" Kevin asked as he stood in the back of the truck, sweating profusely, even though the cold in the warehouse was fairly intense because of the open door.

"Johnny's behind me somewhere with it. I told him to take it slow, since the roads are rather slick." Looking over the equipment contract on the clipboard, I noticed that several more amplifiers had been requested and added, "What in heaven's name do they need all this for? You could play an arena with this amount of gear."

Hamed took the clipboard from me and checked off another three amps. "That's exactly what they're doing. Apparently they have actors who can actually play a bit, and they're going to stage a sort-of-real concert at Maple Leaf Gardens, or what's left of it. They need the equipment for an extra week, too," he grinned.

I'd actually played The Gardens with Neurotica back in the day. Partially dismantled, it was now a sad relic of the past, with all of the concert action having moved south to the Air Canada Centre and the super-large nightclubs on the waterfront. I hardened my resolve *not* to visit the movie set.

I found a week's worth of phone and e-mail messages waiting

when I sat down at my desk, and it took quite a while to wade through it all. January was normally a pretty slow month, but the amount of business coming through the door was either a fluke or a very gratifying upturn.

Writing up work orders took pretty well the rest of the day, and after filling out a deposit slip, I decided to cut out a bit early to stop off at the bank on the way home. As I headed for the back door, Johnny was the only one around. The other lads hadn't got back from the movie shoot delivery and would probably be several hours yet, since they'd have to set up all the gear and test it. That would be duck soup for Hamed, who could play guitar pretty well (imagine a Palestinian heavy metal guitarist, if you will) and loved showing off with some hot licks on a high-volume rig. Kevin could play bass well enough, too, so if a drummer could be found kicking around the set (not such an impossible thing), they would have everything needed for an impromptu concert. If there were some babes hanging around (also not hard to imagine on a movie set), so much the better, as far as they were concerned. I wished them well.

"Can we crack open the mellotron case tomorrow and take it for a test drive?" Johnny asked.

"Sure. Get out one of the Hiwatt stacks and a drum stool. Don't turn it on, though, until I go through the check list the Rugely lads gave me. We *don't* need the mellotron to eat its tapes as soon as we hit the mains switch." I took a look at the next day's duties on the clipboard. "If you want to get a jump on things for tomorrow before you leave, there's that Hammond B3 and Leslie going out early. Make sure it's working properly. I've marked which one I want you to send." Handing Johnny the board, I walked to the door. "And don't forget they want bass pedals. For heaven's sake, send the good set!"

The cold hit like a hammer blow as soon as I opened the door, making me wish I'd decided to settle someplace like southern California.

On the way, I stopped at a supermarket for a few things, including a frozen meat pie for dinner, then made a beeline for home and warmth. Tonight was an evening for a roaring fire and a good book.

After dinner and a glass or two of wine, I wound up behind the piano instead. I noticed with some disgust that the tuning had slipped again, mostly because I'd turned down the heat when I'd left for the UK.

I had a Mozart sonata I'd been casually fooling around with lately, and that kept my fingers and mind occupied for over an hour. Gradually, though, my thoughts started wandering into other channels, and my fingers followed suit. First it was a couple of jazz standards: "What's New?", "Lover Man", moody things like that. Then the rock and roll started creeping out of the dark recesses: a mindless boogie progression in G. Finally something, from where I have no idea, insinuated itself into my brain, and my fingers began following its trail. A melody popped into my head, and I began humming over the chords. It started so innocently, and it felt like it always had in the past when the creative juices began flowing.

I jumped violently to my feet, knocking the piano bench over. Slamming down the keyboard lid as if the piano were somehow responsible for what had happened, I stomped over to one of the windows overlooking Lake Ontario, pulled the curtain aside and stared out. A few stars gleamed brightly in the cold, hard night sky. The air was so clear, you could actually pick out several craters on the nearly-full moon.

I stood looking out for a long time, thoughts both good and bad flipping through my brain at ninety miles per hour.

Next morning, I got my sorry arse out of bed at a reasonable hour. After taking a long, steamy shower and actually stopping for breakfast on the way, I arrived at the shop even before Johnny. As I had feared, the fourteen-foot van was not in its usual spot blocking the loading door. Hamed and Kevin had probably made a late night of it.

If someone were really determined to steal equipment, I didn't harbour any illusions that it couldn't be managed. I tried to make things difficult only to keep the casual thieves at bay. Good locks, an efficient alarm system and a big truck in front of the loading doors saw to that. Even if Kevin had gotten well into the booze or drugs, Hamed, who didn't indulge in either, should have driven the truck back. I'd have to speak to them.

Two years earlier, I'd moved Quinn Musical Equipment out of an inadequate and over-priced space in downtown Toronto into one of those anonymous industrial malls that any big city has springing up in its nether regions like pimples on the landscape. I sometimes suffered a guilty pang from the knowledge that my business stood on what had once been a productive farm, but the mall had already been built by the time I leased space, and if it hadn't been me doing it, someone else would have set up shop regardless. The farm was gone forever.

Almost the whole of our three thousand square-foot space was taken up by floor to (twenty-foot) ceiling shelving units containing amplifiers of all descriptions and wattage, speaker cabinets, drum kits, various keyboards old and new, monitor systems, a few small mixing desks, in short, anything that might be needed on a stage during a musical performance. Quinn didn't supply sound reinforcement systems or stage lighting, since they were too specialized and needed trained crews to set up and operate them, but if a client requested it, I knew people in the business whom I could book for those duties. Recording studios were increasingly renting our vintage equipment, mostly keyboards, for various projects. Those contracts were lucrative and easy to deal with. The tough ones were one-day concert rentals. The first few of that type of gig I'd done when I was starting out made me aware of how much Neurotica had owed our road crew. Talk about a thankless job. Try moving a few tons of equipment twice in one day.

The front of the building housed my small office and a rehearsal studio/demo room, where clients could try out equipment before renting. I attempted to keep everything orderly but had given up most of that fight long ago. As long as the condition of the place didn't cross the line into squalor, I could live with it.

In my office, after bringing my computer to life and checking e-mails, I listened to the answering machine. With nothing urgently needing my attention, I went back out into the warehouse area, where Johnny had taken my latest acquisition out of its baby-blue flight case. One of his mates must have picked him up the previous evening, since he couldn't have opened it by himself. From my briefcase, I got out Rugely Electronic's list of "Things to check before switching on your mellotron" and had the back off the cabinet with my head inside when Johnny arrived.

"Absolutely amazing," he said, peering over my shoulder. "Who would believe that something like this could actually work! Does everything check out, boss?"

I flipped off my pocket torch and stood up. "Seems so. Connect a jack to the line out, and let's fire her up." Johnny had gotten out a classic Hiwatt stack to use for amplification. The mellotron had its own onboard speakers, but they'd sounded pretty wimpy when I'd briefly tried the instrument before buying it. "Turn it up to five," I told him and switched on the mellotron.

It made an odd, soft clanking noise as it sprang to life. I glanced at the sheet Rugely had provided listing the voices and their location on the mellotron's tapes.

"What do you want to hear first?" I asked Johnny.

"It's got to be those violins."

The classic mellotron sound. I looked at the sheet: right-hand keyboard, Station 2, Track A, and checking again to make sure I was doing it correctly, pushed the required buttons. The mellotron whirred and vibrated under my hand. Sliding back the cover, I could see the right rear cylinder turning. Everything seemed to be doing what it was supposed to do. Sitting down on the drum stool, I put my foot on the volume pedal and depressed it halfway. Fingers over the keys, I pressed down the notes for an open F Major triad.

That sound filled the room. Johnny's jaw literally dropped open, and I have to admit that my heart beat a bit faster. I played a couple of chord progressions, and had just started the opening to King Crimson's "Court of the Crimson King" when Kevin and Hamed arrived.

"Jesus..." Kevin said after I'd finished.

I stood and bowed, using my hand in a sweeping gesture to indicate the instrument in front of me. "Gentlemen, the Mellotron MkII."

"It is very impressive," Hamed added, coming around to look at the control panel. "How does it work?"

I handed him the repair manual I'd also purchased. Turning back to the instrument, I consulted the track sheet, pressed another button and began the opening to "Watcher of the Skies" by Genesis. The sound was even more spectacular.

"How come you know all this old stuff, boss?" Johnny asked.

I answered, sounding more disgusted than I wanted to, "Because it wasn't *that* old when I learned it."

On and off during the day, we all kept gravitating to the mellotron, putting it through its paces. Every sound was tried, and none found wanting. Some seemed like old friends because of the number of times we'd heard them on recordings: cello, mixed choir and flute ("Strawberry Fields" anyone?), but several were new to me, bass flute and French horn being the standouts there. Hamed liked the sustained guitar (another new one), and we all especially liked Gothic, a huge sound that was a blend of string section, mixed choir and pipe organ—very atmospheric and creepy to the point where it actually made the hair on the back of my neck stand up.

Shortly after Johnny had left with the organ delivery to a studio downtown, the buzzer on the back door sounded. I'd built a small room with a counter to keep customers out of the warehouse proper, so we couldn't see who had entered. Hamed trotted off to find out. I had my head down fiddling with the reverb control on the mellotron when two sets of footsteps approached.

When I didn't look up right away, Hamed cleared his throat. "Michael, this woman says she'd like to speak to you."

I looked up distractedly, and there stood Regina.

She didn't really want to speak to me. She just reared back and gave my face the kind of full-handed slap you only see in movies.

CHAPTER 5

We all stood frozen as the sound of Regina's slap seemed to echo around the warehouse.

My first thought was how much it hurt! My face burned, but not simply from the force of hand meeting flesh. Kevin and Hamed stood shuffling awkwardly, eyes down. Regina stared at me, her expression daring me to say something, at which point, I had no doubt, she would have slapped me again.

After a good fifteen seconds of uncomfortable silence, Regina turned, and with her head held high and her body stiff, started back across the room. The sound of the outside door slamming followed shortly after. At the same time, the three of us started breathing again.

I knew I deserved what I'd got, but why had she come all this way to deliver her rebuke for my caddish behavior? Princess indeed! I guess I had delivered the ultimate insult, and at all costs, it had to be redressed.

Partly without willing it, my feet began moving, following in her footsteps. I had no idea what to tell her, but I owed Regina more than stunned silence. As I crossed the room, I could hear Kevin say softly to Hamed, "What the hell was that all about?"

"A woman scorned is my guess," Hamed answered.

Without a coat, the extreme cold hit like a hammer as I left the building. Hair streaming behind her, Regina stood hunched into the wind in the middle of the driveway.

I walked forward and touched her shoulder. "Regina..."

She turned slowly, and her face had an odd expression. If I hadn't known better, I would have said it looked something akin to triumph.

"It's cold out here," I began lamely. "Come inside, and I'll call you a cab."

"You hurt me!" Regina said savagely. "I gave myself to you, and you just walked away."

"This isn't the place to discuss my shortcomings, certainly not in this weather. Why don't you come into my office, and we can talk?" I grabbed her arm, steering her back to the door. "Please, come inside."

Regina resisted for a moment, then sagged. "All right. It's too damn cold out here."

Hamed and Kevin were where I'd left them as we re-entered the warehouse. Without a word, we passed through, entered the office and shut the door. I knew they'd be speculating themselves into a stupor, and without a doubt, the story would be all over town in short order. Even though it had been years since I had been in the limelight, people still seemed to take inordinate notice of my comings and goings, as if they were expecting me to break out at any moment and become a Rock Star again. In the past, it had been sort of amusing, but this time I dreaded the chatter. Well, the damage was done, and I would have to live with the fallout, even if a report surfaced on that damned Neurotica fan website that had appeared a few years previously.

"Would you care to sit down?" I inquired politely.

Regina, arms crossed, stood for a long moment glaring at me, before taking the offered seat. I thought it best to put the desk between us, so I sat in my own chair.

"You are a total bastard!" she spat out.

"You came a long way just to tell me that. A phone call would have been easier and a hell of a lot cheaper," I answered, rather coldly and immediately regretted it.

For several seconds she didn't say anything, and I thought she might start crying, but although her eyes brightened, Regina maintained her composure and said quietly, "Angus warned me you could be like this."

I ran my hands over my face and back through my hair, then looked across my desk at her. "Regina...I know it won't mean very much after the fact, but I regret what I did. I really do." A bad thought crossed my mind. "What else did Angus say about me?"

Regina's eyes drifted away to a poster of the Red Hot Chili Peppers behind my desk. "Angus cares about you very much. To be honest, I wish I had a friend like him."

"You're stalling. Come on. What did he *say* about me?"

"He told me that, regardless of outward impressions, you have no idea what you're doing with your life, that I shouldn't take what you did personally. You've been running away from things for years. Well, I'm sorry, but I *did* take it personally."

"I didn't make any promises," I said, but it sounded lame even to my ears.

"And I didn't expect any! But the least you could have done was woken me up and told me that it had been fun, but you really had to be going. You made me feel cheap, slinking out like that!"

"Regina, that's the *last* thing you should feel. The problem was all at my end. I guess I just freaked. It was a stupid thing to do."

"Yes, it was. I came here to get back a measure of self-respect!"

I rubbed my cheek reflectively. "You certainly made your point."

"Good! You damn well deserved it."

I sighed, knowing that this was my just desserts for letting my gonads make decisions for me.

Checking my watch, I said, "Let's get the hell out of here. Can I, ah, take you to dinner or something?"

I didn't know why I'd said that last bit—probably another pang of guilt—but it slipped out before my brain got hold of it, and once said, it wasn't in the realm of possibility to take it back. My only hope was that she'd decline.

She didn't.

"That's the least you can do," Regina responded primly. "I haven't eaten anything all day."

"Okay, I know just the place. Great food, and we don't have to be dressed up."

"That's good, because I don't have much more than I did when I jumped into your car. I did a little shopping at the Glasgow airport, but that was basically just to get a few necessities."

The lads were in the entry room and fell silent when they heard our footsteps crossing the warehouse.

"I have some things to take care of," I told them as we came through, "but I'll be here first thing in the morning. Kevin, could you pull the file of what we rented to the jazz festival last year? We need to come up with a quote, and I low-balled it to help them out. This year they'll have to pay the full freight. Hamed, could you take a look at that Twin Reverb amp that isn't working right? It may just need a new valve—"

"Tube, boss," he grinned. "They're called tubes on this side of the Atlantic."

"You know what I mean, so there's no need to correct me!" I shot back. "We'll need to get it fixed immediately if it's something more."

Regina had been standing by the door looking amused. While I was giving orders, I noticed the lads' eyes flicking in her direction speculatively. Certainly, they were eager to know if their obvious suppositions were true, but that being the case, they'd need to get used to disappointment.

Regina kept her distance as we walked to my car. She wasn't about to make this any easier.

III

I took her to a nearby steak house where I often dine. During the drive over, I commented that I hoped this ride wouldn't turn out like the last one. She made a sour face, which put an abrupt halt to any attempt at making small talk.

Dinner continued in the same stiff manner, and I began to wonder why Regina had agreed to let me take her out. All of my conversational attempts were met with minimal answers.

Finally, after the table had been cleared but coffee hadn't yet arrived, I made one last stab. "So where are you staying?"

Regina looked at me and yawned. "Excuse me! I guess the jet lag is catching up. I also didn't get much sleep last night." She yawned again. "When I got into Toronto this afternoon, I just told the cabbie to take me to the nearest hotel. I'm afraid I don't remember which one."

If that was an overture, I wasn't having any. "Fortunately, the ones near the airport are pretty well along one road, so we shouldn't have much trouble finding it."

During coffee, she actually asked a few polite questions about my business, but because of her continued yawning, I gave short answers and got us out of the restaurant as quickly as possible. I'd done my chivalrous duty, and now was the time to see her to her door, then get the hell out while the getting was good. I did *not* want her to do something silly like ask if she could stay with me. One mistake was enough for this week, thank you.

The drive to her hotel was more relaxed than the earlier one to the restaurant. Regina actually began talking about having visited Toronto one summer eight years earlier to spend time with a school chum.

"I've been thinking about trying to look her up, but we lost touch when we both went to university, and her parents were getting on in years. They may have retired to Florida by now."

"What are your long-range plans, though?"

"I wish I knew." Regina was silent for a couple of minutes. "I quit my job in Paris. It wouldn't have been fair to make them sit around, waiting for me to come back—even if they would have. I don't think I want to work there anyway, since it was my father who got me the job. They probably are aware of who he is, and I couldn't stand being around them, knowing that they know." I could see from the corner of my eye that Regina was shaking her head. "I don't think he'd leave me alone anyway, *especially* after what happened back in Birmingham." She suddenly pointed. "Oh, look! There's my hotel."

The Constellation. I pulled in and stopped at the front entrance. The doorman was nowhere to be seen, and Regina suddenly seemed reluctant to get out of the car. "Michael..."

Not wanting to give her a chance to say something I didn't want to hear, I interrupted. "Regina, I can't say that it hasn't been interesting. We met under the most bizarre circumstances imaginable."

She smiled for the first time that evening. "Relax. I just wanted to thank you for the meal—and what you did for me in Birmingham."

"Yes. Of course."

She leaned over and kissed my cheek. "Thank you for everything, Michael. You're a good man."

"I'm sorry for what happened between us."

"Well, I'm certainly not!" Another smile flitted across Regina's face. "You must be wondering what you did to deserve all this."

She got out of the car, and I watched her slim form as she disappeared through the doors.

That thought *had* crossed my mind once or twice.

The ringing of the telephone felt like a quarter-inch drill bit going directly into my right ear. Rolling over, I groped around on the bedside table and only succeeded in knocking the cordless off its stand. With a colourful oath or two, I got out of bed and began feeling around for it on the floor more by sound than anything else, longing to put it out of its misery. I might have thought of turning on the light if I hadn't been so soundly asleep when it had gone off.

Finally, I located it halfway under the bed. "Hello?"

"Michael?"

"Yes, this is Michael," I said very patiently.

"It's Regina. Look, I'm sorry to be calling at such an ungodly hour—"

"Just for the record," I interrupted, "what time *is* it?"

"Four a.m."

I sat down on the edge of the bed, rubbing the sleep from my eyes, and finally turned on the light. "How did you get this number?"

She hesitated for a moment. "From Angus."

"And why are you calling me in the middle of the night?"

"I wouldn't have called if it wasn't really important," she said a touch resentfully. "It's just that I can't reach Angus on the phone."

Looking heavenward, I answered, "He's probably out somewhere. Why do you have to speak to him so desperately?"

"Angus wanted me to call after I saw you. I promised I would. I've been trying for the past two hours, and no one answers!"

"Okay. Let's go through this step by step. Were you supposed to ring him at a particular hour?"

"He said to call any time since he was planning on being home, but I thought it would be better to wait until I wouldn't be waking him up. If I called at two a.m., that would be five hours later over there, and he'd be sure to be up."

"I *am* aware of the time difference," I responded dryly, thinking that Regina hadn't shown the same compunction about waking *me*.

"He was very adamant that I should call."

"That's odd. Angus is usually pretty reliable that way. Is the phone line still working? It could have gone down in the storm. Happens once or twice a year."

"I checked. Everything's fine, according to the operator. I'm worried, Michael."

There was no need to ask why. We both knew that if the blokes we'd tangled with in Birmingham got a good look at the license plate on Angus's Jag, it wouldn't take them long to track down who owned it. I felt a knot forming in the pit of my stomach.

"Michael?"

"Yes."

"What do you think we should do?"

"There may be a perfectly innocent explanation, but I'm going to ring the Dunoon police and ask if they'll send a car over to make sure Angus is all right."

"Please call me as soon as you know anything," Regina said firmly. "I won't be able to sleep at all until I find out he's okay."

That was the end of any hope of sleep for that night.

Naturally, as soon as I rang off with Regina, I tried Angus—with no result. After making a pot of tea, I sat at the kitchen table brooding. At half four, having had no better luck with a further try, I rang up the Dunoon Police.

The officer who took my call, while very polite, made it quite clear they had their hands full at the moment but promised someone would look in on my friend as soon as they could spare the manpower. I got the strong impression that they wouldn't be getting to it any time soon.

In a bit of turnabout, I called Regina, and while she claimed she'd been awake worrying, she definitely sounded groggy. I rang off feeling distinctly *un*-guilty about waking her.

The phone rang again shortly before nine.

"Mr. Michael Quinn?" a voice asked in about as thick a Scottish accent as I've ever heard.

"Speaking."

"And are you the Michael Quinn who rang the Dunoon Police earlier with concerns over the well being of a Mr. Angus MacDougall?"

Finding the pedantic manner of the caller extremely irritating, I answered back sharply, "Of course I am, otherwise you wouldn't have this number, would you?"

"What gave you reason to be concerned about his welfare, *sir?*"

"Angus didn't answer his phone when I was certain he would be in. Has someone been up to his house?"

Again the pause. "Yes, they have, Mr. Quinn."

"And is my friend all right?"

"Did you have reason to suspect that he wouldn't be?"

I felt as if a cold wind had blown through me. "For God's sake, tell me what's going on!"

"I would first like to ask you a question or two if I may, Mr. Quinn. Did your concern for Mr. MacDougall come from any fear that someone might wish to harm him?"

"Why are you asking me that?"

"Please answer my question."

I considered well before answering. "No, not really. I had just promised to call him, that's all, and when he didn't answer the phone after repeated tries, I rang you folks up. Now can you tell me what's wrong with Angus?"

"This is not normally something we like to do over the phone, you understand, but the constable dispatched to the MacDougall house found him dead in his sitting room."

I slumped back on my chair. Even though I had been expecting bad news, I had not been expecting anything like this.

"Did he have a heart attack or something?"

"We can't be sure about the cause of death until we have the results of an autopsy."

"What? How?" was all I managed to get out.

The voice on the other end now sounded more patient—probably from too much experience at this sort of news-breaking. "Take a few deep breaths, Mr. Quinn. When you're ready to continue, I have a few more questions I would like you to answer."

"Anything."

"Very good, sir. Now, when did you last see or speak to Mr. MacDougall?"

"I was at his home two days ago before returning to Toronto. He drove me to the ferry."

"And did you speak with him since?"

"No."

"Why specifically were you to call him today?"

My brain switched into high gear again. "I had borrowed his car, and it had got damaged. I was calling to find out how much the repair bill would be."

"You're speaking of the blue Jaguar XKE, 1967 with damage to the bonnet, farside wing and farside window?"

That was pretty thorough! "Yes. Why are you asking me all this?"

"It's necessary considering the situation."

Lack of sleep and tension, guilt, grief, whatever, caused me to snap, "Would you *kindly* tell me *what's going on?*"

The voice answered, not unkindly, "Our investigation up to this point has been very preliminary, but we're treating this as a homicide."

I felt as close to passing out as I ever have, with one other exception. I took a few deep breaths before asking, "Your name is?"

"Detective Chief Inspector Campbell, sir."

"I will be on the next plane leaving Toronto for the UK."

"A very wise decision, Mr. Quinn. It will save us a great deal of trouble."

After hanging up, I completely fell to pieces.

CHAPTER 6

I've never particularly enjoyed flying. There's the interminable waiting at the airport, then there are the planes themselves: claustrophobic, noisy and uncomfortable. Between connecting flights, I had too many hours alone with my thoughts, none of them even remotely good. Angus's death was clearly on my shoulders.

Immediately after getting off the phone with the Scottish detective, I'd called my travel agent. In short order she'd booked me on a flight to Manchester, with a connection on to Glasgow which would get me in at eight a.m. the following morning.

Regina's first reaction to the horrible news had been a desire to accompany me, and I only *just* talked her out of it. If what we were surmising was correct, the bad guys could quite possibly still be around and on the watch for her. If they identified me, then there wasn't much we could do, because I *had* to go.

Everything that day took on an air of unreality. The last time I'd felt this detached from normalcy was five years earlier when my brother Bobby had suddenly passed away. No one expects a brother to die of a massive heart attack two days before his fiftieth birthday. My reaction to my mum's call had been the same: I'd taken the first plane.

Some people never learn.

Far too early the next morning, I got into my hired car with a heavy heart and headed west for the Calmac ferry dock at Gourock. My mood was not improved by the fact that I'd have to brave crossing the Firth of Clyde yet again. The day was fine and clear, though, and I spent the twenty-minute ride with hardly a lurch of my stomach. That didn't stop the dread creeping up on me as the boat neared the end of its journey.

One of the ferry employees pointed me in the direction of the police station. I'd already arranged to meet Detective Chief Inspector Campbell at eleven a.m., which gave me time to find a café for a spot of breakfast, nothing more than a bap and a cup of tea, since my nerves were completely on edge.

DI Campbell turned out to be a tall, slender man as overly fussy in person as he'd sounded on the phone. I gauged him to be in his mid-fifties, although that could have been due to the fact that he seemed so bloody dour.

He didn't greet me particularly warmly, considering that I'd flown across the Atlantic on short notice to try to help him. He did offer me coffee, though, which I accepted, although I don't often drink the stuff. A good-looking female constable brought it in, then sat down in the corner with a pad and pen. Campbell took almost no notice of her.

"Now tell me, Mr. Quinn, about your relationship with Angus MacDougall."

"Angus is...was one of my oldest friends. I was a member of a band when I was younger, and Angus was our road manager."

"The name of the band?"

"Neurotica."

My statement elicited no reaction from Campbell, but the constable taking shorthand looked up inquisitively.

"And what was the purpose of your visit earlier this week?" he asked next.

"I had to come over to look at an instrument I was considering purchasing, so I also took the opportunity to visit my old friend. I arrived a week ago Thursday, stayed with Angus for a few days, then borrowed his car to drive down to Birmingham to purchase the instrument and visit my mum. I drove back on Monday and left early on Tuesday morning."

He was silent for a moment. "I will ask you again if you had reason to suspect that your friend was in any sort of trouble."

"No," I answered perhaps too quickly, then stopped to consider. "What sort of trouble do you mean?"

"Did he have financial problems?"

Shaking my head, I answered, "No. He bought his house outright, and his needs were very simple. If he required money, he only had to hire out again as a road manager. Angus had a very good reputation in the business. Any number of bands would have hired him if they knew he was available. He'd done that often in the past."

"What about drugs? Did he have a drug problem?"

"No. Angus was very anti-drug. Why do you ask?"

Campbell looked down at his hands. The office was obviously not his. I felt certain that his own would not have had so much as a paperclip out of place, and I doubted if a backwater such as Dunoon would have warranted its own Detective Inspector anyway. Considering its close proximity to Glasgow, he'd probably been brought in from there. Consequently, Campbell seemed ill at ease.

Finally, he looked up. "I'm going to take you into my confidence. Certain bits of evidence have come to light since we spoke yesterday, and they have led us to believe the people who visited Mr. MacDougall on Thursday evening are involved in the drug trade." Campbell fastened his eyes on mine. "In light of that, would you like to revise what you just told me?"

"No. I wouldn't. Angus had nothing to do with drugs of any sort."

"Excuse me if I find that a little hard to believe. After all, he worked in the pop music business—"

"Yeah, yeah," I interrupted, "to hear most people talk, you'd think we...*they* did nothing more than get wasted and defile young women. Well, I was there, and yes, there was some of that to be sure, but most of us took our job seriously, and you can't play well when you're wrecked. Angus's job was very tough, and he couldn't have done it either, if he'd had a drug problem. What makes you think Angus's killers were part of the drug trade?"

"As I said, various bits of evidence. Things that were done. We have a national computer database where we can input facts we discover and it will tell us if this sort of thing has been reported before. In your friend's case it has. Three other unsolved murders. These were criminals who came to his house. If you're telling me the truth, why did those particular people come there? It's that question I most want the answer to."

"What in God's name happened? You keep hinting around, but you haven't really told me anything."

Campbell considered for a moment, then came to another

decision and abruptly stood. "Constable Dickson, could you see about getting one of the pool cars to drive us out to the MacDougall place?"

"Right away, sir." Dickson closed her pad with a snap and left the room.

$$\blacksquare$$

The weather and the drive out to poor Angus's place was a far cry from my last trip there. The roads were completely dry, and as a passenger, I could watch the scenery go by. The cold, clear air, cloudless sky and distant vistas gave me a lot to look at, but I cannot say I enjoyed the trip.

A road block had been set up at the beginning of the one-lane road to Angus's.

"Can't have media vans clogging a one-lane road, can we?" Campbell said as we passed, and I slumped down in the seat, hoping the few newshounds wouldn't somehow spot me. Earlier, I'd slipped into the police station right under the noses of several. I knew that sort of luck wouldn't last forever.

Campbell sat in the front while Dickson drove. We spoke very little. I got the feeling that the detective was letting me stew in my own juices in the hope that I might reconsider what I'd told him. I had a pretty good idea of why he was taking me to the crime scene.

As we came to the last mile of our trip, Campbell turned around and said, "We're fairly certain your friend let his killers in, since there's no evidence they forced their entry."

I shook my head. "Wouldn't have been a need. Angus seldom locked his door."

Campbell, unperturbed by my correction to his hypothesis, scribbled in a small notebook he took from his jacket pocket. "There appears to have been a struggle once they were in, though. Papers were scattered all over the room, and—"

"Papers were scattered all over the room when I was there," I interrupted again. "Angus was attempting to do his own taxes."

This time Campbell looked up sharply, and I could have sworn Dickson snorted, but if she had, it was quickly covered up by snuffling and other cold-type noises.

"We found broken furniture and a bookcase knocked over. He fought back hard, it seems."

"Doesn't surprise me. Angus was a big man and wouldn't back down from anyone."

Arriving at the farmhouse, we pulled into the spot where I'd parked the damaged XKE just a few days earlier. It felt like a lifetime. Climbing out of the back seat of the police sedan, I looked out at Loch Striven. The scene was still beyond description, the hills as forlorn and forbidding as ever. The gulls still wheeled, crying in the air above. But something had gone, and everything felt as if it were rapidly receding into a distant memory. I knew I would never return here of my own volition.

Yellow crime scene tape snapped noisily in the steady wind. A blast skittered down my neck, causing me to shiver, but out of proportion to how cold it actually was.

Angus's Jag wasn't parked in its usual spot, nor was the beat-up Land Rover. Both had probably been carted off somewhere for examination. A white van stood there instead, along with a blue and yellow checked Strathclyde police sedan. As we'd pulled in, a sleepy-looking constable had jumped out of the driver's side. This time Dickson snorted for sure.

Campbell walked over to me. He had to raise his voice against the wind. "As near as we can figure, three people arrived here shortly after eight on Thursday evening. We've spoken to a witness who drove by a bit earlier, and there were no strange cars parked here. An hour later there were. These visitors probably didn't leave until the wee hours of the morning. The Medical Examiner thinks your friend died sometime after two a.m."

"How did Angus die?" I asked.

Campbell fixed me with a curious gaze. "Sure you want to know?"

"I can handle it."

Campbell looked at me assessingly. "Your friend was tortured and eventually had his throat slit."

Campbell's blunt, matter-of-fact delivery caused me to feel like I'd been kicked in the stomach, even though I should have been prepared by all his dark hints.

My legs suddenly felt as reliable as overcooked spaghetti, and I had to lean heavily against the police car. The world spun crazily as I forced myself to take some deep breaths.

As if from the far end of a long tunnel, I was aware of Constable Dickson saying to her counterpart from the squad car, "Bet you five quid he loses his breakfast. Seems like the kind."

That pulled me out of my funk. With my eye on the big-mouthed constable, I straightened and said, "Right, then. Shall we go inside?"

Campbell and I had to put on the white crime scene suits you see on the telly.

The place certainly was a mess. On the right as you entered the sitting room stood a large stone fireplace with bookcases on either side. One of these was down completely, and the other leaning precariously. I'd been so wrong in my assessment of the tax documents piled everywhere earlier in the week. It had been nothing like what I saw now. The big table in front of the windows had been smashed, chairs overturned and the fireplace poker stuck out of a wall at a crazy angle.

What caught my attention, though, was a wooden chair from the kitchen which stood in the middle of the room. On the seat and streaked down the legs to the floor where it had pooled, I could see the very obvious remains of a whole lot of blood.

Campbell let me take in the scene for several moments before speaking. "I know that it's nigh on impossible to tell from the state of the room, but do you notice anything missing?"

I could only manage a shake of my head.

"Follow me then, and please stay close to the wall. We've cleared a wee path through the mess."

Campbell led me into the kitchen. Everything there looked pretty well as I'd seen it last. On the stove stood a half-cooked dinner its chef would never eat. A bottle of Scotch on the table had the cork out, although the glass next to it was empty. If I hadn't known better, I'd have thought Angus had just stepped out for a moment.

I became aware of sounds from Angus's bedroom, directly above us. "What's going on up there?" I asked.

"Scene of Crime lads. They have to go over the whole house. You never know what you might find, although I'm not holding out much hope in this case. You being here is a good thing for us, since you knew MacDougall well, and you were here recently. Anything missing or out of place in this room?"

"No. It looks much as it always did."

Campbell took me through the entire house, including the basement which I'd never seen, a place filled with junk pre-dating Angus's tenure. I felt distinctly uncomfortable when we went into the bedroom I'd last used and saw the bed I'd shared with Regina. The sheets and blankets had been removed, making it appear even more forlorn.

We stood in the doorway for several moments longer than was necessary. "You say the linens were fresh when you went to sleep the last evening you were here?" he finally asked.

I almost fell into it, realizing only when my mouth had actually started to form the word "yes" that I hadn't said anything about bed linens. Only then did I realize what even a forensic buffoon would have known: two obvious sets of hair in the bed, since Regina's was chestnut to my light brown and a lot longer.

"Ah, no, they weren't," I answered casually. "I'm afraid Angus wasn't much into housekeeping, and I was far too shagged from the drive north to even begin to think about changing them myself."

Campbell hid his disappointment quite well, and as we went on to another room, I looked heavenward and said a silent, "Thank you!"

In the bathroom, I found out that I'd been correct in my assumption when Campbell asked, "Did MacDougall have any lady friends who might have visited him recently?"

I pretended to think for a minute. "Not that I remember him mentioning. The last lady friend I knew about was probably two years back. That wouldn't have stopped him picking up someone down at the boozer, though, in all likelihood. Why do you ask?"

"We found hair samples in the shower here and also back in the bed in which you slept. Anything you'd like to add to what you've told me, Mr. Quinn?" Campbell asked with raised eyebrows.

"No."

Campbell shook his head and turned towards the stairs.

As we headed back outside, I asked him, "You said earlier that you thought there were three men. How did you figure that out?"

He turned to face me. "Certainly it would have taken at least two strapping lads to subdue a man the size and apparent strength of MacDougall. In my experience, these people prefer to work in groups of three. Two to hold the person, and one to soften him up. You'll be happy to know that at least one of the intruders got what looks like a very bloody nose, and one may have cracked his head on the bookcase before it fell down. We won't know for certain until the laboratory results come back, but that's my feeling based on the evidence collected so far."

"And so these three bastards burst in on my friend," I said carefully as we stared out at the sunlight reflecting off the loch below. "What could they have wanted?"

"That's why I asked about money or drug problems. This is the approach used by people such as those mixed up in the drug trade when they want something. Send some lads over to scare the person, hurt him enough to let him know they mean business. The average victim crumbles pretty quickly under that sort of treatment and soon coughs up what's wanted. Occasionally, I've seen them do something like this when they don't get what they want, or to send a strong message through to someone else." Campbell again peered at me in that uncomfortable way of his. "Any idea who that might be?"

I wasn't about to tell him anything more at that point. Possibly later. I'd have to see how things shook down. It's not that I wanted to hinder the investigation and see the bastards get away with it. I wanted to see them get the full measure of the law, but I did feel I had to protect Regina—for the moment at least.

"So they pounded Angus around then slit his throat?"

"As I said earlier, he was tortured. That's why I think they wanted to know something."

"How did they torture him?"

"Cigarette burns. The poor sod's body was covered with them. MacDougall was either very stubborn, had a terribly high pain threshold—or didn't know what they wanted to hear."

I hoped poor Angus had been all three in this case.

Campbell next went to the largest of the two outbuildings on the property, this one located west of the house and slightly further down the hill.

I'd only been in it once when Angus had first moved in, and it had been in pretty rough shape. The walls, probably stones cleared from the surrounding fields, had been well constructed and were still sound, but the roof had holes, the doors leaned at crazy angles, and the building had contained rusted farm implements, doves and cobwebs.

As we approached it now, I noticed that it had a new roof, and the wide doors had been rehung. A large, shiny padlock now kept the world at bay. Odd for Angus to lock this when he didn't lock his house.

On finding the padlock secured, Campbell, with some irritation, turned and bellowed up the hill, "Dickson! Some idiot has locked this bloody thing again. Fetch the key!"

Dickson and her comrade held a hurried discussion, with the result that they trotted off to the house and returned shortly with a large ring of keys. "Here they are, sir," she said. "Would you like me to open it?"

Campbell snatched them out of her hands. "I think I'm capable of opening a padlock!"

With the number of keys, though, it took him nearly a minute to find the right one.

As he worked, I asked, "What is it you want to show me?"

The detective ignored my question, and Dickson started to speak when Campbell glared at her over his shoulder. Her mouth shut with an almost audible snap.

The padlock didn't give up the fight until only the last few keys remained. Campbell grabbed one door, Dickson took the other, and they swung them back. Sunlight flooded into the room.

It took my eyes a few moments to adjust. The room gradually revealing itself was completely different from the wreck I remembered. Even though everything was covered with sheets to keep dust out, it was easy to see that Angus had built a rehearsal hall.

He'd cut two large windows (curtains closed at the moment) into one of the long walls. They'd have fine views of Loch Striven. The ceiling had been closed in (no more open rafters and roosting doves), and the floor had been carpeted. Scattered in a rough circle around the walls, I could see what looked like a complete band set-up: three amplifier stacks, a large drum kit, mics, a fair-sized mixing desk, monitor speakers. But it was something at the far end of the room that caught my attention.

I threaded my way around the drum kit and crossed the open area, barely avoiding tripping over a mic cable. Lifting a sheet, I stood gazing at something I never thought to see again. My interior emotions were surprisingly strong, but outwardly I only smiled wistfully at what Angus had done.

The two cops stood in silent bemusement as I went around the room removing all the sheets. Finally I stood in the middle of the circle, slowly turning to look at what surrounded me.

Angus had all of Neurotica's original equipment. The battle scars on each piece spoke to me of half-forgotten memories. All I'd have to do was flip on the mains, and everything would work perfectly. Angus had always seen to that. The crowning glory and what had set my heart rate through the roof was the fact that my old keyboard rig still existed. He had everything: Hammond C3, Wurlitzer Electric Piano, Minimoog and a Yamaha DX7, set-up as they always had been, seemingly waiting for me to come in and pick up where I'd left off twenty-four years earlier. When I'd beat my hasty retreat from the band, I'd left everything behind, not caring what happened to it. I'd assumed it had all been sold or junked or stolen years ago. And now here it all was again.

Looking at the set-up, it felt as if the lads and I had merely nipped down to the nearest pub for a pint and a pie and would be returning shortly to run through the tunes for our latest album or rehearse for our next tour. Everything came flooding back, whether I wanted it to or not.

As I stood gawking like an idiot, someone crunched along the gravel outside and stopped in the doorway. I turned, only seeing a silhouette against the glare from outside, but I *knew* who it was regardless. The only living people I'd known longer were my mum and my auntie.

"Hello, Michael," said my former best mate and comrade, Rolly Simpson, lead singer of Neurotica.

CHAPTER 7

Roland Paul Simpson was the reason I still had an unpublished phone number. After walking out on Neurotica in the middle of the tour which, according to our record label, would have made us one of the top five acts in the world, Rolly started calling me on a daily basis. "The band can't go on without you." "You can't just walk away from us; we're mates!" "How can you be so hard-hearted and selfish?" "You're killing Neurotica, you know." Or variations on the theme.

I'd taken a bit of the money I'd made and gone off to be alone. I suspect that Rolly's success in always tracking me down regardless of where I was hiding out had been because he was able to buy the info from my perennially-short-of-cash brother. It made no matter where I went, a small hotel in Paris, a pension in Vienna, an island in Greece, Thailand, even Achiltibuie in remote, northwestern Scotland, sooner or later I'd get a call from Rolly. When I'd finally emigrated to Canada, he'd obtained my phone number within a week.

Twice he'd tried confronting me: the first time I walked away without saying a word, the second time, I popped him one.

Since then, I'd only seen Rolly in photos or occasionally on the telly (much less so in recent years), and what I'd seen hadn't been good. He'd had a bloated, pasty look due to his hard-living lifestyle. In his case, all the royalty money we'd received over the years had not been well spent.

The Rolly Simpson in front of me that day was slim and looked fit and clear-eyed, although undeniably older than his forty-nine years. Tall, with a hawk-like nose, piercing blue eyes and blond hair (now back in a ponytail), his rugged good looks and devil-may-care attitude had been attracting women by the score for as long as I'd known him.

"Hello, Rolly," I said neutrally. "Didn't think to find you here."

"Angus's old dad wasn't up to officially identifying the body. Since you were en route, DCI Campbell, here, asked me to deputize. I happened to be in Edinburgh, so it was no problem to pop over." He went up and shook the cop's hand heartily. "Top o' the mornin' to you, sir!"

Campbell beamed at Rolly in a way that I hadn't yet seen from him—certainly not towards me. In fact, I had the feeling he would have regarded me as the prime suspect if I hadn't been so firmly three thousand miles away in Canada.

Rolly turned his smile on Constable Dickson. "And how are you today, Michelle? I've never seen any woman look so good in a uniform."

The constable dropped her eyes, blushing furiously.

Rolly hadn't changed one jot over the years: same bad lines delivered with such ease they could charm the pants off any woman inside of ten minutes. Judging by her reaction, he might possibly already have accomplished it with PC Dickson, or was well on the way.

"So what do you think of poor Angus's little museum, Michael?" Rolly asked.

I smiled, despite my mood. "It's like seeing old friends again."

Rolly looked at me sharply. "Does that include me?"

Noticing Campbell's attention on us, I chose my words carefully. "Yes, Rolly, that includes you."

He strode forward and gripped me in a bear hug, patting my back heartily. I tried to look as if this were all normal.

Rolly stepped back with his hands still on my upper arms, looking me over. "The years have been kind to you, haven't they? You look almost the same, Michael. God, it's great to see you!" Turning back to Campbell, he asked, "Have you finished doing your worst on my mate here? If so, I'd really like to get him alone somewhere for a long jaw about the old days."

Campbell nodded, but added, "If Mr. Quinn doesn't mind, I will probably wish to talk with him again, and I'd like to know if he makes any plans to return home."

Not so much the words, but the way Campbell said them, brought me up short. I still couldn't shake the feeling that he'd divined some of the part I'd played in Angus's murder. He'd managed to come close to tripping me up a few times, and I wasn't eager to give him any more chances if I could help it.

"I will certainly be here through the funeral," I said, then turned to Rolly. "I'm assuming there will be a funeral?"

"Angus's father would like one—even if Angus himself would have thought the idea bloody stupid. I'm to call later today and find out what's been decided. One of Angus's sisters lives in Australia, you know, so it will still take her a bit of time to get here. My guess is the funeral will be the day after tomorrow at the earliest, assuming that's all right with you folks," he said to Campbell.

"It should be fine."

"Great! That's settled then. Michael, do you feel up to some grub?"

I suddenly realized that I was indeed hungry. "All right. I'll also need to arrange for a place to stay."

"No problem! You can stay with me at the Hilton in Glasgow. I'll just change to a suite. It'll be like old times."

I didn't want those old times—for several reasons. "No thanks, Rolly. I'd rather stay someplace nearby like Dunoon."

He flashed a quick smirk over at Constable Dickson, and I was certain from the looks that passed between them, that he'd bedded her. "Right, I remember now: your seasickness." He turned to the two cops. "Once we decided to cross the Channel by boat, and Michael spent the entire trip with his head in the—"

"I'm sure they don't want to listen to old war stories. Besides, I left the car I hired back in Dunoon at the police station."

Rolly realized from my tone that he'd overstepped the boundaries and did a deft about-face. "Right. Let's go, then."

As I would have expected, Rolly's car was fast and expensive: a bright red Porsche Carrera coupe. His driving hadn't changed, either: too fast, too careless and still way too lucky for him to think of smartening up.

He didn't take the road back to Dunoon, though, turning instead to the left in the direction of the Isle of Bute.

"Where are we going?" I asked.

"I'm taking the road up the side of Loch Fyne to a little place I know. They serve great seafood, especially oysters."

"*Oysters?* Good lord, Rolly! When did you start eating anything like that? You always said that plain old pub grub was good enough for the likes of you."

"Yes, and all it got me was good and fat. Now that I've got back to fighting trim, I'll stay that way, thank you very much."

In better circumstances, I might have enjoyed the meal. The location was fabulous, even in winter. Loch Fyne Oyster Bar is right across the road from its namesake, and framing the scene across the water were the high hills of Argyll. It was a bit of an upmarket sort of place, but one where you felt the food was more important than the decor.

The meal was astounding for another reason: I watched this person, whom I *thought* I knew, negotiate things about which he should have known absolutely nothing. He was on first name terms with the female waitstaff (not surprising), but he also knew all about what shellfish to order and could discuss the relative merits of various vintages of champagne. In short, Rolly was the complete opposite of the roustabout Brummy lad I'd grown up with.

Two things hadn't changed, though, his talk was still pungent with expletives—and he still drank too much.

"You know, Michael," he said at one point, punctuating his comments with his fork, "the world will treat you like shite if you let it. Look at us. We got fucked over by the record company. Do you realize that we paid for recording all our albums out of our advance money, and then at the end of the day, they owned the bloody masters? How do you figure *that's* fair?

"Confront them on that and they'll tell you this is the way these things have always been done. Take a naïve group of lads with stars in their eyes, and while you're shaking on the deal with one hand, you're picking their pockets with the other."

I nodded. "These same record companies hit me up for freebie equipment rentals all the time. And what do they plead? Poverty! It would make me laugh if it weren't so unbelievably pathetic."

"How right you are! My lawyers *still* can't get a clear accounting of what they owe us."

"And at the time, if someone had told us the way things worked in this business, would it have stopped us for one second from signing on the bottom line? I don't think so."

"I can't help wondering how much we got cheated out of."

"You and I have done all right out of it, haven't we? Let it go. It's all in the past, Rolly."

"Maybe for you, Michael, but I still get a charge out of standing in front of an audience, doing our music. People want to hear it again, and me and the lads want to play it."

"I don't," I said with resignation, knowing all along that this was coming.

"Have a heart, lad! Why do you always stand in the way?"

"Get Drew Whatsisname to play keyboards for you."

"It's not the same! Don't you get that yet? It *has* to be the original line-up, or it isn't worth doing. Yeah, yeah, Drew's an okay player, but it isn't the same. You're one of the great ones, Michael, and he's not."

"Why don't you add that he can't write?" I spat out sourly. "That's the real point, isn't it? You've told me enough times in your phone messages, comments to the press and through Angus that you don't want to be a 'museum exhibit'—isn't that the term you use?—and for that you need *me*. Don't deny it!"

Rolly flashed one of his thoroughly disarming smiles—disarming to everyone but those who knew him well. "I won't, Michael, because we both know it's true. Listen, I just had a terrific idea! Why not get the band together for a memorial concert for Angus? I think we owe him that much. I know the other lads would be up for it. Just one gig to salute our fallen comrade. It would be a great send-off for him. What do you say?"

Under different circumstances, I might have said yes. In a very real way, I thought it would be a gesture Angus would have appreciated. I would probably have agreed because of the responsibility and guilt I felt at Angus's death.

But Rolly had been in the music business far too long, and even though he would have heartily denied it if I'd pointed it out, he'd absorbed too much of the thoroughly false *bonhomie*, its way of saying one thing and meaning something totally different. I still dealt with this crap every day at work, and I had a very low tolerance for it.

"What do I have to say?" I ruminated. "I have to say no."

He looked at me closely, his gaze a bit unfocussed due to his intake of champagne. "You've always been a right bastard, Michael. I guess I'd forgotten." He got up from the table, motioning for the bill. "All right! Have it your way. We'll do a concert, and I'll make it clear that you were asked but declined to participate."

"That's great, Rolly," I said, also getting to my feet. "You know, you may think you've gotten sophisticated in your old age, but one should never try to get the server's attention by snapping one's fingers." I turned on my heel. "It's very clearly the mark of a boor."

He made me wait out at the car for a good ten minutes. Typical. At least he had the good sense to allow me to drive. It seemed that the awareness of mortality which age brings—either that, or Britain's DUI laws—had put a curb on Rolly's characteristic recklessness with booze and cars.

I took the inland road along Loch Eck back to Dunoon. We didn't meet many cars, and I made the most of having a Porsche that handled beautifully.

The steep sides of Loch Eck, barren, brooding pieces of rock and scrubby grass rising up six hundred feet or more, make the narrow road a winding, exhilarating sliver of pavement to drive—especially when taken above speed, which I did that day, trusting more to luck than I should have.

Within minutes of leaving the restaurant, Rolly had begun snoring, giving me plenty of time to think while I drove.

Back at the dock in Dunoon, I drove the car onto the waiting ferry, paid the fee and left Rolly sleeping off the champagne with a note stuck in his shirt pocket telling him I'd call in the morning to find out about the funeral arrangements. What happened when he got to the opposite side of the Clyde was not my problem.

The duty officer at the police station recommended a few places that were open during the off-season, and I booked into the nicest one: the Argyll Hotel in the high street.

Once settled in, I rang the shop back in Toronto first. Since it was Saturday, only one employee needed to be present. Kevin had not been happy when I'd asked him to work, but I wanted my senior man on the spot when I was out of town.

He sounded exceptionally bored when he answered. "Oh, it's you. How's everything going?"

"As well as can be expected. It's all rather gruesome. How's everything there?"

"Fine. The jazz festival got back in touch, complained about the quote, but accepted it anyway."

"I figured they would," I answered, taking notes. "Anything else?"

"Well, it's the usual slow Saturday. As a matter of fact, I've been taking the time to do some poking around inside your mellotron. It is *quite* the machine."

"Is that order for Montreal ready to go out on Monday? They're coming early for it."

"Pulled it all this morning. I'm sitting on one of the amp cases, as a matter of fact."

"And you gave them plenty of extra cables? I told you what happened last time they rented."

"Yes, they had four cables that didn't work," Kevin answered in a sing-song voice, indicating I'd pounded it into their heads perhaps a bit too hard. "I gave them double what they needed and tested everything. All the paperwork is complete. We *do* know what we're doing, you know."

I ran my hand through my hair. "Yes, I know, and you all say behind my back that I worry as much as an old woman."

Kevin laughed. "I never have!"

"Well, you're going to have to keep the place running without me until at least Tuesday, probably Wednesday."

I was ready to sign off when Kevin said, "Just a minute, boss. There is one thing that happened yesterday. Someone came around asking questions."

I was instantly wary. "Tell me about it."

"Well, I was putting away some drums when this guy strolled through the back door. I didn't even know he was there until I looked back. He started talking to me as if we were old buddies. He might have been a cop."

"Did you see any ID?"

"No, but he had that sort of feel. You know what they're like: big, clean cut, and even when they're wearing blue jeans and a flannel shirt, it looks like a uniform. Said he wanted to rent some equipment for a charity gig he was involved in. His accent was sort of strange, too, like he was trying to imitate a Canadian."

"What sort of questions was he asking?"

"How long I've worked there. Do I like the job. Stuff like that."

"And what did you tell him?"

"I told him you're the best employer in the world and that I love working for you."

I snorted. "Anything else?"

"He wanted to know how busy we are and whether we rent stuff internationally. I thought that was a bit odd."

"And how did the conversation end?"

"He took the price list I made up for him and said he'd get back to us after he'd checked around with some other places."

"And you think he *was* a cop? Could he have been something else?"

"Like what?"

"I don't know..."

"Are you in some kind of trouble, Michael?" Kevin asked, actually using my name for the first time in memory.

"I wish I knew." I made a decision I'd been mulling over since the conversation had taken this extreme left turn. "Did he ask about that young lady who came in the other day?"

"You mean the one who slugged you?"

I winced. It was only natural that Regina would always be 'the woman who slugged the boss' to my staff. "Yeah."

"The subject never came up."

Something about the way he said it made me think that Kevin hadn't been completely truthful.

|||

I had too many things to ponder to sit still in a hotel room, and since I'd told Regina that I'd call her at one p.m. Toronto time, I decided to take a walk through Dunoon and try to sort things out in my head while I waited.

Dunoon had once been a "holiday destination". Being close to Glasgow and on the water had assured it of a steady flow of visitors during the high season. When that had collapsed due to the rise of cheap package holidays to Spain, the nearby US submarine base had picked up most of the slack. With the Yanks now also gone, the little town is slowly slipping into the twilight.

I stood for over an hour at the sea wall looking out over the Firth of Clyde. It struck me ironically that I enjoy being around open water, but somehow just can't manage to be *on* it.

Across the firth, I could see the lights of Gourock in the early winter evening, and my thoughts were drawn back to the scene etched in my memory by that morning's trip.

What had happened at Angus's farmhouse? I was certain it had something to do with Regina, but which group of men was it? Was her father responsible for the murder? Was it the other group of men, and who were *they* anyway? Most importantly, had Angus told them what they wanted to know before they killed him?

Then there was DCI Campbell. I could hear Angus's voice in my ear. "Never trust a Campbell, laddie! As it was in Glen Coe, it shall always be with that clan." Clearly Campbell, trustworthy or not, had guessed I knew more about the murder than I had told him. That had been why he'd taken me up there, why he'd shown me everything. Had he expected I'd fall to pieces and confess?

Looked at logically, if I had told him what I did know, where would that put him? Regina would probably be able to identify someone out of the six who'd accosted us in Birmingham, but how could we know if they'd been the ones who'd shown up at Loch Striven?

If Angus hadn't been slain by "Group #1", then what? Neither Regina nor I could identify the other three. I don't think I would have recognized any of them if they'd walked up to me right then and there.

Suddenly, looking around, I realized that I was the only person in sight at the moment. If those blokes *were* around, I'd be easy pickings. With untoward haste, I scurried to the nearest pub, where I would hopefully find safety in numbers and elucidation at the bottom of a pint glass.

III

"I've been on pins and needles all day long, Michael!" Regina exclaimed when I got her on the phone. "What's happening?"

It took me a good thirty minutes to lay it all out. I knew which way I was hoping she'd jump about what to do next, and I tried to angle the discussion in that direction, but she didn't pick up on it.

"Poor Angus," she said softly when I'd finished. "Do you really think it could have been my father's men?"

"That's where we're in pretty murky water. It could have been...and it would explain why Angus had to die. If he'd been left around to tell someone what information they'd wanted, they would be in serious trouble. If it was the second group of men, then I just don't know. But whoever was responsible, the sad truth is that Angus had to die."

"Why?"

"To keep the information from the other group."

Regina didn't speak right away, and when she did, it had a quiet intensity I could hear clearly from three thousand miles away. "In your heart of hearts, do you think Angus would have told them what they wanted to know?"

I had known she would ask that question, and I'd been pondering it all day myself. Angus would have been aware of how dangerous that would be, but he had no idea at the time they showed up at his house where Regina was. He only knew where I was.

"I certainly hope not."

"What about the man who came to your business today?"

"Perhaps Campbell has someone nosing around. He kept bringing up drugs. Maybe he thinks Angus and I are...were involved in the drug trade, something like that. If it was the police at my business, they're looking for something on me. It won't be long before they're also looking for you, though. They know you exist—"

"*How?*"

"You left hair samples all over Angus's house. In the shower, for instance. Other places, too."

"They know about that?"

"Not from anything I said. I told them the sheets weren't fresh, and I'd been too lazy to change them. If they wanted to press things, though, I suppose I could be asked to give a DNA sample, and that could be matched up to what we undoubtedly left on the sheets, and then with the hairs you left in the shower. My employees can identify you. How do I explain all that?" I ended bluntly.

"No, Michael! I do *not* want to be brought into this. I can't be. These people are after me!"

My anger with Regina, building as the day had progressed, suddenly boiled over. "I certainly wish you'd thought to tell Angus that before you left!" I spat out angrily.

"And what's that supposed to mean?"

"It means, even though we *both* should have thought things through a lot better, it's *you* those thugs were after. Don't you regret anything about what's happened? My friend is dead because I brought you to his house!"

"Michael I...I know that. It's just..."

"Whose side are you on, anyway? Are you trying to protect your father or something?"

There was a long pause before she spoke. "Okay. You're right. Tell the cops. Just don't tell them about me."

I looked heavenward. "Can't you see that's impossible?"

"Can't you just ride this out?"

"I don't want to. I want Angus's killers to be brought to justice! Don't you want that, too?"

"Yes, yes. Of course I do," she answered, but it sounded reluctant.

"Then you have to agree to help the police."

"You're definitely going to tell them everything?"

"Yes," I answered, suddenly certain of the way forward. "There's no other choice. And you must help. You have valuable information."

"I don't know if I'm ready for that... There's my, um, father to think about in all this. I don't know if I'm ready to...you know..."

"Say you'll help!"

"I'll think about it. Call me tomorrow."

"What's there to think about? How can you be this ungrateful?"

"Goodbye, Michael."

The line went dead, and I sat there stupidly until the dial tone returned.

Damn her!

Damn myself.

CHAPTER 8

It didn't surprise me to get a phone call from the Dunoon police at half eight next morning.

"DCI Campbell would like to see you as soon as possible, sir."

I didn't feel up to what was coming, having been awake almost the entire night. No doubt about it, I'd landed in a right mess.

As I walked up the hill to the Dunoon police station, I kept a wary eye out for the media. It was only a matter of time before they got wind of my involvement in Angus's death. Even though Neurotica's story was firmly in the past tense, they wouldn't pass up the opportunity to troll for juicy info. A bit of digging, and I'd be nailed.

I strolled by several cars and vans parked on the street, their occupants keeping warm while they waited for something to happen. They wouldn't be happy when they discovered their big story had walked right under their noses, twice.

The duty officer at the station told me to sit on one of the benches lining the walls of the gloomy room. Ten minutes later, Campbell himself came to retrieve me. I stood to shake hands but couldn't read anything useful in his expression.

We went to a different room that morning, bare except for an ancient wooden table, three unmatched plastic seats and a metal waste basket that looked as if it had been booted more than a few times. A constable came in to take notes almost as soon as we'd sat, but also—to my mind more ominously—he placed a recorder on the table between Campbell and me. Having seen the BBC's *Prime Suspect* series, I knew full well what that meant.

"So, Mr. Quinn," Campbell began, "did you spend a comfortable night?"

"Not really. What is the recorder for?"

"We have moved on to the second stage of our investigation, and since we may require it later, I thought it best to have it on hand from the beginning."

Up to that point, I hadn't *quite* decided what I wanted to do, but the appearance of the recorder settled it. Not telling the detective what I knew was getting me deeper into it with each passing moment.

In hindsight, I probably should have had a lawyer with me, but since I felt I had nothing to hide, and I had done nothing wrong except to be a bloody stupid git, I got ready to spill the load.

"I, ah, may not have been as forthcoming yesterday as I might have been," I began.

Campbell didn't make an outward sign, but I could detect a satisfied reaction. After a long moment of staring, he reached forward and switched on the tape recorder, stating the date, time, circumstances and people present. Then the detective leaned back in his chair, folded his arms across his chest and nodded, making it clear I wasn't going to receive any help with this.

I took a deep breath, said a silent Hail Mary and began. "When I returned here from Birmingham, I had a woman with me."

His face was unreadable. "We were aware of that."

"You were?"

He smiled, but it wasn't friendly. "There were two condom wrappers under your bed, as well as one recently-used condom stuck in the toilet, which is an old one and doesn't flush very efficiently."

"You looked in the toilet?"

"We *removed* the toilet. Since discovering that, we spoke to the ferry workers, and one remembers your friend's Jaguar making the crossing with its memorable damage as well as a rather good-looking young lady accompanying you."

"And that's why you asked me to come in this morning?"

"Partially."

"What do you mean by 'partially'?"

"Look, Mr. Quinn. Why don't you just tell me your story, and then we can clean up any remaining questions when you've finished."

Trying to stay relaxed and look decidedly *not* guilty, I fixed my eyes firmly on the opposite wall and told Campbell everything I could remember, starting with Regina jumping into my car in Birmingham in the early hours of Monday morning last.

It took quite a long time.

III

They didn't let me go until almost half two. After I'd finished my story, Campbell had a multitude of questions. He asked if I thought I might be able to help a police artist sketch any of the six men who'd tried to stop us that night in Birmingham. He even had my fingerprints taken to help with identification of what they'd found at Angus's place. Finally, they typed up a statement for me to sign. No one made any indication as to whether what I'd told them had been believed.

If I thought I'd been exhausted before the interview, I'd been wrong. Part of my fatigue was hunger, so I stopped at the same café as the day before and ate a bowl of soup and a sandwich, hardly noticing what any of it tasted like. Still, I felt better for eating—and for finally doing something positive to help the cops catch the bastards who'd murdered my friend.

When I got back to my room, I immediately tried Regina to give her the lowdown on how things had gone. Even though he wouldn't say how he was going to proceed with the information I'd given him, I felt certain DCI Campbell would try to get someone in Toronto to interview Regina. She needed to know exactly what I had said so there wouldn't be problems with conflicting stories.

With a sinking heart, I received the news that the person in Room 517 had departed the previous evening—almost as soon as she'd got off the phone with me, as it turned out. "Did she leave any messages for people calling?"

The desk clerk's reply sounded tentative. "I will check, sir, but somehow I doubt it."

"What do you mean?"

"She left without settling her bill."

"She skipped?"

There was a pause. "Yes, and I'm afraid the credit card she gave me when checking in was not, ah, active."

"Did Miss Mastrocolle leave any forwarding information?"

"I'm sorry, the guest in that room used a different name. Are you sure the guest you're inquiring about was in 517?"

"Of course I am! I spoke to her yesterday afternoon." I squeezed the bridge of my nose between thumb and forefinger. "How much does she owe?"

The voice on the other end sounded very much relieved, and I suspected that he'd screwed up and not handled her registration correctly. Most hotels check credit card information when guests register, *not* after they've skipped out on their bill.

Filled with disquiet, I replaced the receiver. Several things didn't add up here. I should have expected Regina to register under an assumed name if she could, but the bogus credit card was a really stinking bit of evidence. If she was what she'd told me, she wouldn't have phony credit cards.

Dialing the operator, I asked for directory assistance for Paris. Several minutes later, my disquiet had ramped up alarmingly. The place Regina had told me she worked, Galerie Longchamps, had never heard of her and had never in their history had an American working for them.

I called back the hotel in Toronto. "Could you tell me what name the woman in 517 used?"

The desk clerk sounded more friendly this time. "This is about more than her hotel bill, isn't it?" he asked candidly.

"You could say that."

"Sorry to hear that, sir. I don't think it would be *too* far beyond hotel policy to tell you that she registered under the name of Genevieve Fleury. Had all the papers, too, *and* a very charming French accent. She certainly fooled me."

I was stunned. "Where did she say she was from?"

"Boy, you sound as if you're in the same boat I was! Sure hope you weren't taken for much. Her driver's license said Montreal."

After hanging up, I lay back on the bed, staring at the ceiling. Something was very wrong, and it was obvious that, even after coming clean with Campbell, my situation had now become considerably worse.

What did I *really* know about the girl? Only that two groups of men had chased her and been quite ready to use force (or worse) to get her. Past that, I could be sure of nothing—except that she was a damned good liar.

I rang up Campbell, only to be informed that he'd gone to the divisional headquarters in Dumbarton and wouldn't return until the following morning. I asked if they would have him call me as soon as possible, that it was quite urgent.

Nothing more could be done on the Regina front at the moment, so I next tried the Hilton in Glasgow, only to be told that Mr. Simpson was not accepting calls, but they agreed to deliver a message. It took Rolly only ten minutes to ring back.

"Michael! How are you?"

"I've been better."

"Have you reconsidered what we were discussing yesterday?"

"There is nothing to reconsider. Let's just drop it, Rolly, okay?"

He didn't answer immediately, and I could distinctly hear a female voice giggling in the background. The lovely Constable Dickson?

"Sorry, Michael. What was that you said?" Rolly asked.

"Nothing. So when is the service for Angus?"

"Monday at the RC church in Dunoon. The body is to be cremated, according to his wishes and that will be done in Greenock. Has that solicitor chap been in touch with you?"

"What solicitor, and how the hell could he ring me up if no one knew where I'm staying?"

"Good point. Give me your number, and I'll pass it on to him."

"What does he want?"

"Didn't Angus ever tell you? You're his bleeding executor."

I spent the late afternoon dozing on the bed, only making a quick trip out to pick up a copy of the *Glasgow Sunday Herald* and a quart of orange juice.

It must have been a slow news day, because the coverage extended beyond what one would expect for a fairly sensational murder. There was a nice article about Angus the Road Manager, mentioning all the acts he'd worked for, with some very gracious quotes from some of the artists. It didn't surprise me that there were extensive quotes from Rolly. Most of the photos were from Neurotica gigs as well, including one of Angus, Rolly and me with one of the Beatles who'd once visited us backstage in London. The caption referred to me as the band's "reclusive keyboard player". All in all, it was a nice write-up and one that painted Angus in a flattering light.

Since it was approaching dinnertime, I flipped on the evening news, and sure enough, Angus's murder was the third item dealt with. This coverage I was a lot less happy with. One reporter had managed to corner DCI Campbell as he'd left the Dunoon station that afternoon. In reply to the reporter's question, Campbell said, "We have received new information, although we don't know how reliable it is at this point. I expect more news will be forthcoming in the next day or two."

The clip ended with Campbell requesting "anyone with information to please come forward to assist the investigation." The next clip was a brief interview with Rolly in his hotel room, something I'm sure he'd been very accommodating about.

To my horror, he told the reporter that the original members of Neurotica had expressed a desire to perform a memorial concert for their fallen comrade. When the reporter questioned my involvement, Rolly replied, "I'm certain Michael will want to be part of it. He and Angus were very close. As a matter of fact, he was visiting a few days before this senseless killing."

Rolly came off as very concerned and generous, but knowing him as I did, I could detect the smugness in his expression. To add insult to injury, the reporter closed the segment with some coverage of my sudden and mysterious departure from Neurotica, complete with a clip from the press conference the band's management had called after it had occurred. The reporter closed with the statement that I was currently living in Toronto.

I flipped off the telly and angrily threw the remote across the room, where it shattered against the wall.

Rolly had just completely screwed me.

If I didn't take part in his little memorial concert, I would come across looking very churlish indeed. Angus *had* been my best friend since I'd left Neurotica, and what excuse could I give for not performing? Rolly knew quite well that my reputation was very important to me.

As I stewed about the situation, it suddenly dawned on me that anyone who had seen the broadcast (or others like it which undoubtedly would be shown) would know more than enough to be able to find me. Those people who'd killed Angus could now come after me with little trouble.

I went to bed early and felt like pulling the covers over my head. Sleep didn't come easily, but I was used to that.

▌▌▌

The next morning was clear and bright and, feeling the need for a bit of space, I took my hired car and went for a drive up the peninsula as far as Rest and Be Thankful, where I pulled over and looked out at the world. Scotland on a beautiful day can be breathtaking and today it was at its best.

The glorious view didn't clear my head, though. My life had gone completely down the crapper. I was in trouble with the police, I was being manoeuvred into doing something I'd sworn I'd never do, and I was partially responsible for the death of a very good friend. The worst thing was I'd found that the one person who could verify everything I'd told the police had disappeared, after feeding me a complete pack of lies. Could things get any worse?

Back in Dunoon, it took me a bit of time to find the church and a place to park. A lot of people Angus had worked for showed up, so naturally the press was out in force, snapping pictures of rock stars uncharacteristically wearing dark suits or sombre dresses. I managed to get in with only one or two snaps being taken, and none of the TV people could corner me for an interview, since the service was ready to begin.

Raymond MacDonald, the solicitor Rolly had mentioned, had been on the lookout, though, and cornered me in the vestry for a quick update. Angus's will stipulated that it was to be read at his home. Unfortunately, the police had forbade use of the house, so helpful Rolly had suggested the outbuilding where the instruments were kept. It wasn't hard to guess his reasons.

The less said about the service itself, the better. Angus would have killed himself laughing, being about the most un-religious man imaginable, who always took great glee telling everyone that he wouldn't be caught dead in a church. That caused me a wistful private smile because here he was, caught dead in a church, complete with choir, pipe organ and a grandiose coffin.

I hoped the service was a comfort to the family, since it didn't seem to do a lot for most of the music business people I was observing.

I sat alone at the back, but it wasn't long before the Neurotica crew started motioning for me to come forward to join them. I couldn't graciously say no to that, so during a break in proceedings, I scooted forward, sliding in at the end of their aisle.

Quietly shaking hands with Tommy (the drummer) and his wife, Margaret (better known as Mags), and nodding over at John (guitar), without his wife, and Lee (bass), perennially divorced, I stared at Rolly down on the end, who kept his gaze steadfastly forward and fidgeted. I found out why when he got up to deliver the eulogy.

Tommy leaned across Mags and whispered, "How come you're not doing this?"

"Wasn't asked."

"Figures," Mags grumbled, then added pithily, "I wouldn't be surprised if the wanker gave the eulogy at his own funeral. He always was a conceited arse."

Tommy looked heavier and had lost a good bit of hair on top. He'd stopped playing professionally, joining his dad's plumbing business. I remembered Mags as a stylish, leggy blonde in her twenties, and while she'd put on a bit of weight, she looked pretty good. Her tongue was still as tart as ever. I liked them both and was glad things had worked out between them.

John had always been dark and brooding, and that hadn't changed. He remained rake-thin and still wore his hair long, although it was now greying and pulled back in a ponytail like a lot of other aging rockers. He naturally tended to regard everyone as being less intelligent than he, but he was undoubtedly a brilliant guitarist, and the most musically successful of the group, post-Neurotica, having become a sought-after studio musician.

At nineteen, Lee had been the youngest of us when we'd hit it big. I remembered him as a gawky free spirit who'd needed a lot of looking after. Lee was a good enough player when he kept his mind on business at hand. Apparently, he'd spent the last ten years kicking around the UK with various club bands, since, with three marriages behind him, he was also completely broke. He'd never written any of

Neurotica's material, and we hadn't shared writing credits as some bands do. Other than Rolly, he was (naturally) the most interested in a Neurotica reunion. I was sad to see that he now looked older than any of us. The years had not been kind.

Rolly's eulogy was as bad as might have been expected—but only to insiders. On tour, Rolly had been a very demanding performer who'd required a lot of Angus's time and attention and never made anything easy. His words that afternoon made it sound like the glory days of Neurotica had been a case of "all for one and one for all". I remembered it as a hard slog: long days stuck in buses (and later, planes) and even longer nights, where the only places I felt truly comfortable were on stage or in the studio. Rolly made it all sound like a mad lark. Perhaps for him it had been.

At the conclusion of the service, we naturally congregated at the front of the church, speaking quietly about our departed friend and renewing our acquaintance. They'd seen each other far more frequently, but we easily fell into our old speech patterns and attitudes.

"I wondered if you'd show," Tommy said, looking toward the street, where our lead singer was surrounded by the media. "You must be mad as hell at Rolly."

"You figured it out, then?" I asked.

"Rolly told me he was going to do it. I told him it was a bad idea."

Lee sidled up next to me. "You *are* going to play, though, Michael, aren't you?"

I sighed. "I have to now. Angus always wanted it. But I'm *not* going to get involved in any of the planning, and we have to find an appropriate charity to give the proceeds to." I stopped and smiled at them. "Unless we're all willing to foot the bill and make the gig a free one."

Mags guffawed, and the others, especially Lee, looked unhappy. It had been a childish thing to say, and I was immediately sorry I'd needled them, a bad habit from times past.

Before I could apologize, the coffin came out of the church, carried by Angus's five nephews and his old dad. It was apparent that he shouldn't have attempted this, but the man was as stubborn as his son had been.

I stepped forward and said, "Please, sir, allow me. It would be a shame if you stumbled. You can follow behind."

He must have been thinking the same thing, because he acquiesced immediately, and I took his place, unfortunately providing a terrific photo-op for the media who surged forward.

Once the coffin was safely in the hearse, the family got into the three waiting limos behind and headed off for the ferry dock. The cremation ceremony was for family members only. Rolly and I went back into the church to join the others. The press called after us to no avail, and the cops kept them well away. Several of the stars who'd come to the service nodded at us as they went by and thankfully gave the news-hounds something to do.

"You've met MacDonald?" Rolly asked me.

"Yes. And from what I gather, everyone is invited to the reading of the will. I still have no idea what's in it, though."

"Angus was tight-lipped about it, but knowing him, there'll be a zinger of some sort." He turned to the other Neurotica members. "We don't have to be back to Angus's until three. What do you say we get a bite and hoist a few pints? It will be just like the old days."

They all looked at me to see my response, and I suppose I looked suitably perturbed, because Tommy hastily added, "It will be an opportunity to talk about Angus and remember the good times."

"I'll drink to that!" Rolly said—something I hoped he wouldn't do to excess.

During the remainder of that day, Neurotica had its first meal together in twenty-four years (missing Angus mightily), and found out that our road manager had left an estate surprisingly larger than one would have imagined. The instruments were to go to each of us, but they had to be off the premises as soon as possible, because the family was going to sell the property.

As executor, I found I didn't have much to do. MacDonald explained that my job was simply to make sure the estate was concluded properly, all the death duties paid and Angus's wishes followed.

It also turned out that Rolly and Lee had, to no one's surprise, engineered the meeting *not* to be held in Glasgow simply to get all of us (primarily me) out to where our instruments were kept, hoping that it would be a simple matter to have an impromptu jam session . Having been manipulated far more than I liked the past two days, I declined and managed to piss off everyone but Tommy, who later confided that he was so out of shape, he didn't think he could play the old material without making a fool of himself.

To soften the blow of my refusal, I again confirmed that I would do the concert and would also take care of getting the instruments safely stored somewhere in Glasgow so they'd be handy for rehearsals.

Everyone left fairly quickly after that, except for Tommy and Mags who stayed to help put the equipment into the flight cases. Lee also stayed, but only because he was forced to. John had made it perfectly clear that the extra seat in Rolly's Porsche would be taken up by *his* bum, not Lee's. In consequence, Lee had to wait around for Tommy, Mags and me. He wandered around for a while, rolling up the odd guitar cord, but eventually disappeared outside to have a smoke, not returning until we were finished.

"You have a drum kit at home?" I asked Tommy as we lowered the flight case lid over the organ.

"Yeah, but it's not mine. My son's taken up drums, don't you know. Quite good, really." He stopped and looked long at me. "I can't believe you're actually going to do it."

"I can't believe I'm actually going to, either, to be honest."

"Is there any hope of this becoming something more involved?"

I took a deep breath. "I know how much this means to the rest of you, but no. I feel I owe this concert to Angus, and that's the start and finish of it. He wanted it more than any of us, and now he's the only one who won't be there to see it."

Tommy clapped me on the shoulder. "Well, I for one am happy that you're at least able to do this much. We can crank up the real Neurotica one last time and give Angus a send-off that would make him proud!"

It took over an hour to get everything in the cases. Lee stuck his head in the door from time to time, grumbling about how long it was taking. Mags told him to shut his gob and help. Several times I caught her smiling at Tommy. It was clear she knew how much playing around with these instruments and re-living his glory years as a musician meant to her old man.

Tommy and I were pretty sweaty by the time the gear had been stowed in the flight cases. Now I'd only need to find someone to pick it up and cart it off to storage. While that would probably take a few phone calls, with my connections in the business, I could get the job done without much trouble. At the top of my mind, though, was making arrangements for my flight home.

We were putting on our overcoats when Tommy turned and said, "Rolly told me yesterday that the coppers have been talking to you."

Probably to keep me in a good frame of mind, nothing had been mentioned about that all day. "Yeah. I was here two days before the poor sod bought it."

"Do you have any idea what happened?"

I could only stare. How the hell do you respond to a question like that?

Tommy's face grew hard. "I'd like to kill the bastards who did it," he growled.

CHAPTER 9

My old nightmares returned with a thumping vengeance that night, as I'd feared all along they would.

A week earlier, I would have smugly stated that I'd laid all my demons to rest years ago. I guess seeing all the old faces, combined with the horrendous circumstances that had returned me to Scotland, allowed my "night horrors" to creep so easily out of their dark hiding place. I can see now they were never really defeated, simply waiting.

To be afraid to close your eyes, to know that as soon as you drop off, you're going to face the same gut-wrenching product of your tortured conscience yet again is no way to live. For someone who's never suffered through more than losing the odd night to bad dreams, there can be no comprehension of how debilitating having the same dream night after bloody night can become. For years after leaving Neurotica, I'd been a walking zombie, living in a mental and physical twilight. Sleeping pills (even prescribed ones) did no good. Hypnosis, ditto. I'd even tried drinking myself into oblivion in the hopes that passing out would give me a few hours of blessed relief. The images my brain treated me to on those occasions were even more awful, distorted grotesquely through the haze of alcohol. The only thing that had gradually allowed me to resume a normal life had been distance and time.

There had been nothing I could do when it had been fresh and raw in my brain, and I had the horrible feeling that there would be nothing I could do now.

So I lay futilely on the bed that night, scared to drop off, with my mind a hopeless jumble of half-formed suppositions and even more fragmented conclusions. It felt as if someone had dumped me in the middle of a dark, tangled forest with no way to see or move more than a few feet in any direction without being stopped by a web of clawing undergrowth. One moment my life had been ordered, regular, something which I could stand in the middle of and be satisfied with, and the next moment *everything* had changed—all because of that damned girl who had jumped into my car.

By the time the meagre light of a Scottish winter dawn began to filter through the curtains of my hotel room, the only thing I was certain of was that *this* was one mess I couldn't run away from. The silent phantom of my friend sitting the entire night bound to the chair opposite my bed would never allow me that escape.

|||

Determined to try out that hoary adage that the best defense is a good offense, I was showered, shaved, dressed and sitting on a bench at the Dunoon police station by eight thirty. I wanted to catch Campbell as soon as he returned. I had way too much to do before I could get the hell out of Scotland and begin trying to get my life back on track.

Dressed in his usual three-piece suit (this one dark greenish tweed), Campbell strode in shortly after nine, looking impatient and unhappy, especially when he noticed me sitting in a corner. Without a word, the detective indicated with a stiff flick of his head that I should follow. Once in his borrowed office again, he hung his overcoat on a peg behind the door, carefully smoothing out any wrinkles. Then, taking his place behind the desk, the DCI opened his leather briefcase to remove some papers and his notebook. I tried hard not to smile when I saw it also contained a sandwich and an apple.

Glancing up at me, he said curtly, "Well, come in lad, and take a seat. Or do you prefer standing in the doorway all morning?"

I did as I was told and sat in one of the chairs across the desk from him, trying hard not to look as if I were twelve years old and had just been summoned to the headmaster's office.

"You were on television last night," he began.

"I expected I would be."

"Besides your friend's funeral, they ran some old footage of you playing and being interviewed, followed by a news conference when you quit that pop band of yours." Campbell pulled a fountain pen out of his inside jacket pocket, staring at it for a moment. "Why did you leave right in the middle of a supposedly very successful tour?"

My eyes felt as if they were bugging out of my head, although I'm certain they weren't. Every action and *re*action takes on magnified significance in this kind of situation. This was *not* the way I'd envisioned the meeting when I'd planned it during the dark hours of the previous night.

Struggling to keep my face a blank slate, I managed to say evenly, "It was due to artistic differences." Not a complete lie.

"You walked away from an act on the verge of becoming the biggest thing since, since..."

"Since the Beatles," I finished for him. "Yeah, yeah, I've heard all that before. It was more some publicist's hyperbole than truth."

Campbell looked at me shrewdly, and I wondered if he actually knew something or was just fishing. He put down the pen. "From what I've been told, you *were* this pop band; it was supposed to be your brilliance behind the group's sound. What happened to their sales of recordings after you left certainly bears that out. My question to you is: why haven't you done anything since? If you'd had artistic differences, that wouldn't have been enough to cause you to walk away from a very promising career. I find that hard to fathom. Was there perhaps another reason you left?"

I tried not to bore holes through the detective with my eyes. His probing was hitting awfully close to something I was firmly determined *not* to share with anyone, no matter the reason. "I was totally disillusioned with the music business."

"Yet you're still part of that business, from what you've told me."

"I rent bloody musical instruments! Doesn't that make sense? I know about things like that. It was natural to start that sort of business."

Campbell looked more unhappy, but kept his thoughts to himself.

"What could something that happened nearly a quarter century ago have to do with my friend's murder?" I continued. "Are you interested in finding his killers or just in hassling me?"

"I am interested in getting at the truth by knowing the complete story, and since you were visiting Mr. MacDougall two days before his murder, I need to know about you—especially since it seems this girl you told me about has disappeared." He must have read my expression accurately, because he added, "You see, we have been following up on your story."

"I was afraid this would happen."

He picked up his pen and opened the notebook. For a moment he hesitated with his hand above the phone, probably about to call for a stenographer and tape recorder. "Clarify what you mean."

I snorted disgustedly. "I tried calling her. I didn't want her to freak out if the police came around. She's vanished, and worse, she ran out on her hotel bill. The name she gave me doesn't appear to be good, either. I have no idea if *anything* she told me was true."

"Elaborate, please," the detective said as he readied his pen over a clean page in the notebook.

This time I held back absolutely nothing. Regina could rot in hell for all I cared.

"Do you believe what I've just told you?" I asked him when I'd finished.

"What you've told me *could* explain our lack of success at locating any record of the girl. We'll have to start all over again with this new name—not that she couldn't have used a different false identity to purchase her plane ticket in Glasgow."

"But you *do* believe that I had nothing to do with the death of my friend?" I persisted.

Campbell looked out the window, where the sun was finally making a decent showing, and spoke without turning his head back to me. "I am keeping all options open at this point, Mr. Quinn."

"Did you send someone around asking questions at my business back in Toronto?"

The DCI shook his head sadly. "Surely, you can't expect me to answer that."

"Maybe I should have got a lawyer before I told you anything," I said more to myself.

He finally turned back to look at me. "You have cooperated to a large extent, and I can assure you that if you've told the truth, then you won't come to any harm. But," and his gaze sharpened again, "I believe that there is still more to your story than you've related to me."

"I know nothing more about Angus's death than I've told you. I swear it!"

"I hope for your sake you're telling the truth, laddie. Believe me when I say that if you've omitted anything, I will discover it, then it will go very badly with you. *That* I can guarantee."

"Am I free to go back home?"

"I cannot keep you here."

"Good! You know where you can find me if you want me again."

"Yes, I do."

III

Back at the hotel, I booked a seat for the first flight I thought I could manage—early the next morning, as it turned out. I still had to arrange and supervise getting the equipment moved. Campbell had balked at allowing anything to leave his crime scene, until I pointed out that the storage shed/rehearsal hall had nothing to do with the murder, and if he so desired, he could have his people on hand to see if what I'd be taking contained anything pertinent to his investigation.

Getting that amount of equipment moved in a short time required me to do something I didn't like doing: trading on my name.

A call to Jeremy, a pal in London who ran the same sort of business as I, and with whom I had on occasion traded clients as they toured on either side of the Atlantic, produced a couple of businesses in Glasgow that could handle what I needed. Jeremy had also heard of the pending Neurotica reunion concert.

"You swore up and down you'd never play again!" he said in mock outrage. "Michael, you're letting me down. Is hell actually freezing over?"

I sighed. "There's more to the story than I can say at the moment, but the long and short of it is, I would look like a churl if I refused."

"Well, I was always hoping I'd get to hear the band live, but it's a real bummer that it had to come about this way. Losing Angus is a shame. He was the best. Keep me informed about the concert. I plan on coming, yeah?"

"I'll have tickets set aside for you. And thanks for the info."

The first place I called told me there was no way they could do it for three days.

Upon calling the second number, the male voice on the other end sounded infinitely bored. "Yeah, mate, what can I do for you?"

I choked back a tart comment. If one of my lads answered the phone like that, he'd get a good ticking off, and if it continued, he could expect the sack.

"My name is Michael Quinn, and I got your number from Jeremy Withers in London. I need some equipment moved and stored."

"So?"

"Can you handle it?"

"How much stuff?"

I told the bloke that I figured a twelve-foot lorry would do the job. "It's all in flight cases, packed and ready to go. The problem is that it's at a farmhouse north of Dunoon. It has to be moved immediately."

"You're kidding me. How do you expect that's bloody well going to happen?"

"Look, I know it's a lot to ask, but I'm really stuck. I have to leave for Canada early tomorrow morning."

"You do have a problem, mate," the voice answered insolently.

"Would a little something extra for express service help?"

"Oh, you could expect to pay extra for same-day service without your kind offer."

"Can you do it?"

"Well, I can't say that we can, and I can't say that we can't."

My anger began to boil over. "Can you be any more vague?"

"We usually expect people to plan these things out ahead of time and book in advance."

That did it. "I'm sorry I couldn't be so considerate. Why don't you be a good lad and put me on to your boss?"

"He'll tell you the same."

"I don't think so. Tell him Michael Quicksilver's on the phone."

"You said your name was Quinn."

"My professional name has always been Quicksilver."

The turnaround in employee attitude was truly breathtaking. "You're kidding! *The* Michael Quicksilver from Neurotica? God! I've always wanted to meet you. You're one of my heroes!"

"Well, if you get that lorry out here before I leave for Canada, you'll not only get to meet me, but I'll help you load the equipment!"

"Bloody hell! Wait until I tell the boss. This is all Neurotica's gear, I take it? I heard on the news you were going to play again."

"Yes. Now when can I expect you?"

"The old man will want to speak to you. Just a sec."

The boss sounded as enthusiastic as his employee, and I eventually had to cut him off. I could see the lorry showing up at midnight if I let him talk any longer.

It never made me comfortable to hear people go on about me, and I was especially uncomfortable now, since I didn't want to be playing with Neurotica anyway.

Before heading back to Angus's for the equipment pick-up, I tried the office, hoping my lads wouldn't be tardy because the boss didn't happen to be around to crack the whip. Surprisingly, Hamed, always the last to show up, picked up on the first ring.

He assured me everything was going swimmingly, nothing out of the ordinary. Even though I wanted to, I didn't ask if any more cops (or anyone else, for that matter) had been nosing around. The less my crew knew about my troubles, the better.

"I should be back tomorrow around closing time."

"Hey, boss," Hamed said just before hanging up. "I caught a report on the radio this morning that said you were going to play a concert in Glasgow with your old band."

I sighed deeply. Bad news travels faster than ever in our electronic society. "Yes, it's true."

"Do we get to come?"

"Only if you pay for your own plane tickets," I said, surprised by his cheek.

"Everyone always says you're a cheap bastard," Hamed shot back.

"Nobody says that, and you know it. You'll have to find another tack if you want a transatlantic ticket."

"We can hump the gear for you, then."

"That's more like it. I'll think about it."

The equipment got moved, the cops didn't bug us in the slightest (although they did watch the goings-on closely—probably out of boredom) and the flight back to Canada the next morning was uneventful. The temperature, too, had risen. Things were looking up slightly.

Even so, by the time I got through customs and retrieved my bags and car, it was well past three p.m. Having spent a second almost sleepless night, I really wanted to just head home, but thought it would be a good idea to check in at the business, since I'd been away so much.

I also had another reason.

Hamed had not been exaggerating. Everything was ticking along quite well without the skipper at the helm, although my desk was covered with papers requiring my attention. All hands were present, and they'd even swept the place *and* cleaned the bathroom.

Telling them I had business to take care of with the landlord who kept an office in the complex, I went out the door, but instead of heading off to see Jerome, I walked to the far end of the building, where an investigative service rented space.

The office I entered was small and bare-bones in decor, with a rather beat-up desk, a long row of filing cabinets and stackable plastic chairs for the clients to park their bums on. The walls had been painted white quite a while ago, and the carpet was a bilious green with a lot of salt stains near the entry. A fake redhead in her late twenties sat behind the desk, busily tapping on a keyboard. The room stank of burnt coffee and cigarettes.

"I, ah, would like to talk with someone," I said, standing in front of her desk.

The girl looked up and was about to speak when the phone rang. Holding up a finger in a waiting motion, she answered it.

"Good afternoon, O'Brien Investigates... Just a minute, Mr. Saunders, I'll see if she's available." She pressed a key on the phone. "Shannon, it's our Mr. Saunders. Are you in?... Okay. I'll connect him. Oh, and there's someone out here who wants to speak to you... Just a sec." She turned back to me. "Your name?"

"Ah, Michael Quinn. I own Quinn Musical Equipment at the far end of this building."

The information was relayed, and I was asked to take a seat.

Ten minutes later, a woman who looked to be in her late thirties came through the door behind the secretary's desk and walked over, extending her hand, then stopped dead, staring at me. "Hi, I'm Shannon O'Brien. Please step into my office."

The inner sanctum wasn't much more plush than the reception

area, adding to my misgivings.

"You own this business?" I asked bluntly.

"Yep, every last stick of crummy furniture."

If my question bothered her, it didn't show.

"What kind of, ah, investigations do you handle?"

She stared at me again for a very long moment with her head tilted to the side and something unreadable in her eyes. "Well, Mr. Quinn, I think we could handle whatever it is you need. I've been a private investigator for seven years, and I come from a long line of cops. Please don't let the fact that I'm a female—"

"No, no," I interrupted. "I meant no insult. I just have no idea how these things work. You see, I've never needed an investigator before."

She sat down tiredly behind her desk. "Sorry. I've been in this business long enough to know better than to make stupid assumptions."

Shannon O'Brien didn't look like any private investigator I'd ever seen on the telly or read about in paperback novels. Rather pretty, with shoulder length honey blonde hair held back by a clip, no make-up and wearing jeans, a blouse and trainers, she seemed more like a mum about to pick up her kids from swim lessons. Although she was tall and appeared quite fit, I did wonder how she could have landed in such a potentially dangerous line of work.

"Tell me what you want, and I'll tell you whether we can handle it."

Something about the intensity of her gaze stopped me from giving the whole thing up as a stupid idea and bolting out the door. She leaned back in her chair, waiting.

"This is all going to sound rather confusing. You see, there's this woman, well, more of a girl actually..."

She smiled grimly. "There usually is."

"No, no," I corrected, "it's not like that at all."

As I sat trying to gather my scattered wits, the woman leaned forward and folded her hands in front of her. "Mr. Quinn, let me assure you that by now I don't think you could say anything that would shock me. Everything you tell me will stay between us—unless what you want done involves something criminal. I'm not a lawyer, doctor or priest, so that sort of thing can't be kept confidential."

"It does involve a crime, but I had nothing to do with what actually happened."

"Okay, start at the beginning," she said, leaning back again. "I'm a good listener. Would you like a cup of coffee? Tea?"

Remembering the odour of burnt coffee when I'd first entered the building, I politely declined.

I took a deep breath and ran down the story pretty well as I'd told it to Campbell. Unlike the police detective, she asked no questions, made no comments and only took notes, so subsequently, it became easier to talk as I went on.

When I finished, she cut to the chase. "And how do you see us being able to help you?"

"I want you to find the girl. I don't know if the police in the UK will be able to do that. There are too many diplomatic hoops to jump through, aren't there, since she's over here?"

"Is part of this because this Detective Chief Inspector Campbell seems to think you're more involved in what happened?"

This woman was pretty darned sharp. "Yes."

"Do you think *anything* the girl told you was true? We don't have much to go on. Did Campbell say whether they'd gotten any prints of hers from the crime scene?"

"I didn't think to ask."

"Okay. Here's the way I think we should proceed." O'Brien ticked off the points on her fingers, something I was going to discover she did quite a bit. "First, I'll go to the hotel where the girl stayed and see what I can find out. There's probably not much to learn, but you never know unless you try. First rule in this business is 'Expect you'll get lucky'. It's amazing how often you do. Next, I will get in touch with a colleague in New York to see what he knows about the Mastrocolle crime family. At least we know they exist, so that's one truth she told you. Who knows, maybe she *is* the man's daughter. There has to be some reason why she gave that name and not another."

"It can't be true."

"We won't know unless we ask, will we?" She looked over at me for a moment, sizing me up. "In the meantime, I'd watch your back. These guys will likely come after you next. It might be a smart idea to get out of town for a while."

"I'm not running away. I can't, anyway. I have a business to operate."

Where the hell had *that* response come from? Straight out of the id, and it really surprised me, considering that getting myself out of harm's way would have been my first reaction two weeks earlier.

O'Brien continued to gaze intently at me across her desk. "That could prove dangerous."

"Yes, it could. I can take suitable precautions."

"Do you want me to arrange for a bodyguard?"

"That won't be necessary. I usually have two or more people around me at work. Surely these thugs aren't going to take on all of us."

"What about at home?"

"No one knows where I live."

She began ticking off points on her fingers. "How about if they follow you, how about—"

I held up my hand. "I've gotten pretty good over the years at knowing when I'm being followed—even by professionals. I doubt if these blokes are better than journalists!"

"Okay. I get the picture. Just be *very* careful." She picked up her pen. "Now give me the numbers where I can contact you, *and* I'll need your home address, too." After copying it all down, O'Brien added, "I'll also need a retainer. A thousand ought to do it. You'll receive an update every few days at the very least, along with a rundown of what we've spent money on. And I should warn you; this could get expensive."

"I want to find that girl, whatever it costs. I'm good for it."

"I'll bet you are, Michael Quicksilver."

I started at her use of my stage name. "You knew who I was when I walked in?"

Shannon O'Brien laughed. "As soon as you walked in my door, but I had no idea you were my neighbour!"

"You know about Neurotica?"

"I was the president of my high school's Neurotica fan club," she said with a grin. "I finally had tickets to hear you guys, and then you left the band. I was heartbroken at the time. Why did it happen? The reasons I heard didn't ring true."

I sighed. "That's a very long story."

She looked at me with that piercing gaze. "You'll have to tell me some time."

CHAPTER 10

Remembering the neglected paperwork that had been piling up on my desk for almost two weeks, I felt a twinge of responsibility. If another sleepless night lay ahead, I could at least get something useful done. I shoved my cars keys back into my pocket and headed for the shop.

I'd been talking with the surprising proprietor of O'Brien Investigates far longer than I'd realized. Day had faded to winter night, with clouds rolling in from the northwest, the direction that always brings snow. Not having heard a weather report since arriving back in Canada, I had no idea how much of a dump had been forecast. With several pick-ups and deliveries scheduled for the next day, even a small amount of snow could throw a major spanner in the works. Quinn prided itself on always being "On Time and On Spec". The next day might well turn out to be more interesting than I'd have preferred.

The running of my business was too much on my mind as I turned the corner and arrived at my side door. It was locked. With snow on the way, the lads had probably bolted as soon as they decently could.

Fumbling around in my coat pockets for my keys, my mind occupied with mundane matters, I never heard them approaching.

Next thing I knew, someone grabbed my shoulder, spun me around, and a quick shot to the gut had me gasping for air. I went down on one knee, but they grabbed my coat and yanked me roughly back to my feet.

There were three of them, all big, all mean-looking. Two had me firmly by the arms. The third one stood back a few feet towards the middle of the driveway. This bloke was dressed better, and I got the feeling from his demeanour that he'd organized this little party. After peering at me for a good, long moment, he nodded once.

The blond one grabbed a handful of my hair and smacked the side of my head smartly on the metal door frame. It connected with enough force to make my ears ring and my eyes smart. Everything got very wobbly for a moment, but they held me up firmly.

The other one, an ugly dark-haired brute a with ponytail and a squashed nose that spoke of many fights, then said softly into my ear as they continued holding my head against the frame, "The keys, friend. Unlock the door."

I didn't like my chances *anywhere* with these three blokes, but I liked them even less if they had me alone in the warehouse, where they could leisurely beat the snot out of me—or worse. The memory of that blood-stained chair in Angus's sitting room was still fresh in my mind. Even out here, I was in great danger. At the far end of a deserted industrial mall, meagre light coming from a pole too far away, the possibility of someone seeing what was going on and coming to my aid seemed pretty remote.

I made a show of searching for my keys, and the thugs loosened their grip a bit. When I finally pulled the keyring out of my pants pocket, I quickly shoved the blond one and flung the keys high over my head, where they thankfully landed on the roof, twenty feet above.

"That's going to cost you," Blondie said as he recovered his balance and his grip.

He and his chum slammed me against the door frame again, much harder than the first time. I saw stars.

At a signal from the leader, the ponytailed one on my right let go of me and slapped my face hard. The shock of the blow was really quite astounding, partly because of the noise, and partly because I'd figured the next hand laid on me would be a closed fist.

Then he stuck his face into mine. "Where is she?" he hissed.

"Who?"

With no warning, he jabbed his fist hard into my gut. This time I did fall to my knees, but was quickly dragged upright again.

"That's to let you know we're serious. Now do you feel like answering the question?"

"Not particularly," I answered without thinking.

He grabbed me by the hair and rapped my head against the door jamb several more times.

"Wrong answer, pretty boy. Now if you want to *stay* pretty..."

I knew I didn't have many options. These idiots might have instructions to get specific information, or they just might be fishing.

How was I to know? The worst part was that I really didn't have much information they would want. I might actually have even less than they did. Would they be satisfied with almost nothing?

I didn't think so.

As big as the two knocking me around were, the third guy scared me more. Not as big, he somehow exuded far more danger. Perhaps he had been the person who'd tortured poor Angus. The curious smile on his face told me that he'd enjoy doing things like that.

An SUV rounded the corner at the far end of the building next to the one where we were standing. Sometimes the other tenants use the driveway that passes the side door of my shop in order to exit to the street, and if this were the case, it would mean he'd pass us. Only a dolt would not recognize that something bad was going on. The vehicle slowed for a moment, as if the driver were hesitating.

We all seemed to be holding our breath, but for completely opposite reasons. Would he or wouldn't he? The ringleader uttered his first words, "Get him into the auto. We can't stand out here—"

That's as far as he got, because the driver of the SUV suddenly floored it, and with squealing tires, came directly at us. Both the ringleader and the dark-haired flunky reached into their jackets.

The ringleader, standing out in the driveway away from my side door, made the easier target, and the SUV appeared to be aiming for him. At the speed it was moving, the guy wasn't going to be able to attempt to get out of the way *and* get a shot off. The one with me, however, *would* have a chance to fire.

Within the blink of an eye, the SUV came screaming to a halt, dividing the three of us at the door from the bloke in the driveway. In my impaired state, I tried to help by stamping down as hard as I could on the instep of the one with the gun. I was dimly aware of a noise from the other side of the SUV as I turned to the blond guy.

He'd snapped out of it, all right, and gave me several quick jabs to my face with hands that felt like concrete blocks. I went backwards and bumped into the one whose instep I'd nailed so well. Being up on one foot, while holding the damaged one, he easily overbalanced and went down in a heap with me fortunately on top. My head hit something very hard. Maybe it was the driveway, maybe it was the guy's head, but I must have actually blacked out for a moment.

The next thing I was aware of was a shape coming around the back of the SUV. In the dim light and with my stunned brain, that's all that registered. Blondie turned to face the newcomer, ready to do battle.

Something flashed in the light as the newcomer came in fast and low, leg swinging wide. The next thing that registered was a dull thud, and Blondie was down on his side. A strong hand grabbed me, pulling me to my feet, and dragged me into the passenger seat of the SUV. In a flash we were underway in a second tire-screeching take off. A hard left, which had me falling against my saviour, who was behind the wheel again, had us accelerating down the back of my building towards the street.

"Hold on to something, because I'm taking this turn as fast as I can without rolling," the person said, which we did with a god almighty bump as the vehicle clipped the curb.

We sped off west towards Woodbine Avenue, the main north/south road in the area, going right through the stop sign a block away from my shop. The light was with us at Woodbine, so with a sharp left and little slowing of our speed, we were heading south towards civilization.

My saviour was keeping a sharp eye in the rear view mirror, and I couldn't believe it when we quickly pulled into the parking area in front of a line of stores (closed for the night) only two blocks south. The SUV halted next to a small stand of fir trees which partially blocked it from the street. Our headlights and the engine were switched off, and the driver slouched down in the seat, pushing down on my head so I'd do the same. For a moment, it was silent, except for some pinging as the engine block began to cool.

"What in God's name are we doing?" I asked.

Shannon O'Brien looked over at me. "We're watching to see if they come by. I want to make their tags if I can."

"What?"

"Get their license plate number."

"Do you think this is wise?"

"Relax! It's the last thing they'll expect. I'm sure they figure we're either hightailing it to safety or the nearest cop shop. So without knowing it, they're going to provide us with the first solid lead we have in your little problem."

I rubbed the back of my sore head. I didn't want to think about what my face looked like, but everything could have been a lot worse. "Thanks for what you did back there. I was in a pretty tight corner."

"Well, I should have been quicker on the draw. When you said someone had been nosing around your shop, that was a strong indication you could find yourself in a whole lot of trouble in a big hurry."

"Looked to me like you were doing just fine back there. I think two of those bastards had guns."

The blonde detective sighed. "I wouldn't be surprised if all of them did, the way things are in Toronto these days. We're lucky they didn't just heave you into the back of their car and take you someplace a little more private. I guess they figured your warehouse would suit for what they had in mind." She sat up a little. "And here come our boys, if I'm not mistaken."

I sat up in time to see a nondescript white car pass by. They made it even easier by having the car's dome light on. The dark-haired one was driving, and Blondie was partially turned in the passenger seat, talking to his boss, who sat slouched in the back with a hand to his eye.

Shannon took out a pen and wrote on the back of her hand. "Made the tag! It was *so* kind of them to wash the car recently." She turned the key in the ignition and the SUV roared to life. "Let's follow these suckers and see where they go!"

"I'd rather not. I've had enough for one day."

As the shock of what had almost happened started to sink in, *I* felt like crawling in the back and hiding under the seat. Shannon was almost vibrating with excitement, and I realized she had a real love of the chase and not a lot of fear. Interesting woman...

She suddenly seemed aware that I had been pretty badly knocked around. Switching on the dome light, she fished around in the back seat for her purse and produced a wad of tissues. "Here. Use these. I don't want you to bleed all over my upholstery."

I took the tissues, not knowing if she were serious. Touching the right side of my face gingerly, I realized it was damp. With the sun visor down on my side, I saw in its mirror that my head was indeed bleeding—and swelling up nicely in the bargain. I'd look *really* terrific by morning.

My detective switched off the light and put her vehicle in gear. "We should get that looked at."

"No," I answered firmly. "I don't want to take the chance."

"You think they're going to be watching all the hospitals for you?"

I shook my head. "No, not them. Reporters. I'm worried about publicity. I don't want any. You never know who's going to come around to dig up the dirt."

Her face took on a quizzical expression. "You *have* been out of the spotlight for quite some time, you know."

I explained to her about the proposed Neurotica benefit concert. "Look at it this way: I'm involved in a murder, and then this legendary band announces it's going to play with all the original members for the first time in twenty-four years. It may not be big news here yet, but it is in the UK. I just don't want to take any chances with somebody finding out what's happened tonight. You don't know how these things can get twisted around."

"Oh, I think I do."

"Just take me back so I can get my car." I stopped as memory seeped in. "Wait a minute. My keys are on the roof of the building. Damn!"

"Michael..."

I turned stiffly in my seat to look at her. "I hate to ask, but can you drive me home?"

"What are you going to do there?"

"Clean myself up and go to bed."

She shook her head. "You're too much. What if the bad guys show up at your door?"

"They can't know where my apartment is."

"Do you want to bet your life on it?"

That brought me up short. "I see what you mean. Well then, drive me to a hotel. There's one just down the road."

"I have a better idea. I'll take you to my place." I must have telegraphed what shot through my mind, because she laughed. "Have you got the wrong idea! I have two children, one of whom crawls in my bed most nights because he's been having bad dreams, plus, my mother lives with us."

I felt kind of stupid jumping to conclusions like that. "Well, I did notice you don't wear a wedding ring."

She stopped smiling. "My husband and I divorced last year." She started backing out of the parking place, a little quickly to my mind. "So, will you take me up on my offer? I have a big old farmhouse with lots of spare rooms. The bad guys won't find you there, and I can keep an eye on you. They thumped you pretty good. You might have a concussion."

"You really know how to cheer a bloke up."

She raised an eyebrow. "So what'll it be?"

I shrugged. "Take me to your place, I guess."

Shannon explained as we drove that she lived northwest of Toronto in an area of Peel Region where they still have farmland.

"My family has lived there for almost a hundred and fifty years. We haven't farmed it since my dad passed away. A neighbour leases the fields from us now, so my kids get to see the land being worked, and we still keep some chickens, a cow, a few sheep. My youngest, who's eleven and named Robbie after his dad, loves the outdoors and really 'gets it'. My daughter Rachel thinks living off a dirt road and sharing her yard with a bunch of animals is 'boring', just like a lot of other fifteen-year-olds—bright lights of the big city and all that."

We were speeding west along the 401, Toronto's main superhighway, at well above the speed limit. Shannon seemed quite competent behind the wheel, but it still made me a tad nervous the way she wove in and out of traffic. Snow had begun falling again, and I knew how quickly it could get slippery.

"May I ask how you got into the investigation business?"

"Got a couple of hours?" she laughed. "I had a grandfather, father and uncle who were all cops with the Toronto force. My ex-husband was a detective. I guess you could say it was pre-ordained."

"What about siblings?"

"Two brothers. Oh, they considered it, but chose other paths. One's a university professor in Ottawa, and the other works for a bank in Vancouver. It really disappointed my dad, though."

"How did he feel about you becoming one?"

"He didn't like it at first, but he got used to it. He'd retired by then and was trying his hand at running the farm. He wasn't very good at it, I'm afraid, and it eventually killed him."

"So how long were you a police officer?"

"Nine years. I stopped shortly after my son was born. It seemed the smart thing to do. Policing in Toronto was getting more dangerous. My husband quit soon after, and we started the agency. He felt there was better money in it, and we could set our own hours, rather than always being at the mercy of whatever shift we were assigned. Boy, were we naïve!"

"And he's...?" I started, but the sentence was left dangling for several seconds.

Shannon sighed. "Gone," she said wistfully, then her voice and expression hardened. "Let's just leave it at that, okay?"

We continued our drive in silence, lost in our own thoughts. I distractedly watched the Toronto landscape slide by as we turned north on the 427 to skirt the eastern edge of the airport, then west when the 427 ended, then north again, up a two-lane road.

The weather worsened the further we went. Once clear of the housing developments, the snow swept unobstructed across the flat acres of fields in a blinding, white vengeance. With my winter experience shaped by city living, I was becoming uneasy. Go off the road out here and it could be hours before they find you—long enough to freeze to death.

"Is it much farther?" I asked.

"Just a kilometre or two."

We slowed to a crawl as another buffeting of wind made the road disappear in swirling white.

"Now I know why you drive one of these things."

"Sometimes I think a snow plow would be more appropriate," she responded, leaning forward in an attempt to see better.

A few minutes later, we stopped, then slowly turned right. How Shannon could see where we were was beyond me. Creeping forward, the wind died for a moment, and I could make out a farmhouse a few hundred feet ahead.

She cursed under her breath as she pulled up next to the house. "Darn kids must have every light in the house on!"

It certainly was a handsome building. Made of brick with all the gingerbread trim, white shutters and a big porch, it looked well loved and well lived in. Long ago, someone had planted a windbreak of pines, which had now grown tall and protected the house from the worst of the storm. As we got out of the suv, you could hear the wind thrumming through the branches as the trees tossed to and fro.

Walking to the back of the house, I frowned as my shoes—good for travelling, bad for winter walking—filled with snow. I got the feeling I might not be going anywhere in the morning.

A light clicked on as we approached the back steps—motion detector. Shannon hopped up all three athletically, and I followed slowly. I still felt rather wobbly, and during the long drive, I'd stiffened up quite a bit.

Shannon opened the door, and life and warmth erupted from the kitchen beyond with a loud cry of "Mommy's home!" and the tail-wagging fury of two dogs of uncertain parentage. "Mommy" quickly closed the door, shutting winter firmly outside where it belonged.

The kitchen of the O'Brien farmhouse had been built for a time when large families and farm labourers were the order of the day, and as such, it was a generous size and dominated by a rather grand old table much scarred by years of service. I imagined it was as old as the room itself. At the moment, the table had been turned into a homework station, and Shannon's two kids' textbooks, papers and a laptop were spread haphazardly over its surface.

The inevitable questions started immediately. "Who's he?" "Mom! You could have told me you were bringing someone home!" "Are you on a date?" "He looks as if someone punched him out!"

An odd expression flashed across Shannon's face as she turned away from the coat pegs by the back door. "Kids, you're not being very polite! Where are your manners?"

"We don't have any!" the little guy shouted, then dissolved into laughter. I got the feeling I'd just experienced a well-rehearsed and often-played scene.

On the opposite side of the room, a short, stout woman with her grey hair done up in a tight bun was busily putting the last of the dinner dishes into the dishwasher. She turned to face us, wiping her hands on a towel. "Are the roads bad?"

Shannon smiled tolerantly. "I feel like I'm holding a press

conference! Okay, everyone, this is Michael Quinn. He's a client of mine, and he owns a business at the opposite end of the building my office is in." She turned to me. "And Michael, this is my son Robert—but everyone calls him Robbie—and my daughter Rachel." Shannon walked across the room, putting her arm around the older woman. "And this is my mother, Mary Cathcart, without whom this household would grind to a halt in about one hour flat!"

Rachel, growing tall like her mum but with dark hair and less delicate features, looked at me levelly before asking, "Why did you bring him home with you?"

"He couldn't get home on his own, and I didn't want to drive him all the way downtown where he lives, so he's staying in one of the spare rooms tonight."

Robbie, who shared Shannon's fair skin and hair, sat once again at the table. "Did my mom save you from getting beat up?"

Out of the mouths of babes...

Mom, probably used to dealing with awkward comments from her child, did. "He had a bit of an accident, that's all."

"But he's bleeding!"

Grandma Cathcart said, "He should have that looked at."

Shannon stepped to the other side of me, and after a closer look said, "You're right. You'd better come with me, Michael."

Three sets of eyes (five if you counted the dogs) watched silently as Shannon led me out of the room.

While she was busy rummaging in a built-in cupboard up in the farmhouse's enormous bathroom, I took a peek at myself in the mirror over the sink. The side of my head which had been bashed repeatedly into the door frame had quite a gash, and it was still dripping. The blood had flowed down just in front of my right ear, and the collar of my shirt had soaked it up, leaving a brilliant crimson stain. To top it off, I was showing all the signs of a nice black eye, and my face looked lopsided from the swelling. Lovely.

"Sit here on the toilet seat," Shannon said as she flipped it down. "The light's better."

I did as I was told and wished I were a million miles away as she snipped away a bit of hair, dabbed and otherwise tended to my wound. Even though she tried to be gentle, the swelling made the whole area quite sore, and I winced several times.

As she finished up by applying a couple of butterfly bandages, Shannon said, "I want to apologize for what happened tonight."

"Apologize?" I answered disbelievingly. "You got me out of a damned tight spot!"

"You wouldn't have been there if I'd been a little bit more on the ball. *I'm* supposed to be the expert you hired. Tomorrow we're going to arrange for a bodyguard, and we're going to the police about what happened."

I shook my head, a bad idea because I was developing a thumping headache. "No. No police."

"But that's nuts! You could have been killed."

"I already told you why not. There's been no mention on this side of the pond about the murder case I'm messed up in, and I'm not about to add any fuel to the publicity fire. But I'll think about the bodyguard."

Shannon started slamming things back into the medicine cabinet. "You're just too stubborn and unreasonable for words! Michael! You're not even listening to me!"

My mind had definitely slipped sideways. When Shannon had mentioned what had happened earlier, the scene had sprung into my consciousness, everything vivid like a video playback. The two men holding me and the one in charge standing back.

"I've seen one of those men before."

She turned to me. "What?"

"It just came back to me. The leader tonight. There was something in his eyes. I should have realized it earlier, but I guess those knocks on the head distracted me. The last time I saw him, he had a length of pipe in his hand and was standing in front of Angus's Jaguar. He had no fear of me simply flooring the car and squashing him all over the pavement. You could see it in the way he looked at me."

I stopped and looked through my memory at both times I'd seen him, looked deep into those bottomless eyes again.

He knew I was terrified of him.

CHAPTER 11

I actually slept for five uninterrupted hours that night, a good thing, since I'd felt about ready to fall on my battered face. More importantly, what woke me was not the same boring nightmare, but the blizzard outside, its wind rattling the windows, sounding like some hungry animal circling the house to find a way in.

Not wanting to disturb the family by wandering around their house in the middle of the night, I remained in bed thinking, my brain turning over what had happened in the previous two weeks.

When I was a child, I used to have a recurring dream where my bedroom window would suddenly be sucked away by a violent storm. I knew a malevolent force out there was after me, even though I couldn't see it. The furniture in the room would begin disappearing, crashing out through the ragged window opening as the force searched for me. I would usually be left hanging on to the light fixture on the ceiling or the doorknob in an attempt to save myself. Sometimes I made it, but often I didn't. When I didn't, I'd always wake up just as I was clinging by my fingertips to the window opening.

That night, snug in a warm bed in that old farmhouse, the wind outside brought back the memory of my childhood nightmare for the first time in many years. My present situation resonated strongly with that old dream. What I didn't know was whether it would be better to hang on with all my strength or let myself get sucked out to discover what it was that was after me.

Eventually, I slipped back into a light doze without having seen any clear way forward.

By morning, the storm had blown itself out, and even though it was still dark when the O'Brien household began stirring, I could see from my room's window that the day would be bright and clear, but probably all the more cold because of it.

After ducking into the bathroom for a quick shower, I slipped into the same dirty clothes I'd been wearing since leaving Glasgow two days earlier. At least my shirt was clean. Shannon had washed it the previous evening and left it hanging on the doorknob. Downstairs in the kitchen, I found only Shannon's mum, sliding a pan of muffins into the oven.

"Sleep well?" she asked without turning around.

"Well enough, thanks."

"There's a pot of fresh coffee. If you want tea, I'm sorry to say that we have none. You can wait for the muffins or have some toast now. Toaster, bread and coffee are all over there," she said, indicating a side counter with her head.

"Coffee's fine," I answered as I picked up a mug and poured some. It was deep black, scalding hot and very good.

Finding a seat at the far end of the kitchen table, I sipped my coffee and watched Mrs. Cathcart bustle efficiently around the kitchen making lunches and getting breakfast pulled together. I would have offered to help, except from the way she kept stiffly silent and her back to me, I got the distinct feeling that it would not have been welcome.

Upstairs, the sound of pounding on a door and irritated shouting told me that young Robbie was up and Rachel was being hounded to get out of the shower. Shannon called out that he should use the downstairs bathroom if he really had to go that badly, then slammed a door herself.

Grandma put two cloth lunch bags on the table and looked across at me, her expression pinched and unfriendly. "My granddaughter told me who you are," she sniffed. It sounded from her tone of voice as if she thought that being me was something criminal. "You just make sure my Shannon doesn't regret taking on your job. You were a hero of hers when she was in high school."

"Mother!" Shannon said, appearing in the kitchen doorway.

Mrs. Cathcart was unrepentant. "I'm only saying what any mother would. You've been through too much this past year."

"That's enough!" Shannon walked farther into the room. "Michael, please forgive my mother's—"

Her son's noisy entrance cut her off. I kept my head steadfastly down, sipping my coffee while life went on around me. When Shannon asked about completed homework, Robbie sounded rather dodgy on the subject, a lot like I'd been at his age. Rachel, who arrived shortly after with damp hair and a petulant expression, wanted to go to a party on the weekend, something that would obviously require further discussion. In the background, the radio was set to CBC's *Ontario Morning,* with news of the past night's storm, as well as what was cancelled and what was not.

Rachel asked if I wanted a hot muffin when they were ready, looking at me with a comically raised eyebrow as she held it out. "You look really ratty this morning, Michael."

"Rachel O'Brien!" an outraged Shannon said from her spot at the opposite end of the table. "That is *no way* to talk to a guest, especially an adult!"

I smiled. "It's all right. Rachel can call me Michael if she wishes, and she's absolutely right. I'm probably not the picture of vibrant good health this morning."

"I checked out your band's website last night," Rachel continued.

"I've never looked at it, in actual fact."

"It's a fan website. It has all sorts of things about this concert you're doing."

"I prefer not to live in the past."

"Well anyway, you don't look all that different from the old days, except for the lumpy face."

Shannon continued to glare at her daughter, and Rachel flashed a grin across the table. Obviously, she hadn't formed as strong an opinion about me as her grandmother had, although I could see from her expression that the jury was still out on one Michael Quinn.

Eventually, the kids had books and lunches stuffed into their backpacks and were hustled out the door to make the long trek down the driveway to wait in a little shed for the school buses to arrive. Robbie looked particularly downcast, since he had been counting on school being cancelled, a wish probably due to partially-completed homework. As soon as the kids had gone, Mrs. Cathcart took off her apron and left the room.

Shannon got up to pour a second cup of coffee and brought the pot over to me. "I guess Rachel ratted you out while we were upstairs tending to your cuts."

"I'm sorry your mother is upset. What was that all about anyway?"

"Well, the long and short of it is," Shannon began as she returned to her seat at the far end of the table and busied her hands with pulling a muffin to shreds without any noticeable intention of eating it, "I told Rachel about you a year or so ago. She'd had her heart broken when her favourite boy band split up just before they were to appear in Toronto. It was the first concert her dad and I were going to allow her to see, and the concert got cancelled. So I told her I'd been through the exact same thing myself."

I nodded, remembering what she had said the day before about my departure from Neurotica.

Shannon finally looked up. "My mom is just remembering how it was when that happened to me. And," she sighed, "it was also a reference to the fact that my marriage imploded this past year. The concert thing seems pretty silly now, doesn't it?"

"Finding out your heroes have feet of clay?"

She frowned and nodded, seeing something that I could only guess at. "You could say that." She looked at the clock over the sink. "God! Look at the time! We've got to get a move on."

"What's on your agenda for the morning?"

Shannon, rinsing our dishes in the sink, said, "A couple of things. I want to check out the tag number we got off that car last night, and I want to see what I can come up with at that hotel where your girlfriend stayed." She turned and must have seen something in my expression, because she quickly added, "Just a figure of speech."

I vowed inwardly not to be so transparent in my feelings. "Count me in on the hotel."

"You sure? You said last night that today was a busy one for you."

"I want to be there," I said firmly.

Using my cell phone as we drove towards the airport, I mobilized the troops back at the shop to get work underway without me.

"Shame about your car," Kevin said. "You must really be pissed."

"What's wrong with it?" I asked sharply.

Kevin sounded surprised. "You don't know?"

"No. I, ah, couldn't get it started last night, so I called a cab."

"Well I'm sorry to be the one to have to tell you, but it looks like someone took a baseball bat to it. All the windows and headlights are smashed, and there's a hell of a dent in the hood. The inside's filled with snow, too."

After hanging up, I let loose a string of very ungentlemanly words.

Shannon looked at me, her eyebrows raised. "What's up?" She whistled after I'd told her what had happened. "I'm more convinced than ever that you should speak to the police. These are dangerous people you're playing with."

"I'll just have to be more careful."

"You're pretty stubborn."

"So I've been told."

III

Even though there had been more than a foot of snow, we made decent time on the drive down to the airport strip.

Regina had stayed at one of the more expensive hotels. Judged by the line she'd originally fed me, it had made sense at the time she'd checked in there. Somebody who'd been brought up the way she had wouldn't have considered the cost. Now *I* was paying the freight for her expensive tastes.

As we pulled into a space in the hotel's parking garage, Shannon turned off the engine and looked at me. "This could be a little tricky. Hotels don't like giving out information on guests—especially if they've been scammed. It may be helpful that you've tagged along. I can use the fact that you bailed them out as a wedge to get their cooperation. I generally fly by the seat of my pants on these things, though. You'll have to listen very carefully and follow my lead wherever it goes. That's very important. No matter what I say, support it. We can't afford to disagree or start bickering in front of someone we're trying to get information from."

"What do you mean?"

"Michael, even though I've only been around you a short time, I can safely say you're pretty straight-laced." I thought she was going to say something else, but she finally added, "Like I said, I fly by the seat of my pants. If I feel that a certain line will get us results, I'll run with it."

"What does that mean?"

"That could mean anything. Just go with the flow."

"I understand."

Shannon's expression as we walked across the parking garage clearly said that she thought I didn't.

We entered the hotel's revolving doors with purpose, Shannon setting the pace. I liked that. People who dawdle when they walk make me very impatient.

The lobby was quite nice, bright and airy, and since its clientele was primarily drawn from Canada's biggest airport on the day after a heavy snowfall, predictably busy.

Approaching the front desk, Shannon said, "It's too bad you didn't get the name of the person you spoke to when you called from Scotland. You have no recollection of his name?"

I shook my head and frowned. I should have been quicker on the uptake that day, but at the time I'd been too stunned to think clearly.

We only had to wait for a few people ahead of us to check out. I was quite curious, and a bit apprehensive to see what this rather odd private investigator I'd hired would do.

There were two desk clerks that morning, a male and a female, and Shannon had juggled things so that we'd get the male, since there was a chance he was the person I'd spoken to on the phone. With her nicely tailored slacks, silk blouse and suede coat, she looked businesslike and competent.

"We'd like to see the manager, please," she said to the clerk.

"Are you a guest here?"

"Not exactly. We were bilked out of a fair bit of money by someone who was staying here."

"I'm afraid it's against the hotel's policy to—"

"You see, when she ran out on her bill here, this gentleman made good on her charges."

The clerk's tone shifted to something more officious. "That sounds like it should be something handled by hotel security." He moved his hand to reach for the phone.

"No, we'd like to see the manager."

"And you are?"

"A private investigator. We need to find this woman. We played ball with you by paying her bill. Don't you think it would be the right thing to do to play ball with us?"

The clerk picked up the phone. "The guest's name, please?"

"Genevieve Fleury," I told him.

Within thirty seconds, a tall man in a dark suit glided up. "May I be of assistance?"

"Are you the manager?" Shannon asked.

"Ah, no. I'm Don Clark, an assistant manager," he said, all oil and smoothness. "Our manager will not be in this morning. Why don't we go to my office and see what can be done about your problem?"

As we walked around a corner, Shannon moved in next to me and said into my ear, "Is he the one you spoke to?"

I shrugged, but it was tentative. How can you tell these things from a cell phone across an ocean?

Obviously, our assistant manager had not risen very high up on the hotel totem pole. His office was tiny and cramped with a desk, two filing cabinets and three chairs.

Once we were seated, he produced a legal pad and a pen from his desk and looked at us. "Why don't you start from the beginning?"

Shannon's eyes were constantly moving as she took everything in. Then, pursing her lips, she reached into a back pocket and flipped a leather case onto the desk. "I'm a private investigator," she said. "You are aware of why we're here?

Clark nodded. "The desk clerk informed me who you were inquiring about."

I started to say something, but Shannon flashed me a look that clearly said, *Shut up and pay attention.* "This man is my client."

Clark nodded again, looking more uneasy. I'd finally placed his voice as the one on the phone. I squeezed Shannon's arm, and when she looked at me, I nodded as discreetly as I could.

Shannon leaned forward, fixing Clark with her eyes. "My client generously paid the Fleury girl's bill—and it was a substantial one—when he was not obliged to. That got someone in this hotel off an extremely sharp hook. We'd like to exchange that courtesy for some information."

"It is strictly against hotel policy to give out any information concerning our guests."

Clark's attempt to put Shannon off fell on deaf ears. "If you would prefer to wait until the police and your boss need to get involved…"

"No, no," the assistant manager responded quickly, as fine beads of sweat appeared on his forehead. "That won't be necessary." He looked at us apprehensively. "What kind of information are you looking for?"

"What can you tell us about her?"

"Not much, I'm afraid. I checked her in. She was quite, ah, distracting. It wasn't until later that I realized that her charm had a purpose. Of course, no one saw the woman leave or had any more to do with her during her stay."

"Too bad." Shannon smiled. "Well then, Mr. Clark, hopefully you *can* give us two things. How about the address the Fleury girl gave when she checked in, and I'd like to take a look at your security tapes. I assume you have cameras in the elevators?"

Clark nodded, not looking happy. As he opened the top drawer of his desk, Shannon flashed me a grin and a quick thumbs-up.

After taking out a folder, Clark handed two small pieces of paper to Shannon, one at a time. "This is her registration card with the address she gave in Montreal. And this is a photocopy of her credit card imprint. He flipped through a few more pages then pulled a larger sheet out. "This is from a security camera in one of the elevators. We made it for our use in case she ever returns."

Shannon passed it to me after she'd looked at the printout for a long moment. It was a good likeness.

She took the paper back and looked at Clark. "May I keep this and get photocopies of the others?"

The assistant manager shrugged with resignation.

Shannon stood and reached over the desk to shake hands. "You've been most helpful, and we really appreciate it." Once we left the office, she was buoyant. "That went very well indeed. It was a good thing you so generously paid that bill," she added with a smirk.

"What's up now?"

"I'm heading downtown to check on that license plate. I should be back at my office by mid-afternoon. If I'm not going to make it, I'll call. Okay?"

"Well, the airport is as good a place as any to hire a car, since it looks as if I'm going to need one for a few days."

Just before we split up in the lobby, Shannon touched my arm and I turned. "Michael, be careful. You don't want those guys to catch you alone, and *don't* think that they've given up. They're still around. Don't stay in your warehouse by yourself."

I had a lot to think about while waiting for the shuttlebus to pick me up for the ride over to Terminal 1.

My car was in worse shape than Kevin had suggested on the phone. Since the snow was not the heavy, wet variety, I probably wouldn't have to replace the leather interior, but the bonnet and boot lid were write-offs, as was every window and light and the trim around them. The bastards had been thorough.

Trudging through the snow back into the shop, I called a towing service, then the car dealer to let them know what to expect. I toyed with the idea of calling my insurance company, but that would invariably mean the police being called in. My bank account could handle the repairs, although it would probably make a sizeable dent.

Neither Kevin nor Johnny said anything about the state of my face, but I could tell they were dying to find out.

After answering some phone messages and emails, I took a look at the schedule to see what was coming up over the next week. Business looked to be going through a boom period at the moment, and fortunately things so far had been easily handled by my experienced crew, since I hadn't been of much use to them lately.

Even though Hamed had to babysit the instruments we'd rented to the movie shoot (they had to work flawlessly whenever the cameras rolled), at least one of my crew would be around the whole day. As I settled down to try to make some progress on the mountain of paperwork, I had to admit to myself that Shannon's warning as we'd left the hotel had me pretty spooked. The condition of my BMW had driven the point home smartly.

By two thirty, I'd gotten all the invoices finished and readied the deposit for the bank, which I'd take care of on the way home. Other than a half sandwich Johnny had given me when he couldn't finish what his mom had packed, I hadn't eaten anything since early morning, and frankly, my stomach was making rude noises.

In the middle of trying to decide what to do about it, my reverie was interrupted by the unmistakable sounds of the mellotron. Someone out in the warehouse seemed intent on butchering the Moody Blues' classic "Nights in White Satin".

Coming out of the office, I was met not by Kevin or Johnny as I'd expected, but by Hamed with three other people.

Hamed looked up at my footsteps. "Hi, boss. We can't shoot until this evening, so we thought we'd come up and see the Beast."

The three that Hamed had brought certainly looked Hollywood. One was the producer, a short, roly-poly man with a glib tongue and sharp eyes. The director had come as well. He was big, balding and bearded, with an overwhelming air of being the most important man on the planet—or at least the warehouse. The young guy behind the tron attempting a "Moody Blues moment" turned out to be an actor from the movie. He didn't seem impressed with himself, probably because he didn't have a big enough role. I got the feeling he'd just tagged along on this excursion.

"Quite a machine you've got here," the producer said. "Your boy's been telling us all about it. Is it true that the Beatles used it on *Magical Mystery Tour?*"

I looked sharply at Hamed, who was standing at the back of the group. He flashed a wry grin.

"Not this particular one," I replied.

He'd got them up to the warehouse (even if his story might have stretched the truth), and it could be worth a pretty penny if the movie shoot wanted to add my latest acquisition to the rental agreement, so why not *really* show them what a mellotron can do? Not many people have ever heard one of the big brutes live.

As Hamed set up an amp and plugged it in, I explained how the tron worked, showed them the Rube Goldberg-like inner workings, then fired it up.

It helped that I'd played it a few times since retrieving it from the airport, so I was able to put on a pretty good show. It was my take on the tail end of the intro to "Watcher of the Skies", using the famous mixed choir sound on one keyboard and the brass/violin mix on the other that sold them. I must admit I felt the hair on the back of my neck stand up, too—but that just might have been the volume.

The director was beside himself. "I have *got* to use this in the movie. The unit is so...*substantial*, it will look terrific on screen and will absolutely *make* the big concert scene! It fits into the time frame of the storyline, and this thing *sounds* as magnificent as it looks! How long can we have it for?"

The producer added, "And for how much?"

Surprisingly, I was suddenly hesitant to hire it out. "Actually, I was thinking of using it for a gig I'm doing in Glasgow next month."

Where the hell had *that* come from? My mouth had moved seemingly without the expressed consent of my brain—or was it just my subconscious speaking out of turn?

The director was adamant. Sensing my hesitation, he offered me a ridiculous sum. The producer grimaced but stayed silent.

"What concert?" the director finally asked, exasperated by my continued refusal.

"It's in Glasgow with my old—"

The actor snapped his fingers. "*Now* I know where I've seen you! You used to be in Neurotica. Man, I thought you were dead!"

That really hurt—probably because it was so close to the truth.

CHAPTER 12

As she headed downtown from the airport strip, Shannon felt as if her head was going to explode.

Driving was not easy, and she was having trouble concentrating properly. Most of the snow had been stripped from the roads, accomplished by the application of salt by the ton. So the sludgy, grey spray the cars threw up around her meant she had to clean her windshield every thirty seconds.

I should have checked the fluid level on the last fill-up, she thought sourly.

Part of Shannon's thoughts was occupied with the usual worries of any mother. Robbie seemed to be having such a hard time buckling down in school this year. Rachel had now become *really* interested in boys, and with her wild streak, Shannon was bracing for a lot of trouble over the next few years. She hoped the problems with both children were not further fallout from the divorce. She and Rob had done their best to keep personal acrimony separate from their roles as parents, but you never knew with kids. Sometimes she thought hers had come with built-in radar.

In her shoulder bag she now had a good likeness of the girl Michael had gotten himself mixed up with. Men could be so damn gullible! With that thought, the inner spotlight immediately turned on her, though, and she had to admit that some women could be pretty damn gullible, too. Sighing heavily, she forced her thoughts back to more constructive channels.

She had come up with a workable theory on why the girl had shown up in Toronto. She'd known the goons after her in Birmingham wouldn't give up easily. If they'd been only *reasonably* smart, they'd have gotten the number of the Jag, and armed with that, Shannon knew how easy it would have been to get an address in Scotland.

Knowing what might soon go down, the girl would have needed a solid alibi. Who better than Michael in Toronto? Then there was what she'd done in the hotel's elevators. If she'd wanted to avoid detection, could have used the stairs or averted her face rather than staring brazenly upward at the security cameras in the elevators the way she had—unless she had wanted a hard record of her visit to Toronto.

How much of what she'd told Michael had been the truth? That was what Shannon really *had* to find out, something that would likely prove very tough. Montreal was the only lead she had. Unfortunately, on the home front, it couldn't be a worse time to be out of town.

Shannon felt certain Michael was in real danger. The creeps she'd caught off guard the night before meant business and wouldn't be such easy marks next time. She would have to be very careful about this. Michael still had no idea what he'd gotten into.

God, he had a stiff neck. And all that false bravado! It didn't impress her one iota, and besides that, it was stupid. Thugs like the ones after him wouldn't think twice about lopping off a finger or two to get the information they wanted. After that, Michael would have to die. She somehow had to make him understand.

Swinging onto the eastbound QEW from the 427, her thoughts drifted sideways again. It was so bizarre to be working for someone she'd idolized so long ago, actually talking to him like he was just a normal person. He obviously thought he *was* normal. She didn't know if she could ever completely feel that way about him.

During her last two years in high school, she'd been absolutely *smitten* with Michael Quicksilver. Her bedroom ceiling had been covered with posters of Neurotica so she could look at him as she lay on her bed. All her friends thought Rolly Simpson was the hottest thing ever, but Michael with his dark good looks and that faraway stare had always enthralled her. She'd seen him do that a few times during the past day, and it still brought on goosebumps, remembering how she'd fantasized about him, learned everything she could about him.

She realized now that she'd known only the things breathlessly imparted in fan magazines. She really had no idea who this man was—other than someone in a pack of trouble, and he was counting on her to get him out of it.

So the great private detective was now getting the chance to help her teenage heartthrob. Life could sure take some strange turns...

Shannon spent a useful two hours at Toronto's police headquarters, calling in a few favours in order to get information on the thugs who'd attacked Michael. That tag number had been easy to make. The car belonged to a punk named John Smith, of all things. He'd been busted for boosting cars and was suspected of a couple of break-ins, but so far he'd managed to stay out of the slammer, except for two short stretches. It didn't surprise anyone she spoke to that Smith would do strongarm stuff for hire. As for "known associates", there were several, including a guy who'd recently arrived from somewhere out west and who sported a ponytail. The latter had the reputation of being more than a little nuts, and the person Shannon spoke to about him thought he might be capable of almost anything given enough exposure to the "poorer elements in Toronto".

"Watch out for Andrew Stokowski if he's involved with this," Shannon had been told. "He's a bomb waiting to go off."

Stokowski's mug shot (two arrests for aggravated assault) confirmed that he'd been the dark-haired one knocking Michael around with great gusto the evening before. Smith had been the blond one holding him. Shannon drew a blank on the third goon, not unexpected if he had come in from Britain.

As for the girl, she hadn't expected to get any information. Everyone promised to keep their ears to the ground for her.

Shannon had a lot more to think about as she started up the Don Valley Parkway—not least because three people had asked after her husband, unaware that they'd split up.

I went back into my office, shut the door against the aural onslaught of the actor trying out one of our bigger guitar amps in the warehouse, sat down behind my desk and took a deep breath.

It had suddenly hit me that I'd be performing in a few weeks and with sentiments like, "I thought you were dead," I would have to be more than good when I hit the stage in Glasgow.

Rolly had left messages twice with updates on the concert preparations and to try to nail me down for rehearsals. So far, I hadn't returned his calls, but I couldn't decently hold my mates up any longer, regardless of what was going on in my life.

I felt like a bug facing an oncoming windscreen.

I'd kept my chops in shape over the years and actually played a lot better technically than I had in my Neurotica days, but I had a spotty memory of most of our material. Being a keyboard player, my parts were often too far back in the mix to hear clearly, and I dreaded the effort I'd have to put in to lift them off the recordings. Lastly, there was my reluctance to just play the old tunes without taking a fresh look at them. Twenty-four years on, I felt we certainly owed it to ourselves to do a lot better than that.

Once Elvis had left the building, and it was safe to go back out to the warehouse, I assembled the troops, telling them which keyboards and monitoring system I wanted. It only took us a few minutes to move everything into the front room, which would have been the reception area if I ran a normal business. My employees mostly used it as a lounge/lunchroom, though we'd often press it into service to demo instruments for clients if they wanted a spot of privacy.

Once we had the Hammond organ and mellotron in place, I told everyone to clear out, since I could set up the four synthesizers and the digital piano alone.

A short while later, I fired everything up and tried a few hot licks. Since it wasn't the set-up I'd used in the past, I thought the change might help me re-think things as I went along. Pretty soon, I realized that I liked what I'd come up with; the only change I would make for the concert being to use a real piano in place of the digital one.

I was playing the few Neurotica things I *did* remember when I felt someone watching me. I looked up to find Shannon standing in the doorway.

"Please don't stop!" she said. "It was really fascinating. And don't roll your eyes at me, either! You were playing 'Don't Push Me', weren't you? Boy, does that bring back memories! But I've never heard it like that. It was so slow."

I began shutting down the keyboards. "That's the way Rolly and I originally conceived it. If you pay attention to the lyrics, it's not a particularly happy song. The producer on our first album made us do it up tempo, and I guess he knew what he was talking about, because it *was* a big hit." I shrugged. "But I still hear it slow in my head."

"You should talk the band into doing it that way for your concert. I bet it would set a few people back in their seats."

"Not likely. Audiences like their favourites played straight up."

"No, no. I've just had a brainstorm. You could play the slow version in the middle of the concert somewhere then do the hit version as an encore. I bet the audience would go nuts. I know *I* would."

The years had fallen away from Shannon, and I could see the seventeen-year-old she'd been when Neurotica was in its prime. Then I flashed to her as I'd seen her the night before: dedicated mom talking to her kids about their homework. If Rachel could see her now, *she'd* probably roll her eyes.

Do we ever really grow up? Is the younger person always lurking inside just waiting for a chance to get out?

"What?" Shannon asked when she caught me staring intently.

"Nothing," I answered as I checked to make sure the mellotron and organ were turned off.

Shannon, leaning against the door frame, related what she'd found out downtown as I again studied the photo of Regina the hotel had provided. Her expression as she looked up at the camera made me feel very odd, almost as if she'd known I'd see it eventually.

"So it seems pretty obvious to me that your girl—"

"She's not 'my girl,'" I interrupted rather harshly.

"The girl we're looking for then, if that suits you better. Anyway, as far as I'm concerned, the only reason she had for following you to Toronto was to get herself an iron-clad alibi. She knew she'd be nabbed if she stayed with Angus, so she had to get away—"

"Yes, and leave poor Angus with his head in a noose!" I interrupted again.

"You don't know that. Maybe she tried to get him to leave."

Shannon was probably right. A mere slip of a girl like Regina couldn't make Angus do anything he didn't want to. No one could. "So where do we go from here?"

"To Montreal. Well, at least I go to Montreal. I'm not counting on much, but who knows? I may get lucky."

I was about to ask how long she'd be away when the bell for the side door rang. "Why have those boneheads locked the door?"

"Perhaps because they were leaving for the night?"

Looking at my watch, I saw that it was after six. How long had I been playing? "Wait here a second. I'll see who it is."

My private investigator shook her head. "Not a good idea." She indicated the other door out to the front of my building. "Do you have the key to that?"

"Of course. Why?"

"I want to sneak around to see who's bothering you after hours."

We always kept the curtains closed in this room. To be on the safe side, I'd also changed the lock, so a key was needed to go in *or* out.

Before disappearing into the night, Shannon said with surprising earnestness, "Lock this after me. If I'm not back in five minutes, call the police. Whatever you do, don't come out looking for me! I'll give three quick knocks when I come back. You don't hear it that way, you don't open the door."

Eyes glued to my watch, I waited a very long two minutes before hearing three soft raps. Shannon slipped in and switched off the lights as I relocked the door. She was breathing hard as she sat on the floor to brush the snow off the bottom of her jeans and out of her trainers.

"Just what I thought. They're out there. Must have been waiting for your crew to leave, either hoping to follow you or catch you alone."

"How many?" I asked, trying not to act as scared as I felt.

"Just the two bozos who manhandled you last night. The big shot isn't here. That's probably why they tried pretty much the same stunt."

"What do we do now?"

She sprang lightly to her feet. "We sit and wait. Sooner or later they're going to try this door. I don't want to take a chance on going out until they do."

I went over to the far corner and grabbed a stray mic stand, turning it upside down. With the big weight on the bottom, they make a very effective weapon and have been used by many a musician in bar fights.

"If they come through that door, I'm going to put a world of hurt on them."

"Nice sentiment, Michael, but I don't think they'll want to risk setting off any alarms. I just want to be sure they're gone when we leave."

"What about your footprints in the snow?"

She snorted. "I'm one step ahead of you. It'll look like someone left and didn't come back."

"You think of everything," I shot back.

"No. I blew a stake-out once by not remembering about footprints in the snow."

Sure enough, we soon heard noises outside the door and detected a faint shadow on the curtain where someone was trying to see in.

"Skinny guy," Shannon whispered. "John Smith, by name. Not too smart by all accounts, but good with his fists. Him I'm not worried about. It's the other guy. Everyone tells me he's nuts. That kind is always dangerous."

"How comforting..."

"Do you have a flashlight handy? I want to go to the side door, and I don't want to risk turning on the warehouse lights."

I couldn't put my hands on a flashlight quickly, but I did have a lighter a client had left on my desk a few weeks earlier, so we used that to light our way across the warehouse. John Smith was reporting back.

"I don't think anyone's in there," we could hear him say through the door.

"You sure?" his companion asked.

"There weren't any lights on. Looks like he snuck out the front."

"Are you *absolutely* sure?"

"There were footprints by the front door."

"The big man ain't gonna be happy about this, and we don't get paid until the job is done."

"The guy split, I swear! Let's get the hell out of here. I'm freezing!"

Then the crazy one said something that froze my blood. "When we get our hands on that little shit, maybe I'll cut off a few of his fingers so he'll remember it don't pay to mess around with people like us."

That's all we heard, until a car started up and drove off. I reached for the lock, but Shannon grabbed my forearm.

"Wait!" she hissed. "I think they're pretty dumb overall, but let's not find out we're dumber. Besides, the front door is a better bet."

We waited fifteen minutes before Shannon felt it was safe to leave.

During that time, she used her cell phone to call home. Her mother didn't sound happy about having to babysit: bingo night.

"I suppose they could," she said into the phone. "Look, put Rachel on. I want to talk to her." While waiting, Shannon, dimly seen in the light as I held the curtain back a little to survey the parking lot outside, rolled her eyes at me. "Rachel, honey, Gram wants to go to her bingo night, and I'm not going to be home for a while yet. I'd like you to take care of Robbie until I come home... Yes, I will... No!... You may *not*!... Am I going to do *what*? Young lady, we're having a *long* talk when I get home. A *long* talk!... Yes. Now put Gram on again."

I unlocked the door, and Shannon stalked out with nary a look to the left or right. I followed as she headed down the sidewalk to her office. A gentle snow had begun to fall, and it felt as if the temperature was dropping again.

When we got to her business, she walked through the reception area, into her office and shut the door behind us. "Right. We've made it this far." She then opened up a closet and started taking things off the shelves, handing them to me to lay on her desk. Most looked like pretty serious tools of the trade.

"Do you have a computer at home?" she asked over her shoulder.

"Yes."

"And high-speed internet?"

"*Yes!* What's all this for?"

Shannon turned and looked at me with X-ray intensity. "You're paying me to look after you as well as finding that girl?"

"Yes..."

"Well, I'm just doing my job!"

With that, she turned back to the closet, rummaging around in some boxes on its floor. By the time she'd finished, she had littered her desk with equipment. Hands on hips, she looked at the pile for over a minute, then nodded. "That's about it."

"Are you going to tell me what you're up to?"

She took a folded gym bag out of the bottom drawer of a filing cabinet. "Like I said, I'm being paid to look after you. That's what this stuff is for. I have to go to Montreal tomorrow to try to pick up the trail of your little friend, and I want to make damn sure that nothing happens to you while I'm gone. These little babies," she continued, handing me a palm-sized thing with a lens, "are going to be watching your apartment. Ever get one of those internet ads for a spy camera? What you're holding is a lot like those, just with a few more bells and whistles."

"Like what?"

"Infrared and sound activation. We'll put a couple inside the apartment and one out in the hall, and you'll be able to see what's happening on the home front from the comfort of your office. If you spot any hanky-panky, you just call the cops."

"What if I'm at home, and they're out in the hall?"

"Same thing."

"And the rest of this stuff?"

"Mostly the electronics to connect everything." Shannon looked over at me. When I nodded, she added, "Good. Let's get going. I want to get home at a decent hour!"

My hired car was parked on the front side of the building near the door we'd exited from earlier, but Shannon insisted on going out to check things over. Since she was the expert, I humoured her, but I did have to admit that the events of the past twenty-four hours were making me very uneasy, and the sooner we got to the bottom of the whole mess, the better I would like it.

We drove downtown in tandem. Halfway down the Don Valley Parkway, Shannon pulled up next to me, honked and made actions like talking into a cell phone.

I flipped it on, and it rang almost immediately. "What?" I asked.

"I just wanted to let you know that there wasn't anyone following, in case you're concerned about that." With that, she slipped back behind me.

The lights of downtown Toronto sparkled as only a large city can on a cold, clear night. Some would comment on all the electricity being wasted lighting empty buildings, but I thought it looked lovely. Swinging west onto the Gardiner Expressway, I had the whole of downtown spread out next to me. Beautiful!

Exiting at Jameson, we doubled back along King to the street past Dufferin where my loft was located. Shannon had never been right behind me, but she somehow stayed with me and pulled into a visitor's spot outside as I shut off the engine.

The basement of the renovated factory had been turned into parking, and the upper part of the walls had been cut away to let in a bit of natural light. It was a nice effect, since it made the garage seem less like a cave. Shannon appeared on the ramp, slipping a little on some ice, and I stepped forward to take her surprisingly heavy gym bag. She didn't look particularly grateful, but she didn't say no.

As we headed for the lift, her eyes were constantly moving, assessing possible places to attack from, I supposed. Taking out my key, I used it to summon the lift. By the time the door opened, Shannon was fairly vibrating, but as it shut she slouched against the back wall and smiled tightly.

"Are you really that worried?" I asked.

By way of answer, Shannon produced a palm size black box from her coat pocket. It looked as if it had been stepped on. "I found this stuck under the back of your car. Global positioning..."

"Hmmm..."

"My sentiments exactly. That's why I was being so careful on the drive down." The lift doors slid open again. Shannon stepped out first, looking in both directions down the deserted hallway. I picked up the bag and showed her to my door.

She turned to me. "You said there's always a security guard in the lobby. Are they strict about who gets in?"

"They have to be around here."

"Don't trust them."

Shannon unzipped the bag and took out a plastic pouch. Inside was a coiled thing made out of metal with an eyepiece at one end. "Fiberscope—great for checking things out if you don't want to be seen." She uncoiled it, slipped it under my door, and stood looking for a few moments. "Everything seems okay."

The next two hours were pretty eye-opening. Shannon checked the apartment over for listening devices and plugged a gadget into my phone that would instantly tell me if anyone was listening in. The motion detector video camera she put in the living room looked for all the world like a clock radio, and the one in my bedroom looked like a vase, complete with silk flowers. Out in the hall, she found a dark corner by a heating duct to put a third camera, then everything was connected by a some sort of box to my laptop.

"You're lucky you don't have a cat or dog," Shannon said as she installed some software. "We had a client once with several cats, and my husband and I had to wade through hours of them chasing each other around the poor guy's house!" She crawled under my desk. "Now you must leave this on all the time if you want to be able to check out what's happening here while you're away. This gadget I'm connecting to your line will allow you to use your phones to listen in on what's going on in the apartment."

"Why do I need that with the cameras?"

"Because you can use your cell phone from down in the garage to do a last minute check on whether someone has recently arrived."

"Do you normally use this gear for protecting people?"

Her eyes shut for a moment. "No, mostly we use it in suspected infidelity cases."

"Do you handle a lot of those?"

She suddenly busied herself with putting tools and things back in her gym bag. "I try to do as few of those as possible." Her voice sounded tired.

At the front door, Shannon looked around the living room once more, satisfied. "I've done what I can. I still think you should leave town until I can sort this out."

I sighed. "You know that's not possible."

"Thought I'd try once more. Look, Michael, I don't want to sound paranoid, but take this threat seriously. Look over your shoulder. Don't go *anywhere* alone. You may think no one knows where you live, but they can find you if they're determined."

"When will you be back from Montreal?"

"Tomorrow evening, unless I run into a hot lead." Her expression softened a bit. "Take care of yourself, Michael. I want to get you to that Neurotica concert in one piece."

"Good luck on your trip," I answered in return.

Shannon looked grim again. "I'm going to need it. Now I really must be getting home. I promised I wouldn't be too late."

I watched as she walked down the hall to the lift, gym bag slung over her shoulder. Shutting the door, I went to the kitchen and poured myself a stiffish glass of Highland Park single malt, my drink of choice, and leaned against the counter sipping it.

Strange woman. Something had set her off tonight. Shannon had been so friendly when she'd caught me playing, but shortly afterwards she was treating me as if I were a client she didn't like very much. The really odd thing was that while claiming to be a huge fan of my band, she hadn't once glanced at any of the awards lining the hallway.

march 15, 1981

Oh my god! I just can't believe it! Dad finally agreed that I could go with Randi and Jill to the Neurotica concert next month. He even talked to someone he knows and got us the BEST seats!!! We girls are gonna rock out that night!

The outrageously coolest thing is that we'll be on the side of the stage where HE is. You certainly know who I'm talking about by now, diary!

On the way home today, Cathy asked what I would do if I ever met one of them. She said we should find out what hotel they're staying at and hang out. I can see him in my mind now, though. I'd have to look up at him since he's 6' 1½". He'd never dye his dark hair blond like Rolly and Lee have (yuck!) His would be long and flowing, down his neck— moving a bit as he strides across the lobby towards me. He has that cute nose and high forehead, but it's those big green eyes that would sink me. I'd look into them and just turn into a quivering pile of jello.

Michael, I love you!!!!

Shannon Quicksilver Cathcart

CHAPTER 13

Shannon's gadgets didn't do much to help me get a good night's sleep. Every creak and sigh the old building produced had me wide awake, straining to identify sounds that might mean I wasn't alone.

About the time the sky started brightening, I finally drifted off into a very deep sleep. Like so many early morning dreams, it was very detailed, almost like watching a movie.

At first it was enjoyable. I was back playing music again. The other musicians were not my old mates from Neurotica, but the tune was something we had been working on about the time I'd left the band. The room looked like a hotel ballroom, and we were set up in the centre. I'd get wrapped up in what I was playing then look up to find that one of the musicians had been replaced by a "Neuroticand", not as they were back in the day, but as they had looked at Angus's funeral. This happened over and over until the group was completely Neurotica, and I began growing anxious that I'd be forced to keep playing with them.

We finally took a break, and everyone decided to go out for a pint, but I stayed back in the darkened, empty room, suddenly engulfed by anguish. I realized that I should be with my mates and not alone, so I yelled for them to wait, but they took no notice. By the time I got into the hall, they were nowhere to be seen.

I wandered endless, deserted hallways for what seemed like hours, all the time tense and nervous. Turning a corner, I ran into Angus, but Angus as he'd looked twenty-four years earlier.

"Quicksilver! Thank God I've found you! You have to come and help me. Something dreadful has happened!"

I started backing away, knowing what would come next, but a wall I hadn't remembered stopped me.

Angus grabbed me by the shoulders and looked into my face. "Michael, you're the only one who can help! Don't back out on me now, man! Follow me."

He stomped off down the dimly-lit hotel corridor, not looking back to see if I was following. Again, it seemed to take hours. Finally, the dream-Angus stopped in front of a door, motioning silently. Reluctantly, I moved forward. As I got close, he swung the door open and gestured inside.

I wanted to run, to be anywhere else on the planet, but I'd been through this so many times that the next sequence had become ingrained on my psyche. I began taking the final steps to the door, my heart thundering in my chest, dread filling my heart.

That morning, though, something wonderful happened. I suddenly woke to find myself in my own bed.

Closing my eyes, I blessed Shannon for making me so anxious about those brutes. I'd been spared from the conclusion of my horrible nightmare so few times that it felt as if a huge weight had been lifted from me. The sound that had wakened me was caused by an icicle. Warmed by the morning sun, it had broken off and clanged on the window sill as it splintered into a thousand pieces, much like my nightmare had just been shattered.

Feeling more peaceful than I had in a long time, I lay back, smiling. A glance at the clock told me that it was almost nine a.m, and I should shift my lazy arse. Shannon would be in Montreal by now.

I wondered what sort of information she'd bring back.

▌▌▌

Shannon glared at the seat back in front of her as if *it* was responsible for the way she felt that morning: majorly cranky. Yeah, yeah, it could be put down to having to pry herself out of bed at five thirty after only four hours sleep in order to catch the seven thirty flight, but she knew it went deeper than that.

The evening before, she'd had the worst fight ever with her daughter over what Rachel had said on the phone. The girl had defended herself by saying that she'd only been kidding.

Shannon didn't take the offered way out. "You had no right to say something like that to me!"

"Yeah, and now you're going to tell me that it's because you're my mother. That's a bullshit excuse, and you know it. Be honest! You like him. You told me once how you thought he was 'dreamy'."

"Rachel! Good God, I felt that way when I was seventeen!"

"So? I saw the way you were staring at him the other night. Look me in the eye and tell me you wouldn't like to sleep with him!"

Shannon couldn't clearly remember the sequence of what happened next. Suddenly Rachel was standing there with a hand-shaped red mark on her cheek, and Shannon's right hand was stinging. She'd never struck one of her children before.

Rachel ran from the room, leaving her mother standing there, feeling empty and sick.

Later, when she'd pulled herself together, she had gone to Rachel's door and tapped lightly. "Rachel, honey, can we talk?"

Silence.

Robbie opened his door and peeked out, then quickly shut it when his mom glared at him.

"Rachel, please open up. I'm sorry I got so angry. That was uncalled for, and I apologize."

Silence.

Shannon had finally given up and gone to her own room. Flopping crosswise on the bed, she'd stared at the ceiling late into the night.

Not knowing where the trail would take her that day, Shannon picked up a rental car and a map of Montreal. The fact that she had several identical maps back at the office from previous investigations didn't improve her mood any.

The address Michael's chickie had given the hotel was in the city's east end near Rue St. Denis, an area familiar to Shannon. Even though she had to fight rush hour traffic, she made pretty good time.

However, Montreal had received the brunt of the recent blizzard, and driving on the back streets proved slow and laborious. Because of the mounds of snow, parking places were at a premium, so she grabbed the first one she saw, leaving her a walk of at least three more blocks, judging by the street numbers.

She had an ambivalent relationship with the city, this neighbourhood especially, and old memories weighed on her mind as she slipped and slid along the sidewalk.

Her ex's family had settled in Montreal after emigrating from Ireland, and "Big Rob" had lived in a flat near St. Joseph and Papineau for most of his childhood. Soon after they met, he'd talked Shannon into visiting his old stomping grounds. At this point, Shannon had thought of her fellow officer as a buddy. Since they had coinciding vacations and she had nowhere else to go, she'd agreed, never having seen Montreal. Since they'd be staying with his "sainted widowed grandmother," Shannon hadn't felt the least bit awkward accepting the invitation.

The drive from Toronto had been great fun, with Rob in high spirits, and as usual, driving way too fast. They'd gotten pulled over on the 401, but he'd talked his way out of a ticket, being a "brother officer".

Visiting at the height of summer, Shannon had been charmed by the city. These old neighbourhoods lined with very distinctive buildings, their outer staircases curving up to the second- and third-floor flats reminded her of something right out of Europe. Even though her high school French was not very good, the people had made Shannon feel comfortable, and besides, Rob spoke the language well enough in a rough and ready style. Most nights they spent clubbing on St. Denis or visiting his old chums. Days were spent with him showing her the tourist sites. She'd especially loved Old Montreal.

Looking back on it now, Shannon realized how thoroughly she'd been seduced. Rob had a rather overwhelming personality and was very handsome, in a roguish sort of way. At thirty, he was already a high flying veteran on the Toronto police force and possessed that presence that comes with being a cop.

The melt-in-your-mouth summer nights, the laughter and camaraderie, Rob always hovering close, making sure her glass was full, had completed the job on a relatively unworldly twenty-five-year-old. That, and a *very* deaf grandmother who went to bed at nine p.m.

The last night of their trip they'd been sitting on the front stoop talking when Rob had leaned over and kissed her cheek, then her lips. It had been so soft and gentle, Shannon had immediately responded. Her weak spot had already been sussed out somehow, because if Rob had grabbed, she would have bolted. Indoors, as the kissing continued in the doorway to his room, she had let him touch her, and she was soon his. With her head spinning from a bit too much wine and young lust, she'd wound up in his bed, making love for only the second time in her life.

They'd only had unprotected sex that once, but that was all it had taken. Six weeks later, Shannon had received the bad news that she was pregnant. Rob had "done right" by her, and they'd married. At the time, she felt she'd married the love of her life.

She purposely walked down the opposite side of the street from her target address, so she could get a wide angle view of the building. Situated near a corner, the brick building was four stories, taller than the neighbourhood standard of three. Other than that, it looked pretty undistinguished, a good place to "blend in". She wondered if any of the windows facing her belonged to apartment seven.

She crossed the street, dodging a taxi that had run the light at the corner, getting sprayed with slush in the process.

The spartan foyer needed of a good coat of paint, and the floor had several tiles missing. She could see through the glass of the inner door that the first floor hallway wasn't much better kept. Only the cocoa husk mat at her feet looked new. The intercom was built into a dented row of steel mailboxes on the right side. Sure enough, the listing for number seven was G. Fleury.

Shannon buzzed, but not surprisingly, didn't get an answer. With a shrug, she pressed the button next to the listing for Concierge.

After cooling her jets for a minute or two, she was about to press again when an old man appeared at the far end of the hallway. She tried hard to wait patiently while he shuffled down the length of it.

At 5'9", Shannon was tall and positively towered over the little man who had answered her summons. He *might* have been 5'1".

Looking to be around seventy, he had started out stocky, but that had degenerated into fat. He also needed a shave and reeked of tobacco. After a closer whiff, Shannon also realized that a shower was long overdue. Equally unappealing were his dirty, grey track pants, stained white T-shirt and a ratty flannel bathrobe that should have been thrown in the trash years ago.

He squinted up at her through a haze of smoke. "*Oui?*"

Realizing that discretion was the better part of valour in this case, she tried something in her high school French. "*Je ne peux pas parler français très bien.*" She flashed him an apologetic smile "*Vous parlez anglais?*"

Le petit concierge puffed twice on his cigarette and nodded once.

Shannon tried not to cough. "I was buzzing someone who told me they'd be at home today. There was no answer, and I wasn't sure if the intercom worked, so I tried you."

"Which apartment?" His English was French Canadian, thick and difficult to follow.

"Seven," she answered.

The concierge stopped puffing, looking her over from head to toes. "You are to meet with the woman in number seven?"

"Yes."

"That is very interesting." Taking a pack of Gauloises from a pocket of his robe, he lit a new cigarette from the stub of his current one, which he threw on the floor, grinding it out with a slippered foot. A few more puffs. "So you know Mademoiselle Fleury?"

She weighed possible answers carefully. If this vile-looking little man liked the Fleury girl, he would probably lie to protect her. The way he'd given Shannon the once-over told her he probably enjoyed ogling *les jeunes filles,* so she decided to try charming *and* telling the truth. Flashing her widest smile, she relaxed her body a bit, leaning in conspiratorially. "We haven't met, but she was in Toronto recently, and I wanted to speak to her about something that happened there."

"Toronto? That doesn't surprise me."

"Why do you say that?"

"That girl is always off to someplace, Europe, the States, always someplace new with her."

"What does she do for a living?"

"You *la police*?"

Shannon thought before answering, then reached into her purse, pulling out a business card. "I'm a private investigator." Shifting gears and trying to sound more like a cop, she said, "I'm trying to track down the Fleury girl. She may be in some trouble."

"What kind of trouble?"

She couldn't decide if the little concierge looked wary or interested. Either way, she didn't want to scare him off. "Some people were looking for her in Toronto. They bothered a friend of mine there, thinking he might know where she is."

The little man nodded sagely. "You are not the first to ask questions about her, you know."

"Who else has been looking for her? A cop?"

The old man snorted. "*Ben non!* Two big men, English—from England, you understand. They came yesterday," he snorted indignantly, "and said to me they were lawyers and had news of a possible inheritance. *Tabernac!* What did they take me for? *Un idiot?*"

Now *this* was interesting! "So what did you tell them?"

"I told them nothing! I said she wasn't here, which is the truth. I said she may lose her apartment because she has not paid her rent for two months, and that is all I said to them!"

"They asked for nothing else?"

"Of course they did! I said I was busy. They offered me money to tell them if the Fleury girl returns. 'It is very urgent that we speak to her.'"

"And how are you supposed to contact these men?"

"I do not know. I sent them away without asking!"

Shannon, observing the concierge closely, noticed his eyes flicker sideways and a slight shift in his weight. *He's lying,* she thought.

"You said that she has not paid her rent recently."

"Two months! She is fortunate I am so understanding. When I saw her in the hall three days ago, she promised that she would drop off a cheque before she went out for the evening! *Pah!*" The little man punctuated his disgust by spitting on the floor.

"What does the Fleury girl do for a living?" she repeated.

"She told me she is a...how do you say it?...stewardess, but I've never seen no uniform."

"And three days ago was the last time you saw her?"

The concierge could only nod his answer as he started coughing. "You must excuse me, *madame*. I am just getting over *la grippe,* and it is not very warm in our foyer."

The pair was moving into the lobby as a man exited the elevator, mumbling a *bonjour* as he squeezed past in the narrow hallway. They both turned to watch him cross the street.

She really wanted to get into the girl's apartment and saw an easy way she might accomplish it. So she opened her ski jacket and immediately felt (rather than saw) her companion's eyes checking out her chest. Going shamelessly with the flow, she started to remove her jacket and dropped it "accidentally" behind her. Smoothly turning away, she bent over at the waist to pick it up, giving him a good view of her jean-covered butt. *Hope this does the trick*, she said to herself as she straightened and turned back.

The dirty old man was practically salivating. "Is there anything else I can do for *madame* this morning?"

She feigned indecisiveness. "Well...there is one thing. Would it be possible to see apartment seven? I would, of course, pay you for your trouble. No, no. That is to much to ask. Please forgive me!"

A big grin split the man's face. "No. It would be *très possible*. And you say you have never met *Mademoiselle* Fleury?"

"No," she answered, her pulse quickening. "I was told about her and offered to speak to her, since I was going to be in Montreal."

The old man's grin widened. "Then it is no problem! I told her that if she did not pay the rent, I would be forced to start eviction proceedings against her. You will be someone who is looking at the apartment in the hope of being able to rent it. *Non?*"

She reached out and touched the man's arm in a gesture of concern. "I would not want to get you in any trouble!"

"I assure you, *madame*, I can do what *I* wish in this building." He motioned across from the elevator. "The elevator is very slow. It would be best if we took the stairs."

Yeah, right! she thought as she started up the stairs in front of him. *He just wants another butt shot.*

He made it up the stairs surprisingly quickly, considering the way he'd puffed down the hallway earlier. Perhaps it had something to do with the speed at which Shannon took the stairs.

The old man sorted through a ring of keys, squinting at each as he held it up to the light. About five from the end, he found it, then opened the door to number seven with a flourish. "*Voilà!*"

She hadn't known what to expect, but the apartment came as a shock. Considering the rundown nature of the building, coupled with the fact that the old man had told her that the girl was away more than at home, the furnishings were opulent. Obviously, this mysterious girl had exquisite taste along with *quite* a lot of disposable income.

The little concierge whistled. "*Tabernac...*"

Shannon knew she had little time and wanted to see as much as possible. Knowing she couldn't do a real search with company present, she made the best use of her time by just wandering through the rooms as if she were enjoying all the fine furniture, carpets and *objets d'art*. What she was actually doing was trying to get some sort of a lead as to where the girl might be, or at the very least clues as to who this mysterious girl was.

On a tall dresser in the bedroom were several photos, the only ones she'd seen in the apartment. Five were of the girl at various stages of her life, bare-assed at two or three opening a screen door, one at about eight or nine with a pretty white dress and a bouquet of flowers, probably a confirmation photo, and two of her as a teenager, gawky and still with baby fat, but becoming a fairly attractive woman. The last and largest photo had been taken more recently, and was by far the most interesting because it showed another person, male, possibly late twenties, handsome, swarthy complexion, very powerfully built. The girl and this male had their heads together. He was sitting, she was bending over and their brilliant smiles filled the frame. The bit of background led Shannon to believe the photo had been taken at a beach.

She turned to the concierge, aware that he'd been staring at her. "Do you know who this person is?" she asked, indicating the photo.

He shuffled forward, craning his neck. "*Oui*. I have seen him a few times."

"Can you tell me anything about him?"

"I was taking the garbage to the curb, and Mademoiselle Fleury and this gentleman they arrived in a taxi and went into the building. Next morning, I was taking the garbage cans back in, and he stepped out of the elevator."

"So you think he stayed the night with her?"

The little man gave a generous Gallic shrug.

"When was this?" she asked.

"Last September, maybe early October."

"Did you hear him speak?"

"*Oui*. He asked me where he could get a taxi."

"Was he from Montreal?"

The concierge shook his head. "The States. He spoke like someone you hear on that crime show from New York, you know, *The Sopranos*."

"You're certain?"

"*Oui*. It was strange, though..."

"What?"

"Another time, I saw them at a bar on Rue St. Denis. It was a fine evening, and they were sitting outside. I stopped by to say hello, and he and Mademoiselle Fleury were speaking Italian. He did not look happy at my interruption. She sounded as if she had been born in *Roma*. I visited Italy once in my youth, you know."

Interesting. "I didn't know she spoke Italian."

"Oh, yes. After that I tried out some of what I remembered on her, and she would laugh. She said she had attended university in Milan. Something to do with economics, I think. Anyway, her Italian is *molto bene*. I also heard her speaking German into her cell phone once. *Ça, c't'une fille brillante, Mademoiselle Fleury!*"

Fluent in at least four languages? She certainly did sound brilliant. "Anything else you can tell me?"

The little man frowned as he searched his memory. "The man from New York called her Julie."

"You're sure?"

"*Oui!* I heard it quite as clearly as I am hearing your voice. Twice he said it."

Shannon kept her face passive, but inside she was smiling broadly. *Gotcha!* she thought triumphantly. *The girl's made her first mistake.* A question flashed across Shannon's mind, one she should have asked a lot sooner. "But she's from Quebec?"

"*Décidément.*"

|||

Shannon spent the rest of the afternoon touring the nearby night spots on St. Denis where a young woman might go for an evening of fun. Besides a few hits of recognition as she showed the girl's photo around, the detective learned only a little more. The Fleury girl occasionally had male companions with her, but usually came in alone. No names, no remembered conversations. One night she'd entered one place by herself but left late with an American tourist who'd been hitting on her all evening. No one had ever heard her speak anything but French—except to the American.

On the drive back to the airport, Shannon's bad mood of the morning grew worse. The trip had certainly not been a waste, but what now faced her was something she'd been dreading would be the next step in this investigation: a trip to New York.

It wasn't the best time for her to be gone overnight, not after the battle she'd had with Rachel. That would be better dealt with right away instead of being left to fester. Shannon had no idea what she was going to say to her daughter, especially if Rachel kept pushing her, as she'd been doing lately.

Rachel was a smart girl and had seen something that her mother hadn't even been able to admit to herself. If she were honest, it couldn't be denied. Michael Quinn *did* attract her, and it wasn't the remainder of a long-ago teenage crush. That puzzled her. She'd felt so certain that she'd hardened herself to anything like that. After the disaster of her marriage, Shannon had sworn she would never allow herself to have those feelings again. It wasn't realistic, of course, considering that she was an attractive forty-one-year-old with a healthy sex drive, but she'd always imagined herself feeling something like this in the far-distant future, when years had healed the wounds to her heart suffered at the hands of the man she had loved so completely.

As she spoke on the phone to her mother, giving her the bad news about the extended trip, a vision of Big Rob floated in front of her eyes, as it had on and off all day. The next call she'd be making would be to him, since Rob was the only "connected" person she knew in the Big Apple. In the past, she'd always relied on him to use his connections when one of their cases had taken them down that way.

One time she hadn't. And now she had to go to him for help.

Shannon again stared sourly at the seat back in front of her on the one-hour flight to New York. Now it wasn't just her kids and ex-husband that were on her mind. What was bothering her was a new and more disturbing problem.

CHAPTER 14

My recurring nightmare doing a crash and burn gave me a terrific lift. Maybe, just maybe, this was a day where things would actually go my way. The blasted dream had never imploded like that before.

Given my state of mind, it wasn't hard to convince myself that my fears of the night, jumping at every sound I'd heard, had merely been the product of an overheated imagination. Things always seem worse in the dead of the night, don't they?

After a leisurely shower, followed by breakfast at the Mars diner on College Street, I zipped along some backstreets, grabbed the Don Valley Parkway off the Bayview Extension, and got to the warehouse in thirty-five minutes flat, no traffic tie-ups. Amazing! I could count on the fingers of one hand the times that had happened.

Surely, I had the world by the tail.

Hamed was still on loan to the movie shoot, Kevin was out with the van, picking up equipment at a studio, which left Johnny and me to assemble the gear needed for two contracts going out later that day. We were both sweating heavily by the time we finished, but we could look with satisfaction at two organized lines of amps, drums, keyboards and their attendant hardware in the middle of the warehouse floor, ready to be whisked into the trucks when they arrived. One of the contracts had even been prepaid.

Life could still have its good moments.

I had just sat down on a flight case with a cold beer out of the refrigerator when the phone rang. Johnny, keen as mustard, jumped for it before I could move a muscle.

"Quinn Musical Equipment... Yes, he is... Sure. I can do that. Whom shall I say is calling?... Really? Wow! I'm sure he'd like to speak with you. I'll get him." Johnny stuck his head out of the little entrance room. "Hey, boss. It's Rolly Simpson on the phone! Do you want to take the call here or in your office?"

"I'll take it in the office. Ask him to hold on," I answered, getting wearily to my feet.

Flopping down behind my desk, I lifted the receiver. "Hi, Rolly. What's up?"

"We're getting a lot of interest in this concert, Michael, and I think you should be aware of that. The phone's been ringing off the hook since the announcement, off the bleeding hook! I must have done a dozen interviews the past three days. This reunion is going to be big, Michael, really big. Has anyone got in touch with you?"

"There have been a few calls, but I haven't returned them. I have no interest in speaking to journalists."

He sounded vexed. "Why must you always be so bloody difficult?"

"I don't like journalists. What's so hard to understand about that? They don't listen, they make things up, and just about every time I've sat down with one, they've made me out to be a lunatic or a hermit or something else I'm not."

"But we all need to promote Neurotica's reunion!"

I was beginning to lose patience. "No, Rolly, *you* need to promote Neurotica's reunion. This *was* supposed to be a tribute to Angus and it should be billed as such. Fine. But I will not kiss the media's arse. You can. You like doing it, and I bloody well don't!"

"All right, all right," he said soothingly, but still with an undertone of impatience. "That's actually not why I was calling. We've got the dates set and—"

"Wait a minute, Rolly," I interrupted. "Did I just hear you slip a plural in there?"

"I told you there's been a lot of interest. We couldn't get the SECC as our venue, so we're doing the gig at Braehead Arena. It's a nice place, but it only holds fifty-five hundred, so the proposal now is to do four performances over five nights. The others have agreed to it. Besides, why go to all that trouble for one kick at the can?"

Rolly did have a point. If I were going to take the time and expense to put my end of this together, playing only one night would be less than satisfying. "I don't know..."

"Oh, come on, Michael! You know it makes sense. You're not going to have to do any of the slug work this time. I'm working with the promoter, and a mate of John's is providing the lighting and sound. All you have to do is turn up and play. If we only do one concert, our fans who can't get tickets are going to lynch us!"

"Okay," I sighed, "I'll do the four bloody shows." Picking up a pen, I added, "Give me the dates."

Rolly actually had a schedule all organized, a first for him.

I'd need to be gone for nearly a fortnight. Hmmm... "Getting away for that long might be a problem."

"But you've given your mates your word! Don't you dare try to back out on us, Michael, or I swear to God—"

Lord give me strength! "I'm not remotely trying to back out. I'm just telling you that you're asking for more than I was expecting."

"We have to allocate enough rehearsal time. We haven't played together in so long, and our material isn't easy. We'd look a right bunch of prats if we're playing duff notes all night long."

"Okay, point taken. Look, why not write out a set list and pass it around, then we can all dis—"

"Check your fax machine, mate. You'll find one there. The rest of us have agreed on it. Long as you're happy, that's what we'll be playing."

I yelled for Johnny to bring me the fax. Upon looking it over, I noticed it contained two songs I hadn't written and consequently had never played.

"Do you have access to the masters for these?" I asked, even though I had zero interest in playing them. They were total shite.

"I don't think that will be a problem. Why do you want them?"

"Actually, I'd like copies of the multi-tracks for *all* our material. I simply don't remember handfuls of it, and it's always hard to pick out the keyboard parts. If I can isolate the keyboard tracks, it will speed up my practising. Can you get them?"

"If it will make you happy, Michael, I'll fly them over myself!" Rolly said. "The record company is behind this, so I'm sure they'll play ball."

"Have them transferred to files I can read with ProTools."

"Sure, and I'll let you know when they're on their way. Michael..." Rolly paused and I waited for the inevitable announcement. "The record company wants in for a live recording and DVD."

I'd known this would be coming the moment I'd agreed to the concert.

"Look, Rolly, this is way more than I agreed to. I said I'd do *one* concert, and now we're doing four. I understand that. Now, you're throwing a CD *and* a DVD at me. And weren't you the one who was telling me recently that our record company were a bunch of crooks?"

"But there's money to be made here, mate!"

"I thought we were doing a charity gig—or are you saying that the charity will get all the proceeds from any recordings?"

"Well..."

"I thought so. No recordings, full stop. That's my final word on the subject. And make certain the other lads are practising. I don't want to waste time while they relearn their parts at rehearsal. You know who I'm referring to!"

And with that, I slammed down the phone.

My day now pretty well a ruin, I decided to go for total martyrdom and do some work on the business's books, something I detest, but with tax season approaching, I didn't have much choice. However, I detest it much more when I get so far behind that I have to spend days getting caught up.

Throughout, I kept a weather ear open for anyone entering the building. I'd decided if I didn't like what I was hearing, I'd be out the front door in a flash, dialing 911 as I ran. Getting smacked around the other night had been more than enough to cure me of any idea of wanting to play the hero. My feet had never failed me up to this point, so why shouldn't I keep relying on them?

I found it hard to concentrate, though, and that made the job far more onerous as I continually lost track of what I was doing. A thousand things kept flitting through my head, and none of them were productive. I also began to get the overwhelming feeling that events were catching up with me. The next time the bad guys made an attempt, they'd be a lot more circumspect. That didn't bode well for my health.

I was hoping my private investigator would discover the magic bullet that would put an end to this mess, but an address in Montreal from a bogus driver's license was not much to go on. She'd probably find an empty lot where the address should be.

Kevin returned shortly after one, and once we had the truck unloaded, I called out for pizza rather than sending him as was our usual practice. With people around, I felt reasonably safe.

The afternoon was spent over more paperwork, with the guys checking equipment, then putting it away and helping to load the outgoing orders. I tidied up the last of the paperwork, filled out the week's paycheques, then decided to look over Rolly's set list again.

Frankly, it was not very imaginative. If I was going to go to all this trouble, the gig *had* to be something special, something that stretched us. Shannon's idea about the alternate way we could play our defining hit was a start, but we'd have to dig a lot deeper than that. Would the rest of the band be up for it?

I spent the next few hours in the front room working out a few ideas on my keyboard rig. The mellotron gave rise to a number of interesting alternatives. In the past, I'd always used electronic samplers. Using such an archaic keyboard would raise more than a few eyebrows, but there was just *something* about the sounds the mellotron produced that really excited my imagination. Neurotica had never sounded like this, and people would know I was back. Trouble was, I had to convince the band to try what I had in mind. Maybe a call to John or Tommy to sound them out would help.

Before closing up for the day, I remembered that Shannon had those spy cameras set up all around my apartment, so I went back into the office, and using the instructions she'd written out for me, I soon had my computer showing me the page on her private website giving me access to anything that had been recorded.

Four minutes later, I was very glad I'd looked. The two locals had showed up at my door about ten minutes after I'd left that morning.

I wouldn't be sleeping there tonight.

A call to Shannon's cell caught her about to board a plane to New York. She agreed I should check into a hotel and stay well away from the warehouse, at least until she got back.

"And when will that be?" I asked.

She sighed. "Tomorrow or Sunday. You should hope for Sunday, though, since that would mean I'm having some luck. I'm not staying in New York a moment longer than I have to."

"You have hopes then?"

"I don't want to jinx anything. Let's just say I ran across a few things today that made my antennae twitch."

"What?"

"I'd rather not say." She paused, and I knew what was coming next. "Michael, you really *should* go to the police, you know."

"Let's not get into that again. You know why I don't want to."

"You're being pigheaded about something that's getting more and more dangerous."

"I know, I know, but it can't be helped."

"Let me hire a couple of bodyguards, then."

I rolled my eyes. Danger or not, *that* would be too much. Staying at a hotel, I should be plenty safe. Anything to do with my business could be handled over the phone... "Damn and blast."

"What's wrong?"

"If I can't come to the warehouse, how am I supposed to practise for the bloody concert?"

"Aren't there places that rent rehearsal space?"

"Word I'm practising someplace will be all over town in a flash. I'm hot news at the moment. The *Globe* and *Toronto Star* and some Brit papers have already requested interviews. No, I can't rent space."

"Leave this with me until I get back. I may have a solution."

Shannon's voice had seemed rather clipped and strained during our conversation, so before signing off, I asked, "Sounds like you've had a rough day."

"What?" she said, startled, as if I'd cut in on some inner reverie. "I'm fine, fine. I just have a lot on my plate at the moment."

"Speaking of plates, I think I owe you a good dinner when you get back into town. You've done a lot for me the past few days."

"Dinner? Me?"

"Yes, dinner, you," I laughed. "What do you say?"

"Just try to keep yourself alive and in one piece, then we can talk about dinner. Okay?"

As I put down the phone, I wondered to myself, *Where had that come from*?

I took the paycheques out to Johnny and Kevin, who were sitting in our entrance room shooting some late Friday afternoon bull.

"I, ah, have some appointments tomorrow morning and Monday, so I'm going to leave Hamed's cheque in the drawer here. I'll be available by cell, though, if anything should come up."

"Does that mean Hamed is going to be back here to carry his weight?" Kevin asked.

"No. Hamed is at that shoot for the duration. Tell him it's waiting for him if he calls."

Kevin seemed pretty put out. "How come I don't get a chance? He's not doing anything I couldn't do, and I've worked for you longer!"

"He's the one who is on the job until I say so. Okay? Besides, tomorrow is your turn for the Saturday opening."

"Hamed didn't do his turn last week!"

"I don't want to hear any more about it."

As I drove downtown, I decided that maybe it hadn't been the best way to handle things. Kevin was my employee of longest standing and possibly deserved more consideration. Regardless, that didn't give him the right to shoot off his mouth. Even though I didn't have to force the issue very often, I was still the owner of the business. Kevin just needed to be reminded of that, and if it didn't suit him, he could find employment elsewhere.

III

I checked in at the Four Seasons in Yorkville, normally out of my price range, but a place used to dealing discreetly with celebrities.

"Excuse me," the middle-aged desk clerk said, "but has anyone ever told you you look just like the keyboard player in the band Neurotica?"

So much for discretion...

"I have heard that, yes."

After signing the registration card with my real name and handing it back, she looked up at me again. "The resemblance is really uncanny." Then after another glance at the card, she said, "You actually *are* him, aren't you?"

With a grim smile, I answered, "Most of the time."

"Wow! I've always been a huge fan."

"Really."

"Ever since I was in college! Is the band going to tour again?"

"I rather think not."

"That's too bad. I certainly don't have the money to go to the concert you're doing in Glasgow—even if my husband would allow me!"

"Yes, it is rather far."

"Well, Mr. Quinn, it's a pleasure to have you stay with us. If there's anything we can do, just let us know." She pushed over a pen and piece of paper, and with a shy smile, asked for my autograph.

I obliged, and we proceeded with the check-in without further comment. Her eyebrows did rise, though, when I told her I had no luggage.

That was something I'd have to rectify the following morning. There was no way I was going out on the streets at night.

Dinner consisted of a club sandwich ordered from room service washed down with a beer from the mini bar.

Shannon was right. This cat and mouse game couldn't go on.

For years now, I'd been able to go where I wanted with little fear of being recognized. There had been a time when our photos were in all the music magazines, on billboards, and I often had to deal with fans and autograph seekers. The rest of the band had loved it; I hadn't.

Yes, I could have been rude and told them to bugger off, but I didn't like doing that either. So I'd put up with it. After I left the band, it had continued for a while, but eventually the public's memory faded. Now I could go months without anyone asking me for anything but directions or spare change.

Angus's death and my agreement to do the bloody concert had changed all that. I had figured that there would be *some* interest in a Neurotica concert, but it seemed to be arousing far more notice than I would ever have imagined—and a lot of questions about why I'd left the band in the first place were being asked once again.

If word now got out that gangsters were after me, my car had been trashed and I'd been beaten up, I'd find myself in the centre of a media frenzy. The sooner I could get everything behind me, the happier I'd be.

Disgusted that my life had been reduced to this, contemplating the long night ahead and feeling in need of a soporific, I switched on the telly and flopped onto the bed.

CHAPTER 15

Shannon O'Brien arrived at LaGuardia shortly before six that evening, her first time in New York since 'that day'. With disgust, she noticed her palms had become sweaty, a sure sign of nervousness. What did *she* have to be nervous about?

After getting some American cash at an ATM, she headed straight for the taxi rank.

New York had also received the same dump of snow that had buried Montreal and Toronto two days earlier, but the Big Apple never coped with winter's vagaries the way her Canadian cousins could. In other words, traffic was still badly snarled, and even though the roads themselves were clear, the entrance and exit ramps were a mess, with barely room for one vehicle.

Shannon sat back in her seat with a sigh and fished her cell phone out of her purse. After dialing Rob's number, she waited about five rings before someone picked up.

"Hello?" A woman's voice.

Damn! Shannon thought, *the last person I want to talk to is that cow!* Not identifying herself, she asked to speak to Robert O'Brien.

The voice sounded put out. "Yeah, he's here. I'll get him."

Shannon's ex came on the phone a moment later and said in his loud, blustery way, "Is this my little Shanny?"

The former Mrs. O'Brien swore sharply under her breath, causing the cabby to look back through his rear view mirror with interested eyes. She should have expected the woman to recognize her voice.

"Cut the crap, Rob. I'm in town for one reason only, and we both know that it isn't you."

"You hold a grudge an awfully long time, you know that?"

Mister, if you think this is a long time, you don't know jack! she thought, then said out loud, "Did you get a chance to ask around about those names I gave you earlier?"

Shannon had spoken to her ex from Montreal shortly after lunch, giving him the meagre amount of information she had, which basically amounted to not much more than a few names.

The New York mob heavy the girl had told Michael was her father Shannon already knew was the real deal, although she doubted they were related. The rest were just names, and she'd made the trip south, hoping she might be able to add a bit more flesh to the bare bones. If this lead proved to be a dry well, then all she had left was the fifty bucks she'd invested in the old concierge to call her if the girl showed up at her apartment. Whether he'd do it or not was another matter.

"I made inquiries around town with people I know," Rob told her, and she heard the rustling of paper. "Yeah, here it is. This guy Angelo you asked about, got a last name for him yet?"

"No."

"Well, it might be Angelo Spadaro, a low life scumbag who does 'errands' for the Mastrocolle family."

"That part fits in with the information I have," Shannon answered. "What else you got?"

"Nobody's seen him in over two weeks. Rumour has it he may have met with an accident."

"Really," she said, scribbling in her police pocket pad. Old habits die hard. "Did your contact give you any other details?"

"Some merchandise may have gone missing."

"What kind and how much?"

"Don't know the answer to the first question, and as to the second, apparently plenty." Rob was silent for a moment. "Say, Shan, could we do this in person? Seeing as you've come all the way down here, it might be easier."

A wicked thought flashed through her mind. She seldom got Rob alone, and she'd been wanting to discuss their kids. Whenever she had him on the phone, he always found some excuse to sign off when she brought up those kinds of problems.

"Sure. Where can we meet?"

"How about your hotel?"

Not a chance, buster! she thought. "Know a good restaurant around midtown? I'm starving."

"Seeing as we're talking about Italians, how about a plate of pasta and some vino?"

They arranged to meet at eight, and Shannon told the cabby to take her directly there, since time was short and she wanted to be seated when Rob arrived.

She'd ordered a decent bottle of red wine and had drunk about half a glass and eaten a slice of hot bread when he made his big entrance. Some things never changed.

The maitre d' had a backslapping hug put on him, and Rob shouted his name as if they were best friends who hadn't seen each other for twenty years. Every eye in the restaurant turned to look—which was the whole idea. Shannon refrained from rolling her own eyes as he also shouted the length of the restaurant to her.

Sitting down at the table, he leaned across to give her a kiss, but that was short-circuited by Shannon taking another sip of wine.

"You're looking really good, Shan," he said, sitting back in his seat. "Really good."

She looked across the table at her ex, wondering why she'd never noticed what a complete phony he was. It was like standing behind a magician, watching him do his tricks and being able to see how it all was done. Rob hadn't changed; it was Shannon's perspective that had.

After pouring him some wine, she did relax enough to clink glasses.

The waiter came by for their order, and after he left, they stared at each other for a few moments. They really hadn't shared any time alone since she had found Rob with another woman. Everything about this meeting felt foreign to her, as if it were on the edge of being out of control. One thing she'd prided herself on since the breakup was *always* being in control, and she wasn't about to let that slip as she had the previous evening with Rachel.

"Thanks for agreeing to help," she said, and stifling a grin, added, "and asking me out for dinner."

The man across the table obviously thought she was on an expense account and would be picking up the tab. He didn't hide his frown quickly enough by sticking a piece of bread in his kisser. Feeling more at ease, she pulled out her notebook as their salads arrived and continued to pump Rob for details throughout the dinner, much to his obvious annoyance.

"So who haven't you asked for information yet?" she inquired at one point. "I don't want to leave any stone unturned on this."

"You always were a little bulldog," Rob said, then shrugged. "You seem to think that I'm as well-connected in this town as I was back in T.O. Working for the agency now, I don't meet with cops the way I used to. Plus, I'm Canadian, and that doesn't help in some circles."

"You've come up with a fair bit since my call at two o'clock."

"Look, Shan, what is this all about? You're moving into some pretty deep waters here and—"

"Think I'm not equipped to handle it?" she shot back.

"No, no. That's *not* what I'm saying. The people you're asking about are the roughest players in town, and they have a long reach. I'm talking about southern Ontario. Cross their path and you're really asking for trouble."

"I've already crossed their path, or at least my client has. They seem to have some interest in him, and he isn't sure why. I'm trying to help him find out."

"Who is it?"

"A guy who rents space at the opposite end of the building where the office is."

"That music warehouse? Is this about drugs?"

"Why does everyone think that music and drugs *always* go together? The guy's clean in that regard."

His response was a knowing smirk.

"Why did you mention drugs? she asked.

"Because a little bird told me that's what's missing. You call me up and ask about some people, and one of the answers that comes up is drugs. You've been hired by someone in the music business, and I just think 'bingo': cause and effect." Rob looked hard at her. "I know you're still really pissed at me, and probably always will be, but we shared something together once, and it was a fine thing. I care about you. You're the mother of my children. Have you checked this guy out *really* carefully? Is he on the level?"

"Do you think I'm *that* inexperienced? *Of course* I checked him out!"

Some of Shannon's heat in her response came from the fact that she had taken Michael Quinn at face value and hadn't done any kind of background check on him—not that she'd ever admit it to Rob.

"Is he from Canada or the States?"

"Britain originally, but he's been in Canada for a number of years."

"Any connections down here? I could check up on him for you. What's his name?"

Shannon didn't want to tell Rob, but couldn't think of an excusable reason not to. "Michael Quinn."

Rob whipped out his notebook and started to write. "Any aliases?"

Dammit! How had the conversation gotten away from her? "Well..."

"Well what?"

She sighed. "I guess there's no reason not to tell you, but I want this kept quiet. He's also known as Michael Quicksilver."

His face went blank.

"Remember me talking about a rock band called Neurotica?"

Still a blank.

"That band I told you about that I liked so much in high school."

The light bulb finally went on, and Rob's expression was rather comical. "*Not* your teenage heartthrob?"

Shannon couldn't do a thing to prevent her blush.

Rob knew he finally had an opening. "Still stir your blood?"

"Give me a break, Rob! The guy's a *client,* and he's got his shorts in a knot because some mob types tried to rough him up!"

Rob's expression told her he didn't believe her. She wanted to wipe it off with a good right jab. Even though *he* would never tell anyone how it had happened, she knew how Rob had gotten his crooked nose. Never condescendingly offer to teach the tomboy daughter of a cop how to box.

When their main courses arrived, she turned the talk to their children. Since Rob seldom came to back Toronto, and the kids were only free during school holidays, he didn't see much of them. He didn't seem pleased about the news he heard.

"Okay. I'll talk to Little Rob and get him to straighten up and fly right. All boys go through this at some point or other. I'll give him a fatherly boot in the rear end. That's all he needs."

"And Rachel?" Shannon asked, gazing at him steadily.

"She's your department. You know she has me wrapped around her little finger. There's too much of you in her."

"What's that supposed to mean?"

For only the second time she could remember, Rob seemed unsure of himself.

After a long minute of silence, he spoke. "Look, Shan. I know I made a complete fool of myself, that I never should have done what I did. I hurt you, and you didn't deserve that. It was just a stupid fling. She really—"

She held up her hand, pain showing clearly on her face. "No, Rob, don't."

He didn't seem to notice. "I've been planning on coming up to Toronto to see the kids, to see...you. I thought maybe we could all go to my family's cottage in the Gatineaus and—"

The anger she'd kept bottled up for so long boiled over. "You sonovabitch!" she shouted as she sprang to her feet. Shannon didn't care that everyone in the tiny restaurant had stopped talking. She just wanted to strike back at the person who had hurt her so badly. "Don't you dare think you can do this to me! I'm not the gullible fool I once was." She leaned forward, her face inches from his, and hissed, "You see, I made it my business to find out about the others."

Struggling to hold back the tears until she was out of the restaurant, away from him, she grabbed her coat and overnight bag and made for the door.

Out on the street, she looked around hopelessly for an empty cab. The last thing she wanted was for Rob to follow her out. It had been a *huge* mistake to ask him for help. All this time she'd thought the wounds had healed, but now she knew they had only scabbed over.

Using her fingers to whistle, she finally managed to get the attention of a passing hack. He crossed over dangerously right in front of another car, whose driver blasted his protest on the horn, and pulled up, and slid to a halt in the slush covering most of the road.

"Where to, lady?"

She told him and slumped back, trying to slow her rapidly beating heart, more angry with herself than she'd been in a long time.

Checking in at the hotel was mercifully quick, since most guests for that night had already arrived. Because she didn't feel comfortable wasting Michael's money on classy digs, the room was tiny, its double bed leaving barely enough room to squeeze around the walls. At least it was clean.

She dropped her coat on the one chair, flipped on the door's safety catch and flopped onto the bed.

"Well, you really screwed *that* up!" she said to the ceiling and squeezed her eyes shut as more tears threatened. She was determined not to cry, even if no one would ever know.

Her cell phone rang. She knew she'd hear Rob's voice.

"Shan... I just want to apologize. I'm really sorry I upset you so much. I didn't mean to; I just—"

"No. Drop it. This conversation is over." She was in the act of hanging up when she heard his tinny voice squawking at her. "What is it?" she asked tiredly.

"I was trying to tell you that someone put me on to another person after I spoke to you earlier. You ran...ah, I upset you at the restaurant before I could tell you about him."

She sighed, figuring this was another little ploy of Rob's to keep her on the line. She was well aware the man didn't give up easily, regardless of the fact that he'd earlier referred to *her* as a bulldog. "Tell me about him."

"I don't know much," he admitted. "I only got his name and the fact that he might be interesting to talk to about Angelo Spadaro."

"Can you arrange a meeting?"

"Might be possible. When?"

"Tomorrow morning. Call me if it's a go," she added and hung up as he was still trying to say something.

That at least had felt good.

|||

Shannon spent a restless night. The radiator in her room clanked intermittently, and the corridor outside her room seemed to be party central until well after two a.m. A call home had told her that Robbie's teacher had called, and Rachel hadn't even wanted to talk to her. If Rob didn't come through tomorrow, this entire trip to the Big Apple would have turned out to be worse than a total waste of time.

Finally giving up trying to sleep around five thirty, she sat up in bed making notes about everything she'd learned concerning Michael's case. She routinely did this as a way of clearing out her brain. Writing things down in an orderly fashion also often suggested new lines of inquiry that she might otherwise have missed. Her ex had preferred "brainstorming" through problems by sitting around and talking things over. Shannon had always thought of it as "bullshitting" your way through the problem. For years she had continued to make her detailed notes, while Rob would lean his chair back on two legs and poke fun at her "bookish" ways.

An hour later, she took a shower, dressed and went down to the hotel's coffee shop, continuing to work on her notes throughout the meal. One jerk businessman tried to sit down at her table, but she quickly sent him packing with a baleful expression and a tart putdown. At the end of the meal, her bad mood was still intact.

On the way back up to her room, she looked at her reflection in the fingerprint-spotted, polished metal of the elevator doors. *I'm not normally a bad-tempered person,* she thought. *What's wrong with me?*

Her cell rang shortly after ten.

"Shan?" Rob's voice.

"Yeah. You got anything for me?"

"The guy said he'd talk."

"When?"

"Soon as we can get there," he replied.

"Where is that?"

"Up north a ways. Westchester. It's about a forty-five minute drive. We're also taking along someone to make the introductions. Do you have a problem with that?"

Shannon was relieved by that last bit of news. After the previous evening's festivities, she really hadn't been relishing being alone with her ex for an extended car ride.

When she hopped into Rob's car fifteen minutes later, the passenger was introduced to her simply as Frank. She knew better than to ask questions.

He looked to be on the far side of fifty, skinny and had definitely seen his best days. His thin hair was grey and combed straight back. His shirt bore several stains, as did his tie. It was obvious he had a complete set of dentures, since he constantly sucked on them.

As they drove north to a town called Port Chester, the men in the front seat talked about nothing but sports, leaving Shannon to go over her notes and look out the car window. The skies were leaden, heavy with more snow. The only thing looking up was the temperature, now hovering near freezing, which felt absolutely balmy after the recent deep freeze in Canada.

Port Chester was a down-at-the-heels, small city hard on the Connecticut border, and it didn't surprise her when they pulled up in front of a seedy-looking bar.

Frank finally turned around and spoke to her. "You know, Ed Sullivan came from Port Chester."

"Really? That's very interesting."

"Quite a man was our Mr. Sullivan. Quite a man."

It didn't say much for the town if Ed Sullivan was its most noteworthy export.

The interior of the bar was dark and stank of stale beer and cigarette smoke. Frank immediately lit up, as did Rob, which surprised her. He'd proudly been smoke-free since they'd met, and she wondered if his new floozy was also a smoker.

They paused at the door while Frank's eyes got used to the dim light. He saw who he was looking for and led them to a table in a back corner. The person sitting there looked to be the same sort of person as Frank, except he was bigger, overweight and gave off an aura of being much more dangerous. At a nod from the man, they all sat down.

"Eddie, this is Rob, the guy I was telling you about," Frank said by way of introduction.

"Who's the fluff?" Eddie asked, glaring at Shannon. "You didn't say nothing about her."

Before Frank or Rob could answer, Shannon leaned across, sticking out her hand and said, "I'm actually the one who wants to hear what you've got to say."

Eddie just stared at her hand. "You're from Canada."

Shannon pulled it back. "Yes, I am. You've got a good ear."

"Nah. My second wife was from there. Could talk the hind leg off a mule. Believe me, I heard *plenty* of her damn accent. You one of them Mounties?"

"No. I'm a private investigator."

"A female dick? That's a laugh." Eddie pulled out a pack of cigarettes. "Anybody mind?"

Shannon shrugged, resigned to her fate. All three males at the table had now lit up, and the air became that much thicker.

Eddie tapped the side of his fat nose. "I can smell cops, you know. That's why I ain't never been in the slammer. We're talkin' twenty-nine years, missy."

"Impressive," she answered, meaning it. In Eddie's line of work, you had to watch out for everybody, especially your friends, who would shop you in a minute if they thought it would save their own skin.

"So I guess you want to hear about my boy Angelo."

Shannon nodded as she took out her notebook. "Yes. Anything you can tell me."

Eddie raised his empty beer glass and wiggled it. "Anybody else joining me?"

Frank also ordered a beer, but Shannon and Rob both declined. As the bartender brought over two bottles and a glass, Shannon paid and fat Eddie began to talk.

"I don't like to talk behind nobody's back, but sometimes you gotta, know what I mean? Angelo's my sister's kid, and he never had much up here," Eddie tapped his head. "I brought him into the business and figured it was up to me to keep an eye on him.

"Angelo's a good lookin' kid, but too often he let his 'little head' do his thinking for him, meaning no disrespect, but that's what happened this time. You see, old man Mastrocolle had a bit of a problem, and Angelo got caught up in it."

"What sort of problem?" Shannon asked.

Eddie looked at his buddy Frank, who nodded slowly. "Some stuff went missing." Eddie leaned forward, and so did everyone else. "Actually more than some stuff. A lot of cash, too, and as you might guess, Mastrocolle was *not* happy about it. You see, he's very old school. It's all about honour with him, and he figures that someone has dishonoured him. Heads roll when that happens."

"Can you give me any details?"

"With borders being watched more closely these days, you gotta be smart if you want to move merchandise. In the old days it was easier."

"You got that right, Eddie," Frank said between swigs of beer.

"Was the shipment coming in or going out?" Rob asked, speaking for the first time.

"Coming in. Now that Afghanistan is back in the game, and Europe one big country more or less, some guys arranged for the shipment to come through England. That's usually a tough route, 'cause them Limeys ain't no fools, but like I said, it's tough everywhere."

"So you're saying Mr. Mastrocolle lost his money and didn't get the shipment either?" Shannon asked and Eddie nodded. "Know how that happened?"

"Somebody in the organization was playing for their own team, know what I'm saying?"

"Can you tell us more?"

Eddie lit a new cigarette from the stub of the old one, which he then stubbed out rather hard. "I'm getting on. I don't like to admit it, but it's true. Right, Frank? You and me are on our way out. Anyway, I'm not privy to much that goes on any more. Mastrocolle still calls on me when he wants something special, but day to day? Nah."

"So you don't know what happened?"

Eddie smiled. "I'm not saying that. I just want you to know that I didn't see nothin', know what I mean? I only *heard* about it."

Shannon had forgotten all about her notebook. She was sitting forward, certain that Eddie could deliver the goods.

"Not having dealt with these Limeys before, they wanted cash from Mastrocolle, so he put his most trusted person on the job. The deal was that the payment would be made here in the States and given to a trusted third party for safekeeping. Then Mastrocolle's man would go to England to arrange the shipment. When it was on its way, the deal would be concluded. It was a risk, having something go down that far from home, but the old man felt good about it.

"Problem was, Mastrocolle's man, the one who arranged the whole thing, had a different idea. He diverted the shipment and substituted sugar. Then he went to collect the payment and managed to sweet talk the third party holding the cash into giving it to him to take to the Limeys—which wasn't part of the set-up. It would have been a hell of a sweet deal if he had pulled it off. The guy would have walked off with the cash *and* the stuff."

"What went wrong?" Rob asked.

Shannon felt like kicking him under the table. He knew better than to interrupt when someone being questioned was on a roll, as Eddie clearly was.

The old hood called for more beer, and it was little wonder that he looked so rough, if this was the amount he normally consumed—before lunch. Shannon reluctantly paid again.

"Sure you folks won't have anything? No? Okay, where was I? Yeah. What went wrong...

"When you want to pull off something like this, timing is everything. You know how this caper got blown all to rat shit? A goddamn better delivery than anyone would have expected! From what I heard, the merchandise should have taken at least a week to get to the States."

"So the guy Mastrocolle trusted was still around when the fake shipment arrived?" Rob asked, butting in again.

Eddie smiled at Shannon, and it made her skin crawl. Fat and old he may have been, but he was still plenty dangerous.

After pouring his beer, Eddie tipped his glass and drained half. Then, wiping his lips on the back of his hand, he smiled across at Shannon again. "Thanks." He made a display of gathering his thoughts, maybe as the prelude to asking for some cash for his story. "Yeah, Mastrocolle's 'trusted guy' was still in town when the shipment arrived. Seems his Limey friends were a little too efficient, or actually paid off the right people for a change. I gotta tell you, the 'package' must have sailed through security and customs unchecked—at *both* ends of the trip.

"As you can imagine, Mastrocolle was not pleased when the switch was discovered, that he'd bought some awfully expensive powdered sugar. So he sent a few of his *very* trusted men to the guy's apartment.

"They were only just in time. Caught the slippery bastard and his know-it-all girlfriend with their bags packed and ready to disappear for points unknown. They were brought to Mastrocolle none too gently, I hear," Eddie ended with another of his shark-like smiles.

"Did he have the money?" Shannon asked.

"Nah. That would have been too much to expect. Also, by this time, the Limeys had discovered they'd also been had and figured it was a double-cross by Mastrocolle. To top it off, the old man couldn't be sure that *he* hadn't been double-crossed by the Limeys. It was a frigging mess."

"At least Mastrocolle had the brains of the scam," Rob pointed out.

Shannon frowned as she thought about what she'd learned about the girl. "I wouldn't be too sure about that."

Eddie guffawed. "You're too smart by half, little lady! It's obvious now the girlfriend had more to do with the scam than anyone realized.

First of all, it was her that found the Limeys to do the shipping."

"What happened next?"

"The usual: bring him in, sheet of plastic on the floor with a chair in the middle. Let him know they really meant business. He knew he was done for, and also that he could make it a lot easier on himself if he spilled his guts. Funny thing is, he never did, and believe me, from what I heard, he got worked over good. Real good."

Shannon could feel she was getting close. "So how did your nephew get mixed up in it?" she asked casually."

"Like I intimated before, it was a long pair of legs."

"How so?"

"Angelo was told to watch the girl while her guy, Paul, was 'talked to'. Seems they got a bit cozy in that bedroom while they were waiting. Angelo had a shit-eating grin I should have noticed when I checked on them at one point, but I had other matters on my hands."

Shannon noticed Eddie's slip but let it slide right by. What happened in Mastrocolle's office wasn't her business at this point.

"You mean the girl had been giving herself some 'other alternatives' while they were alone."

Eddie guffawed again. "I like the way you put that! That's *exactly* what happened. She had my Angelo pegged right. Give a fool a taste of honey, and he'll always want more—*especially* when it's good."

"Angelo let her get away."

"Exactly. She spun him quite a yarn about how she didn't know nothing. Made arrangements to meet him in Atlantic City." Eddie shook his head sadly. "Angelo was a complete *stunat*. There wasn't nothing I could do for him."

Shannon reached into her coat pocket, unfolded the printout of the girl's image from the security camera at the hotel in Toronto and slid it across the table.

Eddie suddenly grew very still, and anything in the way of good nature disappeared from his face, as if it had never been there. Shannon saw his hand slide off the table ominously, and it seemed as if the room had grown very quiet indeed.

The old, fat hood leaned forward, and as the beer fumes wafted across the table, said in a surprisingly gentle voice, "I think you need to tell me where you got this, little lady."

CHAPTER 16

Saturday, a day which *should* have seen me practising for many hours, instead got spent in time-wasting activities, considerably worsening my mood.

The previous night, my recurring nightmare had steamrolled my tired brain over and over. It was caused primarily, I suppose, by having spoken with Rolly.

Around noon, the need for a change of clothes finally pried me from my hotel room. I had the doorman hail a cab. A short ride got me to Stollery's at Yonge and Bloor. Since it was a Saturday, I knew it would be crowded, and if the bad guys somehow were on my tail, they'd hesitate before coming after me there.

Forty-five minutes later, with three days worth of new clothes I didn't need nor want, I had the store call another cab to take me directly back to the hotel. My neck was aching, though, from having to watch my back.

Periodically, I'd have a room service delivery, but my time was taken up watching a succession of mind-numbing shows on the telly after I'd exhausted the few good movies on the hotel's pay-per-view.

Saturday night was no better than Friday: eventually doze off, have bad dream, wake up, eventually doze off, have bad dream, wake up...

By Sunday morning, after two nights and a day filled with boredom, frustration and almost no sleep, I was near my breaking point. Through it all, I couldn't see any way out of my mess. I had a business to run, and in only a short time, I'd be front and centre on a rock and roll stage—and life would get even *more* weird. Unless my luck finally turned, eventually I'd be run to ground by those after me. It was a pretty bleak prospect.

Shannon finally rang my cell at ten a.m.

"Michael? Where are you?"

"Trapped in a hotel room and getting bloody desperate!"

"Well, for *once* you made a good decision about something."

"How do you figure that?"

I could hear the tap, tap of a computer keyboard in the background. "Well, for instance, I'm checking on the cameras in your apartment right now, and if you'd been dumb enough to be home the past two nights, you would have entertained guests. Let's see, last night they came around three a.m. Two of them...no, all three. I'm watching them plant two bugs, one in the living room and another in your bedroom. Pretty clumsy, too. Using the inside of a lamp shade went out in the sixties! Oh-ho! You've also got a bug on your phone."

"Bloody lovely."

Shannon finally twigged to the disgust in my voice. "What's wrong?"

"I *don't* appreciate having to live my life this way, hiding out in some hotel room."

"I understand your frustration, but I have been making progress."

"Will it give me back my life?"

"Not yet."

"Then what bloody good is it?"

"Michael, that's being rather unfair. I'm doing pretty well, considering what we had to go on."

I got off the bed, walked over to the window and looked out at snow falling in big, lazy flakes. "You're right. I'm behaving like a prat."

"Look, I have a lot to tell you. Do you have some time later on in the day?" She sighed. "Sorry. Dumb question."

"When can you come and spring me?" I answered dryly.

"That bad?"

"Yes, that bad."

"I have reports for a couple of other cases to look over and phone calls to make after that, and I also promised to take the kids out to breakfast, but I should be able to make it down to you by mid-afternoon. Is that okay?"

"Just get me out of here for a few hours!"

"I don't know if that's a good idea."

"Look, what harm can it do if we just drive around? Bring a gun or even a rocket launcher for all I care, if you think the bad guys will give us a hard time. I just cannot stay here much longer without going bloody mad. Call when you're near the hotel, and I'll wait in the lobby. No one will bother me there. I'm at the Four Seasons on Yorkville."

At five minutes after four, I hurried out the entrance and jumped into Shannon's waiting SUV, feeling a bit of a fool and sure that everyone could see how jumpy I was.

She had on a pantsuit which looked much more businesslike than her usual jeans, sweater and ski jacket. "I had to see a client I've left hanging a bit too long."

"On a Sunday?"

She shrugged. "That's how it is sometimes." We turned up Avenue Road. "Where to?"

"Anywhere. I'm just happy to be out of that hotel room." I sat back with a sigh. "You said on the phone that you'd made progress."

She zoomed ahead to make it through the light at Davenport. "Yup."

"So you know where the girl is?"

"Well...no. But I do know *a lot* more about her."

"Tell me—and don't spare the details. I want to know everything about the person who stuffed my life into a blender and hit frappé."

Shannon snorted as we charged up the big hill towards St. Clair.

Her monologue lasted for a good hour, during which we wandered all over the Forest Hill neighbourhood, then up the Allen Road to Highway 401 before circling around to the bottom of the city via the 427 and Gardiner Expressway.

"Let me get this straight," I said when she'd finally finished, "you're not even sure the girl is American, Canadian, *French* Canadian or Italian? She sounds like a damned chameleon!"

She nodded in agreement. "That's *exactly* what she is, Michael. I'm finding it impossible to tell where the truth stops and the lies begin. I'm sure you've noticed that parts of what that hood in New York told me sound like the story she fed you. She got away by, um, talking one of Mastrocolle's stooges into helping her. But even though I now know more, everything I learned leads to more questions. Somehow I've just got to find her."

"Any ideas how to accomplish that?" I asked.

Shannon shrugged. "Not a clue at this point, but I've baited my hooks and may catch something yet. That's how these things often work."

I tiredly rubbed the bridge of my nose. "You know, Shannon, you're always telling me that I'm taking risks. Sounds as if you took a big one meeting with that hood."

"I did have a bad few minutes when I showed him the photo. He thought I'd been stringing him along, that he was being set up. He thought I knew where she was, and I was totally blindsided by the ferocity of his reaction. He *really* wants to get her. She set his boy up when she talked him into letting her get away. All I've got to say is that I wouldn't want to see the results if he does catch up with her!"

"Shouldn't you tell the police about what you learned?"

"Eddie certainly played some part in the killing the girl's accomplice, but now is not the time to turn him over to the cops. I know it sounds weird, but that wouldn't be, well, ethical. We now know exactly why the heavy hitters are after the girl. There's big money involved with what went down. Several million, I'm sure. There's also a whole honour thing involved—especially with Italians."

"I think we need to get that surveillance footage from my apartment to DCI Campbell in Scotland. The big man that's the brains of this crew is from Birmingham, a Brummy like me," I clarified. "We've got the same accent, although his is stronger. I'm betting he's got a record, and maybe Campbell can dig up something on him."

"You could be right."

"Would it be difficult to send it?"

"Easy. I've got a recording on the laptop I have in the backseat. All I need is his address."

"Could I watch it?"

"Sure."

We were going up Bay Street. Shannon pulled over and reached around me for her laptop. We sat there for about twenty minutes, watching the bad guys roam around my apartment, my *private* space, as if they owned it. I felt ill.

Suddenly, I felt her stiffen next to me, and I immediately began looking around for the bad guys, but she was still staring at the computer screen, swearing softly to herself.

"What is it?" I asked.

"I am such a dunce! I should have spotted it right away!"

"What?"

"They're not wearing gloves!" She smacked her forehead. "They're leaving fingerprints all over the place. Now we have them!"

Her attention was back on the screen. "Look at that. They're leaving without wiping anything down. Fools. Now, if the big man left some prints, we could have a *very* useful gift indeed. The Brits have a nationwide computer program that tracks stuff like that. If we're lucky, we'll have a name attached to that ugly kisser. I just can't tell if he's got gloves or not. His hands are usually in his pocket."

"I don't want you going to my apartment alone."

"No, Michael, I know what I'm doing, and I can take care of myself. They'd be stupid not to have the place staked out, bugs or no bugs. I know how to do these things. You don't."

"But I need to get into my apartment to pick up some things. I had to go out and buy the clothes I'm wearing today. See if you can figure out a way to get me in there safely."

Shannon held out her hand. "Just give me your keys. I'll pick up whatever you need."

"I'd rather get them myself."

"I've said it before: you have a stiff neck, Quinn." Her hand remained out. "The keys."

Seeing her hand, her fingers wiggling to prompt me to do something yet again I didn't want to do was suddenly just too much. Days of worrying and looking over my shoulder with no end in sight, the pressure I was under with those damned concerts and having almost no sleep for the past two nights, caused me to finally snap.

"You *don't* order me around!"

She got right into *my* face. "And you don't tell me how to do my frigging job!"

With that, I stepped out of the car and began walking. Shannon yelled something after me. I just kept walking.

I was *not* going to be pushed around any more! Not by her. Not by anyone. I almost wished the three blokes after me would pull up. In my mood, I would have taken them all on.

With no place else to go, I eventually ran out of steam, hailed a cab and went back to the hotel.

‖‖

Someone knocking on my door woke me at half six. I'd fallen asleep sitting up in bed, and now my neck had a bad crick in it. Groggily rubbing it, I made my way to the door and looked through the peep hole. Shannon. Shit. I saw her arm balloon in the fisheye lens as she raised it to knock again.

In an effort to gain time, I asked, "Who is it?"

Her response sounded put out. "I'm assuming you're looking through the peephole."

"I'm not dressed."

"I'll wait."

Clearly, she wasn't about to bugger off, so I threw on pants and shirt and opened the door.

"Michael—" she began.

"I give up."

"What?"

"You were right. I should listen to my hired expert."

"Michael, that's not what I came here to tell you. I should *not* have said what I did. It just sort of slipped out before I could stop it."

Two people were coming down the hall from the lift.

"Get in here! I really don't feel like airing my dirty laundry to everyone coming down the hall."

She entered and looked around.

I stood leaning against the closed door. "Casing the joint? Sizing up the suspect?"

Her face fell. "You have every right to be angry with me."

"I'm not angry. I'm just so frustrated I could scream! I want to fight back and hurt somebody, but that somebody shouldn't be you."

"And I have to remember not to yell at clients who have every right to be frustrated and irritated." She sat down in the chair by the window and looked up at me. "What?"

I smiled. "Are you aware that whenever you walk into a room, your eyes go into laser beam mode? What the heck are you staring at?"

"It's a habit," she responded with a hint of embarrassment. "People pay me to notice things. Would you be happy if I was always walking around in a fog?"

"Certainly not. Anyway, that was a serious question I was asking. What do you see?"

Shannon looked around the room a bit more. "Same things I did in your apartment. I see someone who is very neat and orderly. I'm assuming you have more clothes than what you're wearing. They're all put away, your jacket is hung up and the things from your pocket are laid out in a row on the bedside table. The bathroom, from what I saw walking by it, was also tidy."

"And what does all this tell you?"

"You're either anal about neatness, or you're hiding away anything that might reveal something about you personally."

"Anything else?"

"Yes. The only place I've seen where you allow *any* mess is your desk at work. Your office is a pig sty, as a matter of fact."

"Meaning I don't care as much about my work as I do my privacy?"

"Maybe." Silence fell awkwardly between us. "So where do we go from here?"

"If you think I'm about to go off and find another investigator-slash-bodyguard-slash-psychologist at this point, you're more screwed up than I am."

Shannon took a deep breath. "Good. I've been afraid I'd blown it."

"No. Just the opposite." I stepped over to the bed and sat down on the corner closest to her. "So where do we go from here?" I asked, repeating her words.

"I really studied the recordings made by the cameras in your apartment, and I'm afraid your Brummy friend is too clever by half, as you Brits say. He had gloves on the whole time, as far as I can tell, so that's probably a dead end if we were hoping to send Campbell fingerprints along with the face."

"But you still want to go down there?"

"Might as well get whatever prints I can." Shannon looked up at me with a challenging expression.

I got to my feet. "Let's get that dinner I offered you the other day, and while we're doing that, you're going to figure out how to get me in and out of my apartment without getting caught. I really do need some clean clothes, and no, I'm *not* going to let you choose them for me. And that's final!"

"You've got a stiff neck, Quinn!"

"Not as stiff as yours, O'Brien."

▯▯▯

It wasn't hard deciding that the hotel's restaurant was the easiest place to eat, considering the weather, which had been deteriorating throughout the day as the weather reports blared winter storm warnings.

We actually had a nice meal together, talking about her kids and how much they got out of living on the family's old farm—even Rachel, who daily went from one teenage crisis to another.

My hired car was the best choice to get to my apartment, since the bad guys had seen Shannon's SUV. She would drive, and I'd keep my head down in the back seat. Make a quick circuit of my building's basement car park to see if anyone was lurking, then it would either be a quick exit, or we'd be home free.

Snow was really coming down, and driving was treacherous. There were very few cars on the road.

"How come they won't recognize you?" I asked as we drove south on University Avenue.

"Simple. I'll put a scarf on my head. It's amazing how something that basic can throw off a man."

"As opposed to a woman?"

"Women notice more than men do. It's a proven fact!" she said, laughing at my doubtful expression.

Once we got past Bathurst, King Street looked like a vast snowy desert. Anyone with a modicum of sense had long since headed for the shelter of home and hearth.

Sliding in the deep snow that had collected under the railway overpass just east of my building, we both began to tense up, but not due to the weather. My confidence was seeping away faster than the snow was falling.

"It's a known fact in police circles," Shannon had said as we'd come out of the hotel's underground parking lot and surveyed the condition of Toronto's roads, "that crooks and bad guys don't like to be out in miserable weather any more than the rest of us—less, probably, because they're inherently lazy. Break-ins, robberies and car stealing all plummet whenever the weather is bad. I'm hoping no one will be watching your apartment tonight. We're about the only ones dumb enough to be out in this blizzard!"

I climbed awkwardly into the back and crouched between the seats as Shannon drove the last two blocks at a circumspect pace, her eyes constantly on the move as we passed parked cars.

We almost got stuck in the driveway of my building, since it had collected a lot of blowing snow, but with a little rocking, we made it to the ramp down to the car park.

She made two slow circuits and saw nothing untoward, but being cautious, she parked in one of the visitor spaces, rather than my reserved one.

While I waited in the back seat of the car, she keyed the lift and got it down, then signalled with a sharp whistle that all was ready. As I scrambled out and ran for the open lift door, I felt as if I'd landed in the middle of a cheap spy novel. We both breathed a sigh of relief as the door slid shut uneventfully.

"First step accomplished," Shannon said tightly.

We got off on the floor below mine and walked up via the stairwell at the opposite end of the building. Shannon insisted on doing a quick reconnoiter down the hall and soon whistled another all-clear.

I tried to walk at a dignified pace to my apartment. I had the door open in a flash and resisted leaning against it once the deadbolt had slid home.

"Here," Shannon said in a whisper as she pressed something into my hand. "Only use this if you have to, and keep the beam low."

It was a tiny torch with a red filter over the lens to keep one's night vision intact. Private eyes get to play with some pretty cool toys.

I followed her into the bedroom. She'd put on a headlamp thing with the same red filter and busied herself in the room with her fingerprint equipment. It took her only a few minutes to find a group of prints on the dresser and my bedside table. Then she gave me the all-clear to get on with my packing.

Contrary to what she'd said about me earlier, I just grabbed two suitcases and stuffed everything in willy-nilly. I was getting spooked being in my apartment under these bizarre circumstances. It felt more like I was in someone else's place doing a bad break-and-enter job.

In the meantime, Shannon had moved on to the bathroom. She was spraying something on the surfaces of everything which made the fingerprints glow under the purple of a hand-held black light. With a tripod, she then snapped photos of them with a digital camera.

I came up behind her and whispered into her ear, "I thought you used some sort of dust for things like this."

"That is *so* last year," came her low response. "Since this is a quick in and out job, *not* evidence collection for a court case, we'll get what we need in a fraction of the time." She sighed. "So far, all I'm seeing are three sets of prints. I'm assuming the ones in the largest group are yours."

It only took a few moments to grab the toiletries I needed once Shannon had finished. Judging by her sighs in the living room as she looked for more prints, she was having no better luck finding fingerprints that might belong to the Brum.

As each minute ticked by, I began to feel more uneasy. The building was quite still and felt completely deserted. Outside there were no noises of traffic. Even the sound of the nearby Gardiner Expressway seemed to die in the rapidly falling snow.

I quietly moved the blinds to look out. It was coming down harder than ever.

Shannon was now working on the front door, and I went over and said into her ear, "If we don't get out of here pretty soon, we're going to be stuck for the night. Remember what the driveway was like coming in!"

"I'm going as fast as I can!" she hissed back.

She again set up her camera to take pictures of everything the magic chemicals had revealed on the door and frame. Seeing it all made me feel my apartment was incredibly filthy.

After snapping a dozen more shots, Shannon straightened up and cast her eyes around the room. Her eyes stopped on my piano over in the far corner.

"Surely you don't think they came here and played a few tunes before leaving!" I said, forgetting for the moment that I wasn't supposed to speak out loud.

Shannon glared at me with one finger firmly pressed to her lips, picked up her equipment and moved across to the piano. I stood at the door unable to relax, jumping at the slightest sound and wanting simply to get the hell away.

Shannon motioned to me. With the help of the little torch, I crossed the room quickly.

She put her lips to my ear. "We may have hit paydirt! I just found a set of prints I haven't seen anyplace else in the apartment. Have you had anyone over here recently, someone who tickled the old ivories?"

I shook my head.

In a minimum of time, she had what she wanted safely stored in the camera and was back at the door with me.

"Everything will look normal if they come back," she said, "unless they have a little light like mine, in which case it will all look like this!"

She flicked on a black light, and little bright green glows came from multiple surfaces around the room. It reminded me of fairy lights.

"I love doing that," Shannon said close to my ear as she slipped out the front door, returning about a minute later. "Well, other than the person down the hall watching a hockey game on TV, it sounds as if this floor is deserted or everyone is asleep. My suggestion is that we do the same thing we did coming in, but in reverse. I'll go down to the garage first and check it out thoroughly before you come down."

"Whatever you say."

I cooled my heels near the third floor lift for a good five minutes, although it seemed more like five hours. Finally the lift moved, and I heard its muffled dings as it passed the ground floor, then the second floor and right past me to the fourth floor. My heart stopped.

Could we have been wrong about the weather keeping the bad guys indoors, or was this just something innocent like a neighbour coming home late?

The stairway door farther down the hall opened, and Shannon stood there waving at me frantically. I grabbed my two suitcases and hightailed it towards her.

"What's up?"

"Looks as if I was wrong. You must have blown it when you spoke out loud. They couldn't have been far away, because they got here fast, considering the weather. I stepped out of the elevator just as they pulled in. Thank the lord I'd put the scarf on."

"Jesus..."

"That's not the worst part. They've parked right next to me!"

CHAPTER 17

What do we do now?" I asked, not caring if I sounded every bit as desperate as I felt.

"All three of them went up to your apartment. What you're going to do is leave by the front door and start moving fast towards King Street, then turn east. Watch for any cars behind. You see any but your rental, you duck. Got that? If I don't show up along the way, grab a cab, a streetcar, anything, but *get the hell away from here!*"

We started down the stairs as rapidly as we could without making noise. At the ground floor, Shannon grabbed my suitcases and continued down towards the garage while I strode off towards the foyer. The security guard was dozing at his desk, the canned laughs of some comedy show on his small TV not disturbing his slumbers. That was a really comforting thing to find out.

At the front door, I turned and looked back. No signs of pursuit.

It was one long block up to King Street, and I struggled to make the best time I could. The snow was deep and underneath was a coating of ice. I fell twice, and my shoes quickly filled with snow. It was one thoroughly miserable person who finally made it to King Street and turned right. The street in front and behind was nearly deserted, the closest vehicle being at least three blocks away. I made it to the railway underpass, having barely managed to keep my feet under me all the way down the incline, before Shannon pulled up beside me and flipped the door open.

"Hurry up and get inside," she said, and oddly she was laughing.

"What's so funny?" I asked as she pulled away with a lot of fishtailing and spinning of tires as she attempted the upward incline.

"You'll never guess what just happened!"

"How about we almost got our arses in a sling?"

"I got stuck on the frigging ramp—and they pushed me out!" She laughed again. "Such kind gentlemen!"

"Are they somewhere behind us?"

"My guess is they're trying to push themselves out. One other thing. Your Brummy friend is not in a very good mood."

"I can't imagine why."

It took us about twice as long to get back to the Four Seasons. Plows were out in force, but frankly, they just couldn't keep up with the snow.

"You're not going to make it home in this weather."

"I know," she said. "My mom told me the same thing when I called home at dinner."

"Look, the least I can do is pay for a room for you tonight."

"That would be very kind of you."

Only problem was, the hotel had no more rooms. Seems a group of psychiatrists had attended a meeting there that afternoon, and most of them were in the same boat as Shannon.

"I'm sorry, Mr. Quinn," the desk clerk said sympathetically. "We don't have a thing. Even our luxury suites are taken."

Shannon's shoulders slumped tiredly. I knew that she really wanted to be home with her children. I took her aside.

"If I could get a cot, would you be willing to stay in my room? It's either that or one of us sleeps in the lobby, and I don't know how the hotel will feel about that."

She looked at me levelly. "I guess that would be okay, considering the circumstances."

I struck out on that, too. Seems there were far more psychiatrists than I'd imagined. The desk clerk gave me a very strange look when I asked her to please check again on the availability of any cots. No dice.

As we made for the lift with my two bags, I said to Shannon, "I can sleep in the chair. I'm not much of a sleeper anyway. To be quite honest, I suffer from insomnia."

She gave me a wry look. "Will you stop? I'm a big girl, and I know you have honourable intentions." As we got on the lift, she added, "You're very sweet to worry about it, though."

As soon as we got to the room, she called home, and from my end, it sounded as if Mrs. Cathcart was quite relieved that her impetuous daughter was not going to attempt any more driving that night. Since school was sure to be cancelled the next day, both children were up well past their bedtime—and loving their gran's indulgence. Shannon didn't protest about that too much.

By the time the call was over, I'd put all my clothes away and laid out my toiletries in the bathroom, realizing as I did that Shannon would probably nod her head sagely, as I again verified her theory about me.

Shannon had put her feet up on the bed and was tiredly rubbing them. "I don't know about you, but I could use a drink. What's in that bar fridge?"

"Beer, mostly poor, red and white wine—"

"Stop! A glass of white wine would be divine."

I poured a glass of white for her and red for me. She leaned back against the pillows I'd put up earlier and sighed contentedly. "Wasn't that great tonight? What a rush!"

"You enjoyed almost getting caught?" I asked in amazement.

"Well, since the kids were born, I've avoid potential hazards as much as possible. But truth be told, they do happen occasionally. When I was younger, though, that was what turned my crank about being a cop. You survive by your wits and skill out on the streets when things go down. Tonight made me remember what it was like."

I shook my head. "You continually amaze me."

She cocked an eyebrow. "Really?"

"To be quite honest, I've never met anyone quite like you."

"Are you making a pass at me, mister?"

"Not in the least."

"Oh." Swallowing the rest of her wine in one gulp, she got off the bed. "Do you have a long T-shirt or something like that?"

"Certainly. Or would you prefer pyjamas? I have them, too."

"No. A T-shirt will be fine."

"You're sure?" I asked as I handed her an official Quinn Musical Equipment tee.

"Thanks," Shannon said as she headed for the bath. "I'm going to have a quick hosedown. Could you pour me another glass of wine?"

She was out again within five minutes. The evening attire I'd provided covered her posterior adequately, but even so, she scooted across the room and was under the covers in a flash.

I took the wine over as she sat up in bed. "You're not embarrassed, are you?" I asked.

A wide grin split her face. "No, modesty forced me to keep my panties on. Sorry. A stupid attempt at a pun..." she mumbled awkwardly when I didn't respond. I was wondering what was going on in her mind.

I went back to my seat, and we sipped our wine quietly. I'm certain the same scenario was going through each of our heads.

Though mostly hidden by the T-shirt, Shannon's body was not a disappointment. I had already grown quite fond of her companionship and agile intellect, and under better circumstances, things might have turned out very differently that night.

Considering, however, what had happened the last time I'd allowed my gonads to make a decision for me, it was ultimately not difficult. Shannon and I were working together. She wasn't some woman I'd met by chance. It was best to keep things on a business footing and not let hormones get in the way.

"So here are the sleeping arrangements as I see them," I finally said. "You can have the bed, and I'm going to sleep in this chair."

"How is that fair?" she shot right back.

"I didn't say anything about fairness, my dear. First of all, I'm not ready to go to sleep, and you were starting to doze off a moment ago. Besides, do you want me to get into bed with you?"

Her eyes got big, and the years slid away from her face. It was very obvious that in her head, Shannon was seventeen again, and her rock star heartthrob was about to make a woman of her. I had experienced that sort of thing before back in the day, and I'd always resisted. Seeing it in her eyes that snowy evening so many years later made it much easier to resist temptation.

"I thought not," I said softly. "I'll tell you what, though: if I get uncomfortable in this chair, I'll come over and lie on top of the covers. Take it or leave it."

She nodded, then lay down in bed and rolled on her side with her back to me. "Good night, Michael." Within a couple of minutes, she had dozed off.

I hoped her rock star heartthrob hadn't proved too big a disappointment.

Shannon woke up in the late hours of the night, disturbed by a movement on the bed next to her.

Michael had been as good as his word and was lying on the bed, fully clothed and on top of the covers. He seemed to be in a very uneasy sleep.

What in God's name had she been thinking earlier in the evening? Had her brain deteriorated so much that she'd been actually *considering* what she knew would have been a very, *very* stupid thing to do?

Shannon remembered back to slumber parties where she and her friends had daringly talked about what they'd do if they ever caught their favourite movie star or musician alone. It had all been silly, totally unrealistic both in form and content, but it had also been been quite exciting. *Surely* she'd moved past that! Still...if she were being completely truthful with herself, she couldn't help admitting there was just a *twinge* of disappointment at how the evening had ended.

Michael was different from any person she'd ever met. He didn't act *anything* like what she would have expected. Now that she'd gotten to know him a bit, he seemed more like—she stopped to think—a university professor or something. That was it. Michael Quicksilver was an intellectual. But every now and then, the rock star would peek out, as it had the other day when she'd caught him practising.

He twitched again and moaned softly. She wondered if he was ill. If not, he was enduring a very powerful, unpleasant dream.

She toyed with the idea of waking him up, but hesitated, remembering that he said he never slept well. From the dark circles under his eyes and the way he'd sometimes sag tiredly when he thought no one was looking, she believed him.

Getting up gingerly, she padded off to the bathroom, shutting the door quietly. She picked up her watch from the counter. Almost six o'clock. Maybe the roads would be plowed enough that she could get home. Traffic would still probably be light, especially if schools were closed—something Little Robbie had certainly been praying for.

She washed her face and quietly left the bathroom. Peeking through the edge of the curtain, she could see that the snowfall had slowed, but far below, Avenue Road looked pretty treacherous, and the sidewalks were knee-deep. The 401 would be in better shape, but

Shannon was concerned about the back roads she'd have to travel to get home. Even with four-wheel drive, that wasn't something to be undertaken lightly. The previous winter, she'd misjudged where the side of the road was after one bad snow storm, and almost rolled the SUV into a ditch.

Not wanting to disturb Michael by turning on the TV, she crawled back into bed but moved her pillows so she could sit up. She had a bit of thinking to do.

Some of it had to do with his case. It had become obvious the previous evening that things *must* come to a head. Quite clearly, life couldn't go on like this for Michael. Sooner or later the bad guys would run him to ground, and the outcome would *not* be good for him.

He was just an unwitting pawn in a larger game. He'd been in the wrong place at the wrong time. In the hands of a person like this Regina/Genevieve/Julia/whatever-the-hell-her-name-actually-was, he'd been an easy mark. He wasn't the first, and he wouldn't be the last. Women like her preyed on gullible men. That hood's nephew Angelo, the boyfriend who'd taken the fall for the drug heist, Michael... Shannon was certain the list of men started much farther back.

The key to resolving the situation hinged on finding her.

To be honest, she fascinated Shannon, and the detective longed to talk to her, find out what made her *tick*. "What does it feel like to actually *live* the way the way you do?" would be her first question.

Her inner discussion was disturbed by Michael, who was sweating profusely, and had begun to mumble and groan in his sleep. Most of the words were too low to catch, but one phrase came through quite clearly, "We're making a big mistake!"

Seeing his increasing distress, she decided to wake him. "Michael... Michael... You're having a bad dream." Reaching out, she touched his face the way she had often touched her children's when they were upset after a nightmare.

She'd meant it to be gentle. His response was anything but a gentle wakening.

His eyes flew open, and his expression was wild as his hand closed on her wrist like a vice, yanking her hand away from his face. "Don't touch me! Stay away!" As he came further out of his dream, his expression changed to one of confusion. "Shannon?"

Shannon had shrunk away from him. Her shock at his response must have shown on her face.

Michael groaned, then said, "I'm so sorry. You shouldn't have seen that."

"Seen what? What's wrong?"

He looked at her for a moment, then got up off the bed, went into the bathroom and shut the door. He didn't come out again for fifteen minutes.

Shannon was disgusted she couldn't get home right away. She'd hardly seen the kids in the past few days, and knew her mom could use a break. When they'd spoken on the phone before she'd left Michael's hotel room, she'd heard Rachel and Robbie going at it hammer and tongs in the background. Rachel had met her mom's request to clean her room with stony silence.

Probably still mad about the slap on her face, Shannon thought as she crawled north on the Don Valley, and immediately felt ashamed all over again.

It was after nine when she arrived at the office, and Janet, her receptionist, wasn't there yet. Not surprising, but she was probably on her way, because she would have called Shannon's cell otherwise.

If she were lucky, today would be a quiet one in the office. Michael's situation had been taking up far too much of her time lately, and a number of other jobs had slid. Her two part-time operatives had picked up the slack admirably, but there were reports that needed to be written up, calls to attorneys who had cases coming to trial, etc, etc.

But first she had to get the image of the girl, the break-in footage and the fingerprints she'd lifted from Michael's piano the previous evening off to the Scottish police to see if they could make some headway where she hadn't been able to.

It was about time Michael caught a break.

I got rid of Shannon as quickly as I decently could. Once the door had closed behind her, it had taken every ounce of self-control not to try to punch a hole through the wall.

The dream that she'd woken me from earlier had been my worst ever. The whole thing had been grotesquely twisted up with what was presently going on in my life. The man who'd opened the door to Rolly's room had been the big goon from Brum. The worst part had been the girl lying in the bathroom. It hadn't been the same face that had been seared into my memory for all those years. It was slowly morphing into something else, something I knew I didn't want to see.

That would have been bad enough, but to wake up and know that Shannon had seen me in the grip of this terrible dream was more than I could bear. Through all the years of therapy, I'd had to make up stories about the dream, and somehow they always fell short of the horror of what had actually happened. The therapists had never understood why I was so overwrought. After that, I had just bottled it up, kept to myself as much as I could, and tried to get on with my life.

Deciding it was high time I called the shop to find out what was going on, I picked up my cell. There were several messages. The first was from the front desk of the building I lived in.

Joe, the daytime security man, picked up. "Oh, Mr Q. Thanks for calling back."

"About what?"

"Well, Mr. Trembath who lives down the hall from you heard sounds coming from your apartment late last night."

"What kinds of sounds?"

"He said it sounded like you were moving furniture. You know, rearranging your apartment. He complained to me about it this morning as he was leaving. I asked the night guy if he knew anything about it. He tells me no."

"Last night I didn't make it home."

"Really? Well, I've been up to your floor, and your door looks okay. No marks, and it's still locked. Want me to call the cops?"

"No. I'll come down there to see if everything is all right."

"Great, Mr. Q. If I'm not at the desk, I'll be outside clearing some of this frigging snow!"

As I put on my coat, I seriously wondered whether it was worth going down there. I bloody well knew what I was likely to find.

CHAPTER 18

Infinitely depressed, I was standing in the hallway of my apartment when my cell phone rang. Shannon.

"Where are you?"

"My apartment," I answered. "I just got here. Old Joe at the front desk called my cell."

"What the hell are you doing there?" she asked sharply.

Thinking her tone indicated I was about to get a ticking off on the dangers of doing something so rash, I snarled back at her, "Looks as if we really pissed them off last night!"

"What do you mean?"

"You know my gold and platinum awards? Every single one of them: destroyed, stepped on, smashed into a million pieces! Other things got smashed, too."

"Oh, Michael!"

"Serves me right for being so smug. After what that bloody *asshole* did to my car, we should have expected something like this."

She was silent for a long time, and if it weren't for the background noise, I would have thought the connection had gone dead.

"You're right, Michael. I haven't been doing a very good job."

"That's *not* why I said it! *I* knew what I was up against. He is an animal. You haven't seen him up close and personal." I leaned against the wall and rubbed a hand over my face. "I've been a bloody idiot!"

"Michael, have you checked out your apartment thoroughly? Is anything missing? Anything else smashed?"

"My computer was taken, but that's all I can see. Those awards were smashed to teach me a lesson. That's three times the bastard has done this to me."

Shannon's voice got suddenly soft and *very* tense. "Michael, are you alone in the apartment?"

"Yeah. Why?"

"They didn't smash those awards to teach you a lesson. They wanted to smoke you out and knew that was the best way. I think they've proven by now they know how to pick your lock pretty easily. Go over to the door and slip on that deadbolt. Now."

I hurried down the hall. "Done!"

"I'm on my other line right now, dialing the police. Do *not* open your door until they get there and tell you that I sent them. I don't care how real they look, if they don't mention my name, you do not open that door! I'll be on my way as soon as they are."

I was still by the door when I heard it: somebody in the hall. There was scratching around the lock, then the door handle went down.

My front door is metal and thick, but I could make out whispering through it. I raised my eyes to the heavens, thanking Shannon's quick wit and the lucky chance that had led her to call when she did, otherwise, I'd have been dead meat.

Somebody pushed hard on the door. I braced against it, just in case the deadbolt had to take more force than it was made for. It was a good thing I had. The whole door shook, and I was certain two bodies had just bounced off. More talking in the hall, really angry now. I began to worry that they might try some shots at the door, and I wasn't sure if the thick metal was enough to stop bullets.

Finally there was silence, but I was far too shaken—and smart—to even consider checking out the hallway. I just stood there waiting for the cavalry to arrive.

They didn't take long: about ten minutes—pretty good considering the weather. Shannon must still have had some clout with her former employers. Since I didn't know how much she'd told them, and figured the time was right anyway, I just told the two constables the whole story. They called for backup, and one went to check outside for anyone watching the place.

Shannon arrived shortly after two detectives did, and even though there was "hail fellow, well met" all around, she still got the third degree. She'd come prepared with all her files and laptop and made them true believers in a very short time.

I sat at the far side of the room on the piano bench, contemplating how quickly one's life can go right into the dustbin.

She confirmed that the prints on my piano weren't from either of the two local bad boys, and weren't mine or hers, either.

"And you're certain no one else has been in your apartment who might have touched your piano?" one of the detectives asked.

I shook my head.

Shannon looked at the prints again. She'd transferred them to her computer. "These are definitely made by a person with huge hands."

"So what do we do now?"

Eventually, we all left for the police station, me with the boys in blue and Shannon following in her vehicle. There, I had to sign some papers, and they asked me if I wanted protection.

"You might seriously consider leaving town for a while," one of the detectives said.

"I don't think it would do any good. They've already followed me from the UK. The only thing I ask is to keep this out of the press. Can you do that?"

"We'll try."

We decided to have the cops drive me back to the hotel. I went in the main door and immediately out the door leading to Yorkville where Shannon was again waiting to pick me up.

"I'll come back later, get your clothes and check you out."

"Where are we going now?" I asked.

Perhaps it was the aftershock of how close I'd come to getting nabbed, but all I wanted to do at that point was sleep.

"I'm taking you out to the farm. They won't find you there."

"Can't they just trace the plates on the SUV?"

"Nope. It's registered to the business." We were stopped at a light, and Shannon reached across to pat my hand. "Remember when I said that I knew of a place you could practise? Well, my ex set up an exercise area in our barn. We *maybe* use a third of the space for our equipment. There's tons of room for those keyboards of yours. You can spend your days practising and running your business from your cell phone. We can make this work!"

"Do I detect just a modicum of guilt involved with this offer?"

She looked down briefly. "No. Well...yes. I should have worked harder to convince you that you needed to go to the police with your problem. *That's* where I've really failed you."

We were now swinging around Queen's Park, heading south to the

Gardiner. "What about all the evidence you gave to the cops? Think they'll come up with anything?"

"Maybe. At least they know who's involved. I also fired off everything to that detective in Scotland. We'll see what he comes up with. If we're *really* lucky, then they will have found matching prints in the house where your friend was murdered."

"Remind me to keep my fingers crossed," I responded dryly, but she took no notice.

It was all a rather good plan. Too bad it didn't work out.

Next morning, Shannon tapped on my bedroom door shortly after eight. "You awake?"

"Actually, I was asleep," I called out.

"You told me you hardly ever sleep," she answered playfully.

"I got to sleep again at 6:12, to be precise." Pulling myself to a sitting posture, I leaned back against the headboard. "Come on in."

She brought in a steaming mug of tea.

"So now that I'm awake, what can I do for you?"

"I just got off the phone with your DCI Campbell."

"And?"

"He has someone working on the fingerprints I sent him. They haven't made a match with anything at the murder scene, but we weren't really counting on that, were we? Anyway, he seemed very interested in what's been happening here in Toronto and what I was able to find out in New York and Montreal. I think they may send someone over, maybe even him. Reading between the lines, it's my feeling that they're not making much progress in their investigation. The people who did your poor friend in are not amateurs."

"Don't go out of your way to fill me with confidence."

"I'm just trying to be realistic. But also remember this: most crooks are busted because they make dumb mistakes. Maybe deciding to touch your piano will turn out to be one of those."

"We can only hope," I sighed. "How are you fixed for my equipment to be delivered this morning?"

"It should be fine. I got the kids to help me clean up the barn after you went to bed last night, and boy, were they thrilled—*not*! You don't have to go help them move it from the shop, do you?"

"Not when I've been warned against going within a league of my business."

"Do I detect a certain lack of approbation on your part?"

"Lordy, woman! It's far too early in the day for big words!"

Shannon laughed. "Look, it's for your own damn good."

She'd already left for the office by the time I'd showered and shaved. Going downstairs, I found her mum in the kitchen, taking two loaves of freshly baked bread out of the oven. It smelled heavenly, and I was immediately transported back to my own Gran's kitchen. She had lived in Litchfield, and we would take the train out from Birmingham most Sundays, the day she baked the week's bread. I hadn't thought about that in years.

Mrs. Cathcart again didn't seem overly pleased to see me. We talked for a few minutes about nothing in particular, then she said she'd take me out to the barn.

She called it a "century barn", and I could see what she meant. Under the coat of red paint, the wood appeared weathered and split, and the roof line was not straight. They had been wise not to sheathe the building with siding, though. It had character this way.

"We still have livestock down below, you know," Mrs. Cathcart told me. "Helps keep the building warmer and moist so the timber doesn't dry out. Hope you don't mind the noise—or the smell."

Grabbing keys from a hook beside the door, she went out without bothering to put on a coat. Tough old bird. Her two dogs piled out with us, romping through the snow like pups.

We tramped through old footsteps in the snow, and I stole a few quick glances out over the barren, windswept fields. About a half mile away, among a clump of firs, a few ragged wisps of smoke drifted up. The nearest farmhouse. The city lad in me shivered, whether from the cold or the desolation, I couldn't be sure.

After opening the padlock holding the two large doors together, Mrs. Cathcart pulled back one, reached inside and flipped on a light.

"This is it. Hope your truck can make it back here. Shovels are over there if it gets stuck. After you've unloaded your equipment, please use the smaller door around the side. You won't let out as much warmth.

It costs a ton to heat this place for more than a few hours at a time," she sniffed.

The upper part of the barn was one enormous room. Opposite, on the long back wall, there was a hayloft (with hay bales!) that came about halfway out into the room. The entire interior had been insulated, but only the lower area had been drywalled. A few grimy windows let in some light from outside, but not much for the size of the room. Four bare bulbs hung down from the peak of the roof. Gym equipment and mats were scattered willy-nilly at one end, leaving the opposite end wide open, except for some gardening tools and a couple of old lawn mowers. Shannon had been right; it was perfect for my needs.

Johnny didn't arrive until one, having had to hump all the keyboards by himself because Kevin was M.I.A. with car trouble, and Hamed was still at the movie shoot. Shannon's two kids got home from school shortly after, and Robbie insisted on helping. He proved surprisingly strong, digging out the van when it got stuck and humping more than his share of equipment. The effects of having a full gym in one's barn, I suppose.

|||

I stood up slowly, carefully stretching the kinks from my back. Now I remembered why roadies are a very good idea—even if they can be a pain in the arse at times.

Robbie popped his blond head from behind the organ. "Could you check to see if I've connected it right?"

He had, and now all I had to do was fire everything up and get the balances adjusted. The time for putting off the hard work was over. No more excuses.

The two of us stood back and surveyed our handiwork. At one end of the O'Brien family barn stood a classic keyboard rig: Hammond C3 organ with two Leslie speakers, Yamaha Clavinova (minus the real piano for the Neurotica gig), a Wurlitzer electric piano, four synths, two vintage Hiwatt stacks, and the *pièce de résistance,* my Mellotron MkII. All right, I'll admit to being an equipment junkie. It goes with the territory.

"Cool..." was Robbie's response, and that was equally good.

As Robbie and I stood admiring our handiwork, Rachel came in with a teapot, two cups and hot chocolate for her little brother. She'd been hanging around the periphery while her brother and I worked. I could tell she wanted to be part of it but didn't want to be caught doing something "uncool". Such was the price of being her age, I suppose. Ten years from now, she'd do what she wanted, not what she *thought* she wanted.

We sat among the gym equipment. Rachel and I shared a bench while Robbie sat cross-legged on the floor in front of us.

The hot liquid felt good going down. No matter how well-insulated the big old barn was, it still let in a lot of cold air. It was rather silly to insulate the whole space, of course, but the sixty-foot room did have a certain grandeur to it, carpeted with tattered broadloom as it was. My keyboard rig at the far end looked as if it belonged. Wonder what the cows would think when I cranked it up? Right on cue, one mooed down below.

After we finished the drinks, Robbie jumped up and said he'd come out here to do his homework if I didn't mind. He wanted to hear "all these cool instruments." After a moment of hesitation, Rachel said she'd do the same, "to make sure my creepy little brother doesn't bother you."

While they were off in the house, I got everything fired up and adjusted, figuring I'd give them a full dose of what I'd brought. The side door creaked, my cue to start playing my little overture of Neurotica's hits that I'd been messing about with.

Both kids stood with their mouths hanging open—even if it *was* uncool. Yes, I had turned the amps up quite high, which helped the effect, but in that old barn, even I was forced to admit my playing sounded pretty damned impressive. I'd show those naysaying journalists who wondered why I had agreed to play after so many years. "Time has moved on, and Quicksilver having been out of the game for so long, has surely been left in the dust." Ha!

As I worked for the next two hours, it was kind of cute watching the kids watching me. Robbie didn't try to hide his interest, but Rachel constantly stole glances at me when she thought I wasn't looking.

Shannon came home about seven and came right out to the barn.

"Look, Mommy, I've done all my homework!" Robbie said bouncing up to show her.

Rachel made a face and began closing her books with a world-weary effort to her movements.

"Go wash up for dinner," Shannon told them, then walked over and watched as I shut everything down. "If I'd known you'd have this sort of effect on Robbie's schoolwork, I'd have invited you here weeks ago."

She actually had a dress on, and I shot a quick glance at her very nice legs. The full effect, though, was ruined by the fact that she'd donned some old wellies for the journey out to the barn.

"Important business appointment?" I asked.

"Court appearance," she answered, making a face. "I had to testify against an employee who was robbing his boss blind. Ugly, ugly case." She smiled at me. "But I'm glad to be home."

As we crossed over to the house, I said, "I get the feeling that your mum has some problems with me being here. Do you think it's going to be cool? I don't want to create any waves."

Shannon stopped and turned. "Ever since my marriage broke up, she's felt she has to be my protector. I think she may view you as an evil influence from my teenage past. Don't forget you're an unreformed rock and roller!"

As she turned to look up at me, her amused face outlined by the light at the back door, I felt something shift inside, something I hadn't felt in a long time. I quickly buried it as Shannon turned, and we continued toward the house in silence.

CHAPTER 19

For the next three days, I tried to stay out of the house as much as I could for two reasons: first, I simply did not want to be underfoot, especially with Mrs. Cathcart casting baleful glances my way, second, I was really enjoying making music again. Ideas had started flowing, and I'd moved past simply practising to working on new material.

The big bummer came when the recordings from Rolly arrived—especially the ones I'd never played on. I'd asked for the original multitracks so I could hear exactly what had been done, and from that I'd be able to decide what I wanted to change. Trouble was, I'd forgotten I no longer had my laptop, so I didn't have the software to play back what Rolly had sent on the discs.

Mrs. Cathcart had trudged out to the barn with them. "I have to feed the animals and collect the eggs anyway. It's not much trouble." Her expression didn't give me that impression, though.

On her way over to the door in the floor which led down to the animals, she cast a very long gaze at my multi-headed hydra of keyboards, her expression unreadable.

I stared stupidly at the package of discs for a long time, wondering how much lower my bank account would have to drop before I saw an end to this mess. The insurance company was giving me a hard time about my laptop, because I hadn't specifically put it on my policy and couldn't lay my hand on the receipt for the moment, so that meant shelling out for a new one.

After an hour on my cell phone, I had everything pulled together. My computer store of choice on Queen near Broadview would give me a package deal on the computer and software, which made the expense a little more bearable, and I'd arranged for Kevin to bring it out, along with a replacement for one of the synths which had developed a rather annoying sixty-cycle hum.

My stomach was making ominous noises when Mrs. Cathcart

stuck her head in the side door. "I've just made fresh soup and biscuits. Would you like some?"

You could have knocked me over with a feather.

Shannon had insisted on me joining the family for dinner every evening, so I knew what a good cook her mum was. I didn't need to be asked twice.

During the meal, Mrs. Cathcart delivered a rambling dissertation on her youngest child, which I suppose was meant as a lecture. I found out a lot about Shannon and what made her tick. Her dad and uncles hadn't wanted her to be a cop. She had become one. Her dad hadn't liked what he'd seen and heard about her choice of husband. She'd married Rob anyway. You could see a mum's pride in her daughter, but you could also sense the frustration.

Eventually, she got to the crux of the matter. "My daughter is becoming interested in you, Michael. I could not bear to see her hurt again. What are your intentions?"

I had no idea how to respond. Mum had obviously seen a lot more than I had. Yes, there was a little "chemistry" between Shannon and me, but that was only natural. She was pretty, and I very much appreciated her agile brain. And I was her high school crush.

"Mrs. Cathcart... I really have to tell you that I have no, as you put it, intentions towards your daughter. I'm her client. She's loaning me a place to practise. Our relationship does *not* extend past that." I took my dishes over to the sink and looked out the window for a moment. "Has she said anything to you?"

"Heavens no! She doesn't have to. I know Shannon's moods, no one better. Quite frankly, I'm not happy about you being here. All Robbie talks about is you. And don't think I haven't noticed Rachel going out to the barn to watch you. Now come back here and sit down. I don't like talking to your back, young man."

That made me smile. Mrs. Cathcart was little more than twenty years older than I. Young man, indeed! I did sit rather smartly, though.

"You've wormed your way into our family."

"I have not been trying to do that."

"But it's happened nonetheless."

"Are you trying to say that you want Shannon to get back together with her husband again?"

"That horse's behind! Absolutely not! My daughter was a fool to marry him, and now that she's finally clear of him, I have *no* wish to see them back together." Her eyes bored holes into me. "Once you leave for England and this concert of yours, what's going to happen then?"

Another question from left field, as the Yanks say. "I really don't know."

"Exactly. How do you think Shannon is going to take it if you decide to start up your musical career again? She can't go out on the road with you. She has a business to run and two children to raise."

"I haven't even said that I returned this...this affection you say your daughter has for me. Heaven knows, she hasn't said anything to *me* about it." I got up from the table again. "Anyway, you don't have to worry about any of them getting hurt. I will make sure they all understand. Now, if you'll excuse me." As I put on my jacket for the dash to the barn, I added, "Thanks for the meal."

"It was my pleasure. And let's keep this little talk between us, okay?"

Back in the barn, I couldn't concentrate worth a damn. The enjoyment of playing had completely evaporated with that "little talk".

Kevin arrived with the replacement keyboard and computer late in the afternoon. I made excuses to Robbie why I wasn't playing, and Rachel was looking at me very curiously indeed. I wondered if she had any idea of what her grandmother had said.

I did have a good excuse not to be playing, actually. The new tracks Rolly had sent were worse than I'd imagined. The parts my replacement, Drew Baines, had played were really quite bad. I picked at one of the songs without much enthusiasm. Eventually the kids left me alone. I wasn't a fun rock star that day, I guess.

Mrs. Cathcart had really stuck a fork in me. Quite frankly, I now realized how much I'd been enjoying being around so many people on a day-to-day basis. The family *had* grown on me. Obviously, I'd have to pull up stakes yet again—only this time it was not really my choice.

Shannon came out as usual to let me know when dinner was ready.

"I'm not hungry, thanks."

She walked over to where I was sitting on one of the weight

benches. "Michael, is something wrong?"

"It looks as if I may have to go to the UK sooner than I'd planned."

"Oh."

Knowing what I did then, the expression on Shannon's face was quite telling.

"I got the tracks from Rolly today, and the new tunes are worse than I expected. If we're going to do any of them, it will take a lot more rehearsal than I thought."

"So when do you leave?"

"As soon as I can get things squared away here."

"Do you want me to leave some dinner in the oven for you?"

"I'll be all right, thanks."

"Mind if I come out to talk with you later?" Before I could answer, she added, "It's business."

For the next hour or so, I made another attempt at working on the newer Neurotica material without much more success, so when she returned, I was sitting at the electric piano, playing a bunch of rambling nonsense to pass the time. She dragged a chair over and sat just outside the ring of keyboards, watching.

Finally I'd had enough. Best to get it over with. "So what do you need to tell me?"

"I spoke to the cops again today. They've looked in all the known places for those two local boys but haven't been able to come up with anything. DCI Campbell has also been in touch with them. Nothing from those fingerprints I sent to Scotland, but they've identified your friend from Birmingham from the video. He's a thug with a bad reputation and long record, name of Martin Bradley."

"Any news of the girl?"

"Nothing. My guess is she's gone to ground somewhere."

"That's just great. We've made zero progress."

"That's a bit unfair, Michael. We've—"

Just then, one of the big outside doors blew open. I had forgotten to put the padlock back on after Kevin had dropped off the synth and computer that afternoon. Shannon got up to close it, and just as she stepped outside, she gave a muffled yelp and disappeared.

I had barely squeezed out from behind the keyboards when three people I really didn't want to see unless there were a lot of cops around stepped into the room. Shannon's limp body was slung over the shoulder of the last one in, the one they said was crazy.

Martin Bradley spoke first this time. "Hello, lad. We came to have a bit of a talk."

I didn't answer, because the gun in his mitt had my complete attention.

Staring down the barrel of a gun is not the best situation in which to start being a hero, so I didn't bother putting up a fight. Even so, the bastard belted me in the stomach, and when I doubled over, he landed a good one on the side of my head.

Bending down, he hissed in my ear. "That was for all the trouble you've been causing me!"

Not able to catch my breath, and with my head ringing worse than the bells of St. Mary's, it was easy for them to drag me to the far end of the room, throw me on one of the benches and fasten my hands and legs to it with plastic cable ties. They'd come prepared.

They tossed Shannon down like a sack of potatoes and fastened her to one of the weight training machines in the same fashion. That showed me she was still alive.

Things looked pretty bleak for the good guys.

Taking a cigarette pack from his pocket, Bradley lit up, as he stood grinning down at my helplessness. After a long drag, he said, "It would have been much easier for all concerned if you'd accepted our invitation that first night, mate. And there wouldn't have been a lot of messy involvement with others."

"Let her go. She's done nothing," I said, indicating Shannon with a movement of my head.

"Bollocks! We're not as dim as all that! She's seen us. She used to be a cop. I'm sure we'd be doing a lot of people a favour if she joined you where you're going."

"If you don't let her go, I won't tell you anything."

"Oh, I doubt that very much."

And with that, he touched the glowing end of his cigarette to my forearm.

I bit my lip to keep from making any noise, but my eyes bugged out with the effort. Bradley's ugly face grinned down at me. He knew what I was feeling.

"That's just a taste, lad, just a taste. Still think you're going to hold out on us?"

I'll admit I've never been more scared in my life. No matter what I told them, it wouldn't do any good. I was going to die, and Shannon too, and there wasn't a thing to be done about it.

Shannon began to come around. There was a lot more moaning than there is in the movies, none of this waking up, realizing you're in trouble and pretending you're still out so you can attack the bad guys when their attention is elsewhere.

The blond bloke, over at one of the windows facing the house, called out, "Some old broad with two dogs is getting in a car and driving off."

Great. That meant Rachel and Robbie were in the house alone. Maybe, if we were really lucky, Bradley and his crew wouldn't check the house before they left. If I could keep *anything* from these bastards, it would be the existence of Shannon's two kids.

The crazy one picked up a glass of water sitting on a pile of weights and dumped it over Shannon's head. That brought her the rest of the way round in a hurry.

"What did you do that for?" Bradley asked.

"All that moaning was annoying me."

"Well, do us all a favour and don't do anything unless I tell you! You got that?"

I could see from his eyes that he did indeed get it, also that he was as scared of his employer as I was. That might work in my favour.

Shannon looked around dazedly as she struggled with her bonds for a moment, then sagged back, glaring at her captors while water dripped from her hair. She knew enough not to cause any trouble. I was praying she had a gun up her sleeve or something. If it were down to me to get us out of this, we were certainly going to die. I could barely move, and my shoulders were beginning to hurt from the strain put on them by my wrists being fastened to the crossbeam between the bench's legs.

Bradley pulled a chair over and sat down. "Tell me where the girl is."

"She's over there," I answered, indicating Shannon with my head.

His reaction was swift. He barely touched the cigarette to my neck, but I wasn't able to stifle a loud yelp of pain this time.

"No funny answers, mate. It's simple: do that again, and I burn you. I get a wrong answer, I burn you. Even if I get a right answer, I might burn you. Thing is, I can make this very slow and very painful. It's your choice."

"Let the woman go," I sighed. "I'll tell you everything I know."

"No can do, mate. I explained already. I could make you watch while these two lads here have a go at her. Would you like to watch that?"

Shannon looked genuinely scared now.

Bradley repeated, "Tell me how I can get hold of the girl."

"I don't know," I said hopelessly.

As the cigarette descended once again, Shannon spoke up. "Wait! He's telling the truth. We've traced her back to Montreal, but there's been no sign of her after that."

The cigarette hovered just over my forehead. "Montreal, you say? Where in Montreal?"

"Just off Rue St. Denis. She has an apartment there."

Brum put the cigarette back in his mouth, got up and walked to the opposite end of the room with the dark-haired one. A whispered conversation ensued. Breathing a sigh of relief at my temporary escape, I tilted my head back to look at Shannon as best I could. She smiled grimly.

The blond one piped up from his lookout post. "Hey, boss! There's a kid coming across from the house."

Now Shannon started to really struggle, as did I. I could face dying, I suppose, but I would not go gently if they were going to take the children too. Sensing there might be more trouble than they had anticipated, Bradley came smartly back over to us and pulled his gun from his overcoat. Sticking the end of the barrel right against Shannon's forehead, he flicked the safety off with his thumb.

"Make one move, one sound, and your kid is going to have to see mum's brains splattered all around the room. Understand?"

She squeezed her eyes shut and slowly nodded her head once.

Blondie went to the side door and stood next to it with his back against the wall. Thankfully, he didn't pull out a gun, although he may have seen no reason to, expecting no trouble from a child. The crazy one had pulled out some serious weaponry, though. The intensity in Shannon's eyes would have bored holes through the lot of them.

As the knob turned and the door began to swing open, I heard Rachel's voice, "Mom, Grams wanted me to tell you that the phone's not working again. She's going out, and she'll call the repair guys, but she won't be back until—"

That's as far as she got before she a) saw the two of us trussed up like chickens, and b) Blondie pounced on her.

I'll tell you I was ashamed of the fight that fifteen-year-old girl put up compared to my meek surrender. Mind you, they weren't about to shoot the kid as they would have me, but I don't think Rachel would have even noticed a gun. She just went berserk. That's the only way to describe it.

She'd obviously been taught a lot about self-defence, because she got several good shots in before Blondie started to take her seriously and keep his distance. Laughing at his predicament, his two compadres momentarily forgot about Shannon and me, so we both started squirming, trying to make the cable ties binding us give way or to break them by sheer force.

Blondie had wit enough to keep himself between the door and Rachel, but as she danced around him, landing good kicks and punches, she was gradually being forced to the centre of the room.

Finally Bradley had enough. Turning to the dark one, he said, "End this foolishness right now."

Shannon and I both froze as the dark one brought up his gun.

"Not that way, you idiot! Go help out Smith!"

It was all over pretty quickly after that.

They finally wrestled Rachel's squirming body to the ground, and Blondie simply sat on her. Crazy Stokowski came around by her head and stuck the barrel of his gun against it. Rachel stopped as if her batteries had been removed.

She got dragged over to the weight training machine and strung up by the arms against a high cross support. After she tried to kick them, they attached her feet to the base.

Then the real torture began. They asked Shannon and me the same questions over and over, and even though we told them the truth, they just wouldn't accept it. So, sadly I accumulated three more burns on my arms. Thank God they didn't do the same to Shannon. Rachel watched silently, not asking what was going on nor why. The expression on her face was unreadable.

Finally, they left me alone, panting and sweating from the pain inflicted by the burning cigarette.

Bradley, with a glance at his watch, apparently decided too much time was passing, so he went over to Rachel. The girl's eyes widened as he reached out to stroke her cheek.

"Nice looking girl you got here. It would be a shame if we had to get the truth out of you by hurting her, wouldn't it?" He took hold of Rachel's chin and forced her head up. "You wouldn't want to be hurt because your mum and her boyfriend have decided to be stupid, would you, girly?"

"Fuck you!" Rachel snarled and spat in his face.

Bradley was completely taken aback for a moment. Then his expression hardened and he backhanded the child across the face quite hard.

"Animals!" Shannon shouted and began squirming again. "Leave her alone. She's done nothing!"

"Then tell me what I want to know!" he shouted right back. "Where's the goddamned girl?"

"We've been telling you, you fool! We don't know!"

Now it was Shannon and me shouting and squirming, calling them every bad name in the book as the bastards gathered around the very scared fifteen-year-old.

It was at that point that a movement beyond the scene of action caught my eye. The piece of plywood covering the stairs down to the lower level raised a little bit, then dropped slowly down.

Robbie, and if God had given him any sense at all, he would be racing to the farmer next door for help.

I stopped struggling and tried to get Shannon's attention. If we could string this out before the bad guys came to their inevitable decision, there might be hope yet.

"Hey, arse!" I shouted, and Bradley turned around, knowing exactly whom I meant. His expression was not kindly. "You know you're not going to get away with this, mate? What do you plan on doing, burn down the barn? You don't think they'll pick up enough evidence to pin it on all of you? Don't you fools know the cops are looking for you right now? We had you recorded when you were in my apartment. They know who all of you are."

The attention on Rachel wavered. Yes, it would certainly earn me more pain and possibly even a bullet, but I had to do something. I had to buy us some time.

The blond one seemed a bit concerned, Stokowski couldn't have cared less, but Bradley looked puzzled as he walked over and stared down at me.

"Why did you say that, mate?"

"I'm not your bloody mate! I'm just telling you the lay of the land, so you'll realize your only course of action is to get the hell out of it and as far away as you can. Or are you too dim to see that?"

My comment earned me a hard slap to my face.

"Keep your gob shut, *mate*," he sneered.

My little speech had at least got them a bit, shall we say, conflicted. If he'd run all the way, maybe Robbie would be at the farmhouse by now. Maybe these idiots would realize their jeopardy and scarper before the cops arrived. I didn't care how they left as long as they were gone.

Glancing over at Shannon, I saw she was very slowly shaking her head, her expression fixed on the far side of the room. The plywood was again rising slowly up.

Robbie had his finger to his lips. Why the hell hadn't he gone for help? Christ! What did he think he could possibly do on his own?

Silently he emerged and let the plywood down again. The little fool was in the building, and there was nothing we could do about it.

Shannon, being quicker on the uptake than me, first started coughing then moaning. "I can't feel my hands. You've got these goddamn restraints too tight!"

"That's right," I chimed in when I realized she was making noise to cover any sound Robbie might make and also to distract our captors. "Why don't you let the girls go? I'll come along quietly, and you can do whatever you want with me. I just don't care any more."

At that point, we all started babbling. The din was enough to cover up any slight sounds a seventy-pound child would make.

Not wanting to give away anything by looking across the room, I instead looked at Rachel and her mum. That would seem natural at least. By the way their heads were moving, it seemed Robbie must have been climbing into the hayloft.

Suddenly, there was a loud creak, and all the noise we were making couldn't cover up the loose board Robbie had trod on.

"Shut up or I'll shoot the lot of you!" Bradley shouted, pointing his gun at Shannon.

"No, you won't, mister," came the squeak of Robbie's very scared voice. "Leave my mom and sister alone!"

All three of our captors looked wildly around for the source of the voice. When I saw that they'd obviously found it, I dared to look up.

Robbie's tiny head and shoulders were right near the front of the hayloft next to a stack of bales. Lying on his stomach, he held a handgun out in front of him. In his small hands, the automatic looked huge, but he seemed to be holding it correctly.

Blondie had a nasty-looking knife in his hand, while the other two now had their guns trained upwards.

"All right," Bradley said. "You've got the drop on us, sonny. We'll leave. You can come down now."

"No! Drop your weapons and step back from them."

"Or what?" Stokowski sneered. "You'll shoot us? This ain't some video game, kid."

With that, he raised his gun even higher, and the unthinkable happened: a shot, deafening even in the large space, rang out.

"No!" Shannon and Rachel screamed in unison.

But I saw smoke around Robbie. He'd fired.

Straining my neck, I looked back at Stokowski. He was standing there with a puzzled expression on his face. In the middle of his chest, a red flower was growing, spreading outward through the fabric of his shirt. Then he simply pitched forward onto his face.

Snapped out of his shock by the shooting of his stooge at the hands of a ten-year-old, Bradley began moving towards Robbie's mother and sister.

"Stop, mister, or I'll shoot you too!" The deadly, grown-up words came out incongruously in Robbie's squeaky voice.

Bradley ignored the warning, intent on getting to his bargaining chips. Two more shots rang out in rapid succession and the big man spun around, his gun flying out of his hand towards me. He landed on his side with a groan, but because of the angle, I couldn't see where he'd been hit.

That left only Blondie, and he was sidling for the big doors. Robbie noticed also, and I could see him swivelling a bit to follow, but not saying anything. All at once, Blondie bolted for the door, opened it in one fluid motion and disappeared into the night.

Robbie finally stood up, a solitary little form who had just saved three lives, but had taken at least one. His face drained of colour and breathing hard, he looked to be on the verge of collapse.

Shannon had seen the deepening shock as well. "Robbie! I need you to come down here right now. Go slowly. There's no rush. Put the safety back on and stick the gun carefully in the back of your pants, then use the ladder. Can you do that?"

His mum sounded completely calm, the professional cop taking over in a bad situation. Her son nodded once and did as she said.

It seemed to take him a lifetime to get down, and all the while I kept my eyes mostly on Bradley, to make sure he didn't make a move for either of the two free guns in the room. The rise and fall of his rib cage showed he was still alive, but there was an ominous gurgling in his breathing.

Robbie walked slowly across the floor, his face a mask of terror. Edging his way around the two thugs, he finally got to his mother. I became aware of Rachel sobbing quietly, her body pressed back against the training machine to which she was bound.

"Robbie," Shannon said softly, "I want you to get the clippers on the nail over by the door and bring them here. You'll be able to cut through these plastic bands easily. Hurry now—but not so fast you'll trip. You've done a great job so far. Can you do that for me?"

"Yes, Mommy."

"Good boy! I'll give you the biggest hug ever as soon as my hands are free."

Robbie had his mother free less than a minute later. Before she did anything else, Robbie did get the biggest hug ever. As Shannon took the clippers from him, I could see tears streaming down her face.

Shannon kicked Brum's pistol under my bench then turned to her daughter. Rachel seemed far more at sea than any of us, so her mum helped her sit before coming over to me.

"You all right?" she asked softly as she knelt to cut my bonds.

"I'll survive. Just focus on your kids."

"I plan to," she answered with a grim smile.

CHAPTER 20

The hounds of the media were baying at the gates within a half hour of the police arriving. As the local reporters began digging into everything they could find about me, the rest of the story began tumbling out. Angus's murder in Scotland got tied in before morning, and the press on both sides of the Atlantic were in full cry as they closed in.

That was the least of my concerns at the moment, however. The life of Shannon O'Brien's family had begun to implode.

Robbie had been more clever than we'd first assumed. Before sneaking back out to the barn to save us, the little devil had called the coppers from the cell phone Shannon had installed in her SUV.

Earlier, he and Rachel had fought over who should go out to the barn to tell their mum about the phones being down. When Rachel had finally stomped over, Robbie had followed behind anyway to make sure his sister didn't get him in trouble. Hanging back and wearing a dark jacket, he had not been visible to Blondie.

From downstairs in the animal enclosure, Robbie had heard everything. His ten-year-old mind told him that since his father had shown him from an early age how to handle and fire a gun, he would just sneak up on the bad guys and get the drop on them. With the *sang froid* the young often seem blessed with, he'd done just that. The end result was one man dead and another severely wounded, but Robbie had without a doubt saved three lives.

After the ambulance left, the police set up a command post in the O'Brien kitchen. We'd all been herded over to the safety and warmth of the house and had been sitting around the big table. Mrs. Cathcart, recently returned, had taken the whole thing in stride and was busy making coffee and hot chocolate. The expression in her frequent glances at me made it clear *her* shit would hit my fan later.

Shannon sat with Robbie on her lap and Rachel cuddled next to her. All three were in a pretty bad emotional state. Every time the back door opened and someone came in, they would cling even more fiercely. The kids had seen plenty of death and destruction on TV, but now they'd experienced it up close and personal, without all the blood and noise and horror sanitized away. I could not imagine what sorts of emotional scars the evening would leave on them.

It could have been much, much worse, though. We were all relatively unscathed. Except for a bandage over a small cut on the back of her head, Shannon appeared to be in pretty good shape, no concussion. The ambulance people had dressed my burns when I'd refused to go to hospital, but clearly felt I was a fool, since none were less than second degree, and a few had spots of charring. I was subjected to the further indignity of having them photographed "for the record".

A burly cop, with a head of grey hair and reasonably friendly manner, had arrived early and taken charge. He also knew the family, which made everything easier.

"You certainly know how to handle a firearm, young man," he said to Robbie.

"My dad showed me all about it before he...before he left."

"And how did you get the gun tonight, Robbie?"

"Oh, that was easy," the boy answered rather proudly. "It's my mom's. She keeps it in a special storage box on the top shelf in her closet. I figured out the combo!"

Shannon stiffened, making it clear she had no idea her son knew any of this. The cop cast her a sidelong glance.

"And how did you do that?"

"Easy! The combo is her birthday!"

As the cop wrote something in his notebook, Shannon looked across to where I stood leaning against a counter. The expression on her face screamed her guilt.

Both children were dealt with pretty quickly and hustled off to bed. Robbie, true to form, asked if he'd be able to stay home from school the following day.

"We'll see," his mom replied, using the standard parental answer since the dawn of time.

There was a brief family hug before Grams ushered them out.

"There's going to be hell to pay for this, Shan," the old cop said with a sigh, "and there's not a lot I can do to shield you. Have you called their father yet?"

Shannon squeezed her eyes shut. "No, Burt. Guess I better get the inevitable over with. Do you mind if I do it in another room?"

He waved her out then fixed me with a steely gaze. "Come over here and sit down, please."

I did, and he began firing questions at me. Even though he took notes, a tape recorder backed up everything I told him.

Partway through, Shannon, looking pretty grim, slipped back into the room.

"He's catching the first plane in the morning," she reported.

"That will be good for you and the kids," Burt answered.

Her expression made it clear this was far from the case. She again left the room, since Burt wanted us to make separate statements.

Neither of us got to bed until well after five a.m. You'd have thought we were the guilty ones the way they questioned us.

III

I kept to my room the next morning, figuring it was best if I stayed away from the family in whose midst I'd thrown such a spanner. Out front, I could see about two dozen cars and broadcast trucks lining the road outside the farm. A police car blocked the long drive, keeping the media away. From the clock radio by the bed, I already knew we were the top story. I pulled the shade down again and dropped onto the bed with a sigh. Trapped for the moment.

Around eleven, there was a soft tap on my door: Shannon with a steaming mug of tea.

"Oh, you're already up and dressed," she said, handing it to me.

Her hair was wet and her skin freshly scrubbed, but the circles under her eyes were deep and large.

"I never really fell asleep."

"Why didn't you come downstairs?"

"Not a good idea. I've caused enough problems here."

"Nonsense! Are you hungry?"

"Well..."

"Then come and have some breakfast. Mom's making pancakes and sausages for everyone."

"I'd rather not."

"Fine!" she said angrily with her hand on the doorknob. "Have it your way."

She slammed the door but returned a little later with a tray of food. "Eat this. And you were right about coming downstairs. You should have seen my mother's expression when I told her this food was for you."

Just after two, I became aware of raised voices in the living room. Shannon's was one, but the other I didn't recognize. The Ex must have arrived.

The argument went on for over twenty minutes, before three more voices joined in, and things calmed down a bit. It took all my self-control not to eavesdrop from the top of the stairs. The only raised voice now was Shannon's, and it was obvious she was very upset.

Shortly after, I was using the bathroom when I saw the children exit the house with two men and a woman. Robbie, crying and struggling, was being held by the larger of the two men, and the woman had Rachel by the hand. They got into a minivan with a lot of backwards glances and started down the driveway, preceeded and followed by police cars. At the end of the drive, the front two cars sped off south, while the rear police car blocked the road, preventing the press from giving chase.

I went downstairs and found Shannon and her mum clinging to each other, both crying their hearts out. Pulling back out of the kitchen doorway without being seen, I returned to my room.

An hour or so later, Shannon tapped lightly on the door again. I was at the window, staring out at the cars (their numbers just kept increasing), wondering how I was ever going to get away from there. I cannot express the depth of my depression.

"My children are gone," she said simply, then sat down on the bed as if her legs had been kicked out from under her.

"What happened?"

Shannon stayed silent for a good two minutes. "My ex-husband, that's what! You no doubt heard us arguing in the living room. He's livid that I'd put *his* children in such danger, and that I'd been so careless with my gun. At the same time, he was boasting how it was his training Robbie how to shoot that saved everyone's lives. His sanctimonious attitude makes me want to retch. He hardly even bothers to call the kids any more.

"To hear him talk, everything is my fault! Problem for me is, he got the right people to agree with him, and now he's been awarded temporary custody. He came here with Children's Aid in tow. Couldn't be bothered to discuss this with me first. Just, 'Here's the order. Tell the kids to get their things. They're coming with me.' *Bastard!*"

I started to speak, to apologize yet again, but Shannon shook her head. "I know damn well what you're going to say. This was *not* your fault. *I* invited you here, and if anyone is to blame, it's me. I just figured they wouldn't be able to find you out here."

"I've spent a good part of the day thinking about just that," I answered, "and I've only been able to come up with one solution, one I don't like very much."

She wiped her eyes with her hands and swivelled to face me. "Tell me, Michael. I need to know."

"Do you think it's coincidence they showed up last night? Yesterday afternoon I had something delivered by my employee of longest standing, and—"

"Michael! You really don't think *Kevin* told them where you were?"

"Can you think of any other way they found out? You've told me that you took every precaution coming and going from here, and I trust your ability to suss out a tail. I haven't been off the property, and heaven knows I've been careful when I spoke to anyone on my cell. So that leaves only one answer."

Shannon's face grew hard. "He's going to suffer."

"Yes."

III

Since it was a pretty well an open and shut case, the cops were out of there by late afternoon. Before he'd finally gone off duty, Burt had arranged for some of his men to stay on the property to keep the curious and the media away. I finally came downstairs to watch the evening news. The events at Shannon's farmhouse got the full treatment. Burt had held a news conference sometime during the day at the end of the driveway. Apparently someone had blabbed, so everyone knew a child had shot a man to protect his mother and sister. The media wanted answers, and the cops decided to give them enough to satisfy them.

One reporter, however, had done more digging, and consequently Burt had to field questions about me and the murder investigation in Scotland.

"Michael Quinn, the musician, was involved in what happened here last night. We've also been in contact with the Scottish Police, yes," he'd admitted, "but whether there is any connection to our case, I really can't say at this time."

"Can't say, or won't say?" a reporter asked.

Burt had smiled grimly. "Boys, make up the answer. You do that nine times out of ten anyway. No more questions."

With that he turned and started back up the drive. The camera followed him for the longest time, while the newsreader talked about me and what was known about my current troubles.

"Well, this just gets better and better," I observed glumly.

Mrs. Cathcart was standing in the doorway to the kitchen. Our eyes locked, but hers looked at me in a more kindly way than I'd seen. "I've made beef stew for dinner. I think we all could use something in our bellies."

It was a good meal, and for a while we *almost* forgot our troubles. Mrs. Cathcart produced a bottle of very acceptable claret. Apple cobbler finished off the meal.

Shannon disappeared into the basement and came up with a dusty bottle of cognac, which she put on the table. The label said 1965. I raised my eyebrows in Shannon's direction.

"Tonight is the night for this," she said sourly.

"What's the significance?"

Her mother answered. "It was the last anniversary present Shannon's damned husband gave her. 1965 was the year she was born." She smiled at her daughter. "I thought you'd forgotten about it."

Shannon was getting out three snifters. "Not forgotten. I just haven't had the heart to open it up before."

Before we could pour it, though, the phone rang. Mrs. Cathcart answered with a scowl, but that quickly changed to a broad smile. "Of course I will, child! Your fish are going to be so fat and sassy when you get home that you won't recognize them. Yes, she is. I'll put her on."

Shannon took the phone eagerly and immediately left the room.

"This is going to be very hard on her," Mrs. Cathcart observed.

"I know, and I want you to know that I blame—"

"Blame no one but Robert O'Brien! This isn't about keeping two children safe; this is about hurting my daughter."

"How can I make this better? I'll do anything."

She looked at me levelly. "Leave as soon as you can. Give my daughter a chance to put her life back together."

Said daughter came back into the room with fire in her eyes. She had the cognac bottle open in short order, poured three generous portions and downed hers in two gulps. No savouring of the subtle tastes and fragrances. That bottle had to be worth several hundred dollars.

"He's got them back in New York already! I didn't think he'd be able to get them out of the country so fast."

"Shannon! Simmer down!" her mother said. "You're doing yourself no good. Tomorrow, you contact that lawyer who handled your divorce, and she'll tell you what you need to do."

Her hot-headed daughter wasn't having any of it, though. She poured more cognac into her snifter, then stomped out of the room. We listened to her rapid ascent of the stairs.

Mum picked up her cognac, swirled the liquid, then put it down. "She's always been pigheaded..."

|||

My aggression comes out when I'm behind the wheel. Not that I drive like a churl, giving everyone who gets in my way a one-fingered salute. I just drive fast. And I have a string of tickets over the years to prove it.

Shannon, who had told me she was too distracted to drive, sat next to me, arms tightly crossed, her mood not improved from the previous evening. "You don't need to set any speed records getting us there, you know."

I shrugged but kept driving the way I wanted to. Shannon's SUV had a lot of pep, and we made it to the shop in damn good time.

"I want to get this over with," I said as we got out of the car.

Kevin and Hamed (now off movie duty) were in the cramped entry room, morning coffee in their hands. Loud sounds from the warehouse showed that Johnny was out there checking an amp.

"Hey, boss," Hamed exclaimed, a broad smile splitting his face, "didn't think we'd see you out here today. Man, that was some crazy scary thing to have happen!" He stood and shook my hand. "We're all glad you're okay."

"All of you?" I asked, staring hard at Kevin, who went quite pale.

Shannon was actually pushing at me, eager to get at the punk who'd put her kids in such horrible danger. I stayed firmly in her way.

"Hamed, would you go and get us some decent coffees? Get a box of Timbits, too," I said as I peeled off a twenty. "Take Johnny with you. All right?"

"Sure, boss," he replied, looking puzzled. "Anything you say."

As soon as they were out the door, I turned to Kevin. "I certainly hope they gave you a lot of money for what you did."

"What are you talking about?"

"Two days ago, you told someone where they could find me."

"Are you kidding? Why the hell would I do something like that?"

"That's just what I've been asking myself." I shook my head sadly. "You almost got us killed."

"And my two kids!" Shannon snarled over my shoulder.

The idiot actually tried to bluster his way out of it. "I don't have to take this shit! You're both crazy if you think I had anything to do with that British jerk and his two bastard friends!"

The look on his face when he realized what he'd just admitted was comical in a very sad way. None of the news reports had come close to mentioning anything like that.

Kevin drew himself up. "I'm leaving, and you can't do anything to stop me. I know my rights!"

Shannon had heard enough. She pasted him with a hard left jab to the side of his head, then a right hook to the jaw. Kevin fell back, knocking his chair over, out cold.

We looked down at him in disgust. "You have the right to remain silent," she said with a grim laugh as she picked up the phone to dial the police.

While waiting for the arrival of the coppers, she shook out both hands. "That was a dumb thing to do. Contrary to what you see in the movies, your hands really take a beating in a fight. Mine are going to look and feel like hell in a few hours.

"I guess you shouldn't have hit him, then."

"You're probably right." Then she grinned for the first time in two days. "But it felt *damned* good!"

III

When we finally headed back to the farm early in the evening, Shannon had lost whatever bounce she'd got from decking Kevin. The news from her lawyer had not been good. Getting the court order overturned would take time, and because of what had happened, any judge hearing the case would take a very dim view of Shannon's suitability as a parent. Of course, that was ridiculous, but at the moment her husband held all the cards.

The cops had been more than happy to hear what my *former* employee had to say. They wouldn't tell Shannon much, but she did find out that I'd been sold out for the obligatory thirty pieces of silver. Kevin claimed they'd told him they only wanted to scare me a little so I'd cough up some money I owed them. He had been the person I'd always left in charge when I was gone, and I felt horribly betrayed.

I'd spent the rest of the day trying to organize everything as best I could during my absence in the UK. I'd have to rely on only two employees, and business was certainly going to suffer. Once Hamed and Johnny got over their shock at Kevin's arrest as an accessory, they began to fill me in on the way he used to complain about me, cut out early and loan instruments to his friends at no charge. I felt a bit of a fool, because I'd never cottoned on to any of it.

"He was certainly upset when you gave Hamed that movie shoot," Johnny said.

"They asked for Hamed specifically!"

Both had also claimed they'd be ready to handle anything. I had my doubts, but hiring someone new as I was about to leave the country did not seem like a wise idea. I put Hamed in charge, wrote out a long list of instructions and gave them both healthy raises in recognition of the tough slog ahead.

"I spoke to Burt late this morning," Shannon said as we waded through the usual rush hour tie-up around the airport. She still didn't want to drive. "They caught up with Blondie trying to hitch a ride into town after crossing two concession roads, and he's going to cut a deal with the crown. Your DCI Campbell is sending someone over to question Martin Bradley."

"When will that happen?"

"No one can talk to the suspect at the moment. The man's doctor says his patient is not in any condition to be questioned. The local cops are pretty frustrated about that. The interesting thing is that someone was quick to pay for first class legal help. He's got the best sleazeball lawyer in town."

"Interesting. Does anyone have any idea who's paying?"

"Lawyers don't admit that sort of thing."

Traffic ground to a halt again, and I looked over at my passenger. "How are *you* doing?"

Shannon shook her head. "I'm still trying to get past blaming myself."

"Me too."

"The worst thing is that Rob has uprooted those kids at the wrong time. They're going to get put in a new school in a new country, and they're both pretty damaged right now. Their dad says he's going to get them counselling, but I wonder if he'll follow through. It's obvious he's very proud of his son for doing what he did."

"Your helping me has turned into such a nightmare for your family. I am so sorry for it."

I don't think she even heard me.

"I miss the kids—even the fighting," she sighed, then turned away, a clear sign that a few more tears were being quietly shed.

About ten minutes later, Shannon's cell rang. She didn't say much other than "uh-ha" and "yes," then finished with, "Yeah, well, thanks for letting me know." Flipping her cell closed, she sat looking at it for a few seconds before speaking. "Someone got to Blondie in the slammer. He's dead. Knife in the back. No witnesses, and I doubt if they'll find any. Well, that was fast work."

The penny dropped. "That means there's someone else around, someone out to clean up this mess."

"Yup. And we're right back where we started."

At that point, we were finally passing the airport. One of the really big planes thundered off into the night overhead.

"So when do you leave for the UK?" Shannon asked neutrally.

"Soon as I can. You don't need me underfoot right now, and I think the farther I am away from here, the better it will be for all involved."

"Care for some company?"

I was momentarily nonplussed. "What do you mean?"

"Michael..." she started, then stopped. "Michael, if there's still someone around that could cause trouble, then I can't bring my children home, even if I can convince a judge to let me. The only way to get my life back to normal, *both* our lives back to normal, is to find that damned girl. And in that regard, the only lead we have right now is in Birmingham. *That's* where she jumped into your car. Why was she really there? She told you she was staying in a B&B. Do you believe it?"

"Well...no."

"Exactly! Birmingham is the only place where I might pick up her trail."

"Don't you think Campbell has already tried to do that?"

"He told me they'd had no luck, but I really wonder how hard they tried. I might do better. Do you have any other suggestions? No?" Shannon tightly folded her arms over her chest. "Then, in that case, I'm going to the UK with you."

Neurotica announces concert dates in Glasgow
Could a full-blown tour be in the offing next?

Rock "legends", **Neurotica** an enigmatic band (to say the least) from the late 70s/early 80s has decided to strut their stuff once again in a Glasgow hockey arena in a few short weeks.

Does the world really need yet another Rock Dinosaur ambling out into the light to see if there's money to be made from nostalgia?

This time, though, it's somewhat of a good cause since it's a charity concert to honour the memory of legendary road manager, **Angus MacDougall**, found murdered a few weeks ago in his Argyll home by persons unknown.

According to front man, **Rolly Simpson**, this "reunion" concert will feature the band's original line-up, including reclusive keyboardist **Michael Quicksilver**, Neurotica's resident genius who has not performed with the band (or any other forum) since his sudden departure in the middle of a 1982 U.S. tour.

But who cares about music from a quarter-century ago? Simpson, guitarist **John Bowen**, bassist **Lee Grainger** and drummer **Tommy Higgins** have toured since as Neurotica a few times, but always to mediocre reviews and worse record sales. Other than their first two admittedly brilliant albums, the band's music has never been first tier.

They do seem to have their fans, though, who snapped up tickets for the first of 4 announced concerts in a record 10 minutes. Mind you, the venue chosen for the gig only holds 5500. Tickets for a further 3 shows have already come and gone, and our big question is whether Neurotica will feel "obliged" to carry on.

Cynical? Yes, but we've seen this happen far too often in the past when there's a few bob to be made.

Michael Quicksilver: interesting in the past

THE DATES

Braehead Arena
Kings Inch Road, Glasgow
February 10, 11, 13, 14
Support by Julia and the Govans

CHAPTER 21

Just what the hell do you expect to accomplish from all this? Shannon asked herself for about the hundredth time.

As the plane bumped along the taxi way, she watched a huge airplane lift off into the night and wondered if anyone on that flight was as conflicted about their trip as she.

This was to be her first time out of North America, and it felt like a very big step. Her previous travels had been confined to the States and one holiday in Cuba with Rob two years earlier.

Now, with almost no preparation or planning, she was jetting off to the UK, with only a goal in mind and possibly no way to attain it: find the girl who'd started this series of woeful events and bring her to justice. Never in any case she'd handled was the detective as personally involved. This was now about *her* family, *her* kids, and she wasn't playing a game of one-upmanship like her damned husband, either.

When she had called New York that afternoon to announce she'd be gone for a while, Rob had sounded suspicious and made a snide remark about "running off with your rock star boyfriend," and how this was further evidence she'd "taken leave of her senses." If Shannon hadn't been so desperate to speak with her children, she would have slammed the phone down on him.

Robbie hadn't said much other than that his dad had been taking him to "a bunch of really cool places," and that he was feeling pretty good. She had felt reassured, since Robbie had sounded his usual chipper self. Maybe he *would* miraculously come out of this without any lasting scars.

Then again, what might the boy go through in the lonely hours of the night, when tortured things were free to slither out from the dark corners of a young mind? Would his dad notice there were problems?

Rachel, on the other hand, had not sounded good.

"Are you sleeping okay, honey?" Shannon had asked.

"Yeah, I guess so."

"When are you starting at your new school?"

"Dad says tomorrow."

"What do you think of Manhattan so far?"

There was no answer for a moment, then Rachel blurted out, "Mom, why does dad have to be such an asshole?"

"Hush! That is no way to talk about your—"

"He knows how I feel. I just got finished telling him!"

"Well, that's not a good way to talk," Shannon answered, even though she felt exactly the same about him. "Your dad thinks he's doing the right thing."

"When can we come home? I *hate* it here!"

Shannon saw no reason not to be truthful with her fifteen-year-old. "My lawyer is setting up a court date, and hopefully you'll be able to come home after that."

"But when will that be?"

"As soon as possible, honey. Grams and I both miss you a lot." She did not want to start crying, further upsetting her daughter, so she changed topics. "I'm going to be away for a few days."

"Where are you going? To England?"

"Yes. I'm going over there to search for the person who started all this trouble."

"Is Michael going, too?"

Shannon hesitated, wondering if Rachel had overheard her dad's "rock star" comment. "Um, yes, we're flying over together, but he'll be rehearsing in Glasgow, and I'm heading south to Birmingham."

"Are you going to sleep with him?"

It took Shannon several seconds to find her voice. "*Rachel!* We've been through this before. You know that is *way* out of line!"

"Don't you want to, Mom? He's a pretty cool guy."

"Rachel," Shannon answered, struggling to keep her voice calm, "you don't take a large step like that just because you think someone is 'cool'. Haven't I taught you *anything?*"

"Relax, Mom. I'm not saying *I'm* going to do it—but I think you should."

Shannon felt completely out of her depth. Sure, she had spoken to her daughter about the birds and bees several times over the years. She'd even bought her a book in case the girl felt uncomfortable talking about those sorts of things. Now here was Rachel counselling her mother to hop into bed with someone! It would not be easy for Shannon to wrap her brain around this turn of events.

"We shouldn't even be talking about this."

"But don't you like Michael?"

"He's a nice person."

"Well, Mom, it's time you moved on. You're too good for Daddy."

Tears welled up again at her daughter's words. Shannon suddenly felt as if she'd been waiting for someone to tell her this. That it was her fifteen-year-old daughter, with whom she hadn't been getting along very well lately, made the remark doubly welcome—and awkward.

"Rachel, honey, I..."

"Mom, I just want you to be happy. Before, I was angry with you for making Daddy leave. I wanted us to be a family again, so I was mean and unfair to you. I'm so sorry about that."

"There's nothing to apologize for. We've all been under a lot of stress."

"I can see now that what Daddy did was awful for you, that he was being an ass—"

"Please don't use that word again. He *is* your father."

"It doesn't change things, and we both know that," Rachel laughed. "Just do your best to get Robbie and me out of here. I am *never* going to be a New Yorker! *Never!*"

"I'm working on it, Rachel, I'm working on it."

"Good! Now go to England and find the person you're after. If anyone can do it, it's my mom."

"I really appreciate your confidence in me. It means a lot."

Rachel giggled again. "And sleep with Michael if you want to."

"You're too much!" Shannon laughed.

"I love you, Mom."

"Oh honey, I love you so much I feel like I'm going to burst!"

"Good night, Mom. Have fun in England."

Shannon had held the phone to her ear until the dial tone came back on, her mind in a complete uproar. Draping a coat over her shoulders, she had gone outside and stood on the back porch looking out over the fields until the cold couldn't be ignored any longer.

Their plane was now in position on the runway, the pitch of the engines rising as it started rolling forward. Shannon said a silent prayer, not for the flight, but for the leap of faith she was making. Not a good flier at the best of times, she reached out and gripped Michael's hand without realizing it.

The plane rose very fast and first circled south, swinging over Lake Ontario, then east. Far below, the lights of Toronto's downtown glowed with almost painful clarity in the winter night as the pilot steered a course for Glasgow, three thousand miles and another life away.

Nine and a half hours later, Shannon, accompanied by Michael, walked into DCI Campbell's office at Divisional Headquarters in Dumbarton, west of Glasgow. Their flight had arrived at eight thirty a.m., and since they couldn't check into their hotel until noon at the earliest, Shannon had made a call to see if the Scottish detective could see them right away.

It was mainly a courtesy call, one investigator to another, something cops always did when they came on to another's turf— especially if they wanted cooperation. Shannon also felt she needed to establish her credentials as a competent investigator.

Campbell rose as they entered his office. Tall, neat and very proper in his manner, he did and didn't look like what Shannon had expected. First of all, due to his accent, she'd pictured him wearing a kilt, as silly as that sounded. Next, even though he was over six feet, she'd pictured him heavier, since he had a "heavy" kind of voice. He had on a heather-coloured tweed suit, accompanied by an immaculate white shirt and silk tie. Rumpled Columbo he certainly wasn't.

Giving the room a once over, Shannon was amazed at how exceptionally tidy it was, quite unlike the office of most other cops she knew. It made her want to begin surreptitiously moving things.

After gravely shaking hands, Campbell immediately picked up a rather impressive fountain pen. While he did use it occasionally to take notes, most of the time he fidgeted with it in the most annoying fashion. Before five minutes had passed, Shannon had to restrain herself from reaching over the desk to take it out of his hands.

The interview started with Shannon bringing the Scottish policeman up to date on things at the Canadian end, and he seemed sincerely grateful for that. He hadn't yet been told, for instance, that the blond henchman had met with a fatal accident.

"This is an unfortunate turn, lassie," he said. "I've just sent one of my detective sergeants over to your country, mainly to have a wee chat with this man. Last I heard, he was going to cooperate."

"I'm sure they have their hands full with this investigation," Shannon answered, sticking up for the home side. "They'll certainly get in touch with you as soon as they can."

"And what exactly do *you* hope to accomplish while over here?"

Shannon laid her cards on the table. With the assistance of her notes, she told Campbell everything she knew, guessed or imagined about the mysterious girl. After a while, Campbell picked up his phone, asking for someone to come in to record the discussion. Other than that interruption, Campbell let Shannon give her report uninterrupted, a mark of respect, she hoped.

"The thing that really puzzles me," she said towards the end, "is why the girl told Michael all that garbage about her supposed father. When I spoke to those hoods in New York, their information about Mastrocolle matched a lot of what she'd said. Why would she have done that? It certainly puts her head more firmly in the noose. She could have made up any number of harmless stories about why those thugs were after her. That makes me suspect there may be more truth in some of the other things she said, as well."

Campbell sat nodding, the fountain pen held endwise between his two index fingers. "An interesting theory, to be sure, but I don't see how finding her would help me solve my murder case. She may have set things in motion, but she was three thousand miles away when the murder happened."

"Are you actually looking for her?" Shannon asked.

"To be sure, lassie, to be sure, but we operate in a different manner over here. We don't hold much with conjecture, no matter how interesting. Our investigation is proceeding down other avenues at the moment."

The Scot got to his feet and stood looking down at her, a standard police tactic to "gain the upper ground." At that point, Shannon would have had to stand on a chair to get the upper ground, and Campbell knew it. Her anger rose.

She looked steadfastly down at her notes, pretending not to notice him looming over her. "Have you looked for the place where she told Michael she was staying in Birmingham?"

"Yes, and it took a lot of hours and energy to come up with absolutely nothing. It's our feeling she lied about that."

"And you've got no further information about her?"

"We've shared that photo of her you so kindly sent us with every law enforcement agency in Europe, with no luck. She's probably gone to ground someplace in North America, and you don't need me to tell you what that means. Finding her is going to be no easy task, especially since, from what you've told me, she sounds like a very resourceful young lady. So, while she's still of interest to our investigation, we've moved on to other areas which we hope will be fruitful." He nodded to the notetaker, who got up silently and left the office. "Why don't we keep in touch? If you come up with anything, you'll pass it along, won't you?"

On the way back downtown to the hotel, Shannon sat on her side of the taxi, arms crossed and severe disapproval on her face.

"Boy, I've been shut down by some smooth ones before, but Campbell takes the cake! Tell me, Michael, is he always that insufferable? About the only thing he didn't do was pat me on the head and tell me to go home!"

"I wonder if he cares whether he solves the case or not," Michael said as the cabby skillfully threaded the vehicle through the traffic flowing toward Glasgow's core, windshield wipers going a mile a minute under a driving rain.

"Oh, he cares. That kind of investigator always does, but he will also proceed as *he* thinks fit. Campbell has already formulated his theories, and he'll follow them until he has no more blind alleys to go down. *Then* he might consider what I told him, but by then the trail will be even colder. If I strike paydirt on my little trip south, I'm going to make certain he has to eat his words!"

By the time they were ready to check in at their hotel, Michael had actually come up with a very good plan. He would check in at the Hilton, where the rest of Neurotica would be staying when they hit town. However, he wouldn't be sleeping there. Where he would actually be was in the much smaller, out-of-the-way boutique hotel where Shannon was currently looking across the counter at a very tall young lady with extravagantly red hair.

"And you are checking in for yourself and your husband?" she asked.

"Yes. He has a business appointment and will be arriving later this afternoon. I'm absolutely beat after the flight and want to get some rest."

"To be sure," the desk clerk smiled.

Shannon was on edge, mostly as a result of her conversation with Rachel the day before.

Michael's idea was to book this room under the name of Mr. and Mrs. O'Brien. With Michael Quicksilver booked into the Hilton, any bad guy wanting a piece of him would naturally try there.

The sticking point, and it was a *very* big one, was that they would have to share a room, unless they were to book a *third* room so that propriety would be served.

"I doubt that I will be sleeping much," Michael had said back in Toronto, "so you can have the bed all to yourself. This damned insomnia, you know. I've brought a few books to read, and all my business materials are on my laptop, and you know how much time I need to put into them. I imagine I'll be very busy."

Up in the room, she quickly stripped and went into the bathroom for a long, steamy shower to soak the kinks from her body and cobwebs from her brain. Even though she'd dozed a bit on the plane, she had missed a night's sleep, and it was beginning to have an effect.

Putting on a robe, she closed the drapes and lay down on the bed, thinking, *I'll just shut my eyes for a few minutes then get dressed.*

An hour later, Michael's knock on the door woke her out of a deep sleep. For a moment she had no idea where she was, and the knocking made her very apprehensive.

"Who is it?" she called out.

"Michael. How about opening the door to a poor dusty traveller?"

She hurried across the room to open the door. Michael's eyes flicked downward for a moment, and Shannon realized with embarrassment that her robe was open at the top a little more than was appropriate.

Pulling it shut, she let him pass into the room.

"Nice digs," he said, looking around. Noticing the state of the bed, he added, "Sorry I had to wake you."

"I was just dozing anyway. You said I should go until I drop."

"Only way to deal with jet lag." He flopped down on the bed, hands behind his head. "I'm all checked in at the Hilton, and I also stopped off to make sure the equipment was at the rehearsal space we've arranged for."

"When is the rest of the band showing up?"

"Rolly and Lee are already here, but I avoided them at the Hilton. John and Tommy arrive tomorrow." Michael looked at his watch. "It's nearly two. Fancy something to eat?"

"The way they fed us on the plane? I may want dinner, but nothing until then."

"How about we eat here in the hotel? I'm told they have a very swish rooftop restaurant. Quite the view of Glasgow. Would you agree to be my guest? It's the very least I can do."

That sounded good to her. While Michael sat at the desk making the booking, she wandered around the room a bit. The bed was quite large. Some sort of drawn up curtain do-dad behind it made the room seem grand enough for the Queen herself. She had never stayed in such a luxurious place. Michael acted as if it were the norm for him. Perhaps it was, considering his background.

|||

They clinked glasses for the second time.

"My feeling is that every bottle of wine should be greeted with a toast," Michael said with a grin. "What shall we toast to this time?"

"Hmmm," Shannon answered. "We can't toast to that unfortunate girl who brought us together. To be honest, I wish I'd never heard of her."

"How about to Scotland the Brave and your first trip to Old Blighty tomorrow?"

"Old Blighty?"

"Native terminology, covers the whole country. You're actually going to Brum, though, as the locals call it, and the Black Hill country. I hope you can understand their speech. They can be quite unintelligible."

Shannon took a sip of wine. "Initiate me then."

During the remainder of the meal, Michael gave her a crash course on Brummy slang. He was really quite funny, and his good mood rubbed off. For the first time in days, no thoughts of her problems cast a shadow on Shannon's mood.

"I have no idea what you just said," she laughed.

"I asked you if you wanted to go to the off-license and pick up some beer."

"It sure didn't sound like that! I guess you have to be born there to understand the accent and local terms."

"The terms I certainly know, but even I have trouble with the accent sometimes. I haven't lived there for a lot of years, after all."

"That's a lot of water under the bridge."

"Yes, it is." He pushed his chair back. "Shall we go?"

They stood on opposite sides of the elevator on the ride down to their room.

He cleans up quite well, Shannon thought, studying Michael's reflection in the polished metal of the door. Noticing he was doing the same, she blessed her foresight in packing a nice dress, even though at the time she couldn't imagine any circumstance in which she might need to wear it.

As Michael shut the door to their room, he said, "You must be really knackered."

Shannon walked over to the window, flicked the curtain aside and looked down at the street glistening with reflected light. "I'm tired but not sleepy yet. How about you?"

After loosening his tie, Michael joined her at the window. "At this point, I'm just pleasantly relaxed."

"Two bottles of wine will do that to you." She pointed through the window to a large square off to the left. "Do you know what that is?"

Michael leaned closer as he looked where Shannon was pointing. "As a matter of fact I do. Neurotica played an outdoor festival there just after our first album came out. 'Don't Push Me' almost caused a riot. It was a great gig. We felt like real rock stars that day."

"You don't sound particularly happy about it."

"I can see now that was the beginning of the end. The rock star lifestyle is what killed Neurotica, as it has so many other groups."

Standing close enough to smell his aftershave, it seemed natural for Shannon to turn her head and kiss Michael's cheek. He stood there for the space of one deep breath, then moved her chin with his hand and kissed her on the lips.

At first, she didn't know whether to respond. Her kiss had been more of a thank you, an acknowledgement of their friendship. Michael's was much more.

He was a terrific kisser, slow and deliberate, soft and gentle. She felt as if all Michael's attention was going into what he was doing, unlike Rob, who always seemed to kiss as if it was the quickest way to getting a girl naked.

They stood there for quite a while, sharing the closeness, savouring the moment.

When things eventually moved to the bed, she carefully took off Michael's shirt. "I'm worried that your burns will hurt."

"I'm willing to put up with that," he answered softly as he turned her to unzip her dress.

He again took his time, allowing her to set the pace of their lovemaking, guiding him to what she liked best. At the end, lying in his arms as he lightly scratched her back, her felt no regrets.

"If I were a cat, I'd be purring."

He covered her with the duvet. "You should try to get some sleep. Your flight is at eleven, so we'll need to be at the airport no later than ten."

"Oh, all right," she sighed, "but be warned: I may need to wake you up during the night."

He chuckled. "I'll try to be ready."

Shannon did wake up in the night, but not remotely for the reason she had teased Michael about.

She was sure he had twitched violently. Not having pulled the heavy inner curtains shut, there was enough light in the room for her to see his eyeballs moving rapidly under his closed lids. Michael was breathing fast, and he was sweating.

Must be another of those dreams he has, she thought.

She debated waking him but didn't want to come across like a meddling mommy.

He began mumbling in an agitated way, and she leaned close to hear if he was actually speaking coherently. At first, she couldn't make out much of anything, but then he began speaking quite clearly.

"She can't be... What are we going to do?... That's absolutely daft, Angus... What if we're caught? Rolly's the one... He should do the right thing... No! I don't want to touch her."

CHAPTER 22

I'd had the dream again, the full-blown version for the first time in several days. That I could deal with. That I'd had it when I wasn't alone in bed was the problem—especially considering that the other person in the bed was an ex-cop of high moral fibre. Lying there for several minutes as I calmed my racing heart, I couldn't tell whether Shannon was asleep or not. Since I had to hit the loo, I tried getting out of bed without disturbing her.

"Michael," she said, making it clear she hadn't been asleep, "you were you having a bad dream again, weren't you?"

"Sorry if I disturbed you. Go back to sleep."

She was staring at me as I entered the washroom.

Once inside, I turned on the light and took a long look at myself in the mirror. Gingerly lifting off a few of the bandages, I saw that the cigarette burns were beginning to heal, although the doctor I'd been to see thought one on my arm might need a skin graft. Despite the previous night's pleasures, I had been in considerable discomfort at times, but I'd managed to hide it reasonably well.

I sighed heavily at the memory. Now I'd landed myself right in the middle of another big problem. What had possessed me to let myself go last night?

An appealing woman, that's what. I'd been denying to myself for days how attracted I was to my private detective, and seeing her framed in the light of the window, I just hadn't been able to resist when she turned to kiss me. Yes, I had quite enjoyed it, but no, it hadn't been very wise. I could have said that she'd started it, but that wouldn't cut it, nor was it quite true.

Was Shannon viewing it as something that just happened, or had it meant much more to her? Knowing women, and particularly her, I suspected the latter.

"Quinn," I told my reflection, "you're an arse."

Turning off the light, I went back out to the bedroom, not sure what to do.

"Michael, are you all right?" Shannon asked immediately.

"I'm fine, really. Go back to sleep."

She switched on the light. "You can't sleep because of that dream you had. Right?"

"Something like that."

"Why don't you tell me about it? That often helps."

I looked down at her. Even with sleep-tousled hair, she looked lovely. I squeezed my eyes shut in an attempt to force that thought from my head.

Her gaze was steady and direct, a challenge as it were. "It had something to do with Neurotica, didn't it?"

She *knew*, and I was instantly appalled. I must have talked in my sleep. It had happened once before, shortly after my split from Neurotica, when I'd carelessly gotten rather drunk in a *taverna* on Crete and wound up in bed with a French divorcée out for a fling. When she'd told me the next morning what I'd said, I'd immediately split, taking the first plane I could get and winding up in Seattle before I'd stopped to catch my breath. For months, I'd lived in fear that somehow the press would get hold of her story.

Now it had happened again, and this time it would be far more difficult to run away from.

"I don't remember."

Shannon's expression made it clear she knew I was lying.

It was a pretty weary pair that arrived at Glasgow airport for the second time in a little over twenty-four hours. Shannon had dozed a bit on the cab ride out, but I think that was more to avoid speaking to me. It hadn't been hard to read her body language. My refusal to tell her anything had left her pretty upset. My own mood was as black as it's ever been.

Shannon's flight to Birmingham would be mercifully short, but at the other end she'd decided to hire a car, and I wasn't of the opinion that one's first experience with left-hand driving should be in the UK's second largest city.

"You won't reconsider and either hire a driver or use taxis?" I asked for the second time that morning. "I'll pay for it."

She shook her head once, a determined look on her face. "No. I can handle driving on the left."

Her frostiness didn't thaw until we got to the security check-in.

"Michael, take care of yourself. Assume that someone is looking for you. Don't let your guard down for an instant."

I'd expected her to say something like that, but the intensity behind her words surprised me.

"I promise to be very careful. The next three days will be spent between the hotel room and the rehearsal space I've booked. I plan on taking my meals in my room." I pulled her into a hug, which she didn't return at first. "You take care of yourself, too. There are plenty of places in Birmingham that aren't all that safe, especially at night. Don't be a hero."

She pushed me gently to arm's length. "We have to talk when I get back, okay?"

"I hope we'll talk before then," I answered, purposely avoiding her implication. "Please call tonight."

Shannon picked up her shoulder bag and walked towards the security gate. "If I get the chance," she said over her shoulder.

The remainder of the day was the best of times and the worst of times. Knowing everything that lay between my mates and me, should I have expected anything different?

We'd hired a space in King Street, just off Trongate, and the area was decidedly seedy, but that was part of the attraction for me: who would be expecting Neurotica to rehearse there?

The crew delivering the instruments from storage had been asked to take everything out of the flight cases, so I had a pretty good start on my keyboard rig by the time the others began showing up.

Tommy had driven up from Yorkshire that morning and had brought his son, a nice looking lad of seventeen, who seemed perfectly happy to help his dad set up the old drum kit. I found out why shortly after. Said son was well on his way to being a terrific drummer.

"Jazz is his first love, though," Tommy said in mock horror. "Where did I go wrong?"

John arrived next with about five guitars and a flightcase full of pedals and effects. He got ready with his usual efficiency, and for once, without his amp turned up to "nuclear meltdown". He even deigned to help me move around some of the heavier keyboards.

By the time we'd set up the vocal monitoring system and were ready to go, Rolly and Lee sauntered in, coffees in hand for just themselves. It was to be expected, sadly. With a disgusted look, Tommy sent his lad out for hot drinks and "something sweet" for the rest of us.

The only fly in the ointment was the mellotron. It had been delayed. The previous evening, I'd rung up the lads at Rugely Electronics to see what the status was. They were loaning me one of their own MkIs (a very large gesture on their part, considering the value of these rare machines), but I needed to have a duplicate set of my tapes installed in it. This was a large favour to ask, and hence the hold-up.

As usual, Larry answered the phone. "'Ello, 'ello, 'ello," he said using a ridiculous Dick Van Dyke Cockney accent, something of which he was inordinately proud. "What's all this then?"

"Larry, mate," I said, "what's the ETA on that mellotron? I really do need it."

"Got it done last night, we did."

"But when will it arrive?"

"Don't get your knickers in a twist. Nigel's decided to drive it up himself. Left early this morning. That arse just loves Scotland. Every chance he gets, he and his old lady are up there tramping the hills and moors. Can't see what they find so bloody fascinating about it, but there you are. I had to talk him out of wearing his kilt."

"You're kidding!"

"Just 'aving you on a bit, mate, but I do think you should take him out for a nice bit of haggis, neeps and tatties tonight before he heads back, sort of as a goodwill gesture."

"I can't thank you blokes enough for this."

"Yes, you can. Make sure we get tickets for this ridiculous concert of yours. I wouldn't want to miss seeing a bunch of old geezers like you ponce around the stage. And mind you take care of that machine!

Even *one* mark on it, and I'll have your guts for garters."

We'd just got tuned and were ready to go when Nigel arrived. The tron was in a flight case and was even more godawful heavy than my Hammond organ, so naturally it took several of us to drag the thing into the lift then to the rehearsal room, every Neuroticand bitching long and loud about me and my "bloody antique keyboards."

They shut their mouths pretty quickly once Nigel fired the behemoth up and pronounced it healthy. After I'd run through all thirty-six sounds that had been loaded, all Tommy could do was whistle softly and say, "Bloody hell! I didn't know they could sound like that."

"Better recordings," Nigel said simply.

Only Lee continued to gripe, and he hadn't carried a thing.

Nigel headed off to look for a restaurant serving genuine Scottish food before turning for Birmingham and home. Larry hadn't been kidding about the haggis.

Rolly got out his signature gold-plated microphone, and we were finally ready to begin. Everyone just looked at each other, then at me.

"What do you want to work on first?" I asked. "The big hit?"

By the time we got to the fourth run-through, "Don't Push Me" sounded as good as ever. I wished that Shannon were present to hear it.

Seven hours later, we were all toast. We'd run through about half the proposed playlist, and I'd broached the possibility of revisiting some of the arrangements and possibly doing a new song or two if there was time to rehearse them properly. Rolly and Lee perked up their ears at that, thinking that there might be a new album in the offing. I just didn't want to do the same old thing.

Since I wasn't quite ready to present my ideas to the rest of the guys yet, I decided to practise awhile longer, which also gave me a good excuse to avoid going out to dinner with them.

John, oddly, decided to stick around with me.

"So, what did you think?" he asked nonchalantly as he looked over the mellotron's control panel.

"Interesting. A lot of the old crap hasn't changed with the passing of years."

John laughed. "I should have put down a fiver that Rolly and Lee would walk in last."

I grinned back. "You wouldn't have had any takers."

"So let's hear some of your ideas."

Taking out my notes to be sure I had all the synths set correctly and the basic levels were right, I ran through my idea for the concert's opening, basically doing an overture of Neurotica's better known tunes. John took his guitar out and began coming up with his own ideas to flesh out what I'd come up with.

This turned out to be the best part of the day for the two of us, and we quite forgot our fatigue as we happily worked for another couple of hours.

"You've not lost anything being away from it for all these years," John observed as he wiped down his guitars.

I nodded, acknowledging his compliment. "And you always were the best player in the band."

"I may be now," he answered simply, "but that's only because I was forced to properly learn my craft when I started doing studio work. That, my friend, is a cut-throat business. Every week there's some new hotshot arriving in town, and you somehow have to stay one step ahead, or they'll flat-out trample you." John sat on a chair and looked at me while I continued making notes on keyboard settings. "Rolly tells me you're against making a CD and DVD of the concerts."

I had realized this would come up again, but I figured it would be Rolly doing it. "Did he put you up to this? Is that why you stayed behind tonight?"

"Don't give me any agro, mate!" John shot back, a bit of his old self resurfacing. "I stayed behind because I wanted to hear what you were up to, but I also thought it might be a good time to discuss this." He sighed and flashed a weary smile. "Look, Michael, I'm not asking for myself. I've done okay over the years. You and Rolly, too, since you wrote all our good material, but Lee and Tommy haven't. The money from those recordings would mean a lot to them."

"I suppose that's why Lee was acting the twit today."

"Partially. You have to realize that you also intimidate the hell out of him. Anyway, neither of them get much in the way of royalties from our recordings. Tommy had to beg his boss for the time off to do this gig. The man's been reduced to being a plumber, for Christ's sake!"

"Let me think about it."

"Don't think too long. This will take a few days to set up." He started to put on his coat. "You up for some grub?"

"No, I want to go over a few things. You go on ahead."

"Okay, Quicksilver. Do your late night thing. I'm not going to stop you. You always came up with your best ideas when no one was around."

I only stayed another fifteen minutes. Basically, I was avoiding having to go back to the hotel with anyone. There was no need yet for them to know what was going on.

Business taken care of for the day, I turned off the lights and carefully locked up. The old building felt rather empty, no noise except for the clank of the heating system. The floor we were on used to house a group of artists and craftsmen who had moved on to better digs. The area was all old factories and workshops in grimy brick buildings. The press would not come looking for us here unless someone blabbed.

When I left the building well after eight on a bitter winter evening, the streets were as dark and deserted as the buildings. What shops still existed were long since closed and shuttered. Two blocks above in Trongate, I could see traffic, automotive as well as pedestrian, but down here, I felt rather vulnerable.

"You better arrange for a taxi to pick you up next time, Quinn, or leave with the others," I said as I pulled up my jacket collar against the cold and damp and headed north for Trongate. Immediately, two blokes came out of a darkened doorway on the other side of the road. When I began walking faster, they seemed to pick up speed. Approaching the first corner, they started crossing to my side.

I was faced with running, hoping they didn't have somebody waiting ahead to ambush me, and looking a bit of a fool if it was just two people on their way home from work. I increased my speed.

"Oi! You there!" one of them said in a thick Glaswegian accent, but I didn't slacken my pace. "Hey, mate! Hold up!"

Ahead of me, someone big came out of another building. Christ! Now I was in for it.

I stopped, not sure what to do. Looking up and down the road, there was no one else around, no one I could call to for help. My cell phone wouldn't do any good. By the time the coppers showed up, I'd have been hauled off to who-knows-where, and it would be goodbye

Michael. Damn and blast! How could I have been so bloody stupid?

The two men were rapidly closing the gap between us. Stepping through the light of a street lamp, they suddenly became tall, skinny youths, maybe eighteen or nineteen with long, unkempt hair and pimply faces. They may have been up to no good, but vicious thugs they were not. Glancing quickly up the road, I could see the burly form up there helping what looked to be his old mum into the car. My pulse began to ratchet down.

"Sorry if we startled you, mate," one of them said. "Just wanted to know if you had a light."

I felt in my coat pocket and found a book of matches. "Here. Keep 'em," I said and began walking again.

Once in Trongate, I got a cab quite quickly, and all the way back to the hotel, I chided myself for the jumpy state of my nerves. It had been a wake-up call, though, and I would be a fool not to heed the warning.

III

Shannon faced yet another airplane seat back.

I loathe flying, she thought.

It was all part of her current stop-the-carousel-I-want-to-get-off mental state which had only been exacerbated by what she'd done the previous evening.

That in itself had been rather nice. As a matter of fact, it had been rather nice, far better than she'd had any right to expect. Basking in the afterglow of their lovemaking, she'd felt calm, very relaxed and at peace. Her key concern was that Michael had lied to her. Regardless of whether they remained just friends or became something more, she could never accept anything less than complete truthfulness, not after what had happened with Rob.

The whole thing went round and round in her tired brain all through the flight south, until she felt ready to scream. Why did life always have to be so goddamned complicated?

As the pilot informed his passengers of their imminent arrival in Birmingham, Shannon tried to force her thoughts into more profitable channels.

It never made good tactical sense to get personally involved in any investigation, but something about this case made it seem inevitable. she had never believed in fate—until now.

It seemed reasonable to seek a breakthrough in the same place where the whole affair had started. Find where that girl had been running from when she jumped into Michael's car, and she'd have the key to finding the girl, the Chameleon, as Shannon had taken to calling her.

If the British police hadn't been able to trace her, why should she, a total outsider, expect to have more success?

"Fate. That's why," Shannon said as she stood waiting to get off the plane, and only realized it had been out loud when several people turned to look at her.

I'll have to watch that, she told herself as the line started moving.

|||

The drive into Birmingham's downtown had been a harrowing experience. Michael had been so right, there was no way she should have tried it by herself. The signs fairly whizzed past before she had a chance to read them and digest their meaning. Having to divide her attention away from the main task at hand (avoiding hitting anyone while she figured out how to drive on the wrong side of a car), she had soon been hopelessly off course. Several times over the next hour, she'd gotten back on and off the web of expressways that wound through the city, growing more frustrated by her lack of success.

It was nearly three when she finally made it off the A38 near the hotel Michael had booked for her. His directions proved accurate, when she had a chance to look at the map, but even if she were to try it again from the beginning, she felt sure she wouldn't be able to get there in one go.

The Macdonald Burlington Hotel proved to be a good choice, near the Ring Road and not too far from the big red "X" Michael had placed on her map of Birmingham.

Even though she felt like sleeping for a week, Shannon forced herself to make a start. With the help of the hotel staff, she planned a straightforward route that would take her to the beginning of her search: City Hospital on Dudley Road, where Michael had been stopped at a light when the girl had jumped into his car and turned a lot of people's lives upside down.

As she got into the car, Shannon crossed herself and wished she had a St. Christopher medal. Her route would take her through several roundabouts, and the ones she'd navigated so far were all black memories.

Perhaps the patron saint of travellers had blessed her, because she actually made it to the hospital parking lot with only one small misstep on the Sand Pits Parade roundabout.

Standing on the sidewalk near the light where Michael's life had taken such a dramatic turn, she looked around.

The Chameleon had come running up from behind, out of Aberdeen Street. Having been through the listings of all the bed and breakfasts in this part of the city, Shannon felt sure that this part of the girl's story had been bogus. It just didn't fit.

Walking down Aberdeen Street didn't provide anything startling, so she walked up and down Dudley Road a few times, clearing her mind and hoping for enlightenment. She found a bench and sat down.

The hoods in New York hadn't been able to tell her anything about how the drugs were shipped, but she presumed it had been by plane, since they'd said it had been quick. That left out ships. For that reason, she'd immediately thought of London as the point of departure.

But what if it had been Birmingham?

That would explain why the girl had been in the city, but why had she been here, in this place? Shannon looked up at the hospital. Could the girl have been in there? If so, why? She hadn't been sick or injured. No, if she'd been in the hospital, the Chameleon must have been visiting someone.

Walking to the entrance to begin her inquiries, she felt oddly confident. Maybe it would be the hospital, the outside possibility being the nearby prison, but she had a good feeling about her chances of discovering something useful.

Presumably, the police had already covered this angle, but Shannon had something in her purse that they hadn't possessed at the time: a photo of the girl.

It could make all the difference.

CHAPTER 23

Picking up the phone, I sat down wearily on the edge of the bed. If this were Shannon, I had no idea how the call would go, considering her mood when we'd parted at the airport.

"Hello?" I said neutrally.

"Great, Michael, you're there." Shannon sounded almost breathless, her excitement obvious.

"Had a successful day?"

"You could say that," she laughed.

"Don't tell me you've found Regina."

"No, but I think I've found the beginning of the story."

"Meaning?"

"I know where she came from. And we've got yet *another* name for her, and I believe it's her real one: Giovanna, last name Vennuti. And believe it or not, she's a Brum, as you call them, born and bred."

"You can't be serious."

"Uh-huh. And I've spent a profitable hour talking to her cousin. I also know what she was doing in Birmingham the day she jumped into your car."

I whistled. "You *have* had a successful day."

"Do you have time to talk now?"

Moving a couple of pillows, I leaned back against the headboard. "I have all night."

Shannon had been very lucky with her hunch, and we both knew it. The difference, of course, between her success and that of the police was the security photo from the hotel elevator in Toronto. When the police had called round at the City Hospital, they hadn't received it yet, and from what he'd told us the day before, Campbell hadn't sent them back after Shannon had provided it to him.

"I don't think they were as thorough as they could have been, either," she told me. "I spoke to the head nurse in the Accident and

Emergency Department, and she'd been on duty at the time the girl jumped into your car. The police had already talked to her about it, and she was quite sure the girl had not been in A and E at any time. The police seem to have dropped it at that point."

"That's pretty sloppy," I said.

"It is, but to be truthful, I don't think their hearts were in it. You have to remember, when they were asked to do the search, Campbell hadn't even seen fit to send one of his own people down, and I can tell you from personal experience, when that sort of thing happens, the effort put in just isn't the same. You've told me you got the feeling Campbell was after you at the time. Small wonder he didn't have the proper interest in finding the girl."

Since City Hospital was a large place, and Shannon couldn't throw her weight around like a police representative could, it had taken her two hours to visit the various hospital departments, showing Regina/Giovanna's photo to any staff member willing to look at it.

Her doggedness had finally paid off in one of the large general wards. The person identifying the girl had been a male nurse, which made sense. Shannon had already mentioned to me she didn't think the girl was all that beautiful. Yes, she was not what would be termed "a ten", but she exuded something powerful which perhaps only males responded to.

"I remember her well," the nurse had said to Shannon. "Visited only once and stayed for several hours with a dying relative, I believe." The man looked off into the distance for a long moment, then added, "Yes, I'm sure that was it."

"Do you remember the patient's name?"

"No, but I can find out for you."

Shannon had been left standing in the corridor for several minutes watching the bustle of a busy hospital: the comings and goings of nurses, shuffling patients and anxious visitors. When the nurse had finally returned, Shannon had experienced enough of the smell of antiseptic and ill patients, most of them elderly.

"Fanny's on today. Bit of luck that," the nurse told her.

"I take it she's the person on this floor who remembers everything," Shannon replied with a relieved smile.

"Got it in one. You're good."

He had begun eyeing her with something a little more than professional interest.

She decided to put a stop to that right away. "I was a cop for over ten years before I went into private practice. Once learned, the skills stay with you." She'd taken out her cop-issue notebook to reinforce her words. "Now, what you were able to find out for me?"

"Fanny says the girl came to see Mamma Vennuti. That's what everyone called her, see? She was this little old Italian lady, very proper, like the kind you see in movies, dressed all in black. Lived in Britain over fifty years but could barely speak English. Stayed with her own kind the whole time. But everybody on the floor liked the old bird.

"Anyway, she'd been in and out of hospital several times the past year, only now it seemed her time was up. Didn't have a lot of family left. Just one daughter and a few younger ones came to see her. So this particular day, it's after visiting hours, and this piece of fluff comes in and she wants to see her grandmother."

"And this was the person whose photo I showed you?"

The nurse had nodded. "Yeah. Fanny doesn't usually cut people a lot of slack, but she did this time. You see, the girl had only just found out her grandmother was dying and rushed here to see her. The girl was weeping and wailing to beat the band, she was. Real broke up. It wasn't until well after midnight that she left. Said she'd be back the next day, but it wouldn't have done much good anyway. The old lady died before morning."

"You said the girl had rushed here to see her grandmother. Do you know where she came from? Maybe the States or Canada?"

"From Germany," the nurse had said with surprise. "This girl you're looking for is German. Leastwise, she had the accent. Kind of strange..."

▌▌▌

I whistled again when Shannon told me that. "You're right when you call Regina, Giovanna, whatever her name is, the Chameleon. Is there any language this girl doesn't speak?"

Shannon clucked her tongue. "There is certainly a lot more to your little chickie than it first appeared. She is something special."

"You sound grudgingly impressed."

"I am."

With a little eyelash-batting, Shannon had convinced Mr. Nurse to provide her with the name of the late Mamma Vennuti's daughter, though she'd cut him off cold when he asked if she wanted to get together later that evening.

Shannon left the hospital at shop-closing time and found a phone booth. One call had led her right to the family. The woman's daughter had just arrived home from work when Shannon knocked on the door. At first, she was reluctant to talk, but Shannon had exuded all her charm and skill and eventually got in the door. Once tapped, the story flowed right out.

"The cousin, Maria Rota, is the same age as Gia—that's what the family calls her," Shannon told me. "The girls were brought up together because—and get this—Gia's mother committed suicide when the girl was eleven. That's another truth buried among the lies she told you."

"Creepy..."

"Both Gia and Maria had been born late in their mothers' lives. Gia's mum had never married, which, as you can imagine, the parents weren't happy about, but she had a 'career', meaning she worked. Her pregnancy was a major family scandal. It had happened on a vacation to the old country, and the mother never revealed anything about who the father was. I saw a photo of her, and there's an amazing resemblance—except for the eyes."

▌▌▌

Shannon gazed at the photograph Maria had handed her.

"The photo was taken when my aunt first got to Italy on her hols that year," Maria had told her. "She met a man who was also on holidays. That's all we know."

When Shannon laid the photo down on the coffee table, her copy of the security photo of the Chameleon was right next to it, and the similarity between mother and daughter was quite striking. Shannon felt Rosa, the mother, had been prettier, but couldn't say why until she concentrated on the eyes. Gia's had a remote quality to them, as if her mind were on something else, something far away. The mother's were clear and open, and she looked very happy. That was soon to change.

Two weeks after she'd come home, she knew the worst. Her family, understandably, had taken it badly. When the pregnancy had moved into its later stages, they'd packed Rosa off to Italy for her confinement.

"I didn't think anyone used words like that any more," Shannon told me, "but Maria was very matter of fact about it."

The mum had stayed in Italy for a year, then had come home. The family had hoped the father would find out and do the right thing.

"They don't even know if she tried to contact him," Shannon said. "She was a teacher, and even though it was hard, she brought her daughter up as best she could. Mamma Vennuti babysat during the day, and when Gia got older, she spent a lot of time at her cousin's house."

Eventually, the attitude of the family had gotten to her, and during the summer of Gia's eleventh year, the mum had taken her back to Italy to find the father and speak to him about his daughter.

Shannon sighed. "I guess the meeting didn't go well, because the next day, Rosa dropped Gia with a second cousin, said she was going shopping and jumped off a bridge."

The family had brought the little girl back, and Mamma Vennuti had taken charge. Maria and Gia had grown up like sisters. They looked quite a lot alike, although Maria was plainer and probably less shrewd, too, according to what Shannon had observed. From an early age, Gia was apparently precocious with languages and accents. Naturally, with the girls speaking English at school and Italian in the home, they were bilingual, but Gia could flawlessly imitate any of the British accents she heard on the telly. In school, she'd quickly mastered French, then German, Spanish, any language she tried her hand at.

"There's jealousy in Maria towards her cousin," Shannon said.

"How so?" I asked.

"Gia must have completely overshadowed her. She was clever, funny and quite a good actress. Everyone in the family thought she'd do well on the stage, or maybe even the movies. Maria's a nice enough young lady, but like I said, she's pretty ordinary: mousey hair, glasses, clothes that don't do a thing for her, but there's a strong family resemblance. I could see how people would think they were sisters. All through the interview, it kept going through my mind, though: why she was telling me all this? I let Maria know right off the bat that I was an investigator from Canada. I got the feeling she was trying to get her cousin in trouble."

"Sounds logical."

"Maybe. Mamma Vennuti, because of what had happened to her daughter, kept a very tight rein on her granddaughter. Gia and Maria were both sent for a good Catholic education, but Gia wasn't allowed to do anything outside of school, unless it involved the church and there was adequate supervision. She wasn't allowed to work when she got old enough. And as for boys, that was a total non-starter. Mamma V. took her to Mass every day, twice on Sundays, and often talked about Gia taking her vows as soon as she became old enough. I guess the idea being she might atone for the sins of her mother."

Gia had soon begun to chafe under her Gran's constant control. She'd started sneaking out at night. Maria went along sometimes too, and covered up for her cousin on numerous occasions.

It was mostly harmless fun: meeting with kids their own age, going to the cinema, occasionally out dancing as the girls got older. There were no drugs and little drinking—at first. As the girls got away with more, Gia began taking chances, and Maria had got cold feet.

"I think that's where the split occurred," Shannon said. "As you can imagine, eventually the grandmother got wind of what was going on, and I got the distinct impression Maria ratted Gia out."

There was a god almighty row, the priest was brought in, the uncles and aunts too, and Gia had stood up to them all. She wanted to live her life her own way. Hard words were said on both sides, and it was then Gia found out her mother had committed suicide. That fact had been kept from her all those years.

"Wow!" I said.

"She shut down immediately," she continued. "Maria told me everyone figured the strong words had finally gotten through. But about a month later, Gia packed a bag and just disappeared in the middle of the night."

"She didn't tell anyone what she was up to?"

"You mean like Maria?" Shannon asked. "Maria says no, but I'm not so sure. I think there must have been contact. How else would Gia have known that Mamma Vennuti was so sick? It seems likely two cousins who were as close as sisters might stay in touch."

"When did all this happen?"

"Gia left when she was just eighteen, and she's twenty-five now."

"A lot can happen in seven years."

"And with her, I'm sure it did."

"So that's it?"

"I think that's a pretty good day's work, don't you?" Shannon laughed. "I'm certain I didn't get everything I could from Maria. She got spooked when her mother came home. I know she works for the family business, a bakery in Broad Street."

"Since when do Canadians say 'in Broad Street'?" I interrupted.

"Since I got over here and cottoned on to how you Brits talk," she shot back. "Anyway, I thought I'd go round to surprise her at lunchtime tomorrow. See what else I can shake loose. I'd also like a go at the mother." She paused for a moment. "How was your day?"

Shannon might have actually wanted to hear what had happened at that first Neurotica rehearsal, but I didn't really think that was what she was asking.

"What happened between us last night has been on my mind a lot," I said.

"Mine too."

"Shannon, I..."

"What?"

"I'm sorry I upset you this morning. I didn't mean to."

"You clammed up on me the way you always do."

"So why did it make you so upset today?"

"Sorry to be blunt, Michael, but are you really that dense?"

"I don't expect you to understand, Shannon, but—"

"But what?" she interrupted. "Was I just another girl in your bed, Michael? Is that it?"

"No, that's not it at all!"

"What am I to you, then?"

That's precisely the question that had been taking up a good part of my thoughts all that evening. It had been so long since I'd let anyone get within more than an arm's length that I wasn't sure if I knew how to do it any more. Right now I had the chance to bring this whole thing to a screeching halt. I felt confident Shannon wouldn't go home, tail between her legs, that I could properly explain things to her. She'd come to the UK to do a job, and it wasn't for me any longer. This was now about her family. I had no illusions about that. But I suddenly could not decide which way I wanted our relationship to go.

"Shannon, you hardly know anything about me, I mean...personally, you know?" Boy, that was a great start.

She wasn't about to make this easy for me. "And I'm supposed to get to know you better when I ask you a perfectly simple question, and you just blow me off?"

"There are things about me I've never told anyone."

"And maybe that's why you've been living your life like a damn hermit! How many friends do you have, Michael? When was the last time someone invited you to their place for dinner?"

The woman was relentless, and I could see what made her an effective investigator—but she was beginning to piss me off.

"Okay! You've made your point. Maybe I don't live the most exciting life in the world. But I'm supposed to tell you all about me? That shoe can also be worn on the other foot! You've never told me why your marriage fell apart."

"You never asked!"

"And if I had, would you have told me?"

"I..." Shannon sighed. "I suppose not. I would have felt it was none of your business."

"That's why I didn't ask. It *was* none of my business."

"Is it now?"

Shannon sounded unsure, almost vulnerable, and I hadn't seen that in her before. Even when her ex had driven off with her kids, she had cried, yes, but it had been out of anger and despair and frustration. This reaction was very different.

"How did your marriage end?" I asked.

CHAPTER 24

Shannon lay on her hotel bed in underwear and socks, one knee up and the other leg crossed over it, yakking on the phone, just as she had done countless times through high school and college. Many, many times the conversations had been about the man who was now at the other end of the line, and to her the experience seemed incredibly surreal. She was actually living out her teenage fantasy.

The subject matter of the present conversation added to that feeling of unreality: the death of her marriage. She was reluctant to talk about it with Michael, but she'd backed herself into a corner.

"If it wasn't so pathetic, it might be funny," Shannon said after taking a deep breath. "Anyway, O'Brien Investigates used to do a lot of marital stuff. I didn't really enjoy it. Something felt, you know, sort of sleazy. Rob was all for it because it paid well and was generally easy. If someone knew we had gotten the goods on their spouse, they'd always pay well and promptly because they wanted that evidence.

"About eighteen months ago, this guy comes into the office late one Thursday, very agitated, as they usually are. He was convinced his wife was having an affair. I'd heard the same story far too often: a sudden, unexpected trip, New York in this instance. He wanted me to find out if she had anyone with her.

"I had a couple of things on the go, but agreed to handle it. Truth be told, I had ulterior motives. You see, my husband was in New York on an embezzlement case, so I decided that it might be really good for us to mix a little pleasure with business. We'd both been working our butts off, and some R&R would be just the thing. I was planning to surprise him.

"When I got to his hotel, he was out, which was not unexpected, so I left a message and went off to do a little work on my own case. The suspected wife was at the Plaza up near Columbus Circle. I went there, did a bit of snooping, got her room number and sat in the lobby waiting to see if she came or went and with whom. I'd snap a few photos and get on to finding out who her guy was. After a few boring hours of waiting, nothing.

"So I decided to scope out her room, see who I might flush out, since I was in a hurry to get the job completed and have the rest of the weekend free.

"Rob had come up with a really clever dodge: call the room, pretending to be the front desk, and tell the person that a visitor had arrived and was on their way up. If any hanky-panky was going on, you'd almost invariably flush out the other party."

Her laugh was harsh and bitter. "It worked like a charm, except the person I flushed was my goddamned, peckerhead husband. You should have seen his face when he saw me waiting at the elevator."

"That's horrible," Michael said. "What a way to find out something like that."

"It's no worse than coming home and catching them in the act, I suppose. That happened to a friend of mine, and she almost killed her husband—literally. I just looked Rob up and down, pointed out that his shirt was buttoned wrong and told him to take the next elevator. First plane back to Toronto, I was on it. And there you have the whole sorry story," she sighed. "It only took a little more legwork to discover two other flings he'd had over the years. Those were the final nails in the coffin. One we might have gotten through, but three, no way!"

Shannon realized as the silence on the line deepened that it felt oddly good telling the story this way: emotionally detached. She'd never been able to manage it before.

"Are you still there, Michael?" she asked after several seconds.

"Yes. I really appreciate what you've just told me," he finally said, "but what you want to hear from me in return is impossibly difficult to tell."

"Michael, I'm uneasy about this, too." She was going to say more but stopped to think for a moment. "Perhaps it's not wise to talk about it now, I mean over the phone."

"When will you be back?"

"Maybe tomorrow evening. Who knows? It depends what I find out from the cousin tomorrow noon."

"We'll talk as soon as you get back."

While the phone call ended without the little words of endearment that might be expected from newly-minted lovers, neither did it end with Michael kissing Shannon off. The whole experience filled her with an uneasy ambivalence.

Had he understood the importance to her of sharing things on equal terms? Or had his question about her return to Glasgow been asked in an effort to buy time?

If what she'd heard from Michael when he'd talked in his sleep had been the recounting of a real event, then this man was hiding a very bad thing indeed.

Looking at her watch, Shannon decided that her kids should be home from school by now. As she dialed she reflected that her life felt as if she had suddenly been put on roller skates at the top of a very steep hill, then been pushed. Perhaps speaking to the two most important people in her life would make her feel more grounded.

Perhaps not.

▮▮▮

Next morning, after a very poor sleep, Shannon ventured down to the hotel's health club to kill a couple of hours before going after Maria for more information. It had been too many days since she'd gotten any sort of decent exercise. Everything about her felt flabby and out of shape—including her brain.

Wearing a pair of baggy shorts and top with her hair done up in a ponytail, Shannon knew she didn't look her best, but despite that, two younger men took an interest in her, providing a boost to her ego. Michael Quinn wasn't the only game in town.

Maria came out of the bakery on Broad Street shortly after noon, completely unsuspecting and fortunately alone. Shannon was on her in a flash, coming up from behind and startling Maria when she put a hand on girl's shoulder.

"I'd like to buy you lunch," Shannon said in a cheery voice.

Maria turned white. "What are you doing here?" she finally managed to choke out.

"I told you I might need more information, and it turns out that I do. It was easy to find your family's business, since I doubt there are too many places called Rota's Bakery in this city."

"Clever you," the girl said sourly.

Shannon hooked her arm in Maria's and started down the street, making it impossible for her to balk without creating a scene. "Now, where's a good place to talk and have lunch? My treat!"

Maria chose a fancy place with an extensive menu and outrageous prices. Shannon got the feeling her choice was a bit of payback.

"So what do you want to know now?" Maria said after ordering lobster thermidor and a glass of the most expensive wine on the menu.

Michael's going to kill me for this, Shannon thought, then said out loud, "We got interrupted by your mother coming home last night, just as we were getting to the interesting part."

"What's that?"

"You know where Gia is right now, don't you?"

"I never!"

"Come on, Maria. I'm not that dumb. How could Gia have found out your grandmother was so ill? By your own admission, you were the only one in your family who'd ever been close to her, other than your grandmother, and she'd severed those ties."

"Okay. I did know where she was at the time, but I don't know where she is now."

"I'll lay my cards on the table than, shall I? There are some very nasty men after your cousin, and if they catch her, she's going to die. You can take that to the bank. Don't you want to help her?"

"I told you I don't know where she is!"

Shannon looked across the table intently. "I think you do."

ˆWhen the food arrived, Maria seemed to have lost her appetite— except for the wine, which she drank down in two gulps. Another was ordered.

Shannon decided to turn up the heat a bit more. "These same people have gotten it in their heads that a friend of mine also knows where Gia is, which he doesn't, and they've played very rough with him, me and my two children. You got that, missy? Two kids! If you know anything more about Gia, you better tell me, and you better do it now!"

As she picked up her fresh wine glass, Maria's hand was trembling, the detective saw to her satisfaction.

She put her hand over Maria's other one in a friendly gesture. "Come on, Maria, do the right thing. I know you want to help. This is for your cousin, too. She's in a tight corner, and I can help her."

A tear ran down Maria's cheek, followed by another, then more. Soon she had her face covered by her napkin, sobbing quietly.

Giving the girl a little more time, Shannon got busy on her salad. Maria eventually returned the napkin to her lap and sat looking off into the distance. Shannon hoped she'd come to the right decision, but if all else failed, she'd play the "Don't force me to go to the cops" card.

Finally, the girl cleared her throat. "All right, I do know where my cousin is, but I want you to know that I promised on that soul of my father that I wouldn't tell anyone. When Gia ran off, she went to London to try her hand at acting. That led to New York and Hollywood, but nothing much ever came of it. She was in a couple of plays, got two bit parts in movies and even did a voiceover in an animated show on the telly. I think it was called 'Happy Submarine.'"

That had been one of Robbie's favourite shows a few years back, and Shannon wondered if she'd ever seen an episode with Gia's voice on it. Maybe the internet would have some information about it.

"After that, I lost touch with her for two years," Maria continued. "I'd get the occasional postcard, and they were from all over. She never explained, but Gia's like that. She's always adored being mysterious."

"But how did you know where to find her when your grandmother took ill?"

"She gave me an email address, one of those Hotmail accounts. If I ever had to contact her, that was the way to do it." Maria looked down at her congealed lobster. "That's all I know."

Shannon took out her notebook and a pen and pushed them across the table. "Write down the email address."

"I don't remember it."

"Write it down anyway."

The girl picked up the pen, made a show of trying to remember then wrote out the address.

"Can I go now?"

"Just one last thing, Maria. Please also write down the address in Germany where I can find her."

That stopped her. "How do you know about that?"

"I told you I make my living investigating. I get paid to know things." Shannon tapped the notebook with her index finger. "Now write down that address, okay?"

With a dazed expression, the girl did as requested.

Shannon reached over for the notebook. Hamburg. She really did not want to do any more globetrotting, but it looked as if a trip to Germany was on the docket. Too bad she spoke zero German.

Doing a bit of quick thinking, Shannon said as if to herself, "Boy, Germany. That trip's going to take me a couple of days to get together." Then she looked up at Maria. "Is your cousin pretty good at answering emails? Perhaps that's the best way to get in touch with her."

The girl just nodded. "Can I go now?"

"Yes."

Maria bolted for the door.

Shannon finished her lunch, then lingered over a cup of coffee, deep in thought.

"Germany?" Michael said that evening when Shannon gave him her report of the day's events.

"Yeah, I know," Shannon replied. "Trouble is, I have no way of knowing whether it's a wild goose chase. I couldn't just ask Maria if Gia was there, since I was pretending that I knew all about it. She didn't contradict me, but she was plenty shaken up at that point, so I don't think she was lying. If money's the problem..."

"No, no, it's not that at all. I'll pay for your ticket and expenses. That's part of the deal. It's just that I was hoping you'd be on your way back here, not somewhere else."

Shannon couldn't help smiling. This was a good sign. If Michael was thinking of giving her the brush-off, he'd be all for a trip to somewhere else.

"Believe me, I'm not looking forward to the trip, but I've got to strike while this info is hot. I tried a bit of smoke and mirrors on Maria today, telling her that I wouldn't be able to get the trip together for a few days. I should be at Gia's apartment before noon, though."

"So this is all on a hunch?"

"It's a good hunch, Michael, the best we have right now."

"I'm certainly willing to bet on you. So far, you've done rather well."

"Thanks. Now, how are the rehearsals going? Is this show going to happen, or are you all at each other's throats?"

"So far, so good. Some things have changed over the years, and some things haven't. I guess my tolerance for the things that haven't is high at the moment."

"Is Rolly behaving himself?"

"You always cut to the heart of the matter, don't you, O'Brien?" Michael laughed.

The simple truth was, the rehearsals had been going suspiciously well, making me wonder when things were going to fall apart.

Based on the previous day's rehearsal, I'd felt confident enough to show the Neuroticands my idea for the show's beginning. John helped out with some of his ideas, and to their credit, the others listened right to the end.

Tommy was unequivocal. "I think it's effing brilliant."

"I think it's shite," Lee grumbled.

"Why do you say that?" I asked.

Leaning against his amp, Lee looked over at me with an insolent expression. "Because this is just like you, Michael. The conquering hero returns, and we should all bow down. You just want to be the centre of attention again, don't you? It's all bollocks."

John said softly, "I'm sorry you feel that way, Lee, but a lot of this is about Michael, whether you like it or not. He and Rolly are the ones who wrote nearly all our material—not that we all didn't have a hand in it—so it seems right that the concert should begin with him. After all, he's the one who hasn't been here since our glory days."

Tommy jumped in. "And I've never heard of anyone starting a concert like this. It's sort of like we're letting people see what it was like when these songs were created. Michael noodling around with our material, John joining in, then finally getting to 'Don't Push Me', with Rolly singing the way it was written. No one's ever heard it like that. The audience will go berserk."

"It's total shite," Lee said again.

I was looking over at Rolly and his unreadable expression. Thinking or just hung over?

The discussion went back and forth between the other three, until finally Rolly looked over at me. "Do you really think this is a good idea?"

"Yes. Did you have something else in mind?"

"Here come the bloody flashpots," Tommy said under his breath.

"I was sort of visualizing starting with a bang," Rolly began.

"Told you," Tommy huffed.

"But we really should save 'Don't Push Me' until the end of the set."

I tried to keep the exasperation out of my voice as I answered, "But that's the whole point! The audience is going to think the bit at the beginning is all they're going to hear of it. We'll tear their ears off with the familiar version as our encore, just like you want."

Rolly thought about it for a moment, then nodded. "I like it."

As we began working on the material we hadn't covered the previous day, Lee was staring daggers at me. I'd have to take him aside when we broke for lunch and talk to him. Maybe I could get him to understand that this wasn't an ego trip for me, that I was just trying to revisit what we'd done through the filter of a quarter century of living.

Maybe I couldn't.

III

"So you see," I told Shannon, "everything's been pretty good so far."

"And Lee?"

"John told me he's unhappy that I'm against recording the gig."

"Why are you?"

I sighed. "I don't quite know. I guess I'm still trying to keep this whole thing as minimal as possible. Maybe it's because a CD and DVD would make it feel too much like the band is back together again. I don't know... I suppose I'm being a bit of a prat."

"Well, for what it's worth, I think it's a great idea. Speaking purely as a fan, I'd love it."

"I have to make a decision one way or the other pretty soon. We're moving into the arena so we can get the sound and lights together. The video people will need that time to get their part happening."

"How are the tickets selling?"

"Rolly's had publicists promoting the hell out of the thing, and our old record company is putting on a big publicity blitz all over the country. Rolly miscalculated and went for a venue he was sure we could fill. It only holds about 5500. The tickets for the first show sold out in day. The other three were added and went just as quickly."

"That's good, isn't it?"

"Not really. There are bigger halls in the city. Rolly could have booked the Armadillo, for instance."

"The what?" Shannon asked.

"It's what the locals call the Scottish Exhibition and Concert Centre or the SECC. The building looks sort of like an armadillo. Now it's too late. Our long-awaited reunion is being staged in a bloody hockey arena. That's pretty rich, isn't it? I could have stayed in Canada and done all the hockey arenas I wanted! John didn't find out until today where it actually was, and he is *not* happy about it."

"On the whole, though, it sounds like thing's are going pretty well."

"Yeah..."

"Now that you're moving someplace where people will know where you are, you're going to have to be doubly careful."

"I'm aware of that."

What I didn't want to tell her was that people had already been nosing around the Hilton asking questions. Yes, they might have been reporters or fans, but the two men who'd chatted up John and Tommy in the hotel's bar the previous evening hadn't sounded like either one. Plus, they were Yanks.

And the rest of the band had figured out that I was not staying in the room that had been booked at the Hilton.

CHAPTER 25

I guess I should have expected it would happen sooner or later.

To be quite honest, I couldn't really figure out Rolly's response to what was happening at our rehearsals. Here the reunion he had been bugging me about for all those years was actually taking place, and so far he seemed emotionally detached from the proceedings. Yes, he sang with everything he had (when it was appropriate), but when we discussed things, got down 'n' dirty in the trenches as it were, he acted as if didn't care. In the dim past, he would have been in there slinging mud with the rest of us. The term "elder statesman" came to my mind as I stole glances at him during our (thankfully) infrequent discussions over what we were rehearsing and how it was turning out.

It really began to get on my nerves as I watched him watching me. What was his game?

Since we were moving the gear to Braehead Arena across the Clyde that day, I went to the rehearsal space to remove all the cables from the various keyboards. I marked them as to what plugged in where and made a note of all the settings on the keyboard mixer I was using. I always have preferred controlling my own mix rather than letting the sound man do it. Rolly had come down to watch the road crew—some of Angus's people who'd insisted they wanted to take part—pack up the equipment and load it into the lorry. Since they knew what they were doing, he really had no reason to be there, and actually, had seldom been around to supervise anything (except the groupies) in the old days.

The air that morning had a damp bite to it, with the sky looking ready to break open at any moment. Pulling my collar up around my ears, I walked over and stood with him next to the lorry. He took a long drag on his cigarette but said nothing.

"So, how do you think it's going so far?" I asked.

Rolly took another drag. "All right, I guess."

"Nothing you'd like to talk over?"

"No."

"Rolly, just where the hell are you coming from?"

He turned and looked at me. "What's that supposed to mean?"

Rolly and I had been mates since we were seven. We'd been in the same grade at school, and we'd become close because I played piano and he sort of played guitar. Our first song had been written when we were eleven, and he'd made my teens bearable with his good humour and devil-may-care attitude, a good antidote to my propensity for being overly cautious and introspective. There was a history between us.

So, standing on a Glasgow street, I told him exactly what I was feeling about the rehearsals. He listened but made no response.

By the time I'd finished my little lecture, the lorry was loaded. Rolly offered to drive me out to Braehead.

"Let's stop for an early spot of lunch on the way," he suggested.

Scotland doesn't really have the same pub tradition England has, although they have plenty of drinking establishments. Knowing that the afternoon and evening would be a long slog, we limited our intake of beer to a pint each. The only decent beer in the place where we stopped was Younger's Tartan.

"So what are you bloody thinking?" I pressed. "You haven't said more than ten words in a row."

It took a good few minutes for him to speak. "To be honest, I keep wondering when you're going to walk out again."

"Really, Rolly, that's bollocks. I stick to my commitments. When I said I'd do the concert, I meant it. Now we're doing four, and you haven't heard two words about it from me. As a matter of fact, I was going to tell the band that I'd changed my mind about recording the gigs. How's that for commitment?"

"There was one time you didn't stick to your commitments."

There. It was out. I could comment or not as I saw fit.

After all those years, Rolly had presented me with the opportunity to discuss what had happened, but I just couldn't think of a way to approach what I wanted to say. Hell, we'd never so much as acknowledged that it had happened, let alone discussed it.

The meal came and went without me being able to pull the trigger.

Rolly drove around back of Braehead Arena to the loading dock, so we mercifully didn't have to walk through the shopping mall to which it is attached. That would have been beyond the pale.

As we pulled up, the last of our equipment was being unloaded, the sound and lighting company that had been hired had already off-loaded, and some fans had actually shown up. It felt very strange to be signing autographs backstage once again.

Rolly had booked the arena for the three days prior to the shows so we could get used to a big stage (about fifty by twenty-five), and the sound and lighting could be integrated into the performance. The band had yet to run through the entire set in one go, and I still hadn't settled on the final version of my intro idea.

Since no one on the road crew had worked with us before (way too young for that!), I had to help set up the keyboards, but once that was done, I headed for the green room: the home team's dressing room. It smelled faintly of sweat and body odour, despite the fact that it had been thoroughly cleaned and nice furniture, carpets and lighting had been brought in, all the rock and roll mod cons.

The band had become very tense. It was one thing to rehearse in a small room with only us present and something completely different to play on a large stage with a crew and the arena staff hanging about. Besides, the material wasn't as solid as any of us would have liked. There would be embarrassing lapses and duff notes.

Tommy, always sensitive to everyone's mood, started rattling on about some of the bizarre things that had happened to us on the road, and like every group, Neurotica had survived a lot of those.

Pretty soon we were all pitching in, and quite often Tommy had to caution his son Ralph not to repeat to his mum what had been said.

Two hours later, everything was ready and we hit the stage. At first, it was the disaster we'd all feared. My hands were shaking, and I wasn't the worst. Tommy's sticks kept flying out of his hands because they were so slick with sweat. Only John seemed unperturbed, but then he'd been working in pressure cooker situations for many years doing studio work.

It wasn't until I called a halt, suggested we should have a beer or two then try "Don't Push Me" that things started to turn around. Tommy counted it in at a slightly slower tempo than we'd been practising it, and that made all the difference. The familiar parts slipped into place like comfortable old shoes, and we just took off. There was Rolly swaggering and strutting up and down the stage. Lee stopped looking like a scared rabbit, and I wasn't constantly on the lookout for flying drum sticks. At the end, the great groove developed into a long jam with John doing some incredible soloing. We hadn't played the song like that since our days making only a few bob in grungy working class clubs.

Neurotica was finally back.

We packed it in ten exhausted hours later. My brain was as sore as my fingers and arms.

"I am completely, and in all other ways knackered," Tommy said, wiping the sweat from his face with an already sodden towel.

Rolly, staring directly at me, said, "All right, lads, everyone back to the hotel for drinks and grub up in my suite. It's all arranged."

"You arrange for any young ladies?" Lee asked and got stared down by Tommy. "Hey, some of you blokes might be married, but I ain't!" He grabbed his crotch. "Playing always makes me horny."

He laughed uproariously at his comment, until he realized that no one else was joining in.

"Hey, I got my lad here!" Tommy said with a disgusted look.

"Well, maybe you shouldn't!"

Before Lee could dig a larger hole for himself, Rolly peeled him off, and they disappeared down the back of the stage. We could hear raised voices from the corridor running around the arena under the seats, but I couldn't catch any words.

As he handed his guitar to one of the road crew, John said to Tommy, "He always was the one to make arse comments. Take no notice."

To his credit, Rolly did have a nice spread of sandwiches, salads and beer and wine back at the hotel, and to *his* credit, Lee apologized to Tommy, although it was obvious to me that Rolly had twisted his arm hard to make him do it.

I tried to be as enthusiastic as the rest of the lads about the concert. True, that day's rehearsal had been extremely enjoyable once we'd gotten on track, but I could not muster the same enthusiasm for the old days as everyone else, even John. To at least appear part of the group, I stayed until well after five a.m., and since it was so late, I stumbled down to my room there rather than make the trek to the other hotel. Flopping down on the bed fully clothed, I almost immediately fell into a deep sleep.

Probably because of old emotions that had been stirred up during the day, it didn't take long for my old nemesis to make its appearance.

Another seat back, another plane, but this time Shannon had a good feeling about the trip. Yes, she was putting all her eggs in the Hamburg basket, but what else could she do? The only lead she had to follow to the damned girl was at the address Maria Rota had given her.

She got through all the usual airport hassles in record time because, coming from the UK, she was already inside the European Union.

I could get used to travelling like this, she thought as she stepped into a waiting cab and headed downtown.

It was barely eleven a.m. when she found herself looking across a busy street at a nondescript, four-storey apartment building. One thing had to be said for Gia: she didn't go for the high life in her living accommodations, outwardly at least.

Shannon's palms were sweaty as she climbed over a snowbank and walked to the front door. Crossing herself, she pressed the buzzer for number 12.

Thirteen hours later, Shannon wearily fell into a cab at Glasgow airport.

She gave the driver the name of the hotel, then added, "Wake me up when we get there, okay?"

"Sure thing," he said and winked at her in the mirror.

Despite her words, Shannon didn't fall asleep on the ride into town. She was far too upset.

Her trip to Germany had been almost a complete waste of time and had cost quite a lot of money. She'd waited around a good part of the day for Gia to make an appearance, once she'd made sure the girl wasn't in the apartment. Using roughly the same dodge she'd used in Montreal, she'd pumped the super (who fortunately spoke passable English), finding out that while the Chameleon did indeed rent the apartment, he hadn't seen her in at least a month and was getting concerned, since the rent had been due two weeks earlier.

Of course, she'd been using a German alias: Johanna Braun. The super had recognized her immediately from the photo and could only say nice things about the flight attendant who'd rented the apartment for nearly a year.

"She keeps an odd schedule, though, not like the other flight attendants I have had in the building. Sometimes, Fräulein Braun is gone for several weeks. I asked her about it, and she told me she replaces people who are sick, and so the airline moves her where they need her, *ja*?"

Clever girl, Shannon thought. Here's yet another person she's completely hoodwinked.

Using his phone, the helpful man had called the apartment and had only gotten the answering machine.

"Has anyone else been enquiring about her?"

The man gave a generous shrug. "I am not here all the time, but I can ask my wife when she returns from shopping."

The wife knew nothing more, so Shannon had stomped back across the street to a little café in order to watch the entrance and think about what else she might try. The person behind the counter had understood almost no English, so Shannon wound up with a double shot of espresso rather than a cappuccino.

It was always possible that Gia/Johanna had been in her apartment recently without the super knowing, but she doubted it. The man seemed to be on the ball and wanted to collect the rent. Sooner or later, he would have seen her.

By six o'clock she knew this had been a dead-end trip. Either the girl had moved on or her cousin had tipped her off. There was only one more card to play.

Giving up her seat by the window, where she'd been for the past four hours, she went downtown to the main police station, a short taxi ride away.

The English of the officer Shannon first spoke to was darned near as good as hers. Looking over her PI license, passport and ID, he seemed very skeptical. Shannon gave him the name of two Toronto cops she knew well and Burt from Peel Regional, and he dispatched someone with the information, leaving her cooling her heels for a good forty minutes. Eventually, she was shown into a small office. A tall blonde woman behind the desk was looking over Shannon's credentials with more than passing interest.

Shannon sat down and said, "Thank you for seeing me. I'm sorry but I don't speak any German, so I hope your English is good enough," she added with a generous smile.

"Frau O'Brien, we do not usually speak with private investigators, but we have been told some interesting things about you."

This was puzzling. "Like what?"

"That you have been following this Fräulein you are after from your city to Montreal to New York, then Birmingham. That you are a most tenacious adversary."

"And from whom did you hear this?"

"I am not at liberty to say."

"But can you help me?"

"I fear not, but I can tell you that Fräulein Braun is of interest to us. She is mixed up in the trade of drugs, no?"

"I believe so."

"We have been keeping a watch on her apartment, but we now think that she has found out that Hamburg is too hot to hold her."

"So she hasn't been seen? How long have you watched?"

The female cop opened a folder on the side of her desk, consulting it. "It has been just short of two weeks."

Shannon's heart sank. Another damned dead end! "You'll let me know if you find out anything? I know this isn't regular, but it's sort of a special situation."

The cop had smiled for the first time, but there was sadness behind it. Because of this, a small bond had been made. "Yes, we will inform you. You see, I am a mother also."

Weary in mind and spirit, Shannon made her way down the hotel corridor to her room, the overnight bag a dead weight on her shoulder. She felt as if she could sleep for a week straight.

She wondered what the hell she was going to tell Michael.

About to slip her key card into the door, Shannon noticed that the green light was already on. The hair on the back of her neck stood up as she backed away. Something was very wrong, and she knew better than to enter that room.

Moving back down the corridor at something between a walk and a run, she found the elevator still at her floor.

Back in the lobby, the sleepy-looking desk clerk didn't seem inclined to believe her when she told him she thought her room might have been broken into.

"So it's normal for the lock to show green before you open it?" Shannon asked peevishly.

"No," he had to admit, "but Mr. O'Brien might not have shut it properly when he came in."

"You saw him come in?"

"Well, no, but I came on at eleven. He might have come in earlier."

"Look, I want someone to at least come up and help me check my room. Is that too much to ask?"

Turned out that it wasn't, but because of the late hour, it took time to round up a couple of people to go up with her. Shannon tried to remain patient. If she'd had her gun with her, she would have done it by herself.

Finally, she was again walking down the corridor to her room, a cleaner and the late-night bellman with her. The bellman at least had a walkie-talkie.

About ten feet away, Shannon stopped her little posse and said to them in a low voice, "When we get to the door, I'm going to try the handle. If the door is unlocked, I'm going in, and it's going to be sudden. I'll yell out if it's clear. No yell and you get on the blower for help. *Don't* come in. Got that?"

"You talk like a cop," the bellman whispered.

As Shannon moved to the door, she said grimly. "That's because I used to be one."

Trying the door handle, she discovered that the door was indeed unlocked. Opening it fast, she dropped down and rolled into the blackness of the room. She felt clothes against her face, but nothing else happened, no lights going on, no drawn guns, just silence. Standing up, she quickly found the light switch by the door. Flicking it on, she told the two out in the hall to come on in.

Someone had tossed the room but good. Clothes were ripped and strewn all over the place, the mattress had been flung off the bed, and all the drawers turned over and dumped.

"Christ!" the waiter said under his breath.

The bellman was on the walkie-talkie, telling the desk clerk to call the police.

Shannon righted a chair and sat in it. "Don't touch anything else," she said wearily.

As she waited for the arrival of the law, Shannon felt sick. Where was Michael, and had he been there when the bad guys had arrived?

My dream that night I stayed at the Hilton was the worst I'd ever experienced. This time, there was none of the distortion you usually get in dreams. The corridors weren't endless and winding, turning in on themselves like a writhing snake. Everything was exactly as I remembered it, down to the cream-coloured wallpaper and burgundy carpet.

It began as it had in reality: Angus waking me from a deep sleep by pounding on my door. In those days I could sleep through an air raid. The bedside clock read 3:18 a.m.

"Michael, you bugger, you've got to come with me!" Angus practically erupted into the room as I opened the door. "Something really bad has happened."

"What? The lads actually went to bed early?"

"This is no time for jokes. Get some clothes on. I need your help!"

He wouldn't tell me anything, but it was easy to see that whatever had happened was bad. Angus was normally the calm centre of the Neurotica storm.

"Where are we going?" I asked as we left my room.

"Rolly's room."

"Is Rolly all right?"

Knowing his propensity for booze, and more recently, drugs, I had immediately thought of an OD situation.

"Rolly's fine. That's not the problem."

"What is then?"

Angus didn't answer, just continued stomping down the hall ahead of me.

Knowing what the band was like on the road, I'd insisted on my room being far away from theirs, and since this hotel was one of the huge American ones, that meant very far indeed. The building was shaped like the letter C, and I was at one end, while the rest of the Neurotica road show was at the other. The walk seemed to take forever.

At Rolly's door, Angus took out a room key and let us in.

The main room of the suite was a mess, showing the obvious signs of a big party. Rolly had been insisting on a suite for a year now, mainly because he liked having the extra room when "friends dropped in". Rolly could take a young lady off to his room for a romp then come back to rejoin the party. Often the sex spilled out into the room, and that's when things could get really out of hand.

"Where the hell is Rolly?" I asked Angus as I righted a coffee table.

"There," Angus said, indicating the closed bedroom door, "along with something else."

Fed up with his dodging about, I opened the door and walked in.

The room looked as if a hurricane had just come through. Clothes, furniture, food, bottles, were strewn all over the place. Rolly, naked and looking totally spaced out, was leaning crookedly against the headboard of his bed, legs drawn up. His whole body was shaking.

I went over to him. "Rolly, mate, you okay?"

He looked up at me, eyes rolling around in his head. "I'm a little wasted at the moment, Michael."

"Drugs or alcohol?"

"Both," Angus said behind me, then reached out and put his hand on my shoulder. "What you need to see is in the bathroom."

Standing to the side, he turned the knob and pushed the door open, allowing me to walk past.

On the bathroom floor lay a girl, and except for the pallor of her skin and the impossible angle of her neck, she might have been asleep.

Up to that point, the dream had been a completely accurate recreation of what had happened that awful, awful night. But so many years later, as I slept in the Glasgow Hilton and my dream self stood there looking down in shock, something was horribly different.

What made this rendition of my dream dreadful beyond belief was the fact that it was Shannon lying dead on the floor of Rolly's bathroom. Not Shannon as she was now, though. This was Shannon as she would have been twenty-four years ago, Shannon at almost the same age as the real girl had been.

CHAPTER 26

Shannon had gone beyond frantic by the time the police arrived. The mess in the room could have been caused by a violent search, or it could have been due to a fight with a search after, as two chairs and a lamp were broken.

Had they finally succeeded in nabbing Michael? The desk clerk swore he'd seen nothing, but the bellman admitted privately that the desk clerk had been known to fall asleep when things were quiet.

"I suppose they could have gone out the back, and if they'd been careful, no one would be the wiser," he'd added.

As the Glasgow police quietly took over, Shannon was taken down to the manager's office to have her statement taken. Her police training began asserting itself as she calmed down. That's when she realized several things she'd seen, but which hadn't registered at the time: Michael's overcoat wasn't there, nor were his computer, shoulder bag and cell phone. Maybe he hadn't come back to the hotel. Of course, another logical answer could be that the bad guys had grabbed him and taken everything else along with them.

She pulled out her own cell. "Mind if I make a call?" she asked the constable taking down her statement, but went right ahead without waiting for an objection.

Shannon tried to keep her hopes down while she waited for the connections to be made. Never had a cell phone taken this long!

Michael's phone rang several times, to the point where Shannon was sure his voicemail would kick in, then someone answered.

She heard heavy breathing for several seconds, then a husky voice croaked out, "Yes?"

"Michael, is that you?"

"Shannon, oh God, Shannon..." he almost sobbed.

"Michael, we may only have a few seconds—"

"What are you talking about?"

"Michael, where have they taken you?"

"Who?"

Shannon realized they were talking at cross purposes. "Michael, where are you?"

"I'm at the Hilton. I came back with the lads tonight after rehearsal, and by the time things broke up, I was too tired to go to our hotel."

She squeezed her eyes shut with relief and turned to the officer. "I've found him. He's at another hotel. He wasn't in the room. You should tell your superior that."

"Who are you talking to?" Michael asked.

"A cop. I'm in the manager's office at our hotel. Someone tossed our room. The place is a disaster. I thought they'd gotten you."

Michael was silent as that sank in. "I should have left a message. I did a right balls up on this one, didn't I?"

Shannon picked up something in the way he was speaking. His voice was pitched too high, and he was speaking quickly, his words tumbling out all over each other. This was one seriously distressed man.

"Michael, what's wrong? You must have been asleep when I called."

"No, I was awake, thank God! I just couldn't find my goddamned phone."

"That's not what I meant."

"Shannon, can you come over here?"

"Right now? I haven't finished giving my statement, and God only knows what we have left in the way of clothes and other belongings."

"Sod all that!" Michael answered, his voice rising. "I really need to speak to you."

"About what?"

"When you get here." He gave her the room number. "Please hurry."

He hung up before she could answer.

I felt truly awful as I opened the door for Shannon. From her expression as she looked at me, I could tell that it showed.

"Michael," she said as she put her palm against my cheek, "what's happened?"

I knew I had to tell her, no matter what the consequences—but how to start? I'd kept the secret bottled up for so long, I found I didn't know how to let it out.

Shannon got me to sit on one of the beds with her. "Now, tell me what's wrong."

When I'd woken from my dream, I'd actually been sobbing, and I lay there sweaty and tangled in the bed clothes for quite some time, unable to pull myself together. In my heart, I was certain my dream meant that Shannon had been killed. Don't ask me how I thought I knew this, but it was beyond a doubt. It was a devastating blow, because until that point, I'd had no idea of the depth of my feelings for her.

"I can't tell you how relieved I am that you're here," I said giving her hands a squeeze, then leaned forward and just wrapped my arms around her, pulling her tightly against me.

At first she resisted, then gave in. I held her for a long time.

"I dreamed that you'd died," I finally was able to say, my face buried in her hair.

"Was it part of a dream like you had the other night?"

"It's almost always the same dream, Shannon. Tonight was different because of the awful twist at the end, something that's never happened before."

"This is all about why you left Neurotica, isn't it?"

Her saying that somehow made it easier for me to continue. If she hadn't possessed that slim wedge, I don't know if I ever could have started—and that would have been the end of any chance of our relationship continuing.

"Yes... Something very bad happened, something I'm so ashamed of... I guess you could say that it's blighted my life—if that isn't too flowery a term."

I suddenly couldn't sit still. Getting up, I walked over to the window. From so high up, I could see a faint glow in the sky on the faraway horizon. Dawn wasn't far off.

"I know I spoke in my sleep the other night."

She nodded.

"What did you hear?"

"You said something about someone being dead, a girl, I think. There were also a few words about Rolly, and you seemed to be talking to your dead friend, Angus. That's all I know."

"Twenty-four years ago...I was party to something that I am totally ashamed of. Even now, I couldn't tell you why I did it. When it happened, I just acted without thinking, like my brain had switched off. I've never spoken about this to anyone, not even the people who were involved as deeply as I was." Taking a deep breath, I plunged on. "And now, I'm petrified of telling you, because I have no idea what you'll think or do after you know."

Shannon nodded, concern on her face. "You didn't kill someone, did you?"

Even though I knew why she'd said it, I was still completely appalled. "No! Of course not!"

"But someone did die."

Now it was my turn to nod. "I'm telling this inside out."

"Starting at the beginning would probably be best."

To gain a spot of time, I went to the bar fridge and took out a soft drink. "Care for one?"

"Yes, please."

I handed her a Coke, and we sat there sipping as if nothing were wrong, but I'm sure both our brains were going a mile a minute. I drained my can before I spoke again. She waited patiently.

"Neurotica was in Chicago. The tour had been going quite well, but things were getting out of hand offstage. Everyone but me seemed to be getting sucked into some bad things. Our manager and the record company execs did nothing to stop it, even though the lads trashed a hotel room in Miami, even though our playing began suffering. My only solution had been to withdraw as much as I could. It was like watching a plane crash in slow motion.

"Funny thing was my withdrawal added to my mystique. Even you've made reference to it. That's what attracted you to me when you were in high school, wasn't it? The lonely genius thing?"

"Yeah."

"You weren't the only one. Every tour stop, the groupies were there. Most of the time, I just ignored them. Most of the time...

"So we were in Chicago, with three days off. I was hoping we'd rehearse and regroup, get our bearings again, but the lads had other ideas. Rolly's suite, as usual, became party central. Being bored, I joined them one night, just to hang out. Frankly, I felt like my band was drifting away from me or vice versa, and I'd worked far too hard to let that happen.

"Rolly was in his bedroom shagging someone, and everyone in the sitting room was completely pissed, high or both. I sat on the chesterfield next to John, who had a girl on each knee. This young girl came over and sat down next to me. She reminded me of a china doll: very delicate features, pale skin, long blonde hair, huge eyes. She was stick-thin, and her jeans looked as if they could have been painted on her.

"Since everyone else was occupied, we began to talk. It took about five minutes before she'd respond in more than single words. I got the feeling that if I'd said 'boo', she would have fainted dead away."

Shannon looked at me, her mouth a tight line of understanding. "You were her favourite."

I nodded. "So I found out afterwards."

"She must have been petrified. I know I would have been."

The final scene of my earlier dream flashed through my head, and it took me a few moments to pull myself together.

"At some point, I went out on the balcony for a bit of fresh air and a little quiet. The girl followed after. She had a joint, and I even took a few hits. For several minutes we stood leaning on the rail, looking out at the lights of the city.

"Finally, I turned to leave. It was late, and I was tired. 'Take me back to your room with you,' the girl blurted out. I actually thought about it for a moment then decided that it wouldn't be a good thing. I wish to God now that I had!

"When I told her no, she got very upset. 'Don't you like me? Aren't I pretty enough?'

"'That has nothing to do with it. I'm tired and want to sleep. Maybe I'll see you around tomorrow, yes?'

"Her lip was trembling, and tears started running down her face. 'I came to see you, to be with you. You can't turn me down! They all said I wouldn't have the nerve!'

"'Who did?'

"'My friends!'

"She cuddled up against me and asked again if I'd take her to my room. The whole situation stank, and I just wanted to get out of there. I pulled myself away, went back into the smoky room and crossed to the door. Looking back, I saw her framed in the doorway out to the balcony. The girl didn't look to be over eighteen. What I should have done was pull her out of the room, but I didn't. I just turned and left."

I couldn't read anything in Shannon's expression, so I plowed on with the story, telling her how Angus had woken me up about an hour later and taken me back to Rolly's room.

"When I saw that poor girl lying on the bathroom floor, I just freaked. Angus told me it had been an accident. After I'd walked out of the suite, the girl had gotten into some of the booze and more drugs. Eventually, she'd come on to Rolly, and when he's had a snootful, he has no conscience, so off they went to the bedroom. Once in there, Rolly had wasted no time in niceties and told her to strip. She'd gone that far, but as the moment of truth approached, she'd freaked out.

"Rolly got upset and told her to get the hell out. The poor thing grabbed her clothes and ran into his bathroom."

"You mean that he raped her?" Shannon looked disgusted.

"Rolly can be stupid, but he's not that stupid, certainly not when there's a room full of willing girls on the other side of the door. Angus told me at the time that Rolly was so wasted, he probably couldn't have done anything anyway. No, the girl just freaked. Her earlier come-on to me had all been bravado. She was only playing at being a 'bad girl'.

"As near as we can figure it, the floor was wet and she must have slipped. It looked like she fell over backwards and her head hit the edge of the toilet."

"How come none of this ever made the news?"

"That's what I'm so ashamed of, Shannon. As we looked down at the girl's body, Angus turned to me and said he had an idea to make the whole mess go away.

"Before he came to get me, he'd cleared the suite, so no one knew anything bad had happened.

"'All we need to do is get rid of the body,' Angus said, 'There isn't even any blood. She simply slipped and fell. The girl came here of her own free will, and it's too ruddy bad what happened, but why should we take the blame?'"

Shannon sighed. "And you swallowed what he was saying?"

"He kept at me for an hour: what was at stake, all the hard work, that it was not Rolly's fault. You can imagine what it was like."

"And you gave in."

A wave of shame flooded over me. I'd been down this road so many times over the years, and it never got any better.

"Angus fetched one of Rolly's wardrobe cases. I helped him wrap the girl in a blanket, and we just wheeled the case out of the hotel. It was that simple. Afterwards, the three of us never discussed it. It was like it never happened. Next day, Rolly was hung over but didn't seem any different. Angus was Angus."

"And you?"

I turned and looked out the window, unable to face Shannon. "In the cold light of day, when I realized what we'd done, I was literally ill. Two concerts later, I bailed. I could not face what I'd done. Nothing was worth that much! If this was what success meant, I wanted no part of it."

"And you never contacted the police?"

"I couldn't! They were my mates! I grew up with Rolly. Besides, it was an accident."

Her next comment was made softly, but its impact was devastating. "Did you ever make an attempt to find out if the body was ever found? There were other people involved in this, you know. It wasn't just you and Rolly and Angus. That girl had parents. She had a family."

Shannon had cut right to the heart of the matter, the thing that had eaten away at my insides for twenty-four years.

"About a year later, I went back to Chicago. It's a big city, and they have lots of murders, but with a little digging, I found a few news reports, but they weren't much. The body was found two days later. She'd apparently gone to Chicago alone. Someone saw her talking to a couple of guys outside the hotel that afternoon, and she'd gone off with them. The cops figured they had something to do with it, but the crime was never solved."

"And the girl's family?"

"Kentucky. Single mom, four other kids. They lived in a trailer park. Dad nowhere to be seen. When I went to check it out, she'd moved. I tried to find her a few times over the years, but with no luck."

"Was the girl over eighteen?"

"By two lousy days! She'd used her birthday money to get to Chicago. She was looking for a way out, a better life, and the silly kid thought she'd find it with me."

I looked at Shannon, but her expression didn't tell me anything.

"There's something more. Tonight, when I had the dream, the ending was different... It wasn't the girl lying on the floor of the bathroom; it was you, you as you would have been at the time that girl died. I've seen the photos on that shelf in your sitting room. I know what you looked like at eighteen. What made it so unbearable was I realized it easily could have been you in that room that night. Tell me it's not true. You've told me yourself how you felt! I just couldn't bear the thought..."

Shannon looked at me for a long time, but I couldn't stand the x-ray gaze and kept averting my eyes. I had hoped I might feel better having finally told the story to someone, but if anything I felt worse.

Shannon got to her feet and picked up her coat. "Michael, I'm going for a walk. I need to do a lot of thinking. I may or may not be back. I really don't know."

"I understand."

At the door, she stopped and gave me a wan smile. "Don't forget that the bad guys are still around. If I were you, I'd be very, very careful. Tonight was a warning. You can't keep dodging them forever."

CHAPTER 27

Rehearsal didn't start that day until noon because Scotty, the lighting designer, needed to make changes to the overhead rig—not that we were in any condition to be out there at the crack of dawn anyway.

In the years I'd been away, a lot had changed, and lighting systems were infinitely more flexible and powerful, with fixtures that could move, refocus, change colour and do just about anything you'd want at the touch of a finger on a computer keyboard. Since it involved computers, that meant programming, and John had hired a really talented person to design the lighting for the concert.

After Shannon left that morning, I had an annoying burst of energy that wouldn't allow me to sit still, even though I should have been dead beat. A long walk would have been a good idea, but after what had happened the previous night in the other hotel, something like that was off the menu.

So I grabbed my laptop, answered a few emails from the shop and made a note to call the lads when they got in. At least nothing was going wrong there. The package I'd ordered from my travel agent would be arriving that morning: two plane and concert tickets for each of the lads, accommodation for two nights, the full monty. I wished I could have seen their faces. Hopefully, being shut down for three days wouldn't screw up anything at Quinn beyond repair.

I had the telly on in the background, hoping something would capture my interest and keep my brain from recycling all the bad thoughts over and over.

When Rolly called from his room shortly after ten to find out if I wanted to take part in an interview for Granada, I actually jumped at the chance, even though I usually wouldn't go within ten miles of that sort of thing.

He was on the second floor from the top of the Hilton and had a splendid view of the west end of Glasgow, fading off into the distant highlands. The weather was finally clear, and the sun shone brilliantly.

A television crew was already set up, and the other lads were present. The taping had begun, and they made a big deal in front of the camera about me being late. It was all in good fun, but I was embarrassed nonetheless, because it made me look as if I were trying to upstage them. The interviewer, a young woman probably picked more for the way she looked than her skill level, asked the usual questions. "What's it like playing together again after all these years?" That sort of crap. She had probably been about two when the original lineup of Neurotica had last played. She'd looked rather disappointed when I'd told her I would not answer any questions about Angus's death or what had happened in Canada. There had already been way too much about that in the British press.

I let the rest of the lads have their fun with the interview and only spoke when directly asked a question. It took her about fifteen minutes to get around to The Question.

"Michael, you left the band right in the midst of its most successful tour, you had a worldwide number one hit album, sold out stadiums. So, tell me, why did it happen?"

The room went dead silent, with everyone staring at me. I don't know if the girl was looking for a scoop or just had no idea what she was asking.

For a brief moment, I toyed with the idea of giving her that scoop, letting her know exactly why I'd left the band, and I think Rolly saw that flash across my face as I risked a quick glance at him. He certainly looked plenty apprehensive.

Since I'd finally spilled my guts to Shannon only a few hours earlier, it still might come out sooner rather than later, but I decided that now was not the time. This was about Angus and what he meant to us. That had to stay top of mind.

"I, ah, guess I just couldn't handle things," I began, and this time I looked at Rolly a bit longer. "It was too much too fast and I, ah..."

Tommy saved me by butting in. "You see, our Michael is a bit of a wallflower and never could handle the rock and roll lifestyle. He'd rather sit in his room and practise or read a book."

It was said kindly, but had a typical barb in it, so I shot my own back, "Well, I know a certain drummer who could stand a little practising in his room."

The rest of the lads hooted, so Tommy chucked a pillow at me, which I caught and chucked back.

John, with perfect timing, said, "See what happens when rockers get on in years? Twenty years ago, we would have trashed the room. Now we have pillow fights."

Things began to deteriorate, so the interview was stopped, but the girl seemed pleased, and her sound recorder gave us a thumbs up from the corner of the room.

As everyone got ready to leave, Rolly came over and said in a low voice, "We have to talk."

I went back down to my room to grab my laptop and jacket, but more to see if Shannon had returned. She hadn't, so I left a note asking her to come out to the rehearsal if and when she returned. I toyed with saying more but decided that wouldn't be a good idea, since hotel staff would certainly see it.

It wasn't hard to get John to give me a lift along with Lee to the arena. Shannon's warning really had me spooked.

On the way over the Clyde to Braehead, John and Lee chatted away, not about the old days, but about what they liked and didn't like with the music being produced now. My mind was back downtown, wondering where Shannon had got to, what she was thinking, but most importantly, what the outcome of those thoughts would be.

Our set, not counting my intro (which still had to be finalized) came in at just under two hours. We ran straight it through, minor warts and all, and with the adjusted lighting and sound system wailing, it was quite a rush. By the end, we were all dripping with sweat as the crew applauded.

"That's a bit of all right," Lee said, wiping down the neck of his bass.

The sound man called out from his desk at the far end of the arena, "Want to hear what the audience is going to get?"

We trooped back, wondering what he meant. I was bringing up the rear with John, who'd thrown off all pretense of aloofness and was wildly enthusiastic about the way the run-through had gone.

Since I was paying attention to John, I didn't see who was sitting next to Randy, our sound man.

It was Shannon.

I guess the lads thought she was with him, because they didn't say anything until she looked up at me and said, "I got your message and came out to listen. Randy let me sit with him."

John, asked teasingly, "So who's the lady, Michael?"

I really had no idea what to say, since everything was upside down at the moment, but Shannon's quick wit saved me.

"I'm the former president of the Neurotica Fan Club at my old high school. I had tickets to hear you guys on the last tour Michael was with the band, and I've never forgiven him for it being cancelled, so I made him bring me to Glasgow."

The sweater Shannon had been wearing lay draped over the back of her chair, and she was sitting there in just a T-shirt.

Lee whistled. "With those biceps, darlin', I can see why he'd pay attention."

She grinned at him, and I felt reassured.

Lee sat down next to her. "So what do the fans think of the way Neurotica sounds now?"

"All of the songs are subtly changed, especially Michael's parts. That big brown keyboard that sounds like violins and choirs is really cool."

"You like the mellotron?"

"Well, it's a bit retro, but it sounds right. Know what I mean?"

John gave me a nudge in the ribs and leaned over. "Next thing he'll say is that it was his idea."

Randy was adjusting the knobs and sliders that covered the big mixing desk and was ready with his demo.

"This, my friends, is exactly what was coming out of the speakers while you were playing. Kindly give a listen and let me know where I've got it right and where I don't."

Without Angus by the desk making sure things were the way they should be, I'd been very apprehensive as to what the sound would be like. Most engineers these days mix very bottom heavy, assuming that it gives the sound presence. It just makes mud as far as I'm concerned.

I needn't have worried. Randy was doing a fantastic job, but then, according to John, he was one of the top audio engineers in the States.

We listened to the whole set, stopping occasionally to discuss the balance of the mix, and the entire time Shannon pretty well ignored me. She could actually have been just the former president of a fan club. Lee and Rolly were busy chatting her up.

It was decided to start again in an hour. Catering had been brought in for the duration, so we could all eat without leaving. Deciding I wasn't hungry, I went to the stage with a mind to working on my intro to the concert. Not looking back, I crossed the floor of the arena alone.

Headphones on, I worked for about twenty minutes, with Tommy's son hanging about. Eventually John joined us, and I was so engrossed in what I was doing, I forgot about being rather angry with Shannon.

As the rest of the band appeared in the corridor behind the stage, I saw Shannon walking along with Rolly, the two of them deep in conversation. I felt a twinge in my gut as I thought of the way my dream had ended the previous night and wondered if she knew the effect her behaviour might be having on me.

She came right up on the stage. "And this handsome young man must be your son, Tommy," she said. "He looks a lot like you."

Tommy laughed. "You mean the way I looked about thirty years ago, maybe." He ruffled his son's hair affectionately. "But he's a great lad. Takes care of this here drum kit better than his old dad."

I decided to try my intro straight through, and Shannon and the lads went out onto the arena floor to listen.

We were using in-ear monitors for the gig, since it kept the sound level down on stage and more controllable out front, so I felt as if I was in a cut-off world of my own. There was actually no amplification around me at all, the organ's Leslie speaker having been moved behind the stage by Randy. The rest of the instruments went directly into my mixing board—other than the "seventeenth century amplification" of the grand piano, the only keyboard on the stage which actually produced acoustic sounds.

Using my laptop to control two of the synths allowed me more complexity and texture in what I'd composed. I'd recorded most of that back in Toronto with only a bit of tweaking here and there. That left me with one synth, the organ, the electric and acoustic pianos and the mellotron to play live—more than enough to manage!

The lighting designer, not having heard it before, was flying blind, but he caught on pretty quickly, starting with a blue wash as the programmed synths did their deep rumbly thing: my impression of the music of the spheres. It echoed around the empty arena like an amorphous mass and proved John's intuition to be correct when he'd said not to give it too much melodic direction.

I started off on the piano, using the synth harmonies as a springboard to what I meant to sound like improvisation, but which was fairly worked out. I'd decided on some keyboard flash here and there to make a personal statement that I was back and better than ever. Conceited? Maybe, but I'd taken a lot of heat over the years from the music journalists.

Little bits of various Neurotica tunes flew out from under my fingers as I pulled more sound out of the piano with larger chords and heavier playing. I also started working in a bit of the live synth to punctuate and enhance. Snippets of "Don't Push Me" began to appear, but never in any sort of cohesive form, more like an elaborate tease.

John, knowing how the thing was put together, got Rolly up on the back of the stage, where he stood, looking like a dark shadow.

As I moved to the mellotron, using the bass clarinet voice on one keyboard and the classic "three violins" on the other, stabbingly bright, very tightly focussed white lights shot down on me from the truss above. Out in the arena, I was peripherally aware of someone clapping and whistling.

Now I used the minimoog to play the melody of the chorus of "Don't Push Me" with the boys' choir voice on the mellotron providing the chordal accompaniment. Out in the arena, I was hoping it had the "celestial" effect I was going for.

As the verse started, Rolly, with impeccable timing, began to sing. Bright red lights shot down onto him.

I'd purposely transposed the song down a third, so he'd be forced to sing it in his heavier midrange, and at the slower tempo, the lyrics took on their original meaning. This was no longer a party song of "let's get it on, baby", but something more moody and filled with longing, the way we'd envisioned it.

As the chorus returned, John and Lee came in with their vocal harmony parts, but the lighting on them was purple and subdued. Where they'd come from, I didn't know, but the whole effect was brilliant.

When I switched over to organ, the background synths dropped out, the riff to our opening number, one of the band's earliest tunes, appropriately enough called "How Did We Get Here?", started with butt-kicking intensity, and the band held off until the tension had reached breaking point before exploding into the song, full up lights and you could almost hear the crowd roar.

Rolly stopped us almost immediately.

I could hear Tommy mutter, "What the hell is this all about?"

Rolly looked directly at me. "Again. We need to do it again."

Would wonders never cease? Rolly actually wanting to rehearse? Unheard of!

║║║

Sometime approaching midnight, in the middle of our third run-through of the set, Tommy just stopped playing.

"Sorry, mates," he said, sweat streaming off his bald head. "I'm knackered."

We hadn't yet got to John's solo spot, an unaccompanied *tour de force* that was guaranteed to leave the audience gasping, and he was clearly not pleased.

Motioning with his head at young Ralph, sitting off to the side, he barked, "How about the kid? Can he do it?"

We all looked over at Tommy's son, who just shrugged, but you could see in his expression that he was *very* ready to play.

"Go on," his dad said, holding out his sticks, "get over here and show them what you can do."

After a bit of adjustment to the drum kit, Ralph nodded and John said, "Right then. Back one verse and pick it up there." Then he counted it in.

The kid was a riot once he got going (which took all of about a dozen bars), not only playing really well, but also imitating all his old dad's mannerisms down to the slightly cocked head that always made me want to go over and straighten it.

Tommy stood off to the side, beaming, and when we finished the set about forty minutes later, he burst out with, "Now you know who to call if anything ever happens to me!"

We all clapped Ralph on the back and told him how well he'd

done, and he beamed back at his dad. When I glanced over at Tommy, he flashed me a wink.

III

Shannon had stuck around, part of the time spent in the adjacent shopping mall, looking for souvenirs to take home to Rachel, Robbie and her mum—a very ominous sign to my mind.

The rest of the time, she was with the other lads in the band. I watched her go from Lee and Rolly to Tommy then to John. She was somewhat flirty with all of them, and that had them rather puzzled as they continually looked over at me, wondering what was going on—precisely my question.

It was half one as we went out the back of the arena. The sky was still clear, and you could actually see a few stars.

Everyone was dividing up into the various cars. Rolly and Lee in one, Tommy, Ralph and John in another.

Lee stuck his head out of Rolly's sports car. "Care for a lift, luv?" he asked Shannon with a broad smile. "C'mon girl! You can sit on my...lap."

She shook her head. "Thanks, but I'll ride with Michael." Then she turned to me and said softly, "If that's all right with him."

I looked at her, unsure what she meant. "If you'd like."

Shannon had hired a car that morning. She tossed me the keys. "You're driving into town. Once today was enough, and I certainly don't want to do it at night."

All the cars left at once, and we were quickly on the M8 travelling downtown. Shannon didn't say anything but kept looking out the rear view mirrors.

About three minutes later, she announced, "We're being followed."

"You're sure?"

"Slow down, and that should answer any questions." She turned around. "Yup. I'm sure. It might even be two cars. That's a serious tail."

"What do you want me to do? Should we find a police station?"

Shannon shook her head. "I want to see who they are, if possible. It helps to know your enemy." We were just to the bend north where the M8 crosses the River Clyde and wraps around the core of downtown. "Take the next exit... No, not that one. It's another expressway... Yeah, that exit coming up. I want some side streets."

"Are you barmy? What if they box us in?"

My passenger looked over and smiled. "Trust me."

I put myself in her capable hands. Even though the hour was late, there was still a lot of traffic around, so I felt pretty safe. We drove aimlessly, passing close to the Hilton but not going in. Finally we reached the road that runs along the Clyde. My only choice was to turn left.

"We're coming up to a stale red light," Shannon said. "Slow down so you're near it but not past and let it turn red, then gun it and take the left there. Immediately pull over to the curb. Got that?"

"What if there's a cop around?"

"Then you'll get a ticket, and the bad guys will leave us alone."

I did exactly what she told me, and it worked a treat. One of the cars following us screeched around the corner about five seconds later and was past us before he could react.

"Now do a U-turn and gun it."

"But this is a one-way street!"

"So? No one's coming."

That turned out to be wrong, as a new car appeared at the corner. I barely avoided clipping his driver's-side wing. Another car turning honked at me angrily, and I responded by putting the left-hand wheels on the sidewalk. Back at the corner, I took a quick left and entered the stream of traffic. My heart was pounding.

"Nice driving, Quicksilver," Shannon said.

"Did you see what you wanted to?"

"Oh, yes. I'll know the driver if I see him again. The passenger, all I know is he's a big man with dark hair. And by the way, they're both American."

"How the hell would you know that?"

"Did you see the way they took the corner? That was a panic turn, and they swung over to the right hand side of the road. No one from the UK would have taken the corner like that."

"And the passenger?"

She grinned at me. "Would they have a Yank driving and a Brit riding shotgun?"

"What about the other car you thought was following us?"

"I think that was the car you almost hit."

"Yanks again?"

"I'm not as sure, but I think so. Two more men, both dark-haired."

We were now driving up towards Trongate.

"Where to?" I asked.

Shannon turned a bit in her seat. "I certainly don't recommend going back to either of the hotels we're checked into."

"How about one out near the airport?"

I got back on the M8 without much trouble, and Shannon kept an eye on the side mirror to see if we'd picked up our tails again.

"What was going on back at Braehead today?" I asked neutrally.

"I was doing what you've been paying me to do."

"And what's that?"

"Detecting."

"What were you detecting?"

"I was talking to the other Neuroticands about you." She looked away for a moment. "You threw me for quite a loop last night."

"And?"

"Let's save it until we get to the hotel, okay? I have a lot to say."

CHAPTER 28

It had been a very bizarre experience for Shannon. If someone had told her when she was seventeen that she'd spend a day hanging with her fave band of all time, she would have completely freaked, and yet that's exactly what had happened, albeit twenty-four years later.

However, that experience was tempered by the reason why she was there to watch Neurotica rehearse. She needed answers to questions that Michael's dreadful story had raised in her mind. She was certainly well aware that all sorts of shenanigans went on when money, youth and sex get all mixed up together, but Michael's story had truly shaken her.

Shannon now saw clearly the reasons behind the way Michael had lived his life since walking out on his "mates".

Checking into airport Holiday Inn, Michael turned to her as they approached the desk, "Do you want me to book one room or two?"

Shannon smiled inwardly. Someone as arrogant as Lee or Rolly would have assumed one room and a night of sex were on the menu. That's one of the things she found so attractive about Michael. He was obviously the major talent in Neurotica and had every right to be arrogant, but Michael was always unassuming and kind, despite his foibles.

Once up in the room, Michael sat down heavily on the corner of one of beds, clearly not the only member of Neurotica who was "knackered".

Shannon sat on the opposite bed. "The first thing I want to say is that I realize how difficult it must have been for you to tell me what you did this morning. For that, I'm very grateful."

"Circumstances didn't leave me much choice."

"Would you have told me anyway?"

He rubbed his face with both hands. "Eventually."

"That's what I was hoping you'd say." She switched beds and sat next to him. "I come from a family of cops. My dad and uncles never expected that the next generation of Cathcarts to be in law enforcement would be female, but they were supportive of my decision.

"And you know what? I'd still be a cop if circumstances hadn't sort of forced my hand. It's tough on a family to have one parent gone at all hours, doing work that can be pretty dangerous, but when it's both, that can be hell. So for the good of our kids, we quit."

"Are you trying to say that you're having trouble dealing with fact that I was involved in a serious crime?"

"In a nutshell, yes."

"I was afraid of that."

Shannon's expression became very solemn. "Michael, what you did might have been far worse than you imagine. Have you ever thought you might have helped cover up a murder?"

He shook his head firmly. "Rolly wouldn't do that."

"By your own admission, Rolly was high on drugs and alcohol. He might not have set out to hurt the girl, but it might have happened nonetheless. I was on the scene for crimes just like that when I was a cop. 'Honest, officers, she fell over and hit her head.' I actually had someone tell me that, and it turned out to be murder. Can you say with certainty the same thing didn't happen twenty-four years ago?"

Michael's shoulders slumped, and he looked every one of his forty-nine years. "Rolly and I had lunch together yesterday. The subject almost came up, but I didn't begin the discussion, and Rolly couldn't or wouldn't. Today, he did say to me that we had to talk."

"Michael, you are going to have to ask him."

"I know...I know." He raised his eyes. "Is that why you were so buddy-buddy with everyone today?"

Shannon smiled, but there was little mirth in it. "I wanted to take the measure of each person in the band. It's quite amazing how you'll all talk about each other given the chance. For one, they've all been dying to know just what the hell happened to you back in Canada, but have been too worried about putting you off to ask about it."

"What did you tell them?"

"That if they didn't want to risk putting you off, they'd shouldn't ask about it."

"So in the end, what did you detect?"

"Lee is eaten up by envy. He knows he's not the heavyweight in the band and resents it. John thinks he has something to prove, that he's every bit as good as you. It's all bull, but that's the way he feels. Tommy is just happy to be there. This is like Christmas for him."

"Did you know he set his son up tonight?"

"Did he? That's exactly what I would have expected from him."

"And Rolly?"

"He's a hard nut to crack. I can tell you that he's tired of being a has-been. He ate more of the forbidden fruit than the rest of you did. For years, he's been faking it. When you left the band, you took the magic. Underneath all the posturing, he knows he's rather pathetic."

"So where do suggest we go from here?"

"Two things need to be done. First, Rolly's given you the opening. You have to discuss what happened in that hotel room. He may not tell you the truth, but you may get an inkling of it from what he says and the way he acts. You're a good judge of character. You'll know if he's telling the truth."

"And the second thing?"

"Get into bed, and I'll show you."

My dreams were mercifully undisturbed that night, but I woke up early nonetheless. Lying in the world between sleep and waking, with Shannon spooned against me, I felt calm and completely focussed for the first time in many years.

Twenty minutes later, I noticed that her breathing had changed.

"Are you awake?" I asked softly.

"Mmmm, yes, but I don't want to be," she answered, then turned over to face me. "No bad dreams?"

"Not last night. I think I was too exhausted to dream."

Shannon smiled. "Do I detect a note of censure?"

"I just had no idea what I was getting into with you."

"And that, sir, is a scandalous *double entendre*. Imagine!"

"You're a fine one to call me scandalous," I laughed. "What would your mother say if she knew what you got up to?"

"What would my daughter say?"

"Rachel? What are you talking about?"

Shannon propped her head on her elbow. "You won't believe this. When I spoke to her the night we left for the UK, she told me she thought I should sleep with you."

"She didn't! What did you tell her?"

"A lot of the things you'd expect a mother to say, naturally. Talk about being scandalized! We're going to have to be very circumspect around her."

Shannon expression suddenly clouded.

"It's not all that bad," I said, putting my arm around her, "or is something else bothering you?"

She looked at me with a serious expression. "With all that's gone on in the last twenty-four hours, I haven't really had a chance to tell you the results of the rest of my trip to Birmingham then Hamburg."

"And those were?"

Shannon held up her right hand, her thumb and index finger making a big, fat zero.

"I've struck out completely. The girl hasn't been in Hamburg for at least a month. I called the concierge of her apartment in Montreal, and he told me he hasn't seen her. Where the hell is she?"

I thought for a moment. "She said she worked in Paris for a while. Might she be there?"

"That damned Chameleon could be anywhere! I'm out of ideas, and those people following us last night showed that the bad guys are still out there, so they obviously don't know where she is, either. Since the Americans are now also nosing around, our problems are getting bigger. There's also another thing."

"And that is?"

Shannon told me about her interview with the policewoman in Hamburg.

"My guess is Campbell has someone tailing me."

"Wouldn't that keep you safe?" I asked.

"It's not me I'm worried about, you big dope!"

"But I've got you."

She snorted and shook her head. "I just wish I could get my hands on that girl."

I got out of bed and looked down with dismay at the sorry state of our clothes strewn about the floor.

"I think we're going to need to do a bit of shopping."

By half ten, I felt as if I'd done a full day's work. I don't know how women seem to be able to spend a whole day shopping and still look bright-eyed and bushy-tailed. All I wanted was a nap.

We were at the far end of Braehead Shopping Centre, near the entrance to the arena, enjoying a bite and a spot of tea before rehearsal began. Below us, a couple of hearty souls were using the circular indoor skating rink, making us both think of home.

So far we'd concentrated on getting clothes for me, since I had to start rehearsing in an hour. Shannon seemed to be enjoying herself. I was glad it was almost over.

"I'll go back to our hotel this afternoon and see what's salvageable. I think staying at different hotels every night is the way to go, so I'll arrange something."

"What now? I asked.

"Well, I need some clothes, and I want to buy something that you'd like to see me in."

When I answered, "Nothing looks good on you, Shannon," she rolled her eyes at my pun.

"I should at least get a couple of tops and another pair of jeans."

Just back down the corridor, there was a store selling what Shannon wanted. I went in and waited while she tried on several pairs of jeans, searching for something beyond my ken—being male and all.

The store was deserted except for us, and I noticed the staff looking at me as I sat and waited for yet more jeans to be tried on and found wanting. The girl who was waiting on us, a mere wisp of a thing with jaggy, fire-engine-red hair and matching eyeliner, was called over to the register by her fellow employees, where all three of them proceeded to stare at me and whisper among themselves before she was pushed back in my direction.

When she returned, she seemed very shy and wouldn't look at me. "They all swear you're Michael Quicksilver. Jody says she saw you interviewed on the telly last night."

"She may be right," I said with smile.

We both looked at the others, who were nearly beside themselves now, and I tried to keep from laughing.

"We knew your band was rehearsing in the arena, but never expected you'd walk into our store!"

"So you're a big Neurotica fan?"

"Not really, but my mum sure is!"

Ouch!

I was signing autographs when Shannon came out of the change room wearing a pair of jeans that looked if they'd been sewn right on her body.

"So what do you think?" she asked, turning in front of me. "It's not the sort of thing I'd usually buy."

The sales girls all giggled, and one boldly said, "They certainly look a bit of all right to me!"

For the next ten minutes, Shannon had all three employees of the store helping her find the perfect tops to go with the jeans. When everyone was satisfied, she stood in front of me, looking as if she might not even be past thirty yet. One of the girls had pinned Shannon's hair up, and she was wearing a fedora. Where that had come from, I couldn't imagine.

I whistled, Shannon blushed enchantingly, and the girls all clapped.

"You look totally different. I swear I might walk right past you on the street and not know you."

"It's amazing how little it takes to look completely different. I've used a disguise as simple as a reversible jacket and a hat, and the person I was tailing never spotted me after the change."

One of the girls asked, "Are you a copper?"

"Used to be. I'm a private investigator now."

"Cool!"

I expected Shannon to laugh at that, but her face showed her thoughts were a thousand miles away.

Suddenly, she was all business as we paid for the new clothes, and the girls were very disappointed when she hustled me quickly out of the store. I did promise to have some tickets sent over, hoping they'd come instead of their parents.

Outside in the corridor, I could feel her quivering with excitement.

"What is going on?" I asked.

"You Brits use a term when you've been clobbered by something right out of left field."

"Gobsmacked?"

"That's it. Well, Michael, I've just been gobsmacked but good!"

"About what?"

"I think I've figured out where our Giovanna is, and boy, do I feel like a fool!"

"Why?"

"Because if I'm right—and I'm willing to bet the farm I am—then I spent my time in Birmingham talking with her!"

"You mean Maria..."

Shannon ignored my question. "I should have seen it. There are a lot of little things that point in that direction, but I was so snowed by her performance I simply never noticed."

"Shannon! *What are you talking about?*"

"Gia is Maria."

"*What?*"

"It all suddenly fits. I just needed your comment about looking different to see what was in front of me all the time."

We found a quiet corner in the food court and sat down, Shannon with her back against the wall and her eyes constantly scanning our surroundings as she spoke, ticking off the points on her fingers.

"I felt really sure I'd find her in Birmingham. The drug shipment must have left the country from there. It's the only thing that makes sense. Since both groups of bad guys are still after you, it seems neither has what they want: drugs *or* money. Why hasn't Giovanna retrieved them and disappeared for good? Well, maybe she can't. Maybe they're someplace too dangerous for her to try.

"Now, here's one of the clues I missed. When I interviewed her that first day, there was a table near the front window of the sitting room completely covered with photos. An awful lot of them were just the two cousins. They look very much alike but also different. Maria has light brown, very curly hair, and in most of the photos it's cut fairly short. Giovanna's is dark, long and wavy. Maria also wears glasses. Get past that and they look very similar.

"My guess is the real difference between the cousins was their different natures. Gia is a classic risk taker. You know all about that. She's more outgoing, probably brighter, too. You can see it in the photos. Maria's a mouse by comparison. Some guy will come along and marry her; she'll live a quiet life, be a good mother, respected by her community. Gia will chew the world up and spit it out. With all I know of Gia's abilities, it would be child's play for her to impersonate her cousin.

"Lastly, when the mother arrived home, Gia-slash-Maria hurried over to her and seemed quite agitated. They spoke rapidly in Italian and looked over in my direction several times. Shortly after, Maria hustled me out of the house. I am such a dunce not to have seen it!"

"So you're saying that was Giovanna posing as Maria and staying with her—do I have this straight—her aunt? Isn't that kind of far-fetched? Why would the aunt go along with this?"

"That's one of the things I'm dying to find out. The whole scenario I've outlined to you is admittedly far-fetched, but it does work. What other explanation is there?"

"So what are you going to do now?"

"I'm driving down to Birmingham."

"Why would you want to drive?"

"Because, dear Michael, two people sitting on the far side, pretending to be enjoying pots of tea, are definitely keeping an eye on us. Don't turn around!"

"How long have you known?"

"I had a feeling when we first got here, but I couldn't make them until we went into that last clothing store."

"Which group of bad guys?"

"Neither. They're cops."

"How can you be certain?"

Shannon gave me a disgusted look.

"So why do you want to drive?" I asked again.

"Because I don't want anybody to know where I'm going. How long will it take to drive there?"

"Five hours, if you don't hit any traffic or bad weather on the way."

"Perfect."

"There should be a map in the glove box."

"Even more perfect."

"If you lose your tail, won't they get suspicious and put out some sort of bulletin on you?"

She flashed a naughty smile. "Then I'll just have to make it seem like they lost me by accident."

"When will you be back?"

"That depends. Keep your cell phone on. I'll call when I can." She looked across the table at me, a serious expression on her face. "Those two over there may be cops, but you still have to be on your guard for the bad guys. They must be getting pretty desperate. Don't take *any* chances."

We stood and Shannon made a big display of kissing me. Not being used to the sort of life I live, she hadn't thought of paparazzi being nearby, but fortunately there were none.

"You know, this is a pretty hare-brained plan you've come up with. If you have discovered Giovanna, what are you going to do with her?"

She shrugged. "I'm making this up as I go along."

Once inside the arena, I was immediately swept away by the juggernaut that is a major concert production. Today was the day for media interviews, and they also recorded a short clip of the band playing. Finally, the riff-raff cleared out, and we got down to the serious business.

The rehearsal the evening before had galvanized everyone in the group, and things that day went even better. The lighting had been rejigged yet again, with more effects turning up, including some rather nifty lasers which bounced all over the roof at the climax of the show. Someone had put in a lot of hours setting up all those mirrors.

As soon as we hit the last note, Rolly disappeared offstage. "Another interview," he told us, rolling his eyes as if he didn't enjoy doing them.

It was no surprise that he'd become completely swept up in the whole publicity thing, conducting innumerable interviews via phone, email, fax and in person. But then, he'd always been the public face of the band, and he was welcome to it in.

John and I kept our heads down, tweaking the arrangements whenever and wherever we could.

"You're bloody confusing the hell out of me!" Lee complained after the break, during which John had yet again completely changed the guitar and bass parts to one of the songs. "Give me a bleeding break here, mates!"

John clapped him on the shoulder. "Lee, old man, it's called imagination and hard work, neither of which you know much about.

Let me show you once again how it fits together. It isn't that complicated, and it will surely impress the fan who comes to see you."

In the past, Lee might have threatened to put out John's lights for a comment like that.

Twenty-four years on, he just laughed and got in a dig of his own. "You always had a bleeding big head, and it's gone and got bigger with all that studio work. Tell me, when you fly, do they make you buy an extra seat for it?"

When we took another break late in the afternoon, I went off by myself to clear my head. Things were going smashingly, and I finally felt we were going to acquit ourselves very well.

The foyer of Braehead arena looks out over the River Clyde. Across the way are docks where they build ships for the Royal Navy. You couldn't see much, because night was already falling, as was a bit of snow. For the first time since I'd entered the arena that day, I thought of Shannon, who should have been on the outskirts of Birmingham by now.

Footsteps approached behind me. I turned to find Rolly.

"You've been keeping yourself scarce, mate."

"It's not my doing, Rolly, honestly. Shall we just say my life is a bit complicated at the moment?"

He shrugged. "Suit yourself if you want to be mysterious." For a bit, we both looked out at the few boats chugging by on the river. "The band sounds pretty damn good."

"Yes, it does."

"I think Angus would be very pleased."

Sadness washed over me. "And he would have liked to be here. We always were his favourites."

Rolly turned to look at me. "You know, it's funny how life turns out. All those years ago, we had the world by the nuts, then everything went into the crapper."

"You, most of all people, should know why that is, Rolly," I said, but with no heat, no accusation. I'd finally moved beyond that.

"Why didn't you talk to me before you walked, Michael? Why

wouldn't you talk to me over the years? I used to be your best mate."

I shook my head. "I couldn't, Rolly. What happened in your room that night in Chicago made it crystal clear what we'd become: so carried away with our careers that a human life didn't even matter. I didn't want to be a part of that any more."

Rolly looked stunned. "You mean it was that thing with the girl?"

"That's a pretty casual way to put something that awful!" I said with my anger rising.

"Jesus Christ, Michael! I've always thought it was the crap we'd been putting you through. You know, the partying and not taking our music—or you—seriously. And now you're prattling on about that girl. Sure, it was a tragedy and all that..."

I started having an almost out-of-body experience as Rolly continued talking. As clearly as if she were standing next to me, I could hear what Shannon had said the night before in the Holiday Inn, and I knew that it was time to ask that question I'd feared for so many years.

Eyes and ears open to pick up any nuance, I held up my hand to stop the flood of words. "Did you kill her, Rolly?"

His eyes bugged out, and his mouth opened and closed a few times, giving him the look of a beached salmon.

He was finally able to gasp out, "You think *I* killed that silly cow?"

I made no response.

"Just what the fuck did Angus tell you about what happened?"

"He told me that the girl had freaked out and ran into the bathroom, where she slipped and fell."

"So Angus never told you."

"Told me what?"

Rolly walked away a few feet, shaking his head, and it was easy to see he was quite upset.

"Oh, lord, I can't believe this is happening!" he shouted, then turned and came back. "Angus had to pull her off me. That girl went ape shit, screaming that I was trying to rape her. That was all bollocks, of course. It's always the quiet ones you have to watch out for. If I hadn't been so out of it, she wouldn't have got the drop on me. By the time Angus responded to the commotion, she was beyond gone: screaming, kicking, scratching, biting. She almost yanked my effing tackle off!

"You know how big Angus was. I remember him coming in and plucking her off me as if she was no more than a bleeding pussy cat. He took her into the bathroom, and a moment or two later, she quieted right down. He came out and asked me if I could help him move her, but I didn't know what he meant. I was too far gone by that time between the coke and the booze, and I think I'd done some pills, too. I couldn't remember my own name too clearly.

"Angus told me to stay put and went to fetch you. I remember you going into the bathroom with him and not much more."

I looked long and hard at Rolly as we stood there. He returned my gaze unblinkingly, and I found that I believed what he'd told me.

"You're right, Rolly," I admitted sadly. "I should have talked with you sooner."

"I've had nightmares about it for years."

I shook my head with disbelief, and answered simply, "So have I."

"Angus told you it was an accident? I suppose it could have been. She was that out of control."

"We'll never know now, will we?"

Rolly looked at his watch, a Rolex and probably fake. I suddenly felt very sorry for him, trying to carry on all these years, get a second chance at snagging that brass ring. It was all rather pathetic.

"We should be getting back inside," he said. "They're probably wondering what the hell's become of us."

"You go in. I need a few more minutes to absorb all of this."

"I need a drink!" Rolly said as he went through the door back into the arena.

I needed some fresh air, so I went into the passageway that ringed the arena under the raised seats. Halfway around was a large room leading to the loading dock. I went out there and sat on a box.

I didn't know whether to laugh or cry. Here Neurotica was doing a concert to honour the man who'd done us the most damage possible.

I was surprised when a car wheeled around the corner. Probably some shopper who'd made a wrong turn trying to get out of the car park. It pulled over at the far end of the dock where the stairs were.

Two men got out of the car. The hairs on my neck stood up. I looked at the doors into the arena, only to see them open and two more men step out.

My luck had finally run out.

I was too far away from anyone to yell for help, and there was nowhere to run, so I just waited. The two groups met in front of me.

"Is this him?" one of the blokes from the car asked. An American.

"Yup," One from inside the arena answered, also American. "Saw him on TV last night."

"Get up!"

When I didn't move, they yanked me to my feet.

One of the Americans stuck his face into mine. "We have someone who wants to meet you."

With them holding my arms tightly, we started moving along the loading dock.

Suddenly, behind us, someone shouted, "Oi! You there! What the bloody hell do you think you're doing?"

I turned my head and said, "It's all right, Tommy. Just go inside. I'll be in shortly."

Thomas Higgins had grown up on the same streets I had, so he knew a good frog march when he saw one. Being big himself, he thought he could stop it.

It was a brave act, but ultimately foolish. As I was forced on, two stood and waited.

Tommy did knock one down with a hard left to the head, but the other was ready, and I saw his arm go up and heard the cosh come down on the back of Tommy's head with a sickening thud. He dropped like a stone.

The arm was going up for another blow when I yelled out, "Bastards! Leave him alone!"

The one with the cosh stopped, then helped his mate to his feet.

They left Tommy lying on the concrete. Alive or dead, I didn't know.

CHAPTER 29

Shannon was pretty pleased with herself as she sped down the M6 towards the Midlands.

Midlands? Damn! She was sounding more and more like a Brit with each passing day.

As she'd pulled out of her space in the Braehead parking lot and slowly made her way to the exit, it hadn't been hard to pick out her tail. She must have been pretty low on the surveillance ladder, because they'd sent out amateurs, who made two *faux pas* before they even got to the M8.

Since this road led downtown, it would be logical she'd take it, so they suspected nothing. The tough thing was to make her losing them seem like an accident. Shannon's chance came when she passed a big transport in the middle lane as an exit approached. She was in the inside lane, and at the last possible moment, she swerved around the transport (causing him to lean hard on his horn), shot across all three lanes of traffic and down the exit ramp. Her tail had to drive helplessly past.

To them, it would seem as if she'd almost missed her exit then done something stupid to get off in time.

By the time she'd made it halfway to Birmingham, she was feeling like an old hand with this left hand driving trick. Also, Brits drove very fast, something she enjoyed.

With only two errors, she made it to the street of rundown row houses where she'd met with the girl whom she'd suspected now was Giovanna Vennuti.

As luck would have it, Signora Rota was home.

"*Si?*" she said upon opening the door.

"Hello. I was here the other day speaking to Maria. May I come in and speak with you?"

She was dressed in black like many older women in traditional Italian families and suddenly wary. Her English was heavily accented but fluent. "What do you want?"

Shannon flashed her most engaging smile. "Like I said, to speak with you."

"I do not have time. I am busy."

Shannon leaned forward. "You should make time. I either speak with you or I speak with the police, tell them what I know. It's your choice."

"The police? Why the police?"

"It's about your daughter."

Now the woman definitely looked scared and stood aside, indicating that Shannon should enter.

She was shown into the same sitting room, but this time Shannon looked around with different eyes, having figured out how the magician's trick worked. The clues were on the table near the window.

Shannon walked over and picked up the large white frame in pride of place at the table's centre: Maria. The photo showed a pretty-enough girl of around sixteen with short brown hair, an enigmatic smile and eyes behind her glasses that spoke of a modest intelligence. There were certainly wheels turning in her head, but she seemed to lack something. The other girl who shared many of the photos with Maria, however, seemed to exude something more vital, as if the sun shone down on her with greater intensity. She had the world by the tail and knew it: Giovanna.

Shannon turned to Signora Rota, who'd come no further into the small room than the doorway. "This is a good photo of your daughter."

The woman bobbed her head once, acknowledging the compliment.

Then Shannon reached into her purse and pulled out a folded piece of paper. Picking up another photo that showed Gia and Maria with their hair up (and judging by their white dresses and age, probably their graduation ceremony), she studied it.

For almost a minute, she scarcely breathed as she tried to take in what the photo was telling her. If she'd felt like a fool before, she was double or triple the fool she'd thought she was. Every time she felt she was getting a handle on things, the damned Chameleon pulled the rug right out from under her.

Never one to hold onto a theory when it had been shredded and thrown back in her face like so much confetti, Shannon took stock on where this new information might lead her. Things were much more complicated than she'd thought.

"Could you take a look at this photo I brought?" she asked, crossing the room to hand it to Signora Rota.

The old woman concentrated on it for several seconds then looked up, perplexed. "I do not understand. The numbers on this photo tell me that it was taken less than a month ago."

"It was."

"But this is impossible! Giovanna is dead."

"I figured as much. Please tell me about it."

"But why would you want to know this? You are with the big international company Maria works for, the one that sends her all over the world to lead training sessions. It's why she only works at our bakery sometimes now. I do not understand."

"Maybe we should sit down," Shannon sighed. "I think this is going to be a long conversation."

The woman perched on the end of a rather worn, stuffed chair, clearly ill at ease.

Shannon took a deep breath and began. "I don't work for any company. I'm a private investigator from Canada."

"Why are you here? What do you want to ask me?"

By way of answer, Shannon fetched the photo in the white frame, and said gently as she held it out, "Look carefully at both photos, especially at the left ear, although on my photo it's more difficult to see."

The woman squinted hard at it. "They look the same."

"Yes, and it's one of the key identifiers to establishing a person's identity. It's as individual as fingerprints. Unless you are really knowledgeable and thorough, the ears are never considered when someone is wearing a disguise. And that's something I should have remembered," Shannon finished, speaking mostly to herself.

"I am confused. What are you trying to say?"

"This is a surveillance photo taken in a Toronto hotel of someone I thought was Giovanna Vennuti. The photo in the white frame proves that it was your daughter Maria."

Signora Rota's expression became firm. "No, no! You have made a mistake. My daughter could not have been in Canada at that time. Her company sent her to Australia. It was all very sudden, and she missed the funeral of her grandmother. Maria was very upset about this."

Australia? The Chameleon didn't lack for imagination, that was for damn sure.

Just then, the sound of someone putting a key into the door broke in on the two women.

"*Ciao, mamma, sei qui?*"

The mother's answer was in English for my benefit. "Maria, I am in the sitting room. Please come in here!"

Maria appeared in the doorway and didn't see Shannon right away, because she was sitting on a chair behind the door. The girl walked over and affectionately kissed her mamma on the head.

Signora Rota stuck out her hand, pointing at Shannon. "Tell this mad woman about the company you work for and where you were two weeks ago!"

Maria turned, and while she was quick, she was not quick enough, and Shannon clearly saw the fright in her eyes for a fraction of a second, then the consummate actress, the girl who had looked so plain and clearly wasn't, slid back into her chosen role again.

"Shannon? What the devil have you been telling my mother, you naughty thing! You are such a tease."

"No, Maria!" her mother continued. "She has showed me a photograph. She said that it was taken of you in Toronto. You told me you were in Australia. What is going on?"

Maria leaned her backside against a low chest of drawers and looked at Shannon. "Do you want to tell her, or should I?"

Having no idea where this was going, Shannon made no response.

Kneeling down in front of her mother, and grasping her hands, Maria looked up and said, "The company I work for doesn't pay me to conduct seminars, mamma. I'm an investigator for them."

It was such a stunning statement, Shannon couldn't decide whether to bust her one or jump to her feet and applaud. The Chameleon was a marvel.

"And that is the truth? I know you, Maria, and sometimes you lie too easily."

"I swear on my father's grave, mamma. I am telling you the truth."

"I am to believe that you are spy?"

Maria laughed easily. "Nothing that grand! Our company investigates industrial espionage and manages security. I'm sorry I couldn't tell you earlier, but it was one of the terms of my contract."

Signora Rota smiled triumphantly over her daughter's shoulder, completely snowed by what she'd heard. "But why has this woman told me all about you if it is forbidden?"

Maria turned and winked at Shannon. "I guess it means that I have got the promotion at last. I will now be a supervisor!"

The girl's audacity was simply amazing. Shannon was about to bring this touching scene to a screeching halt when Maria flashed her a warning with her eyes.

The old woman prattled on how proud her papa would have been, and Mamma Vennuti, too, with the success of her clever daughter.

Eventually, Shannon decided to wrest this out-of-control situation back to more manageable waters and said, "Signora Rota, I have a lot to discuss with your daughter. Perhaps you have something else to do?"

The woman jumped to her feet. "I am forgetting my manners! You would like some espresso or tea, perhaps? I also have biscuits, but they are from a tin, I am ashamed to say."

"Nothing for me, thanks. I really do have a tight schedule."

As the mother left, Maria shut the door behind her.

"That was a close one!" she laughed.

Shannon shook her head in amazement. "You are too much."

Maria sat in the chair her mother had vacated, sprawling in an unladylike fashion with one leg over the arm, her foot tapping the air. "So what gave me away?"

"Your ears."

"Right," she said, nodding thoughtfully. "I should have known better than to beard an ex-cop."

Considering she was in a ton of trouble, Maria seemed quite carefree and chipper. Shannon felt sure she was being treated to yet another role, one crafted to get the girl out of this mess.

"You've created havoc in a lot of lives. People have died because of things you've done, and a number of people are in great danger."

"Your employer, for instance? I'm sorry that Michael had to get sucked into this. He's a genuinely good person. I enjoyed his company rather a lot." Maria looked at Shannon then laughed again. "Have you been bonking your clients, Shannon? Shame on you!"

Despite herself, Shannon blushed furiously. Should she add mind reader to the list of the girl's accomplishments?

Forcing her embarrassment back, Shannon fixed the girl with what she hoped was a firm gaze. "You are going to get Michael out of this mess."

"And how do you propose I do that?"

Shannon felt the ground underneath her firm up. "There are people in Glasgow looking for him. People from Birmingham, too. They all seem to think he can lead them to you. I'm going to give you to them."

"And why should I go along with that?"

"Because," Shannon said leaning forward, "if you don't, I'll break both your goddamned legs! You may be slippery as an eel, but I can still whip your ass. You *are* going to Glasgow."

Maria looked at her for a moment. "I suppose what you're really saying is, if I don't cooperate, you'll turn me over to the police. Don't use this violent crap on me. Once a cop, always a cop."

"Don't bet on it."

"But I am. Okay, so I agree to go to Glasgow. What's in it for me? You're signing my death warrant."

"Not really. We're going to do a deal: the heroin and the money, too, in exchange for leaving all of us alone."

Maria flashed the same smile Shannon had seen in the white-framed photo. "Oh, ho. We have been doing our homework, haven't we?"

"Stands to reason you don't have what you want, because you're still hanging around. So it has to be in Birmingham. Where is it?"

"You wouldn't believe me if I told you."

"Try me."

"No, first we're going to work out how I'm going to get out of this. And do you know why? I get the feeling that the police will be involved somewhere along the line. Like I said before: once a cop, always a cop. You want Mastrocolle's arse as much as I do. Admit it! That would certainly be a feather in the O'Brien cap, wouldn't it? Might even make your ex jealous, eh?"

Shannon had a distinct feeling of vertigo. How did this girl know so much about her? No matter what Shannon did, the Chameleon was always one step ahead. Shannon felt as if she was trapped inside a very complicated piece of machinery, one whose purpose she could barely comprehend and which threatened to spin out of control any moment.

Wheels within wheels within wheels.

An hour later, Shannon was back on the motorway, heading north with Maria at the wheel. She needed to devote all her attention to watching the girl. Trust was definitely not an option where the Chameleon was concerned.

The girl had asked if she could change. Shannon allowed it, but under her watchful eye. Surprisingly, Maria had chosen an old fashioned, flowered dress, mid-calf and quite unsuitable for the cold weather. When Shannon questioned that, she replied simply that it was her favourite.

Maria had told her mother a further series of the most outrageous lies to get out of the house. Shannon (her supervisor) was taking Maria out for a celebratory dinner, then they'd be leaving for the States the next morning, so Maria could begin her new job. Signora Rota beamed and smiled at her marvellous daughter.

Shannon, feeling ill over what she was witnessing, had great difficulty not telling the poor woman what was really going on, but she knew it would have accomplished nothing. Still, as a mother herself, it was very hard to watch. Maria had absolutely no shame.

While she was changing, the girl had pulled an overnight bag from under her bed.

Shannon, not trusting her in the slightest, had taken possession of it, and once back in the rental car, she'd rifled through it.

Maria sat looking on with amusement. "You going to pat me down, too?"

"Yes, but not here. I'll do it when we stop for gas." Shannon had smiled grimly.

At the bottom of Maria's bag, she'd found a kilo of heroin wrapped in plastic.

Maria had shrugged as Shannon held it up. "Thought we might need it to show them we're serious about giving them back their merchandise."

Now, shortly after seven in the evening, they were speeding north to Glasgow, much as Michael had done with the girl not that long ago.

"My sources in New York couldn't or wouldn't tell me how big the shipment was."

"Three hundred kilos," the girl answered casually.

No wonder everyone had their shorts in a knot!

Maria had certainly become involved in very high stakes dealings, and Shannon was dying to know why. She was obviously more than smart. Why play such a loser's game? There was obviously something more to it than Shannon knew at the present time.

Maria pulled the car out and shot around a slow moving transport, clearly enjoying herself.

Twenty minutes later, on the outskirts of Stafford, Shannon's cell phone chirped in her pocket.

"Michael?"

"Shannon," Michael groaned. "I've been—"

She cursed as she thought the connection had been broken, but then another voice came on—an American voice.

"Listen closely, Ms Private Dick. We got your boyfriend, and he's very nicely told us you know where the girl is. We want her. Now."

Shannon managed to keep her voice steady. "I've got her with me, and we're on our way to Glasgow."

"Isn't that convenient," the voice answered sarcastically. "Good thing for you and your rock star. How soon will you be here?"

"Maybe five hours. It could be longer with the traffic we're hitting."

"That's good. Call us when you get closer, and we'll tell you where the exchange will take place. And I don't think I need to tell you what will happen if there's any monkey business, do I?"

"Save your breath. I'm well aware of how these situations work."

"Good girl. Don't forget, we're counting on you. So is Michael."

The connection was severed, and Shannon slumped back.

Maria looked over with one eyebrow raised. "So they've finally snagged Michael, have they?"

The detective nodded.

"Well, that should keep us on our toes, eh, Shannon?"

CHAPTER 30

I was struggling frantically, having seen the way Tommy went down, but the men on each side of me simply tightened their grip on my arms and warned that I'd get the same if I didn't smarten up.

Once in the car, I was squeezed into the middle of the back seat between the two largest ones. They produced a cloth bag and shoved it over my head. I knew better than to struggle.

We drove for a long time to get to our destination. Walking from the car, we crunched across gravel.

I was marched into a room that was quite warm and heavy hands on my shoulders forced me to sit on a hard chair. The crackle of plastic sheeting underneath it made me break out in a sweat. Having heard Giovanna's story, I knew what that meant.

The bag was pulled off, and I found myself in a nicely appointed, slightly damp-smelling room, old furniture, carpets, all very comfortable. To my left was a fireplace with a wood stove attachment, and about five feet in front of me sat a comfortable-looking leather armchair with a floor lamp just behind it, casting a meagre glow. Curtains at the far end were drawn tight, same with a French door in the wall next to it. Over the desk next to me a large clock ticked away the minutes—an ominous sound under the circumstances.

It was one of the Americans, standing behind me, who said into my ear, "Keep your eyes forward or we will hurt you. Got that?"

I nodded.

I was certain two of my captors were American, one a Brit and one a Scot. The Yanks had sat with me in the back of the car. The Scot had driven, and the Brit had ridden shotgun. I thought I might be able to recognize the Yanks again, but that wouldn't do me a lot of good if I were dead—and that's what I fully expected to be in short order.

"Now, are you going to tell us where the girl is?"

I'd been in this position before, but I thought I'd see how far I could play the game this time. "What girl?"

Something cold touched my neck, and suddenly it felt as if my body were being ripped apart from the inside, as every muscle went into one huge spasm. The pain coursing through me defied description, and its effect was so powerful that their strong hands couldn't hold me on the chair. I fell to the floor, writhing in agony.

I must have passed out, because the next thing I knew, I was back on the chair, and my head was wet and dripping. Hands forced my arms behind me where they were fastened to the chair using plastic ties. My legs followed.

"Didn't enjoy that, did you?" the voice said into my ear. "Now, I'll ask again: where is the girl?"

"Sod off."

They must have cranked up the juice on their stun gun, because this time I didn't think I would survive. Three seconds of it seemed like a lifetime and reduced me to a quivering pile of jelly.

As I sat there gasping, the voice said, "Don't make the same mistake again, buddy. Tell us where the girl is."

I'd reached the end of what I could stand. "We...we think she's in Birmingham. The investigator I brought over from Canada has gone down to check it out."

Hands rifled through my pockets. Another American voice said, "Cell phone. Good. Tell Mr. M. we have things under control."

They undid my hands and told me to call Shannon. It took three tries to punch it in. Shaking so badly from the effects of the electro-shocks, it was a wonder I could even hold the phone.

I tried to pass something useful to her, but they grabbed the phone away before I could get much out. From my end of the conversation, though, I got the feeling that Shannon had bagged her Chameleon and was on the way back to Glasgow.

I allowed myself a bit of hope. She was a smart women and would go into this with her eyes wide open.

Then they fastened my hands again, turned off the lights and left the room, leaving me to ponder my mortality in utter darkness.

Shannon's brain was in overdrive as she tried to figure out angles and probabilities. Everything had changed since the phone call, and matters were even less under her control, which had been tenuous at best.

Michael had sounded terrible on the phone. Obviously, they'd been hurting him, and it must have been pretty terrible. The bad guys would keep him alive for the moment, but how far they would extend that depended on the way Shannon handled things over the next few hours. She felt unequal to the task.

Next to her, Maria said nothing but kept glancing over. Finally, she broke the silence. "Each passing mile is bringing us closer to Glasgow, Shannon. You're going to have to come up with something or people are going to die. And I don't plan on one of them being me."

"Me neither." Shannon sat up. "Why did you agree so easily to come to Glasgow with me? I was certain it was going to take some heavy pressure. I don't trust you as far as I could throw you, and I want to make that perfectly clear from the start."

Maria smiled wryly. "I wouldn't trust me either. If I'm to tell you what you're asking, you need to understand why I did what I did in the first place. Haven't you been curious about that, or has the mighty detective already figured everything out?"

"Spare me the sarcasm, okay?"

"Sorry. Bad habit."

"How much of the BS you fed me the other day is true? Every time I've heard something about you or someone has told me something you said, there's been a grain of truth in it, but only a grain."

"Fair enough. Okay, here goes. This is the story, and it's the truth as far as it goes. My cousin Giovanna was indeed talented and beautiful. It was always 'Giovanna this' and 'Giovanna that'. Even my own parents prattled on about her all the time. I was always the 'shy, quiet one', not as pretty and generally just a lesser person. They never came out and said that, but I could tell.

"But as you know, there's a lot more to me than they imagined. Gia was a good actress, but I was better. She could only speak English and bad Italian. It was little Maria who excelled at languages, not Gia.

"She was a good girl for the most part. I was the one always getting her into trouble. I'll bet you thought it was me who ratted her out when we'd sneak out to meet boys, right? It was, but I was the one who set things up. She took the heat because they never for a moment thought Maria would do anything bad on her own.

"Mamma Vennuti was a real hammer with her. One thing I got a charge out of doing was dressing up like Gia and doing something bad, like kissing a boy where the priest would be sure to see it, then Mamma V would find out and the crap would fly, I'll tell you!"

"Didn't you like your cousin?" Shannon asked.

Maria's answer came out almost in a wail. "I loved my cousin! She was my best friend, my only friend!"

"Seems you chose a funny way to show it."

"Maybe, but I also had to put up with a lot because of her. I never got the chances she did. And Gia really didn't mind. She'd do the same to me when she could."

Shannon wondered if that last statement were true but kept her mouth shut.

"The part about Gia running off was almost the truth, only she'd planned on doing it when she was twenty, and not for the reasons I told you. I didn't know any of it at the time, but Mamma V. had told Gia everything about her mother."

"What things?"

"Like who her father really was. That was a horribly stupid thing to do. You see, Gia was a hopeless romantic, and she'd been imagining all her life that her father was a count or something, and someday he'd come to take her away to his magnificent home. She'd have me come with her, and we'd live like princesses.

"Her father *was* wealthy, only it turned out that he was also a very bad man. Gia's mother did come to a sad end when she finally went to confront him. That part was all true. Gia's mum had also been a romantic, and she'd fallen for a mafia boss from New York."

Shannon shook her head in wonder. "Not Luigi Mastrocolle!"

Maria nodded her head. "One and the same. Giovanna's mother didn't know it at the time, and when she went back to Italy to try to meet up with him again, that's when she found out, and I guess that's why she jumped off that bridge—or maybe Mastrocolle helped her. I like to think he did."

"So what happened to Gia?"

Maria went quiet, and Shannon could tell she was feeling a fair bit of emotional stress at the question. It also crossed her mind that the Chameleon's current silence might be just another dodge.

After another few minutes, the girl began speaking again, her voice harsh and grating. "Gia got cancer, the really bad kind. It ate her up in about six months."

"So how do *you* fit into all this, and why the elaborate charade pretending to be your cousin?"

Now Maria *was* crying. "Because when my cousin was dying, she made me swear to get her father for what he did! And I'm about to do that! That's why you're here."

"Whoa! Back up the dump truck. That's why *I'm* here? What the hell are you talking about?"

Maria got control of herself, but her voice still had a sharp edge. "You don't honestly think I'd just bow my head and come along nicely to what would certainly be my funeral, do you?"

"So you're telling me that you've planned all this?"

"Don't be dense. What I did was set certain things in motion, and this is the result."

Now it was Shannon who was silent for several minutes, as she digested what she'd just been told. The conclusion was either the girl next to her was certifiable, or this whole thing had just gotten impossibly complicated.

"Okay, I can see why you impersonated your cousin. You're standing in for her, aren't you?"

Maria was was grim. "Got that in one."

"But you're telling me you set this whole thing up? How?"

"I knew that I had to get at Mastrocolle and make him suffer for what he did. The question was how. It took a lot of careful research."

"Research? What kind of research?"

"I had some money, and Gia left everything she had to me, so I made up a story about a job that would take me all around the world and fed that to my mother. Then I packed up and went to the States. It wasn't hard to meet people who knew Mastrocolle or worked for him, and after several months I managed to worm my way in among them. As you can imagine, I make a pretty good drug mule. At first, I helped Mastrocolle make *a lot* of money."

"What about the boyfriend who was in with you on the drug deal that went wrong?"

"Paul was a greedy fool and stubborn as all get out. I almost lost everything because of him. He had to be played just right. All men do."

Shannon was well aware of what that might mean. She shifted in her seat uncomfortably.

"With Paul, I was closer to the inside of his organization. The Mafia is getting squeezed on all sides: law enforcement, biker gangs, Russian mob, Asian Triads, you name it. The old man needed really a big score. With a little encouragement from Paul and me, that was turned into a huge score."

"Why didn't you work for the police?"

"Only a cop would say that! Look, Shannon, you and I both know there are too many people on the take. That would have been an incredibly stupid thing to do. No, I wanted his own greed to bring him down.

"All the time I was working in New York, I was also setting up my other bases from which to operate."

"How many do you have?"

"I told you about the one in Hamburg, even though I'd already cleared out of there. That was to get you out of the way so the New Yorkers could grab Michael. Sadly, the plan did a ball's up when he didn't come back to his room the other night."

"Why would you need me out of the way for that?"

"I didn't want you to get hurt by doing something stupidly heroic. I actually like you, Shannon. Michael, too, for that matter."

"What if I hadn't figured out who you were?"

The girl shrugged. "I had contingency plans."

Shannon could only shake her head.

Maria continued, "You found the apartment in Montreal, and I also know that in New York you met with those two old drunks who used to work for Mastrocolle."

"You were following me."

Maria's smile reminded Shannon of a fox. "Certainly. And I was cheering from the far side of the restaurant when you had that touching rendezvous with your ex over dinner. You see, it was very useful to have everyone looking around for Giovanna when I could just stand and watch things happen as Maria." A road sign flashed by. "I have to use the loo. Mind if we stop? There's a rest area coming up."

They pulled off and parked near the entrance. Shannon followed Maria in, walking just behind her right elbow and ready for anything to happen. Inside the deserted washroom, Shannon waited outside the stall, not taking any chances.

Maria had gone in, but the girl who came out was a completely different person, certainly not unknown to Shannon, although she'd never met her in the flesh before.

Coolly walking over to the sinks, she opened her purse and took out mascara and lipstick. After a bit of makeup and a quick combing of her long brown hair, she turned around and casually dropped a wig of short brown hair into a stunned Shannon's hand. "Say hello to Giovanna, Shannon. Looks like you missed this when you searched me earlier."

Her voice sounded different: lower, more throaty and far more sexy, her accent slightly less jarring. She moved with liquid grace. The damn Chameleon even managed to seem taller somehow.

Throughout the display, the detective felt as if she'd been clobbered in the gut by a two-by-four and doubted if she'd ever be able trust her skills again. About the only thing she'd done right was realize that something wasn't kosher in the Rota household. Everything else she had missed. Everything!

The Chameleon patted Shannon's cheek. "In a bar on St. Denis in Montreal, you actually asked me for directions back to the airport. Remember the blonde?"

Shannon remembered all right, and her face burned with embarrassment. All the time she'd thought she was being so clever following up her leads. And all the time, the Chameleon had been watching her, no doubt laughing at her pathetic attempts. She was so angry with herself that she had to hit back.

"Do you know what you almost did to my family back in Toronto?"

The Chameleon sighed. "There are only two things I regret, Shannon: what happened to Angus and getting your children tangled up in this. I tried telling Angus that he should leave, but he was a stubborn old goat, you know? As for what happened at your farm, I was in New York at the time, pushing a few buttons, and I don't know what I would have been able to do even if I had been there. Those damned Brums were always the spanner in my plans. There is one good thing that came out of it, though."

"What's that?"

"Michael and you got together." She started for the washroom door and said over her shoulder, "Aren't you even going to thank me?"

|||

I don't know how many hours later it was when the lights went on and the room started to fill up with people.

My hands and feet were numb from the plastic ties being too tight.

I'd spent the time being alternately angry with myself for being taken so easily, worrying about Tommy, worrying about Shannon and trying to come to grips with what Rolly had told me just before I'd been nabbed.

That was probably the most stunning thing of all: to know that the twenty-four years I'd spent in musical exile had been based on totally wrong information. Neurotica would probably have failed ultimately, but we could have had a much longer ride. I could have spared myself anguish that had almost overwhelmed me on more than one occasion.

Angus, how could you have lied to me like that?

The first person to enter the room stuffed the bag down over my head again. It had a musty smell that made me want to gag.

Across from me, the armchair creaked as someone sat down heavily. Several people in the room who had been talking abruptly stopped.

From the chair a voice, American, old and hoarse. "This is him?"

"Yeah, boss."

"And the girl, when's she expected?"

"They should have called us by now."

"You might want to give her a call on loverboy's cell phone and let her know just how impatient we're getting, *capisci*?"

Shannon answered the phone on the first ring. Fortunately, the connection was good.

"Where the hell are you?" the American voice said harshly. "We been waiting too long... Well, you got a lot of driving to do yet. Do you know the area? ...Just a second." One of the locals must have been called over, because the American then said, "You talk to her. I don't know nothin' about the roads around here."

As the Scot gave Shannon directions, I realized that we must be somewhere in Argyll, probably reasonably close to Dunoon, because he mentioned Come By Chance and the road down along Loch Eck.

"...and partway down Loch Eck, there's a restaurant on the left hand side of the road. You can't miss it. When you arrive there, call us. You'll get the final directions then."

The American took the phone. "And no funny business, or your boyfriend won't be playing no more concerts."

They stuck the cell back in my shirt pocket, and I listened to the old man ask questions about what was going on. Things didn't sound too good for Shannon's Chameleon. They were going to make her suffer. Mastrocolle's honour had to be avenged. Actually, he used the word *vendetta*.

It must have been at least two hours later when my cell rang again. I'd sat there the whole time, head still covered by that stinky bag, feeling woozy and terribly thirsty while they all ate and drank. I guess the condemned man doesn't get a last meal in Mafia circles.

The Scot took the call. "Yeah, okay. Now listen carefully, lassie. I'm only saying this once. Here's how you get to where we are."

Now I knew pretty well exactly where we were. I wondered if this crew had any idea how close they were to Angus's place.

"And remember: we have people watching your every move."

Mastrocolle sent the two locals outside to bolster the forces already on guard duty. "Make sure there are no screw-ups. Any monkey business and this guy gets it. Don't take any chances on this deal going bad!... What?... Yeah, okay. I'll put him on."

The cell was stuck under the hood. "Shannon? Be very careful!"

A short time later, I heard a car labouring up a driveway covered with gravel.

In the next few minutes, I'd find out whether we were all going to live or die.

CHAPTER 31

The drive continued north with Shannon in an increasingly anxious state. Struggle as she might, the playing field continued to tilt towards the Chameleon.

Actually, she had no idea what to even *call* the girl any more—other than that. The person sitting next to her now was no longer any more Maria Rota than Shannon was.

That had been the most stunning event yet. Maria had walked into that washroom cubicle as one person and walked out as someone who not only looked different, but *was* different in every way. Either she was the finest actor ever, or...

Shannon shuddered. To be stuck with a person who was at best mentally unstable was *not* a comforting thought—with lives hanging in the balance.

At the top of the next hour she had turned on the BBC news, discovering to her dismay that the kidnapping of Michael Quicksilver was the lead story. Facts were sparse, but it had been confirmed by police that he'd been taken shortly before five. Also mentioned was the fact that one of the other Neurotica members had been injured when he'd tried to stop the abduction.

Her anxiety ratcheted up to teeth-clenching levels, and she knew the Chameleon was fully aware of it.

As they were approaching Carlisle, just south of the Scottish border, the girl looked over and asked, "So do you have any ideas about what we're going to do, Shannon? Because you are going to have to make that call pretty soon, and you'd better have a bloody good plan in place, or this is not going to end well."

Shannon felt as if she was sliding down a steep incline, with nothing to grab on to. Ahead there was a cliff, and she knew damn well she was going to go over.

She bit her lip to keep from screaming. "Just drive the goddamn car and let me worry about what we're going to do!"

"It's obvious that you have no plan."

"Shut up and let me think!" she shouted as she turned away and stared out into the night.

A few miles later, as Welcome to Scotland signs flew past, Shannon knew she was beaten. There were just too many uncertainties to take into account, too many unknowns on which to stake Michael's life—and quite likely her own.

As if reading her mind, the Chameleon said, "Ready to give in now, Shannon, and listen to my suggestions?"

Shannon gritted her teeth. "Sure. Go ahead. I'm all ears."

Gia (Shannon had decided this name fit best if she had to call the girl anything) flashed a cocky smile. "Good decision."

She did indeed have a plan, one that made Shannon's head spin more than before. Every bit as audacious as she would have expected, it also might very well work. That's why fifteen minutes later, Shannon was on her cell trying to raise DCI Campbell.

She somehow managed to cajole one of Campbell's underlings into phoning his home to give him her cell number, only because the person she'd talked to remembered the "guv'nor" mentioning the Canadian ex-cop. From the lackey's tone, Campbell's comments had not been complimentary.

"It's too bad we have to bother with him," Gia observed while they waited for the call back. "He's such a dry old stick."

Was there anything this girl didn't know? Shannon felt more inadequate than ever.

Thankfully, she only had to wait five minutes for Campbell to return her call.

"What do you have for me, lassie?" came the clipped voice Shannon found so irritating. "I don't normally take calls when off duty."

Because of her foul mood, Shannon snapped, "And I wouldn't be wasting your time if this weren't crucial! You've heard of Michael Quinn having been kidnapped?"

"Yes. I'm sure the people who have been assigned to the case will handle it adequately."

The unmitigated gall of the man! "Look, I know who has him. They've contacted me."

"Best give it to me, lassie," the Scot said. "We'll take it from there."

"No! That's *not* what's going to happen!"

"I'm afraid we don't work that way over here. We let our professionals handle things—and we certainly don't need nor want the help of private operatives from Canada."

Shannon's anger and frustration boiled over. "I will be involved, or you don't get the information I have, and when the shit hits the fan, buster, I'm going to make sure you get it square in the face."

Campbell remained stodgily unruffled. "Withholding information from the police will get you in a great deal of trouble."

"Look, do you want to nail the murderers of Angus MacDougall, bust an American crime boss and recover three hundred kilos of heroin? That's what I'm talking about."

He went quiet. After a good ten seconds, Shannon asked, "Are you still there?"

"I'm listening."

She quickly and concisely outlined Gia's plan. "But until I call Michael's cell phone, we'll have no idea where this is going to go down. It could be anywhere, but I'm sure it's reasonably near Glasgow, because I told them in the earlier call that's where I was headed. How flexible can your people be in getting around? If the bad guys get even a whiff of cop, bad things are going to happen."

"We'll be ready. Trust me on that."

She wished she could. She was sure Campbell did everything by the book, and this little caper was likely going to prove to be anything but by the book.

"I'll call your office when I speak to the kidnappers again, and I'll hold off on that call as long as I can to give you time to get your end organized. Agreed?"

"You just do what you've outlined, and we'll manage our part just fine."

She hung up. "I hope Campbell comes through. One thing you can be sure of, he's going to be burning up the phone lines between now and when we call back, checking out everything he can. If he doesn't like what he hears, he'll pull the plug. I've worked with cops like him before."

Gia made a disgusted face. "He is such a bloody wanker! And that's why we're not telling him where we're going until the very last minute."

This time Shannon's jaw did drop. "You mean you know where they've got Michael?"

"Sure. I rented the house for them."

"*What?*"

"Relax. It's all part of my plan. I also have two of my people working for Mastrocolle. You didn't expect he could come over here and not need local help, did you?"

"You mean you knew Michael was going to be kidnapped today?"

She shrugged. "Actually, I was thinking it would be tomorrow or the next day. To be honest, I didn't think you'd figure out so quickly who I really am." Gia patted Shannon's knee. "And it looks like ya done good, kiddo. Know what I mean?"

Gia's accent was dead on New York.

Shannon shivered.

▏▎▏

It took four long minutes for them to bring Shannon and the girl into the room. I know. I felt every single second.

I heard Shannon's gasp when she saw me slumped over on the chair. I wanted the bad guys to think I was a lot worse off than I was. I didn't know what good it would do, but I figured it might give me a little edge.

Someone spoke. "We followed her from before the restaurant, Mr. M. Everything's cool."

The old man spoke. "You might as well take that stupid bag off his head, then."

Mastrocolle was much less impressive than I would have imagined, given his reputation. The American press referred to him as Mad Dog Mastrocolle, but he seemed about as imposing as a beagle. Shrunken and old, his skin had a gray pallor that made me think he might be seriously ill.

Shannon wanted to come over to me, but someone stopped her until the old man gave a signal.

Crouching down in front of me, she said, "You look like hell."

"I've certainly felt better."

Reaching around to my hands, she stood and said, "Can't you cut these ties? His hands are like ice!"

Again, the old gangster waved his hand, and someone came forward to do his bidding. Finally, I could get some relief for the aching muscles in my arms and legs. Shannon kissed my cheek and quickly whispered, "We have a plan."

If it involved running within the next two days, I might not be able to take part.

Someone else was pushed forward, and I involuntarily gasped: Giovanna.

The way Shannon had been describing her, I expected some swagger, but she seemed helpless, completely bewildered and very, very frightened. That night she'd jumped in my car, she had displayed something approaching haughtiness. There was none of that now. Quite frankly, she looked like a scared little girl.

Shannon said to Mastrocolle, "I've brought you the girl. Now I think you should show your gratitude by letting Michael and me go."

One of the Americans handed his boss a flat plastic bag with something white in it. "She had this with her."

"I just wanted to prove to you that the girl still has your shipment. Do we have a deal?"

"You will be silent!" Mastrocolle roared with a strength that belied his physical state. "Or I will have you all killed now!"

The mobster continued to stare up at Giovanna intently, but not just at her face. Her coat was open, revealing a striking, flower print dress. Shannon stepped back to stand next to me, her hand on my shoulder, just vibrating with tension. What the heck was going on?

Mastrocolle spoke to Giovanna. "You look different than the first time I saw you. I never noticed before... Where did you get that dress?"

Her accent was pure Brummy. "It belonged to my mother. It was her favourite."

The old man's eyes grew wide, but Giovanna's answer seemed to snap him out of his reverie. "Where is the rest of my merchandise?" he barked, indicating the bag on his lap.

Giovanna suddenly threw herself to the ground at his knees and began wailing, "Please don't kill me! I didn't know what was going on until it was too late. I didn't know who you were. He made me help him. There was nothing I could do. I swear it!" Then she pointed back at Shannon. "And this is all a set-up. She brought the cops with her!"

"Why you little—" Shannon started forward, then gasped and went rigid before pitching forward onto the carpet. The goddamned American held the stun gun against her neck for several more seconds as Shannon writhed on the ground.

"Stop it, you bastard!" I shrieked, trying to leap to her aid and knock that horrible thing from the man's hands, but two pair of strong arms grabbed me from behind and forced me back down.

The American finally stood up and sneered. "Looking for another jolt, my friend? Well, just come to papa."

To drive his point home, he depressed the button on his baton and blue sparks crackled evilly between the two electrodes.

Knowing I could easily wind up in the same state as before, I gave up struggling. Both of us being down for the count would not be good.

Shannon lay on the rug in a very bad state, gasping and moaning.

Everyone turned back to Mastrocolle and found him sitting rigidly upright in his chair. Giovanna held a thin, nasty-looking blade against his throat.

Guns suddenly appeared in everyone's hands.

Giovanna didn't flinch. "If anyone even breathes wrong, your precious boss's blood will be all over the floor. Got that?"

The change in Giovanna's demeanor was galvanic. Her eyes blazed triumphantly, all weakness and subservience wiped away as she snarled at the roomful of criminals in the New York accent I was more used to. One minute she'd been cowering on the floor, and the next she had a knife, seemingly conjured from thin air, at the old man's throat. It made my poor head spin.

Was it all part of "the plan"? I hadn't got the impression Shannon was acting when she'd lunged at Giovanna.

"What do you want?" Mastrocolle asked tonelessly as he continued to stare at Giovanna with that curious fixed expression.

She bent over and said something softly in his ear.

The old man's eyes opened wide. "You? It cannot be true!"

"Do you doubt the truth your eyes are telling you?" Giovanna asked, then continued in very rapid, angry-sounding Italian.

Mastrocolle answered back in that language, his complexion greyer than ever.

Giovanna shook her head and hissed, "*Vendetta!*" Then turned to me and said, "Michael, pick Shannon up and get her the hell out of here. There's a French door just behind me." Two men in the room took a step forward. "Don't!" she warned.

The knife blade must have moved, because a trickle of blood slid down Mastrocolle's neck.

I knew better than to start asking questions, not in a roomful of thugs with guns in their hands.

Shannon was a complete dead weight in my arms, conscious, but just barely. The blast she'd endured from the stun gun had been longer than either of the ones I'd been nailed with. As I picked her up, I glared at the American, wanting nothing more than to grab that thing away from him, press it against his skin and hold the button down for at least ten minutes. Bastard!

It felt rather strange to be the only person moving in a room of totally frozen people.

I had trouble at the door, not being able to open it and hold Shannon because of my wobbly state, so I had to put her down. It was locked with no sign of the key, so I picked up a nearby chair and smashed out all of the glass

As I picked Shannon up again, all hell broke loose around the house. Shrill police whistles began blowing from all directions.

Pushing through the ruins of the door, I heard a loud whoosh behind me, then guns started going off. I needed no more urging to get my arse in gear, and I trotted Shannon along the front of the house and around the corner.

The house was built into a hillside covered in small trees and shrubs, some sort of garden. Passage was impossible where I was, so I shifted Shannon up over my shoulder and stumbled back a few yards until I found a path going up. The best thing I could do was put as much distance as possible between us and the house.

The night was dark and the ground slippery from a recent rain, but I managed about a hundred feet before my reserves started giving out. I gently laid Shannon down.

"What happened?" she asked in a raspy voice.

"You got zapped."

"Taser?"

"I don't know. Something like that. You okay?"

She managed a feeble smile. "If you define okay as feeling like a piece of overdone spaghetti."

The gunfire had stopped, but there was a lot of shouting down below. I moved a few steps back down the path until I could see the house again. Smoke was floating past the flapping curtain on the door I'd trashed. Below me I saw a shadow flit in front of the meagre light, then another. They were headed my way.

I raced back to Shannon, threw her over my shoulder and took off as fast as I could. Thirty feet farther, the path opened up into a clearing about twenty feet across. Logs were piled up there, as I found when I nearly tripped over some. Putting Shannon down again where she could lean against a tree trunk, I turned my head to listen.

Someone was definitely coming. Needing a weapon, I thought of the logs, not much use against guns but better than nothing. I found something far more useful: a yellow log splitter. I settled back into the shadows beside the path and waited. Someone was going to get it.

The first person was on me before I could even react—which turned out to be a good thing as it was Giovanna.

She saw me move a bit. "Michael?"

"Yes."

"There's someone right behind me. You'd better stop him!"

With that, she took off across the clearing and disappeared into the trees on the far side.

If I hadn't heard her approach, I certainly heard the next person as he huffed and puffed and stumbled in the gloom. I waited until the perfect moment and swung, connecting with his midsection with the side of the splitter, wanting only to stop him, not commit murder. He fell to the ground gasping, and I leapt forward ready to give him another if he needed it.

"You're lucky if you haven't killed him, swinging like that," Shannon called out to me.

His loud groans told me I hadn't.

Going back to Shannon, I asked again, "Are you all right?"

She reached up and touched my cheek. "I'll be fine. Don't worry. We better get back down the hill, though. Campbell must be wondering where the hell I've gotten to."

"He's here?"

"Where else do you think all those cops came from?" The guy I'd slugged moaned a bit, and she added, "You better tie him up with your shoelaces. We'll let Campbell's men fetch him."

It took longer than I would have expected to make our way back down the path. At least Shannon could stumble along with me propping her up. I couldn't have managed carrying her downhill in the dark.

We met two uniformed policemen near the bottom and explained who we were.

"There's a bad guy up the path a ways," I told them. "He's injured, but he's not dead."

They disappeared up the hill.

We made our way past the broken door and along the front of the house to the gravel driveway. It was chock full of police cars, blue lights flashing everywhere, the whole scene looking like a Hollywood movie.

Campbell was standing next to one of the few unmarked cars. "Where did you two get to?" he asked, looking rather put out.

By the time we finished telling him what had happened, he'd had the good sense to invite us into his car, because we were shivering so violently. Pairs of constables kept trooping by with thugs in handcuffs between them, leading them to a paddy wagon parked at the bottom of the drive.

"Well, we've rounded up just about all of them," he said. "Only the wee lassie seems to have got away. We're bringing in dogs, and we'll have her shortly. She won't get far in the woods at night."

I looked at my watch. "It's past two a.m. Do you think we can go?"

"I don't see why not. Your rental is boxed in, but I'll see what I can do. Wait here."

While they moved cars so we could get down the drive to the pavement below, one of the officers brought us mugs of steaming tea.

"Remember me?" Constable Dickson asked. "You still doing those concerts this week?"

"I hope so."

"Great! It would be a shame if it got cancelled. Your Rolly said he'd fix me up with a ticket and all."

"Give me your notebook, and I'll write down Rolly's number at the Hilton for you. Give him a call. I'm sure he'd love to hear from you."

As the excited officer shut the car door again, Shannon turned to me. "Michael, you are positively evil!"

She still looked pretty fuzzy around the edges, but the tea had put a bit of life back into her face.

I put my arm around her. "You know, we've been pretty damned lucky tonight."

She relaxed against me. "You got that right!"

About five minutes later, Campbell returned with news that the rental was now waiting at the bottom of the hill. "You'll be staying in Dunoon overnight then?"

"I guess so."

"Please be so kind as to stop by the police station tomorrow before driving back to Glasgow."

"When we were stumbling back down the hill earlier, we saw smoke coming out of the sitting room. What happened?"

"The girl Miss O'Brien brought with her had a smoke bomb of some kind. When you broke the window, she set it off and got away."

Shannon sat up. "And Mastrocolle?"

"Dead. Someone slit his throat."

She slumped back and put her head down. "I should have expected that would be the inevitable conclusion."

I put my arm around her and gave a big squeeze.

"Silent" Michael Quicksilver of Neurotica Speaks!

(Transcript of an interview broadcast on BBC 1, presenter: James Bailey)

JB: I had the distinct pleasure of speaking with the "silent man" of Neurotica yesterday, the reclusive Michael Quicksilver. Approaching the interview cautiously, since he has a legendary distaste for speaking with my ilk, I found him to be fairly open and relatively warm. This is the first interview he's granted in twenty-two years. Here's how it all went down.

Thanks for agreeing to speak with me, Michael.

MQ: (laughs) Well, I can't say that I've been looking forward to it, but I've agreed to speak to you lads, and that's what I'm going to do.

JB: First off, why now? You're back with your old mates—and sounding every bit as good as ever, I might add—but from what Rolly's said over the years, this wasn't something anyone ever expected. I mean, frankly, since 1982 you've disappeared off the face of the earth.

MQ: Contrary to popular belief, I have been on earth all that time, just not in the music world.

JB: But why now?

MQ: Well, I can't say the event that caused us to do this concert is the sort of thing one looks forward to, but it seemed the right thing to do under the circumstances. Angus was always after me to rejoin the group, but for personal reasons, I never wanted to. I'm only sorry he won't be here to see us—in the flesh, that is. I'd like to think he'll be somewhere around, though.

JB: So tell us what it's like playing the old songs again.

MQ: (thinking) Surprisingly nice. It was quite amazing how fast I slipped into it again—we all slipped into it, I should say. I had to relearn much of the material, of course, but as we rehearse, I find myself playing things that weren't on the original recordings I worked from. You know, my mind just sort of floats free, and all of a sudden I'm playing something different. If I think about it, though, I realize that they were changes I made to my parts after the recordings were completed. It's pretty freaky the first couple of times that happens. I'm going like, "Where the bloody hell did that come from?" Since we're taking a look at the arrangement of each song anyway, a lot of that is getting pulled in and used. I think the audience is going to be pleasantly surprised.

JB: No, you certainly haven't lost anything, to my ears.

MQ: Thank you.

JB: Were you surprised there was enough interest to support doing four performances?

MQ: Quite frankly, yes. Over the years our albums have continued to sell quite well, but I guess it's true what they say about absence making the heart grow fonder. From what I've heard, we could have sold out more than four.

JB: So the next question obviously has to be: is this a one-off? Is there more Neurotica on the horizon?

MQ: (hesitates) I know the rest of the band would like to continue; they always have. It became an annual ritual like sending Christmas cards for somebody to ask me about reforming. It was quite irritating, really. Up until now, I've always resisted. Past the fourth show, I don't want to make any commitment.

JB: Are you going to be glad, then, when it's all over?

MQ: I'd like to hope so. I do want to say one thing, and I hope you understand. I've found in the past number of days, that regardless of the fact that I'm pushing fifty pretty hard, my brain is stuck back in my twenty-second year. That's when Neurotica first broke, and everything was new and fresh and quite exciting. I think I can speak for everyone in the group that we're all still back there. It was the best time of our lives, and something like that makes an indelible impression.

I know that's going to seem rather pathetic to some people, being stuck in a year so long ago, but I think it's a valid feeling. I have a very good friend who probably still feels seventeen inside. The strongest thing in your life is where you sort of get hung up psychically. Does that sound too airy-fairy?

CHAPTER 32

We managed to book a room at the good old Argyll Hotel. The old woman behind the desk looked clearly scandalized because of the late hour, our appearance, but mostly our lack of luggage. Shannon found it amusing.

First thing I did once we got to our room was ring Rolly, knowing he'd more than likely still be up. He fell all over himself when he heard my voice, obviously thinking that I was going to turn up dead. "What the hell happened?"

"It's too long a story to tell now. I'm about to fall over with exhaustion."

"Aw, c'mon mate! You can't leave me hanging like this!"

"Get used to disappointment," I responded with a bitter laugh.

He told me about Tommy: in hospital for observation, hopefully only suffering from minor concussion and a bruised face from having fallen on it.

"Mags is on her way up now to be with him. You'd think the poor bugger had packed it in from the way she carried on! They never struck me as being all that close before this happened. You know how they were always ragging on each other. Goes to show you."

"Assuming Tommy is in decent shape, the concerts go off as scheduled, right?" I asked.

Rolly seemed surprised. "You're still in?"

"I gave my word."

"When I told you what I did today, you looked as if you'd been kicked in the gut, mate. When you disappeared, I thought you'd scarpered again. Even after we found Tommy on the loading dock, I wasn't sure until he started coming around and told us what had happened. Everyone's been in a right bad state since then, I can tell you."

"Tell them I'm all right, but I don't know yet what I can manage tomorrow as far as rehearsing goes. We'll talk in the morning."

"Sure thing, Michael. Sure thing."

The call Shannon made to New York was even more interesting.

She hadn't been able to speak to her children for the past two days with all that had been going on, and even though it was after ten in the Big Apple, she had to speak with them. That part of the call went fairly quickly: Rachel and Robbie both complained about wanting to go back to Canada. Then their father got on the phone. At first Shannon's face registered her disapproval at having to talk to him. As the conversation went on (Rob talking and Shannon listening and nodding her head), she began to look far more cheerful.

Finally, she said, "Well, Rob, you know how I feel about this, and you know that I'll do anything to protect my children. What happened was my fault. I should have known better and taken precautions, but uprooting them the way you did when both were so fragile was equally bad." She nodded a few more times, then said, "Because of what happened tonight... No. I'm sure you'll hear about it on the news... Yes. It involves Mastrocolle. Anyway, I'm committed to be here for another few days. I'll let you know as soon as I know what my plans are... Middle of next week should be fine... I'll call my lawyer tomorrow... Yes. Goodnight."

Snapping her cell phone shut, Shannon leapt to her feet and did a little victory dance. "The kids are coming home! Goddamn, that was out of the blue!"

"What's happened?"

Shannon's face just glowed. "Rob can't handle being a full-time dad, that's what. His lady friend wants nothing to do with the kids, no maternal instinct whatsoever. Robbie's been in three fights at school, and they're threatening to expel him. Rachel just mopes around the house and has been skipping classes. Long and short of it is, he wants to send them back. Now we've just got to convince a judge and Children's Aid that it's a good idea. I can't wait to call my mom in the morning. She will be so excited!

It was about this time that Shannon noticed I wasn't sharing in her joy. "What's wrong?"

"Something Rolly told me this afternoon just before the bad guys showed up. It's about Angus and what happened in Chicago. Seems I was very wrong all these years."

Shannon sat down next to me on the bed, concern now etched on her face. "What are you talking about?"

"I was wrong! All those years..."

The anger finally boiled over completely. Once released, it just roared through me with frightening intensity. I snatched up the nearest thing, the bedside clock radio, and threw it against the far wall. Rage at what Angus had done and sorrow at how his act of omission had robbed us all of the kind of chance you get only once—if you're extremely lucky as we'd been.

Shannon gripped my arms tightly, preventing me from storming around the room, likely breaking far more than a bloody clock as I howled at the fates. I struggled to throw her off as she clung to me with all her strength, not caring whom or what I hurt in my despair.

She was sitting on my chest, holding me down as my strength flagged. Tears came, and I wept uncontrollably for a long time. Throughout, Shannon stayed with me, letting the spasm run its course. Though I couldn't say it, her presence did bring comfort. Maybe because of it, I could let myself go like that for the first time. Giving in to such dark thoughts when alone can be dangerous indeed.

Finally I was able to tell her about what had really happened on that night so long ago. I said far more than I intended, about all my fears and self-loathing over the years. Yes, I still had a lot to answer for, Rolly too. That had not gone away and never would, but Angus had done something terrible, and because of me, he had gotten away with it.

"And this concert honouring him is now a complete farce from beginning to end!" I said disgustedly.

Based on what she had said earlier, Shannon's response startled me. "Can you be sure it didn't happen as Angus said?"

"What do you mean? Rolly told me he dragged the girl into the bathroom, there was some shouting then silence."

"And you've told me that Rolly was completely out of it at the time. Can you be certain that his memory is accurate? Perhaps Angus did take that poor girl into the bathroom to calm her down. It *is* possible she could have fallen. She was high and quite possibly drunk. The problem is you just can't know for sure."

I shook my head. "You're right... But not knowing leaves nothing but a festering wound. It will never heal."

"Sometimes that happens, and we just have to learn to live with it."

III

I woke up late in the morning, aware I was being watched. Turning my head, I saw Shannon lying on her side, head propped on her arm.

"Good morning, love," she said gently. "How do you feel?"

I thought for a moment, taking stock. "Good...and bad." Rolling over, I took her in my arms. "But mostly good. If you hadn't been here last night, there's no telling what I might have done."

"Things are going to get better now. You have your life back."

"And you're going to get your kids," I replied, nodding my head.

"It's more than I could have hoped for."

"I'm very happy for you."

She cocked an eyebrow. "You certainly don't look it."

I got up and stared out the window for a long minute. Farther down the road, the statue of Highland Mary looked out across the Firth of Clyde.

"Why do you think she did it?"

"Maria? I've been thinking about that," Shannon said, stepping up behind me and pressing against my back. "Well, I'm certainly no psychologist, but I think she loved and hated her cousin at the same time. That came through in a number of things she said. Then, you have to realize that she has no morals, or those she has are definitely very, shall we say, shiftable—one mark of the true psychopath. For whatever reason, she fixated on getting Mastrocolle at all costs. Everything she did was a means to that end. And it involved selling drugs herself to finance her plan, right down to using her body to worm her way into Mastrocolle's organization, and then to get away again."

"Does that also include jumping into my car?"

Shannon laughed, but it wasn't a happy sound. "That was the only 'miscalculation' she would admit to. Mamma Vennuti's last hours came as a big surprise to her and she raced to the hospital from Germany with her 'Gia' persona still firmly in place. It was only by chance that her Brummy comrades, the guys she hooked into doing her drug shipment, were in the area at the same time carrying out a completely unrelated errand for their boss. The fact she jumped into *your* car was a total fluke."

"Some fluke."

"Yeah..."

I turned and held Shannon close, the two of us brought together by the oddest, and ultimately most tragic of circumstances.

Eventually, I snapped to. "Wonder what time it is? We promised to meet Campbell at the police station."

Looking over at the bedside table and laughing, she said, "This darn hotel should make sure each room has a clock!"

Getting dressed, Shannon discovered her watch buried among her clothes on the floor. "Jeez! It's almost eleven. We should hustle our butts or they're going to come looking for us."

I drove through the sleepy town and up the hill to the ugly police station, fitting in with its surroundings about as much as a flamingo in a flock of geese.

Campbell was still hard at it, looking grey and tired, but wearing a satisfied expression.

Shannon flopped down onto a chair without an invite. "What's up?"

The Scottish cop actually smiled as he put down his pen. "Well, lassie, thanks to your information, we've done a good night's work. You will also be interested to know I got news from Birmingham, and they've clapped the irons on most of that crew, and a fingerprint of one of the thugs matches the only print we lifted from Angus MacDougall's sitting room. Somehow we'll get the bugger to talk, mark my words!"

"My money's on the guy in the hospital in Toronto being the murderer," Shannon said grimly. "He liked his cigarettes way too much!"

I was confused about the references in the conversation. "How did the Brums get mixed up in what happened last night?"

She sighed. "The Chameleon's doing yet again. As we were approaching Glasgow, she borrowed my cell, made a phone call down south and set something in motion that led the Birmingham crew to where she'd hidden the heroin shipment—yet another part of this schizophrenic plan of hers. The drugs were in the basement of Mamma Vennuti's house. My jaw was down to the floor when she calmly turned to me and announced that the late Papa Vennuti was a bootlegger and smuggler of note in the forties and fifties when rationing was still in effect. Apparently, the Vennuti furnace pivots out from the wall, and there's a storeroom behind it. Unfortunately, for the bad guys, the Birmingham police, having received an anonymous tip, already had the place staked out."

"Caught them red-handed, too," Campbell said. "The one thing that baffles me, though, is how the girl fit in. We've never run across anyone with so many aliases. It's almost comical."

Shannon looked grim. "Maria Rota is the cousin of Luigi Mastrocolle's illegitimate daughter, and there's nothing funny about her. I firmly believe she's psychotic."

"Speaking of the girl," I asked, "have you managed to catch her?"

"No, laddie, but we will. She can't remain on the run for long."

"Did she get off the hill?"

"Aye. Had a car parked and waiting down the road. The local patrol had seen it earlier in the day and thought it belonged to some over-hearty hill walkers. We tracked her up to the forestry road near the top of the hill, then she made her way down through Puck's Glen to the car park at the bottom. We found a flowered dress there that we think belongs to her. She must have driven off right under our noses. Got through our road block and all, too."

Shannon flashed me a look that said volumes.

Our statements took a while, but the process was relatively painless, and at the end, Campbell actually *thanked* us for our help. "You will be called for at the trial, and I'll be in touch if we need anything more in the meantime."

Shannon talked me into taking the ferry across to Gourock to save time. Big mistake. The Clyde was wind-whipped, the sky leaden as a cold rain fell, and I spent another endless sea voyage with my head hanging over the side of the boat.

|||

The opening act, a local Celtic rock band on the way up, was thundering through their final number, and what they lacked in polish, they made up for in gusto. Backstage, they'd been pretty cocky (reminding me of Neurotica in the same sort of situation), and Rolly had been pretty quick to consign them to the "alternate" green room.

The keyboard player had hung behind to talk with me, confessing to being a "bloody great fan of yours."

The past twenty-four hours had felt as if I'd been blown about in a hurricane.

The promo people had talked me into doing a press conference, since there had been much skepticism from certain quarters that my disappearance had been engineered for publicity purposes. A surprising number of journalists had shown up, and we'd managed to cajole Campbell into giving the official version of the story. I'd answered questions from those present as best I could but generally wished I could have been somewhere else at the time.

One thing Campbell did that brought a wry smile to Shannon's face was show photos of Maria/Giovanna asking that anyone knowing of her present whereabouts contact his office.

"Good luck to him in finding her," I said afterwards. "It isn't going to happen. If I know our girl, she's probably on some island in the Caribbean right now sipping piña coladas and laughing at the whole sorry bunch of us."

"I don't know. Maria Rota is seriously disturbed. Frankly, I wouldn't want to be on her bad side. She's very, very brilliant, a genius, I suppose, but reality for her is a very fluid thing, and that's incredibly dangerous in someone like her. If I were in Campbell's shoes, I'd be plenty worried."

We'd managed a run-through of the show late that morning, and I must admit to being disgusted when a photo of Angus was projected on the screen at the back of the stage.

Tommy was out of hospital but still rather shaky. Even though he made a game attempt at playing, it was clear he wouldn't be able to manage the whole set. After a hasty confab, we asked Ralph if he felt up to the challenge and would occupy his dad's drum chair for at least part of the first night. This time, John and I exchanged meaningful glances when we detected mixed emotions on Tommy's face.

"I think I might be able to manage the encores for tonight. It would make a good entrance, wouldn't it?" Tommy said stoutly, then he'd ruffled his son's hair. "But we are keeping it in the family at least!"

Now, as zero hour approached, every one of us was pacing the dressing room like caged lions. Shannon, Mags and John's wife up from London watched us with amused expressions.

Shannon, leaning over, said into my ear. "I'm going out there tonight with my eyes peeled."

"What the devil are you on about?" I asked, my tension showing.

She put her finger next to the side of her nose, a thoroughly British expression. "I wouldn't be surprised if a certain party made the scene tonight."

"You've got to be kidding! Maria's probably on the other side of the world by now."

She shook her head. "It would be *just* like her to show up tonight."

As they left for their seats, Shannon gave me a quick peck on the cheek. "I've waited twenty-four years to hear this concert, Quicksilver. Don't screw it up!"

Tommy, getting his own going over from Mags, laughed loudly as he heard that. "She's a bit of all right is our Shannon, eh, Michael? Fits right in!"

Shannon turned and winked as she disappeared through the door.

Butterflies filled my stomach as we approached the backstage area. The last of the warm-up group's equipment was pushed past, and since they'd been set up in front of us on the stage, all that remained would be to test the mics and electronics one last time. I felt keyed up but very apprehensive at the same time. It had been so many years since I'd last performed, and I wasn't sure whether I still had the *sang froid* to pull it off.

The stage manager walking up, handed me a small torch. "We checked your entire keyboard rig twice, but I'm sure you'll want to do that again yourself," he grinned. "Once you're ready, flash me twice with this and just start playing. We'll handle the rest. You're going to be great!"

I looked around at the others, each as tense as I. Tommy, Lee, John and Rolly, all of us were putting our reputations on the line. Ralph sat off to the side on a flight case, chomping on an apple. He grinned and gave me a thumbs-up as I turned to climb the stairs to the darkened stage.

Using the light, I quickly checked all the instruments, listening through my headset. Then, satisfied with everything, I took a deep breath and flashed twice to stage right. Crossing myself, I started the two midi-ed synth tracks. As their drone rumbled out of the sound system, the wash of blue light came up around me, aided by fog let loose at my feet. The whole keyboard rig glowed.

Deviating from my original plan, I depressed a key on the mellotron, the only instrument, it's said, where you can sound magnificent playing just a single note. The "three violins" sound soared out into the arena as two overhead spots stabbed down on me.

The roar of the crowd was absolutely deafening.

ACKNOWLEDGEMENTS

This novel is wholly a work of fiction, but owes a great deal to a large number of very real people.

As always, my wife Vicki was my front line defense, research assistant, fact checker, reader (and corrector!) and more generous with all-round support than anyone could imagine. My son Jan is responsible for the distinctive handwriting used on the cover and throughout the book. Andre Leduc, photographer extraordinare, again provided some incredible images for the cover. Kal Honey and Kim Kho must be mentioned for design and font consultation, as well as my other son, Karel.

The author also would like to thank Craig Collett of Coll Audio in Toronto for advice on backline rentals, and also for appearing on the cover—and he's not even a keyboard player! In the UK, I relied heavily on the expertise and knowledge of David Younger, Lisa Govan, Bobby Teasdale, Mike Dickson and Mark McAleese for help with the Scottish and law enforcement bits; Martin Smith and John Bradley of Streetly Electronics for all things mellotronic and Elaine Smith and Mary Bradley for Birmingham-centric information.

The following kind people also provided assistance: Lyn Hamilton, Scott Martin, Jamie Goad, Josh and Mike O'Connell, James Bailey, Patricia Gouthro, Louise Pambrun, Dale Lang, Erin Lang, Gary Nagels, Ted Brennan and Raffaella Mio. If I've missed anyone, please forgive me!

And as always, at RendezVous Press, Sylvia McConnell and Allister Thompson need to be especially singled out for their insight, dedication and support in making this book a reality.

Any errors in this novel are entirely the author's own—and have been made despite the very best intentions.

Photo by André Leduc

The fact that Rick Blechta has been a musician all his life is clearly apparent in his writing. All four of his novels, *Knock on Wood* (1992), *The Lark Ascending* (1993), *Shooting Straight in the Dark* (2002) and *Cemetery of the Nameless* (2005), have been critically praised for the insider's knowledge of the music world. He also edited *Dishes to Die For...Again*, a collection of recipes by the Crime Writers of Canada.

Rick, who began his professional music career at the age of fourteen, is accomplished on several instruments. After receiving a B. Mus. from McGill University, he formed one of Canada's finest progressive rock bands, Devotion, after which he taught instrumental music for twenty-three years, and for sixteen years was a member of the faculty at the Royal Conservatory of Music.

For the past fourteen years, Rick has been an active member of the Crime Writers of Canada and was recognized with the Derrick Murdoch Award in 2000 in recognition of his contributions to the organization. He is currently the CWC's president.

He is married to prominent flutist and educator Vicki Blechta and has two sons.

For more information on Rick's writing and music, visit his website: www.rickblechta.com. There you'll also find information on a special contest being held (with some terrific prizes!) to celebrate the release of *When Hell Freezes Over*.

ALSO AVAILABLE FROM RENDEZVOUS CRIME

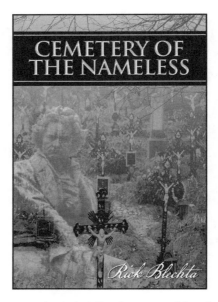

Victoria Morgan, a classical violin virtuoso, and her devoted piano accompanist are on yet another European tour currently stopping in Vienna.

While playing to a full house, Tory leaves the stage and disappears, leaving behind a puzzled (and angry) audience. Why would a professional so intent on maintaining her ascendant career do something so damaging?

Tory's decision to leave proves to be especially fatal to her career, since it is tied to the brutal murder of a high profile Viennese figure.

The action is set around the appearance of a mysterious score for a recently discovered violin concerto of incredible worth. Is it truly by Beethoven as the owner claims, and will Tory be the first to debut this dream violin piece? And who is finding it worth killing for?

"This new novel by Rick Blechta is excellent. Whether it's the terrific plot or the spectacular location, or just plain good writing, the book is hard to put down." **-The Globe and Mail**

424 pages / ISBN 1-894917-17-0 / Cdn. $16.95, U.S. $14.95